Also by Peter David

Sir Apropos of Nothing
The Woad to Wuin

Tong Lashing

Sir Apropos of Nothing
Book Three

PETER DAVID

POCKET STAR BOOKS

NEW YORK LONDON TORONTO SYDNEY

F
D28+L
SF

A Pocket Star Book published by
POCKET BOOKS, a division of Simon & Schuster, Inc.
1230 Avenue of the Americas, New York, NY 10020

Copyright © 2003 by Second Age, Inc.

Originally published in hardcover in 2003 by Pocket Books

ISBN: 0-7434-4913-4

First Pocket Books paperback printing June 2005

10 9 8 7 6 5 4 3 2 1

POCKET STAR BOOKS and colophon are registered
trademarks of Simon & Schuster, Inc.

Cover illustration by Sonia Hillios

Manufactured in the United States of America

For information regarding special discounts for bulk purchases,
please contact Simon & Schuster Special Sales at 1-800-456-6798
or business@simonandschuster.com.

Acknowledgments

Once again the author wishes to thank Kathleen O'Shea for her map craftsmanship, and Albert Alfaro of Imaginarium Galleries for his creation of the Drabits.

Further thanks go to John Ordover, Scott Shannon, and Andy Zack for putting together the one-book-turned-trilogy deal that brought Apropos to life, or at least what he thinks of as life. Apropos' future remains up in the air at the moment, but no matter what that future may bring, it's been a fun ride.

Oh, and movie rights remain available.

—Peter David
New York, June, 2003

'05/$7.99

To all those who had the chance and passed

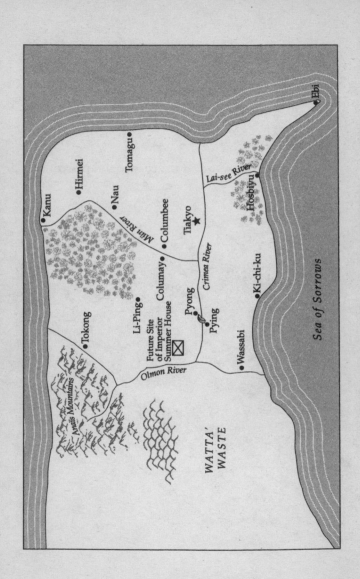

BOOK ONE

Sick Transit

Chapter 1

Ship Rex

*T*otally soaked and certain I would die as I desperately clung to a piece of driftwood, alone in a raging sea while the vessel I'd booked passage on slid to a watery grave, I couldn't help but consider that there was very little upside in playing games of chance with creatures of pure, unremitting evil.

I am not certain if that particular bit of advice will be of much general utility. It certainly lacks the universal appeal of cautions against going out of one's way to annoy magic users, or the hazards of involving oneself in the affairs of such beings. In point of fact, I had no idea when I sat down at a gaming table in the bowels of the good ship *Larp* that I would find myself, barely an hour later, the sole survivor of the poor vessel's explosive and disastrous end. On the other hand, if one had sat me down and told me that such events were about to transpire, I can't say as I would have been all that surprised.

I have that talent. The talent—or insufferably bad luck, if you will—to find myself in the midst of unexpected adventures, or disasters, or cursed happpenstance, despite all my best efforts to stay out of harm's way. As any who have read my earlier autobiographical scribblings know all too well, I make it a full-time occupation to mind my own business, keep my head down, and stay well clear of danger whenever it presents itself. I can only say that danger has become devilishly clever in inflicting itself upon me. I would almost admire the ingenuity ill fortune displays in finding me and inflicting itself upon me if it weren't for the deuced inconvenience. It almost makes me wonder what there is about me that seems worth the trouble. I'm damned if I can figure it out. Then again, for the things I've done in my life, I'm likely damned anyway, so I suppose it all evens out.

I bear the unlikely name of "Apropos," a moniker given me by my long-dead tavern wench of a mother. I was spawned as the result of her gang rape by a group of knights. As a consequence, I have an understandably jaded view of the world. Knights, after all, are supposed to represent all that is good and true, pure and decent in mankind. When a host of these avatars of wonderfulness spend their off-hours brutally raping a helpless floozy, with the end result being me, it should be easy to comprehend why I take the nobility of chivalry far less seriously than the common man. And that's speaking as someone who is as common as they come.

Curiously, this did not prevent my brief tenure as "Sir Apropos of Nothing" in the court of good King Runcible, and my even briefer status as future royal son-in-law. That business came to a fairly disastrous end, and after further misadventures I wound up fleeing the state of Isteria altogether, in the company of a magic user named Sharee.

Sharee . . .

Odd. I thought we'd wind up together.

As I write about my life with the comfortable distance of years between my foolish youth and my positively imbecilic old age, I have come to realize that not only did I expect our union would be the case, but I'm disappointed it didn't turn out that way. I think my life would have been much better had it happened.

I thought Sharee and I would become a couple. I've no idea whether that meant we would have grown old together, indulged each other's foibles and growing infirmities together. Become progressively sick of each other and yet remained together out of a sense of mindless devotion, stale affection, or perhaps simply inertia.

Yes, well . . . even my nostalgia tends to find itself devolving toward unpleasantries. When presented with the question of whether a glass is half full or half empty, I instead dwell on why there wasn't enough liquid available to fill it up in the first place.

Still, Sharee was . . . quite something. A weatherweaver she was, capable of manipulating weather threads in a most expert and occasionally lethal fashion. With black hair and flashing gray eyes, Sharee floated in and out of my life like a butterfly with razor-sharp wings. Our longest separation —up until the time when she left me prior to this narrative—occurred when I was a victim of a sort of temporary memory loss and had become a ruthless warlord (or "peacelord" as I called myself) in an unforgiving land called Wuin. Sharee was one of a group of insurrectionists who sought to put an end to my career through the expedient means of putting an end to me. This plan ran aground when my invincibility was revealed to all and sundry, and from that point on, nothing and no one was capable of stopping me.

Except someone did.

I won't go into detail about it at this point, for the tale was already told once, and I see no reason to cover the gruesome details a second time. Suffice to say that—as is not uncommon in my varied and sordid adventures—a goodly number of people died, and there was much collateral carnage and mayhem.

The grisly business concluded, it was a rather odd trio who set across the land of Wuin, hoping to leave the destruction behind us . . . along with a devastating talisman of extraordinary chaos. But I wanted nothing to do with it, despite the fact that it gave me almost limitless power.

I think, in an odd way, that my decision made me more attractive to Sharee. Certainly after the incident with the gem—the Eye of the Beholder, as it was called—she treated me in a marginally more kindly fashion. She kept her ready tongue and sharp sense of humor, but when she turned her swordlike wit upon me, it was to poke gently rather than to stab. Likewise the barbs that I had once hurled at her were no longer coated with the venom that had used to adorn them.

Plus our new spirit of cooperation might have been aided by the third member of our most unusual trio.

That third member was a drabit, a small, feathered, dragonlike creature that had taken to me during my incarnation as a peacelord. The name I'd given him, or perhaps he'd always possessed, was "Mordant." He didn't speak, naturally, since he was simply a dumb animal, although I would oftentimes find it disconcerting when he looked at me with a sort of cold, calculating intelligence. At such times, he had an almost human look to him . . . except I suspected he was considerably smarter than most humans I'd encountered in my lifetime. In my dreams he would speak to me, making lacerating observations about me or the various choices I made in my existence. In real life, however, he remained mute.

All preconceptions for Mordant, however, were eradicated when, at one point in our sojourn through Wuin, he had opened his mouth and spoken with pure, clear diction. It had come in the midst of a conversation I'd been having with Sharee—one in which I was actually claiming that I had come to believe Mordant was a reincarnation of my departed mother—and I had just accused Sharee of sending me the dreams with Mordant as a way of trying to warn me of . . . well, I didn't know of what.

Sharee, of course, had completely denied it. She pointed out that there was nothing in her history to indicate she had any sort of powers of the mind. A stray squall or passing tornado, yes, those might be laid at her door. But games being played by the sleeping mind were outside her normal realm.

We stood there on a desolate piece of land that really wasn't all that different from the rest of the desolation. Flat, unyielding terrain, tufts of small bits of green giving their all to survive, and most likely losing that all. High, high above us, carrion eaters circled lazily. I endeavored to ignore them. I figured that looking at them would only encourage them.

"Bloody well right I'll deny it," she said. "You've got to start thinking for yourself, and stop ascribing everything in your life to me."

Feeling in a slightly tongue-in-cheek mood, I turned to the drabit as if seeking an ally in the discussion. "Do I have to do that, Mordant?" I inquired.

And without hesitation, Mordant replied, "Absolutely."

As you can well imagine, we stared at him, thunderstruck. For long moments, it seemed as if the world had stopped turning. Sharee's horse even backed up, looking concerned over the fact that the animal nearby had suddenly begun speaking. I wondered wildly if the horse was going to start conversing as well. Perhaps say something such as, "Shut up, you fool! They're not supposed to know we can speak! You'll ruin it for all of us!"

I had never encountered an animal capable of speech

before. The closest I'd ever run into were animal/human hybrids, such as the repellent Harpers Bizarre, or the feral but ultimately tragic Bicce. But Mordant was . . . well, a pet, basically. Although he seemed like a curious combination of reptilian and avian features, nevertheless he was fundamentally identifiable as a sort of dragon offshoot. An animal, pure and simple. So for him to begin chatting with us left us both flabbergasted. Sharee and I exchanged looks, trying to figure out if we were delusional.

"Did . . . you just speak?" I asked.

Mordant looked at me with vague contempt. "What do you think?"

"That I'm dreaming? Owwwww!" I suddenly shouted, looking daggers at Sharee as I grabbed my upper arm. "You pinched me! What did you do that for?"

"To prove to you you're not dreaming," she said with an expression she no doubt thought was mischievous, but I simply found irritating.

"I was willing to figure that out for myself."

"I could bite you, in case there's any doubt," offered Mordant.

"Not necessary." I glanced once more at Sharee, who seemed irritatingly amused. "Are you doing this somehow? Some sort of weaver's trick? Projecting your voice in some manner?"

"Would you be satisfied if I drank a mug of water while he spoke?" asked Sharee condescendingly before turning her attention back to Mordant. "Most intriguing. Your voice is strangely accented."

"So is yours," retorted Mordant.

"Who cares about his accent? He's a blasted talking animal!"

"So are you," Mordant said.

I had no immediate response to that, which was annoying in and of itself. Bad enough to find oneself lagging behind in an oral battle of wits with an accomplished human opponent. Being bested by a creature who, for all I knew, hadn't truly begun vocalizing until a minute or so earlier was a new low in personal esteem.

Mordant's voice was thin and reedy, and without the sibilance that one would have expected from such a creature, presuming one was fanciful enough to imagine him speaking at all. He also did indeed have an unidentifiable accent, as Sharee had noted. She seemed to be adjusting to this revelation far faster than was I, considering that the expression of astonishment she'd shared with me had melted into simple amusement. I was annoyed by that. If I was going to be dumbfounded, it would have been nice to have a companion in bewilderment.

"Why haven't you spoken before this? Openly, I mean?" I asked.

He didn't smile. I don't think he had the muscular ability to do so. His tongue flicked out quickly several times, which I decided was what he did when giving an answer some thought. "Because you're interesting," he said at last.

"I am?"

"He is?"

"Yes. You are. And you know he is," he said to Sharee with faint disapproval. "So don't pretend otherwise." His triangular head shifted back to me. "You're a lost soul, Apropos of Nothing, and I think you're only just now starting to realize it. But you're not sure yet what to do about it. It was entertaining to hear you go on and on about whatever deep emotional conflicts were shredding you. But the only reason you would vent your spleen in my presence was because you didn't really think I could understand you. You might have suspected it at some level, but you did not truly believe it. So on and on you would talk, and it was all rather riveting. You should think about writing it all down."

It was the very first time anyone (or anything, for that matter) had ever suggested that I chronicle my adventures. My immediate reaction was to dismiss the concept out of hand. I thought, Who in hell would be so foolish as to want to spend time involving themselves in the tortured, horrific joke that is my life? And now, having set down my escapades in two volumes so far, with this being the third, I find that I've come no closer to being able to answer that question than I ever had.

"I've often told Apropos he had potential," Sharee admitted. "That he had a destiny. He never seemed to believe it, though," and she looked at me sharply as if daring me to disagree.

I couldn't. Despite the fact that my late mother had said much the same thing, it was a notion I had traditionally rejected, and then later fought against with every fiber of my being. I firmly believed that "destiny" was the excuse given after the fact by people who were losers seeking a way of rationalizing all the disappointments that were their life.

Lately, though, I had begun to wonder. The concept of free will versus what the gods have in store for us had received a good deal of play in my life.

Furthermore, I found myself considering the fact that most men live their lives in quiet Desperation . . . Desperation being the single largest city in all the world, and reputedly the most staggeringly boring. Hence the "quiet" appellation. Situated west of the state of Isteria, quiet Desperation was the capital of the state of Grace, named for the founder's wife (whose name was, curiously, Margaret). People flocked there because of the easy living and usually balmy weather. And those who didn't live in quiet Desperation often aspired to live long enough to earn enough money to move there.

I found myself comparing myself to those who lived in

quiet Desperation, and considered that they truly were destiny-free, because their lives were so damned dull. My life, by contrast, had been anything but dull. Even when it had been dull, it was more along the lines of my life catching its breath before hurling me headlong into the next series of insane events. It led me to wonder, then, whether the very nature of perpetual warped activity that constituted my life more or less indicated that perhaps I did, indeed, have a special fate that was above and beyond what other "mere mortals" faced.

The questions before me then, were twofold: What exactly was the kind of destiny I was faced with, and how much of it was truly in my control? I had the answers to neither, and I think it was the lack of knowing that simply added to my bitterness, rather than exciting me about the possibilities.

I discussed none of this with Mordant or Sharee, of course. Part of me was certain they wouldn't understand, while part of me was certain they would. For the life of me, I'm not sure which prospect bothered me more.

Instead I tried to focus purely on Mordant's background, with the reasoning that people usually like talking about themselves. This notion was thwarted by the fact that Mordant wasn't people. He was disinclined to talk about himself at all. Despite prodding from Sharee and myself, he would not go into detail as to whether others of his species could converse, or how long he'd been speaking, or how he'd come to learn the language.

"Why now?" I asked him. "Why did you suddenly start making it obvious to me now that you could speak?"

"Because she's here," said Mordant, "which means it's unlikely that you'll be forthcoming about yourself anymore. So I felt I might as well join future conversations. Although, frankly, I doubt you'll enjoy hearing anyone converse as much as you enjoy hearing yourself."

"That's reasonably accurate," Sharee said.

My famed glare had little effect on her and, unfortunately, did not reduce her to the puddle of goo I was hoping it would.

We made our way then across the land of Wuin. When we happened to come upon other travelers, Mordant would fall silent so as not to garner further questions from startled passersby. We encountered one or two threats, but it was nothing that a healthy running away from couldn't handle.

The greatest challenge we encountered was trying to steer clear of cities or towns that had known the ravages of my army during my time as a "peacelord." During those excursions, certain magicks had given me an unusual strength and vitality that would have not seemed readily apparent in my more natural form. My red hair and by then thick beard were very easy to spot, but the pronounced limp resulting from my lame and deformed right leg might have put anyone off the scent if they thought to associate me with the more robust Apropos the Peacelord. Nevertheless, we had to exercise great caution, and when supplies were dwindling and water was becoming problematic, we found ourselves depending more and more heavily upon Mordant and his resourcefulness. He always seemed able to find a village or a nomad encampment that he could slip into and out of without attracting attention, with a fresh round of minimal supplies clutched in his claws or mouth.

In this way we managed to survive quite handily our trek across a land that, once, might well have been the death of us. Even the horse survived, although it did still tend to toss what appeared to be suspicious glances in Mordant's direction every now and again.

Eventually, however, matters took an unexpected turn.

We made our way much farther north than even my

peregrinations as the peacelord had taken me. As a consequence, we were able to enter with impunity a particularly sizable port city, Port Debras, renowned for having the largest single dock in the entire land, known as the Grand Jetty.

Since it was a major port, few people there really paid attention to the faces that passed by in crowds. That suited us just fine. It also seemed wiser to keep Mordant out of sight, since there might be some who would associate the drabit with the once-formidable peacelord. We needn't have worried, however. Mordant assured us that he wouldn't be seen if he didn't want to be, and he was absolutely true to his word. As we made our way through the many tents and similar ramshackle structures of Port Debras, I would occasionally spot Mordant flitting from one hiding place to another. But the only reason I saw him was because I knew he was there. Once in a great while I'd see someone do a double take, look again, and then shake their head as if assuring themself that they had merely imagined . . . something. Quite the camouflage artist was Mordant.

It was our intention to try and get the hell out of Wuin while the getting was good. The land certainly had nothing more to offer me, and it was just a matter of time before our luck ran out and someone recognized me as the pillager and plunderer of helpless cities all up and down Wuin . . . to say nothing of my concerted campaign against the Thirty-Nine Steppes. Nor did Sharee have any particular interest in staying. As a weatherweaver, she tended to have more luck with her spells in a clime that wasn't as relentlessly arid. And Mordant hadn't stated any preference one way or the other.

We wound up at a busy pub in the heart of Port Debras. We'd learned that it was an excellent place to find ships and ship captains with whom we could book passage. We were not exactly destitute. I had reluctantly left behind a small fortune in gems, but I'd had access to a significant number of dead bodies (which we'd dutifully torched) before setting out on our expedition, and I'd taken the liberty of relieving quite a few of them of whatever monies they had upon them. Sharee had stood there and scowled as I did so, but hadn't commented beyond that, which I took to be a reluctant but mute admission that we might as well take their valuables since they weren't going to be doing much of anything with them.

Once at the pub, and after having tied off the horse at a hitching post, Sharee and I went in two different directions, asking around, seeing what we could find. Fortunately, I was, and am, a reasonably good judge of character. I was certain that at least two of the men I spoke to were actually of a most villainous nature, who would have been quite pleased to take us as passengers and, during the night, relieve us of our valuables and our lives before tossing us over the side to a watery grave.

What I wound up doing was seeking out people who seemed as if they were having trouble walking. Sure enough, I found a small group of folks who looked a bit shaky on their feet for exactly the reason I expected they would be: They'd been at sea and had just recently come off a ship. Their general deportment, plus their decidedly nonnautical suitcases, told me they were travelers rather than crewmen. If one wanted to be sure that a ship would see you safely to your destination, my reasoning was to seek out recommendations from people who had already made it from whatever port of call they'd just been to, to here.

Inquiring of the new arrivals, I learned that they'd been brought over on a ship commanded by one Captain Stout. A worthy and hardy-sounding name, I had to admit. As it so happened, I found the good captain tossing back some mead in a corner of the bar. Large, gruff, and affable, he struck me as a solid seaman, and his disposition certainly matched the glowing reports I'd received from his recent passengers.

I had no place in particular I was planning to go, which as it turned out dovetailed with Captain Stout's agenda. He had a cargo he was transporting to an island continent called Azure. Azure was, by all accounts, a decent enough place, albeit a bit colder than I was used to. But I believed I could get accustomed to it, and besides, it wasn't as if we'd be staying there permanently. If we liked it, we could; but if not, we could always find somewhere else.

It was at that moment that I abruptly realized I was thinking of Sharee and I as a "we." I had to remind myself that Mordant was part of the mix, but on some level I was starting to regard Sharee and I as a pair. The thought was staggering to me, and yet as the first waves of shock subsided, I slowly realized that it was not an unpleasant notion. I began to wonder if she felt the same way, and decided that she very likely did. After all, I reasoned, I had to be getting the notion from *somewhere*. And where else could it reasonably have been from, if not from hints or subtle suggestions from Sharee herself. And they would have to have been subtle, because she was a magic user, and that's simply how magic users tended to do things.

A loud throat-clearing noise from Captain Stout jolted me back to reality and I realized that I'd drifted off into a daydream about Sharee and me. How truly embarrassed I felt. "What say ye, lad?" demanded Captain Stout. "Any interest in heading to the Azure Island? Quite lovely this time of year, I understand. And we'll have a few other passengers aboard, so you'll have some company other than just my crew."

"It sounds fine to me," I said. "Let me check with my friend and I'll be right back with you. She's just around the other side of the pub."

"She. A lady friend." Captain Stout didn't seem especially thrilled. "Ladies on sailing vessels aren't always a good mix, me lad. Sailing ships are crewed by rough, battle-hardened seamen. Do you know what you get when you put women together with seamen?"

"Pregnancies?"

"You get bad luck," he continued as if I hadn't spoken, which was probably a good thing. "Now, I'm an open-minded man, and I'll bring your little lady along if I must. But just keep her away from my crew. And pray to the water gods for good weather . . ."

"Oh, well, we can guarantee that," I said, "since she's a—"

". . . and, ideally, that no damned or accursed magic-using weavers come anywhere near my ship," he concluded.

My mouth opened and closed without words emerging for a moment. "Weavers . . . are a problem?" I asked.

"You get magic users on your boat, and you're guaranteed disaster," Captain Stout told me forcefully. Then he squinted, apparently processing belatedly what I'd just said. "How can you guarantee good weather? She's a . . . what?"

"An amateur weather predictor," I said immediately. "Charts storms and such. And she told me there's going to be nothing but good weather and smooth sailing for the next three weeks."

"Good weather and smooth sailing where?"

"Everywhere," I told him without hesitation. "Everywhere. In the world. It's the damnedest thing. Never seen anything like it."

His thick eyebrows knit. Then he laughed with such abruptness that it jolted me, and he said, "If that's what your woman thinks, then the odds are that she's going to remain an amateur for a very, very long time." Then he clapped me on the shoulder as if we were old mates and told me to bring my young lady by so he could inspect the cut of her jib.

Personally, I didn't think Sharee was going to want the old salt inspecting any cuts of her at all, but I smiled affably and went off to find her.

I headed around to the other side of the pub and then stopped. There was Sharee . . . but she was going out a side door, in the company of three rather large men.

I gripped my walking staff tightly. The staff was an exceptionally formidable weapon that had been assisting me in and out of scrapes for over half my life. There was a carving of a lion wrestling a dragon on one end, and a sharp blade could be triggered to snap out of the dragon's mouth for use in combat. In addition, with a twist the staff could be separated into two halves and each used as a devastating cudgel.

Not that I was anxious to get into any sort of fight. I never was. Then again, I was hoping I wouldn't have to. If I followed Sharee outside and matters appeared dire, I could whistle for Mordant and he would emerge from hiding and rip the throats out of these likely felons in no time at all, while I would stand by and check over their corpses for valuables. It all seemed a very credible plan to me.

I couldn't tell if the three men were forcing Sharee to go out with them. All I knew was that they were gone and I was going to follow them. I moved quickly, stepping through the door into what turned out to be an alleyway alongside the pub.

What I saw astounded me.

Sharee had her arm extended and Mordant was sitting perched upon it. She had her cape coiled around her forearm to protect it from his rather formidable claws. The three men were making soft noises of admiration, and the largest of them—a broad-shouldered, mustached man wearing a large gray cloak and white tunic—was even scratching Mordant under the chin and being rewarded with gentle "cooing" sounds.

"What the hell is all this?" I demanded, startling them. One of them reached to his side and I heard the unmistakable hiss of steel against leather as he prepared to draw a sword. This didn't sit particularly well with me, as the prospect of fighting generally didn't. But I was just annoyed enough not to back down. Furthermore the weight of the bastard sword I kept strapped to my back was of comfort.

But Sharee put out a hand to the sword-puller and said firmly, "It's all right. This is Apropos. Apropos, these are old friends of mine."

"Are they," I said, in a tone that I wanted to sound chilly, but instead just came out as somewhat whiny. "Imagine running into them here."

"This," she said, indicating the mustached one, "is Rex Reggis. He's a weaver. We received training in the same guild hall, years ago."

"Little Sharee always had a crush on me," said Reggis with the sort of ready smile that just makes you want to rip off the lips of the smiler.

"You," she corrected him in a very arch tone, "had a crush on me."

"I feel the need to disagree," he said.

"And I feel the need to impale myself," I told them, "but sometimes we resist urges."

I didn't like the way she was looking at Reggis. Nor did I like the way he was looking at her. There was something decidedly unsavory about the whole thing, and I couldn't help but feel that the sooner we were quit of them, the better.

"We were just admiring your drabit," said Rex. "Quite an amazing creature. We can use him on our quest."

I had been about to launch on a truly sterling string of snide remarks and cutting insults that would have been among the most memorable ever put forward in the history of condescending discourse. But Rex's comment tossed it right out of my head, leaving my initial response as a sort of inarticulate "Hnnch?" Fortunately I reacquired my ability to speak straightaway, and said, "Quest?"

"They're on a quest," Sharee said eagerly. "Doesn't that sound exciting?"

"Yes," I agreed. "It certainly does. And I have to emphasize here the concept of 'sounds.' As in, is best appreciated second- or third-hand in the telling of it, rather than the first-hand experiencing of it."

"Oh, come now!" Rex boomed. "A man of your obvious quality and sophistication would certainly thrive on a good quest!"

I glanced over my shoulder to see just who he might be addressing, and then realized with dawning disbelief that he was talking to me. I forced a grin, which was more like gritted teeth, and said, "What's obvious to you appears to have slipped right past me."

"Apropos, this is no time to be difficult. It's a once-in-a-lifetime opportunity," Sharee told me.

"Here's the thing about once-in-a-lifetime opportunities," I said. "They tend to shorten the actual lifetime in question."

"I think he's a coward," growled one of the other companions. "A foul character trait to have."

"I prefer to think of it as an alternative lifestyle," I informed the growler.

"Apropos, listen," said Sharee. "What they seek . . . it's the mystic tome of—"

"I don't care."

"It can transform anyth—"

"I don't care! Sharee, what's . . ." I quickly put an arm around her shoulders and pulled her a few feet away from the others. Mordant, on her arm, was rudely jostled by the sudden movement but managed to hold on nevertheless. ". . . what's going on here?" I demanded in a low voice. "We had plans . . ."

She looked at me wide-eyed. "We did?"

"Yes! We were going to . . ."

I stopped.

"Apropos," she pointed out, "we hadn't really planned where we were going. We just decided we were getting out of here. But plans aren't about what you're running from. They're about what you're running to."

"We're going to Azure. It's all arranged."

She blinked in surprise. "It is?"

"Yes. Booked and everything. All set. Let's go."

"And what's on Azure?"

"It doesn't matter."

"It does. Apropos, I thought you understood . . ."

"Understood what?"

Sharee sighed heavily. "Port Debras isn't just a place of comings and goings. It's a place of opportunities. To find possibilities to explore. Rex's quest is an incredible possibility. He's leading a group to one of the most challenging—"

"Sharee, life doesn't have to be about finding challenges. Life *is* challenge. And I . . ."

She stared at me, and I felt her gaze boring through my mind. "You what?" she asked.

And I want to meet those challenges with you. It's taken me this long to realize that the reason you make me so crazy, so infuriated, is because I have incredibly strong feelings for you.

Because lately you've been all I think about, which is incredibly amazing considering that for as far back as I can remember, I've been all I think about. And even a life of supposed boredom would be devoutly to be desired, because no life with you could ever be boring. You're everything I need, everything I could want. I feel as if I'd suffocate without you, I . . .

"Sharee!" It was Rex's voice. He looked hopeful, but also slightly impatient. "The tide will be heading out soon, and we need to be upon it. Are you with us or no?"

I saw the look in her eyes when she glanced in the direction of this fellow magic user who apparently was a great factor in her young life and had never truly been left behind in her growth or imaginings. And in that look I saw, just for a heartbeat, a spark. A gentle, ineffable spark that I instantly, selfishly, wanted for myself. And which I knew, without the slightest doubt, would never be given me.

I realized what a fool I'd been. I was positive that, if I said anything of the absurdly impassioned spew that was rattling around in my head, I would not only sound like a complete idiot, but I would lose whatever shred of respect she might have had for me.

What would have been the point of it? Really? She was still going to go off with Rex Reggis, I knew that with certainty.

She wanted him. I could tell.

And let's face it: It wasn't all that long ago she'd tried to kill me. And not much longer than that that she'd pretty much cursed my name whenever she'd heard it mentioned. There was no reason to think that, sooner or later, she wouldn't want to kill me again. Why shouldn't she, really? Everyone else in my life tried to, sooner or later. Really. Truly. No matter whom I encountered, eventually one or both of two things would happen. Either that person would die, or that person would try to kill me.

What had I done to deserve this fate? Nothing. Be born. That was pretty much it.

And what had Sharee done to deserve that fate as well? Nothing.

I realized it at that moment with one of those flashes of clarity that one has from time to time. Sharee wasn't going to remain with me. Her eyes were filled with Rex Reggis. He was a hero type, a sort I knew all too well, and they had a disgustingly consistent impact on females. Which normally wouldn't interest Sharee, but he was obviously an old love and a mage to boot, and that made him irresistible. But more to the point, if Sharee remained with me, there was every reason to assume that eventually she would join the teeming masses of people who had tried to kill me or wound up dead or both.

Why wish that on her?

Except . . .

. . . I wanted her to say she wanted to remain with me.

To this day, I'm not sure why it was so important to me at that moment. More important to me than anything. Perhaps it was because, since I was long departed from my native Isteria, Sharee represented the last tie I had to my homeland.

Or maybe I just wanted to be loved. Maybe what I was experiencing was the beginnings of being frustrated with the way I was, but having no clue how to change, or even if I wanted to.

She was still waiting for me to finish my earlier sentence. "You what—?" she prompted again.

Why waste the time. It would all end badly, and besides . . . she didn't love me. Didn't want to be with me. Not really. Who would? What did I have to offer? Cynicism and lameness and a deep abiding conviction that I was the only sane man in an insane world, a belief which brought me comfort but oddly was seen as less than flattering by just about everyone else.

Tell her you love her or at least like her, tell her you enjoy her company, tell her you want time, tell her that if she leaves you now you'll likely never see her again and that's unacceptable, tell her anything.

"Go to hell" were the words that came out of my mouth.

Anything but that.

I looked right through her to the drabit on her arm. "Mordant? Coming with me or staying with Sharee?"

Mordant cocked his head slightly, and then wrapped his tail around her arm.

That was my answer.

I shrugged.

"Fine," I said, and something that I hadn't even known was living within me until moments earlier was crushed and died. I turned and walked away without another word to her. Feeling sorry for myself, in an endeavor to look even more pathetic than I felt, I accentuated my limp as I headed back into the pub.

I made my way to Captain Stout. He looked up at me quizzically.

"Just me," I said.

"I see it's just you. Who else would you be?"

"I mean," I sighed, "that I won't have a lady with me on your boat. It'll just be me booking passage."

His face brightened. "Ah! Excellent," he said, and stuck out a hand, which was thick and greasy. I shook it reluctantly and then quietly rubbed it clean on a napkin. "Don't get me wrong," he added hurriedly. "I like the ladies. I do. They certainly have their uses, especially if you need somewhere to dock your dinghy, if you get my drift," and he laughed a raucous laugh.

I forced a smile. "Yes, I get it," I said.

"But really, they've no place on a ship. Just cause trouble. Once you're at sea, mark my words, you're better off without them. We'll have a much smoother crossing with just the blokes running the show."

I marked his words. And some time later, when I was floating in the ocean, fighting what I was certain was imminent drowning, I would have cause to curse them as well.

Chapter 2

The World According to *Larp*

*I*t was some hours later that I brought my meager belongings, in a sling over my shoulder, down to the Grand Jetty. There was an impressive number of ships docked there of varying size and quality. The sky was clear and blue, and the salt of the sea air stung my lungs, but in a refreshing way. I should have felt a sense of exhilaration.

Instead all I had was a distant emptiness.

All the way to the gangplank of the ship on which I'd booked passage, I kept glancing over my shoulder. I thought she would come. I thought she would come dashing down the Grand Jetty, waving and calling my name, and Mordant would be flapping behind her, like the romantic end of some great novel.

There were so many people, hustling and bustling about, and a few times I actually thought I did see her. But it was always someone else.

I shrugged.

"She was a pain in the ass," I said to no one except myself, and even I didn't entirely believe me as I turned and made my way up the gangplank. I knew it was the right ship because I saw the name of the vessel, *Larp*, painted proudly on the side. When the captain told me the ship's name, I asked him from where it derived. He looked at me knowingly, as if waiting for my reaction to his next words: "Say it backwards."

I paused. "Pral?" When he grinned broadly, clearly expecting me to say something more, I forced an expression of comprehension and said, "Oh! *Pral!* Of *course!*" He leaned back in his chair and smiled in triumph, and I never got any more explanation than that.

I boarded the vessel and headed down to the passenger level. There I encountered my fellow travelers. Two of them were traveling together, and they seemed rather chummy with each other in a way that I considered, frankly, a bit unsettling. The one was a barrel-chested, red-haired barbarian named Farfell. His companion was smaller and rat-faced, dressed in shades of gray, and wore his hair long with some sort of thick gel in it that kept it elaborately wavy. He went by the curious name of Gay Mousser. I'd never met a man named Gay. It certainly seemed a convivial moniker.

Still, as I noted, the camaraderie between them . . . disturbed me. When I was but a lad still living in Stroker's tavern, the sinkhole in which I spent my formative years, I once heard mention of men who preferred to be with other men. In my childish voice, I had piped up, "As well they should. Girls are stupid." This had prompted a round of raucous laughter, which pleased me greatly until Stroker cuffed me in the ear and told me to mind my own business.

Later, I asked my mother about it, and after her face flushed with embarrassment, she explained to me the true significance of such preferences. I was appalled, of course. As did anyone else, I knew it for the unnatural abomination that it was. Even I, who challenged the reasons of gods for everything, had to acknowledge that certain things had a right and proper place to be put, and one simply didn't put them in places they were not intended by nature to go. As far as I was concerned, it was no more complicated an issue than that. There was no question of morals or ethics. I simply couldn't comprehend why anyone would choose to do such a thing.

My mother, Madelyne, did not seem to see it that way. Instead she said to me gently, "Strange are the ways of love, Apropos. Very curious indeed. It can propel us in directions that all the great wisdom of youth such as yours cannot begin to envision. You should not be so quick to judge others."

"Why not? If you cannot judge others, who *can* you judge?"

She smiled in that way she had, as if she found adorable everything I said. "Yourself."

"I don't see the point in that," I told her.

"You will."

And eventually I grew up, and she died a violent death, and I had judged myself repeatedly and had to admit I still didn't quite see the point in it.

I encountered a third passenger who was a rather odd individual. Tall, with a distant look as if he felt he should be somewhere else, with stringy white hair and pale skin. He tended to spend inordinate amounts of time adjusting a gold ring he sported on his right hand. I felt a slight chill looking upon it, for rings and I had not gotten along all that well. He was sharing my cramped quarters, which annoyed me. On the other hand, it certainly was going to be easier to be with him than with that barbarian and his hairstyled companion.

"Hello," I said upon first meeting him in our quarters. He had taken the higher-hung hammock and was seated in it, swinging back and forth gently, just shaking his head. "Problem?"

He looked at me and, upon closer inspection, I noticed

that his skin was peeling. Odd condition. "I don't believe you're here."

"Ah," I said, not quite sure how else to respond.

"And I'm not here either," he continued.

"Ah," I said again.

"I am simply an antihero thrust into an enforced heroic situation not of my own making."

"I can certainly sympathize," I said readily, and I could. However, I was becoming equally convinced that this fellow was a lunatic. "I'm Apropos."

"I'm completely irrelevant," he replied.

I stared at him blankly for a moment, and then slowly closed my eyes and cursed under my breath. Then I opened them and forced a smile. "It's my damned name. What's yours?"

"I am called . . . Doubting Tomas."

That was an easy name to believe, although I would have been inclined to switch the letters and make him "Touting Dumbass."

"All right," I said. "I suppose that's marginally better than 'Apropos.' "

Tomas glowered at me. "I do not belong in this world," he told me.

I nodded. "I know exactly how you feel."

He stared as if I were an idiot. "You couldn't possibly. You're *of* this world."

"To be fair," I pointed out, "it certainly seems as if you're of it as well."

"You know nothing."

There was so much I could have said. But then I realized the utter pointlessness of engaging in an extended debate with the fool. So I smiled and simply said, "One thing I do know: This conversation is over."

Whereupon I turned over in my hammock and promptly

fell out as the sling swung out from under me. I hit the floor and lay there as the annoying Tomas guffawed slightly, but offered no other comment. Without a word, I hauled myself back to my feet, balancing myself on my left as best I could, and pushed myself back into the hammock. It swayed violently once more, but the second time I was able to hang on, albeit ungracefully.

I drifted off to sleep and dreamt of Sharee and Mordant. Sharee, who I had thought would be staying with me because she perceived some sort of greatness within me. Mordant, who I had convinced myself was some sort of reincarnation of my mother. Both gone now. Both gone.

No reason for them not to be. After all, wasn't that what everyone in my life did? Leave me, sooner or later?

I took that self-pitying attitude and, even in my sleep, clung to it with as much dedication as I'd hung on to the hammock.

I had no idea what to expect in terms of sea travel. I had never been on a boat in my life, and I had always heard that those who were new to such transport could have some trouble with illness.

I did not have some trouble. I had an excruciating amount of trouble.

We set off and immediately it felt to me as if the entire world was incessantly rocking. I was grateful for the absence of mirrors because, by all accounts, my face was such a repulsive shade of green that rumors began to float around the ship I was some sort of leper (which, for no reason that I could determine, seemed to amuse Doubting Tomas no end). The hammock swayed with the boat, which did nothing to improve my disposition. I started lying on the floor. That wasn't much better. From time to time I would emerge upon the deck, lean over the nearest railing, and be sick into the sea. My discomfort provided endless amusement for the experienced sailors, who walked with confidence, swaying in perfect synchronization with the boat. Every so often one would clap me on the back and say, "Don't worry! You'll get your sea legs soon enough."

I didn't see how acquiring new legs would stop me from hanging over the edge of the boat and heaving into the sea.

After a while I ceased vomiting for the simple reason that I had nothing left to vomit, short of heaving up internal organs.

And then, days into the voyage, as I hung over the railing and contemplated simply throwing myself overboard to terminate my misery, I heard a repetitious thump from behind me that I recognized quite readily. It was the sound of someone moving with the aid of a staff. I managed to lift my head in time to see a man approaching me. He was tall, with thick red hair and bristling beard, and he was wearing what I recognized as an article of clothing called a "kilt." It was red plaid, and he wore a crimson cloak about the shoulders of his thick white shirt, trimmed around the edges with red fur. His staff was ornately carved with images of what appeared to be dancing goblins cavorting its length.

"Ye got a problem, laddie?" he inquired.

I managed a nod, and the world seemed to bob and weave mercilessly, even though the water was remarkably calm. I dreaded the notion of our hitting even a mild squall. Gods only knew what it would have done to me.

He had a pouch hanging on the front of his kilt, strategically positioned over his manhood. He reached into the pouch. I wasn't sure why, and the gesture was disconcerting, because I didn't want to think what he was about to pull out and show me. I was hardly in a position to leave the immediate area, though.

A moment later he extracted a vial with a blue liquid. He looked at it as if to double-check the contents, then strode over to me and extended it. "Drink it," he said.

Now, of course, I had no idea who this fellow was. A total stranger was offering the always-suspicious Apropos some sort of liquid pulled from the general vicinity of his crotch. For all I knew, it would kill me on the spot.

Which is why I took it from him and downed it immediately. That should go to show you just how little affection I had for life at that point. There are few creatures walking the surface of the earth who are more eager to stay alive than me. So if I was so uncaring of life that I was willing to risk throwing it away by swallowing a blue fluid from a total stranger, that alone should tell you a lot.

By way of a stray thought . . . why do we say that, I wonder? "Total stranger." Those words always seem to go together. As if someone could be a partial stranger. Or a half stranger. He's completely unknown to you, except for that torrid weekend you spent in a cabin in the Elderwoods.

Then again, I have had lovers who turned out to be not remotely what I thought they were. And there have been those who called me "friend" who had no inkling of the true depths of darkness and resentment that resided within me. Perhaps we're all strangers to one another in a way, and the only thing that makes someone a "total" stranger is that they haven't yet had the opportunity to betray you.

All that flitted through my mind as the blue liquid burned down my throat, and then suddenly there was an easing of the ache in my stomach and the world seemed to clear. I blinked several times, scarcely able to believe it.

"Good fer what ails ye, eh?" He smiled, displaying large, crooked teeth. He patted his pouch, a gesture that I couldn't help but think he'd best not repeat in mixed-gender company. "Feeling better?"

"I am . . ." I admitted, surprised at the sound of returning strength to my voice. I couldn't believe how quickly the stuff had worked. "I am! Yes! Thank you. I . . . I wish I'd run into you earlier. I could've saved myself days of suffering. What do you call that stuff?"

"Just a little home brew. Frankly, ye looked like a lad who deserved a break from his sufferin'. Ah'm glad Ah could help."

I had to listen carefully to all he said, for his accent was so thick (far thicker than I'm conveying here) that it was all I could do to comprehend. I stuck out a hand. "I'm Apropos."

"Ronnell," he replied. His arm was brawny, his shake firm.

"Whereabouts are you from, Ronnell?"

"Ach," and he shrugged his broad shoulders, "Ah like t'think of muhself as a citizen of the world. It's not where ye've been that matters. It's where ye wind up, ye know what Ah'm sayin'?"

Oddly enough, I felt I did, and nodded. "Will I need more of that stuff?" I asked.

"The dose Ah gave you should last ye about a week. We're supposed t'be at sea fer four weeks, so I'll be happy to supply ye wit' refills."

"You're a gift from the gods, Ronnell," I told him fervently. Then I paused, suddenly suspicious, certain I wasn't going to like the answer to my next question. "How much will it cost me?"

He laughed as if that was the most ridiculous question he'd ever heard, and draped one of his huge arms around me. "Ye needn't worry! We're all travelers together, are we not? Tell ye what. Are ye anxious to repay me?"

I wasn't particularly. I was a big believer in obtaining as much as possible for as little as possible. But I figured I was going to have need of his services and goodwill for a few weeks more. So it made sense to play along with him. "That would be nice," I lied.

"Then join me! T'night. Fer a wee game."

"A game?" I asked cautiously. "I . . . have to warn you. I don't have a lot of money on me, so if it involves gambling of some sort . . ."

"Nah!" he said, forcefully expelling air. "Nah, it's nothin' like that! Ah saw we have some other hardy voyagers aboard, and Ah thought it might be fun to play a wee adventure game."

"I'm not sure what you're talking about . . ."

"Then come down to th' galley this evenin', and ye'll find out." He elbowed me playfully in the ribs in such a way I was sure that I'd felt one break. "Ye'll never ferget it."

That much, he was right about.

It appeared that my newfound friend, Ronnell, was a rather convincing sort. Either that or he had quickly managed to amass a series of debts from the other passengers and conned them, on that basis, to join the festivities. Because that evening I discovered not only myself down in the galley, but also the other voyagers whose acquaintance I had earlier made, and my unwilling roommate as well.

They were already seated when I arrived. The galley smelled of seawater and slightly rotting food, and it would have been enough to send me into spasms of nausea if it weren't for Ronnell's cure-all. So that was enough to remind me that I did owe the redheaded, boisterous fellow, and perhaps participating in his silly game was the least I could do. And as I have made abundantly clear in the past, I always endeavor to do the least I can do.

They were seated 'round a long table that was ordinarily used for meals. None of Captain Stout's dozen or so crewmen were about, presumably having eaten earlier and turned in or gone to their evening stations or gone off to dance jigs and tell ludicrous stories about sizable fish or whatever the hell it was that sailors did at night. It was just the five of us, with Ronnell, who was seated at one end of the table and grinning lopsidedly. I was at the opposite end, Farfell and the Gay Mousser on the right, Tomas on the left. Every so often the Mousser would giggle in a high-pitched tone that made me just want to yank my sword off my back and cleave his head from his shoulders. But Farfell was a brute of a barbarian and would likely have something to say on the matter.

I had taken to keeping my weapons on my person whenever I wandered about the ship. Although Stout's men seemed innocuous enough, I'd heard far too many tales about unexpected mutinies—or even abrupt attacks by pirates—to allow myself to be out of reach of my weapons. The staff was natural enough for me to keep with me at all times. The sword was a hand-and-a-half sword, also known as a bastard sword, given me by one who had every reason to know about such things ("such things" meaning bastards).

"Expectin' problems, Apropos?" inquired the Mousser, giving another of those annoying laughs. I restrained myself, partly out of self-control, and partly out of the firm conviction that Farfell would break me in half if I tried it.

"I expect nothing," I replied, voicing one of my favorite philosophies. "But I anticipate everything."

"A solid philosophy!" said Ronnell. Not that I lived or died on his approval, but the sentiment was appreciated. It was at that point I noticed that Ronnell had set something up in front of himself. He had erected three small upright boards, hinged together, and placed them so that they were blocking from our view the table in front of him. He had an assortment of small scrolls in front of himself, and it appeared to me that they were color-coded in some fashion, with a series of blue and yellow and red ribbons designed to make them easier to differentiate at a glance.

"What are you doing?" I asked.

"I admit to being somewhat curious about that myself," said Farfell.

Doubting Tomas, with a long, drawn look, said, "I have no idea why I've allowed myself to be pulled into this. Bad enough I'm forced to travel this twisted road paved by the sick fantasies of a deranged mind. But now I engage in some sort of nonsensical pursuit purely to provide entertainment value."

"Entertainment, aye," allowed Ronnell. "Then again, perhaps ye will learn something about how ye handle emergencies, and how much risk ye're willing t' take."

This wasn't going to be difficult for me at all. I handled emergencies by vacating the area as quickly as possible, and the amount of risk I was willing to take was near zero. So with any luck, I'd be done with this business in no time at all.

Ronnell pulled a small case from his sleeve, placed it on the table, and opened it. It contained two six-sided black dice. They appeared to be staring back at us, the white dots on their surface glistening in the dim light. I began to get an uneasy chill at the base of my spine, and I glanced around the table to see if anyone else appeared at all nervous. No one did, which either meant that I was getting myself worked up over nothing, or else they were oblivious of some sort of danger that only I was perceiving.

"The name of this game," Ronnell said in a booming voice that caused both me and the Mousser to jump slightly in our places, "is 'Tragic Magic.'"

Sounds like the story of my life, I thought.

"Tragic Magic," continued Ronnell, obviously undeterred by my inner thoughts, "is an adventurin' game."

"A what?" said Farfell, one bushy eyebrow raised.

"An adventurin' game. What happens is, ye use these dice," and he pushed forward a number of the parchments, "and the information on these scrolls to create characters for yerselves. Ye use yer own name, because where would be the fun in utilizing fake names?"

"Where indeed?" I echoed, wondering just exactly where the fun was going to be even if we used our own names.

"These characters will have their own individual abilities and character traits. Ye then send them on an adventure of muh devising," and he held up a large scroll that, unlike the others, was tied off with a black ribbon. The recurring "black" theme was contributing to my overall sense of unease. "The results of yer explorations will be determined by each roll o' the dice."

"This is pointless," said Doubting Tomas, and for once I had to agree with him, although I said nothing. "So we explore this fictitious quest you've fabricated. We kill an evening doing so. What's in it for us, aside from the questionable joy of one another's company?"

"Oh . . . did Ah forget to mention? Just t'make it int'resting, should ye triumph over the challenges Ah present you . . ."

He reached into his cloak, which seemed to have become rather voluminous, and a moment later produced a large leather sack. He upended it upon the table, and gold coins spilled out. It was a most impressive sight, and a pretty formidable sound as well, the coins tinkling over one another with that musical noise that only gold coins can produce. I wondered why I was feeling a burning in my lungs, and then came to the belated realization that I'd stopped breathing. I forced an exhalation and continued to stare at the pile of coins winking at me mockingly.

The others at the table seemed no less impressed than I. "If we win . . . ?" breathed the Mousser.

"How would we split it?" I asked, eyes narrowing.

"Sixty-sixty-sixty?" the Mousser suggested, and I decided right then that, aside from the fact that I considered him an abomination, he was a decent enough sort.

"Splitting it only becomes a consideration if ye all survive," said Ronnell challengingly. "There are many dangers along the way in Tragic Magic. You cannot be certain your characters will make it through."

"We'll take the chance," said Farfell.

"Wait," Doubting Tomas said, "we know what you're putting up. What do we have at stake?"

It was a reasonable question, and one that had occurred to me as well. Ronnell seemed amused by it. "Why, gentlemen . . . the pleasure of yer company would certainly be enough to satisfy any man, don't ye think?"

We all looked suspiciously at one another, probably wondering if he was genuinely looking at the motley crew around the table. But then we collectively shrugged. He was obviously something of a loon, but the stakes he was putting up were sane enough, and there seemed no harm in going along with it.

Following his instructions and a dizzying set of rules, we created characters out of paper and dice rolls. The Mousser reconfigured himself as a thief. Farfell became a bulging barbarian. Neither characterization seemed all that much of a stretch. Doubting Tomas became a cleric, a holy man wielding magic powers.

And I, much to my annoyance, found myself designated as a "jackanapes." "You mean a clown?" I demanded.

"A jester," said Ronnell. "You provide amusement for the crew of hardy adventurers."

Longtime readers of my "adventures" will readily comprehend why this new status was anathema to me. I almost walked out on the game right then and there, particularly considering that my position amongst the group was drawing exceedingly annoying guffaws from the others around the table. Even the consistently dour Tomas thought this was a highly amusing circumstance. Ultimately, though, I kept my peace and forced a grin to show that I was a good sport about it all, even as I imagined what it would be like to yank out my sword and send Ronnell's head tumbling across the deck.

The "adventure" began innocuously enough. I had to admit, Ronnell certainly had a way of evoking scene and mood. In deep, rolling tones he described how we four adventurers first met up in a tavern one cold winter's night, whereupon a dying man stumbled into the pub and presented us with a map. With an "X" marking a spot deep within some place called the Foreboding Mountains (a flamboyant enough name that Ronnell had invented, to be sure, although no more so than some other genuine places of my acquaintance) and a dying warning that failing to complete our mission could result in the End of the World as We Knew It, the dying man fulfilled his function and died. It was up to us to decide the specifics of how we were to go about our quest.

My answer was quite simple: Don't go. It was madness. We were in a warm pub on a cold night. What possible reason was there to go out and risk our necks just to save the world? What, after all, had the world ever done for me?

This line of reasoning proved to be less than persuasive to my cohorts, although they did laugh a good bit on the assumption that I, as jackanapes, was trying to provide some levity. The hell I was. Even in a fictitious setting, the allure of drink and safety was always preferable to deprivation and danger. But they didn't see it that way.

We then spent time wandering about the make-believe village and acquiring make-believe armaments, potions, supplies, etc., using make-believe money. I thought it was all make-believe bullshite by that point, but the others seemed genuinely caught up in the mechanics of the fictitious adventure. Eventually I ceased making snide comments about it because it was having no effect other than to annoy them. One of my general rules of thumb is to avoid annoying people with whom I'm going to be in enforced close proximity for weeks on end. Particularly when I could be disposed of by the simple expedient of being thrown overboard.

The group of us set out on our journey, and throughout our first encounters, we had a fairly easy time of it. We would encounter random threats such as giants or small dragons. At those times, we would develop strategies and the roll of dice would tell us how successful we were. We were consistently able to navigate our way past the assorted dangers, and even I was finding some degree of amusement in the entire process. Having encountered my share of quest-related horrors—an impressive accomplishment considering my near obsessive aversion to quests—there was definitely some entertainment in chancing upon threats to life and limb without any of our lives or limbs actually being jeopardized.

Still . . .

Whenever those dice came down, I felt . . . I didn't know what. Worried. Jumpy. A sensation that we were fish within a net and we didn't even realize it, because the net hadn't been drawn closed yet.

The others didn't notice or care. They became more boisterous, more adventurous as matters progressed. And over it all, Ronnell sat there with a wide grin, watching hawkishly as we rolled the dice one at a time to determine our fates.

We had navigated our way through an assortment of hazards and now stood just within the confines of the Foreboding Mountains themselves. "I think maybe we should leave," I suggested. Naturally no one paid me any heed.

"You are faced with two branching forks," Ronnell intoned, a gleam in his eye. He was leaning forward, wide-shouldered, hunched, looking like a gargoyle or perhaps a predatory bird about to pounce. "Both are illuminated by flickering torches. There is an inscription on the wall just outside the left path."

"I read it," said Farfell.

The Mousser thumped him on the chest. "Your character's a barbarian, remember? He can't read."

"Sorry," muttered Farfell.

"I read it," said the Doubter.

"It's written in runic," Ronnell informed us, and then he lowered his voice and said, "It says, 'Do Not Even Think for a Moment About Going This Way or You Will Die.'"

"That's the way we go then," said the Mousser.

I turned and gaped at him. *"It says not to! It says we shouldn't even think about it!"*

"Obviously," the Mousser told me with great satisfaction, "they're trying to throw us off the scent."

"That's one interpretation. The other is that someone took the time to warn us that we'll die if we go that way. It seems to me damned rude to ignore it if a person went to that much trouble."

"Apropos," Farfell said chidingly, "it's just a game. What's the worst that can happen?"

"Every time I've asked myself that, I invariably find out. And it's usually worse than I could have imagined."

"Nonsense." He looked with certainty at Ronnell and said, "We enter the left branch. We are not put off by the sign."

"Who is in the lead?" Ronnell asked politely.

Farfell hesitated, clearly not expecting the question. It was Doubting Tomas who spoke up, far more into the game than I would have credited. "I will take the lead, since I will be able to read any signs that present themselves."

Suddenly I heard a distant ripple of thunder, and looked around nervously. The ship was beginning to rock a bit more than before. I was more grateful than ever for the medication that Ronnell had provided me. But that gratitude and distant sense of relief was overwhelmed by an even greater sense of foreboding.

It has been said by some that I have a bit of magic in my blood. No weaver am I, certainly, but I can intuit when something is up, magic-wise. I was getting that sense now. That the impending storm stemmed from more than mere weather, or even from an intemperate god who felt like punishing a sailing vessel for no reason other than that it was there.

The others didn't seem to care. If there was anything going on, it clearly didn't register on them.

"The cleric takes the lead," intoned Ronnell.

"Wait," I said.

Ronnell turned and fixed me with a dark-eyed stare and repeated, "The cleric takes the lead." Before I could interrupt again, he continued, "Ye proceed down the hallway. There is a thick mist in the air. Torches continue to flicker on either side. Just ahead of ye, there is a large door made of solid stone."

"Does it have a lock?" inquired the Mousser.

"Aye. Inset into the door. But there is no sign of a key."

"Not a problem," the Mousser said with a confident grin. "The thief comes forward and produces his lock picks. He proceeds to work on the lock."

"The torches grow brighter," said Ronnell.

I could see it so clearly in my mind, the four of us in this scenario, so vividly that it was as if I was standing right there. And when the torches went higher still, I said, "We're leaving."

"The hell we are!" said an annoyed Farfell.

"We've got to get out of here. This thing stinks of a trap."

"I'm still working on the lock," said the Mousser.

"Roll the dice," Ronnell told him. "A roll over eight means the door unlocks."

The dice glittered, and the thunder sounded nearer. I could hear the increasing waves lapping at the side of the ship.

"Don't touch them," I warned the Mousser.

The Mousser looked at me as if I were insane. His expression was filled with disdain. His hair was filled with gel. "Gods, you really are quite the coward, aren't you," he said as he picked up the dice, shook them in his hand, and then dropped them.

A four and a two stared up at us.

"Bad luck," smiled Ronnell, and lightning flashed, illuminating the room through the solitary porthole. "The torches respond to the attempted intrusion."

"They what?" asked the Mousser.

And then he ignited.

His hair went up and he let out a scream like the damned, leaping to his feet, batting his hands furiously at his head, howling for Farfell to help him. The alarmed barbarian upended his drink on the Mousser's head. It made no difference. The flames were spreading, and his entire head was engulfed. The smell was horrific, the screams deafening. Tomas sat there, disbelieving. One had to admire his consistency. Ronnell didn't budge from his place.

Desperately, Farfell yanked off his cloak and threw it over the Mousser's head in an attempt to smother the flame. No good. As if the flame didn't need air to survive—

as if it was feeding off some completely difference source—it engulfed the entirety of the Mousser and the cloak as well. The screams had ceased, probably because his vocal cords had melted, but there was still violent shaking and twitching as the Mousser fell to the floor.

And suddenly an aura of glowing light lifted from the Mousser. It seemed to have form and substance, and yet was without either. It pulled free from the Mousser, mercifully it seemed, for that finally caused his body to cease its trembling. Then the pure, unsullied essence leaped through the air and into Ronnell. His eyes glowed with an inner light, and he licked his lips as if savoring some great delicacy as the aura suffused his very being. Within moments it faded, and Ronnell looked more vibrant, more powerful than he had before.

By this point even the densest of us knew that we were dealing with something truly sorcerous, but there was nothing we could do. For a moment I was terrified that the flames were going to spread to the floor, to the walls. That within seconds the entirety of the ship would be engulfed. Instead the flames appeared to consume themselves, and in seconds, they were gone. What was left was a smoldering pile of cooked meat that didn't look vaguely human, adorned with a few tattered pieces of cloth that had somehow managed to avoid being scorched. The floor all around was blackened, and thick smoke hung in the air, along with a stench that would have made me gag if it weren't for the anti-nausea elixir.

"You right bastard!" howled Farfell, and he didn't have a sword, but he didn't need one. He bore a dagger that was the size of my forearm, and he yanked it from his belt in preparation for leaping at Ronnell.

Ronnell remained where he was, imperturbable. "Sit down, barbarian," he said.

"I'll carve you up for—!"

"*Sit down!*"

The dagger slipped from Farfell's suddenly nerveless fingers, and he flopped down into his chair. His face went beet red, and he strained mightily to stand, but couldn't do so.

"I am the Magic Maestro here," Ronnell informed him coldly. "The runner of this game. The controller of yer destinies. To be the MM of a game of Tragic Magic is t'be the Supreme Being. So I'll thank ye to continue the evening's entertainment."

"Entertainment! A man is dead! *My* man is dead!" Farfell bellowed.

"I found that entertaining," said Ronnell placidly.

Tomas was still shaking his head, his eyes wide. "This isn't happening. I refuse to believe. . . . None of this is real. It's all a fantasy that I'll be awakening from just about any time."

I desperately wanted to share his outlook. Instead I snapped out, "*Shut up,*" and glared at Ronnell. "Who are you?"

"I? I am Ronnell McDonnell!" he said with fierce pride. A crack of thunder obligingly accompanied the pronouncement, as if matters weren't sufficiently melodramatic.

"Ronnell McDonnell?" I said with a grimace. "Of the Clan McDonnell?"

"Aye, the same." Cruel amusement glittered in his eyes. "Ye've heard of me."

"I haven't," said Farfell.

"I have. I just didn't believe a word of it," said Tomas.

I reached over and cuffed Tomas on the side of the head. It just seemed like the thing to do at that moment. Then I turned to Farfell, who looked as if a dozen emotions were warring within him at once. "McDonnell is a weaver I've heard tell of, back when I was an innkeeper in a far-off land. His name is mentioned in whispers, lest saying it too loudly summon him."

Ronnell seemed to find that amusing. "Really. And what do the whispers say?"

My voice low and even, I said, "They say you're insane. They say you seek ways to control men's destinies. They say that normal human sustenance is no longer sufficient for you, and that you consume your victims' vitality at the cusp of their deaths."

"Anything else?"

I pondered a moment. "That you're a hell of a dancer. But I never placed much stock in that."

Farfell looked fiercely in my direction, and then in Tomas's. "Let's rush him. He can't withstand a charge from all of us."

"Fine idea. You first," I said tightly. I was trying to rise from the chair, but having no luck. I was rooted to the spot.

"This isn't happening, this isn't happening," Tomas kept saying, but there was no conviction in his voice. Instead it sounded like borderline panic. I took cold pleasure in that. Misery loves company. Right then I was in the mood for lots of company.

"Ye have submitted yerself to my authority as Magic Maestro," said Ronnell. "By the laws of this game, yer bound t'me, and the game must be seen through to the end."

"And what constitutes the end?" I asked.

"Until ye lose," he replied, which was pretty much the answer I'd suspected.

"And if we win?"

He laughed at that. "Oh, I think the dice will see that doesn't happen. But," he added, "ye never know. They can be capricious." Then he laughed once more, and there was another flash of lightning for further punctuation.

Then, as if further discussion was pointless—which it

probably was—Ronnell McDonnell of the Clan McDonnell looked back down at the adventure he was charting. In a soft, insistent voice, he said, "The entire hallway in front of ye is aflame."

"We back up," I said quickly, "and head for the exit."

"Bad news," said Ronnell, not sounding as if he thought it was particularly bad. "A monstrous cave troll is standing between ye and the exit. He advances on ye. He looks hungry. The chances are that he will devour ye. However, he's a relatively young troll and will likely be satisfied with one of ye."

There was deathly silence for a moment, and suddenly Farfell shouted, *"We toss him the cleric!"*

"The hell you do!" Tomas cried out, doubting less and less by the moment. He lunged for the dice, but Farfell scooped them up and dropped them as if they were red hot. The dice skidded across the table and came up double six.

"The move works," Ronnell said calmly.

"It doesn't work!" Tomas said, and suddenly the front of his body seemed to explode, as if it was being ripped open by a great unseen force. I ducked to avoid the hurtling organs that splattered just above me. Out of the corner of my eye, I saw a glow and then the unbelieving Tomas was gone, his essence ripped from his body with as much force as his body was ripped from itself.

The ship tilted wildly, the force of the storm growing. I heard cries of alarm from the deck above. The sailors were running around to batten down this or tie off that. Their struggle to keep afloat would have been of far more importance to me were I not concerned with my own impending death struggle.

Ronnell McDonnell was grinning viciously. "The monstrous cave troll chokes on the cleric as pieces of him lodge in its throat and it dies . . ."

"We race for the exit," I said.

". . . but it falls in front of the exit, blocking yer way out with its sheer bulk. It's too heavy for ye t'lift."

"I take out my sword of power and start hacking at it," said Farfell. He kept glancing nervously at the charred remains of the Mousser. He looked as if he wanted to start sobbing, but was too afraid to do even that.

"Yer sword deflects off it."

"I hit it again."

"Yer sword bounces away once more," said Ronnell. He was beginning to look slightly impatient. "There is, however, another door down at the opposite end. It appears t'be open . . ."

"I hit the ogre with my sword," insisted Farfell.

Ronnell appeared to be getting annoyed, and I immediately realized why. Farfell had apparently discovered a move he could make that was fairly harmless. If he made no further move in the game, then he would be impervious to anything bad happening to him. He would hack at the unyielding ogre from now until doomsday for all he cared. Meantime, sooner or later, someone who wasn't a participant in this cursed game would enter the room and, with any luck, beat Ronnell senseless. I would have been howling for help the entire time, but the sounds of the storm outside were too vicious. I knew it would have been a waste of effort.

"The blade. Bounces. Off."

His teeth gritted with intensity, Farfell repeated, "I hit. The Ogre. With. My Sword."

Ronnell sat back in his chair for a moment, appearing to consider the situation. Then he shrugged. "Very well. Roll the dice."

Farfell immediately picked up the dice and tossed them. They clattered across the table and came up a two and a three.

"All right," said Ronnell. "Your sword blade bounces off the ogre and stabs you through the heart."

Farfell opened his mouth to protest, but blood began to pour out. His eyes widened and he clutched at his chest. There was more blood oozing between his fingers. His eyes shone with anger and confusion, and then with one final despondent glance in the direction of the Mousser, he keeled over.

Just before Farfell hit the floor, once again there was that glorious glow of light that, under other circumstances, I would have gazed upon with wonder. Now it simply horrified me as the essence of Farfell leaped across the table and into the receptive Ronnell.

He gasped in what sounded like almost sexual delight, and then he sat there, his head lolling for a few moments, rubbing his chest while his tongue strayed across his lips. Then he let out a contented sigh and looked at me.

"You're obviously full," I said. "We can continue this later. I'm sure . . ."

"The door awaits ye," he told me.

I forced a smile, trying to ignore the rapid thudding of my heart. "Yes. Yes, I'm sure it does. And don't think I'm not anxious to get myself killed for your dining and dancing pleasure. But the fact is, I was never much for adventures to begin with. So if it's all the same to you, I'd just as soon shut this one down."

"Tell ye what. I'll make it easy for ye," he said. "Ye suddenly find yerself magically transported through the door into the adjoining chamber. There before ye, ye see a great flaming sword hanging in the middle of the room, suspended by an invisible force."

"And you must think I'd be a great flaming idiot for even considering getting anywhere near it."

"Ye are going to reach for the sword. Roll the dice to see if ye are able to command it."

I still couldn't rise out of my chair. I tried to reach around to yank my own sword from its scabbard in the hope that I could fling it at him, perhaps impale him. But my arm wouldn't move.

"Ye think t'kill me," he smiled, as if able to read my mind . . . which, for all I knew, he could. "It doesn't end that easily, Apropos. Ah am the Magic Maestro. Ah control yer destiny."

Something in the way he said that, the incredible smugness, overcame my blinding fear and ignited my rage, which was always bubbling just beneath the surface anyway. "The hell you do!" I said. "I'd've lived a long and happy life if I didn't have a destiny of any sort. Instead I've spent my entire existence with different people telling me I have a great destiny that I'm supposed to live up to. A destiny I want no part of, thank you very much. But this much I know: I'll be damned if I give a bullying, soul-sucking lunatic like you command over whatever destiny my future holds, great or not. You control my destiny? Gods supposedly control man's destiny, and I've killed a god or two in my time, so don't think you can sit there all menacing and magical and get me to knuckle under to your parlor tricks!"

He didn't seem remotely impressed. "Roll the dice."

"*You* roll the bloody dice!" and I lunged, sweeping my hand back as if to knock them toward him.

And he flinched. His face was still a mask of forboding, but for a heartbeat there was a look of concern in his eyes as he shrank back from even the prospect of the accursed dice coming his way.

That was when I realized. I thought about how he had

never actually touched the dice. He had upended them onto the table from their pouch.

The thunder cracked outside, closer and closer, and there were even more alarmed shouts from above.

A desperate thought flashed through my mind, and apparently it did so at the exact same moment in Ronnell's. We both grabbed our respective ends of the table and tried to upend it, angle it so that we were in the superior position and the downward slope of the table would send the dice clattering toward the other.

The power in my arms, thanks to a lifetime of hauling myself around by them to compensate for my lame leg, is not to be underestimated.

He shoved the end of the table upward, and the dice tumbled toward me. I pushed forward, shoved back, briefly shifting the tilt so the dice began to roll the other way. I tried to shove the table over so the accursed things would fall to the floor. It didn't work. They clung to the table with an uncanny life of their own, which I was beginning to suspect they truly did possess.

We grunted, cursing at each other, trying with all our respective might to bring ruin upon the other. The dice rolled one way and then the other as we jockeyed for position, and the rocking of the boat itself didn't help matters.

The mug of mead I'd been drinking from overturned, falling against my chest and sending foaming liquid cascading into my lap. I jumped from the unexpected coldness, and Ronnell let out a triumphant howl as he thrust upward with all his strength and the dice tumbled right toward me. There was no way I was going to be able to avoid them.

Seized with a final burst of desperation, I grabbed the mug and brought it up to the table level. The poisonous dice tumbled into the mug without coming into physical contact with my person.

For an instant Ronnell hadn't seen what happened, and tried to move the table so he could get a better view. Grabbing the opportunity, I slammed the table forward. The far end struck him full in the face, and I heard a satisfying crack, which I recognized as the sound of a nose being broken (having heard it several times emerging from my own face). I shoved the table aside, the game components clattering to the floor, Ronnell flopping back onto his chair and grabbing at his nose, muttering a string of imprecations.

"*And you can choke on your flaming death sword!*" I shouted, as I swung the mug around and let fly the dice.

For the first roll of the evening, luck was with me, for Ronnell opened his mouth wide to shout something at me, and the dice flew straight in as if they had eyes. Snake eyes.

He gasped, choked, and reflexively swallowed, and I reached into myself and into him with pure force of will and snarled, "The flaming sword of doom doesn't like you."

He coughed, gagged, clutched at his throat, at his chest, as whatever dark magic the dice possessed worked its way and will through him. He began to tremble and toss about, and suddenly I could stand once more, which I did so forcefully that I overbalanced the chair and fell backward out of it. I scrambled to my feet as best I could, clutching my staff. I pressed the hidden trigger and a blade snapped out of the open mouth of the carved dragon on the end.

I wasn't going to need it.

Ronnell fell against the bulkhead, trembling, howling, energy appearing to build up from within him, smoke rising from his open mouth, from his ears. His eyes began to smolder, and jets of flame suddenly ripped from them as he screamed. It was then I realized the significant problem. When others had rolled the dice, whatever horrific circumstance had hit them had struck from without and worked its way in. With Ronnell, it was going from the inside out.

The table was sideways on the floor. I threw myself behind it just as Ronnell exploded with deafening force. The game documents, the partition he'd used, all went up instantly. The incredible power of the energies released slammed the table back against me, and me in turn against the far wall.

I heard a massive roaring and thought it was coming from within my head. Then the smell of salt and spray was overwhelming, and I peeped out from behind my table just in time to see a sight that caused my heart to sink somewhere into my boots.

Ronnell was gone.

So was a good chunk of the boat.

Where he'd been standing and exploding, there was now a vast, gaping hole, and seawater was rushing in with the eagerness of a group of sellswords at a virgins' convention. There was no way out. The water was gushing everywhere, barreling up the steps leading to the upper decks. I did the only thing I could think of: I clutched onto the table for dear life, lying flat on my staff to hold it in position as best I could.

Seconds later there was water everywhere. I took a deep breath, wondering how many days I could hold it, and then I was yanked out of the room, holding on desperately. I had clutched my first lover with less tenacity than I did that large piece of wood.

Water pounded against my face, and I held on all the more tightly. Then I was out of the ship and completely submerged, whipping around, closing my eyes and trying not to gasp reflexively from the shock of the chill water and violence of the spin. I wanted to cry out, I wanted to curse. Either response would have been fatal. So instead I sank my teeth into the inside of my lower lip and found myself praying to beings for whom I'd had nothing but contempt before. At that point I even recalled the time when I'd crossed a stone bridge into the land of Wuin and had fancied I'd seen sea gods raging at me from either side as the waters had surged around me. They seemed rather annoyed with me at the time. I wondered bleakly if they carried a grudge.

I tumbled about, lost track of which way was up and which was down. I figured that I had some measure of safety, since wood floats. Then I thought about the fact that the boat I'd been on was most likely going to sink like a rock, and suddenly the buoyancy of wood was called into question. Trying not to panic even as I felt the air beginning to burn in my lungs and seeking release, I let out a few bubbles and watched them float. They trickled away in the direction that, had I been left to my own devices, I would have sworn was down. Perhaps the gods were perverse enough to reroute air bubbles to lead me astray. I'd put nothing past those poxy bastards. Nevertheless, I decided to trust in what I laughingly referred to as nature and I kicked in the direction of the bubbles, keeping the table tightly under me.

There seemed to be nothing but darkness ahead, and I was becoming more and more certain that I was simply steering myself to a dark and soggy death in the pit of inky blackness that was the ocean. And then suddenly I was up and out, bobbing to the surface under a night sky that was alive with lightning all around. I looked down and saw that my staff was still wedged beneath me. I was relieved. That walking staff and I had been through a lot together, and I would have been loath to lose it.

I bounced up and down like a leaf upon the rough waters. I started screaming for help, why I don't know. I managed to twist around enough to see the ship in the distance. The *Larp* was listing wildly, and I could see sailors tumbling into the water. They were so far away that I couldn't even hear their screams against the storm, and so ceased my own, realizing that all I'd do was hurt my throat.

Then I saw something that will always stay with me. High, high in the crow's nest, I saw Captain Stout. I was certain it was he, even as far away as I was. He was clutching onto the main mast, and he was saluting, making no effort to abandon the ship and save himself . . . not that he would have likely had much opportunity for salvation. For some reason, I was certain that he was smiling as I watched the mast slowly descend into the water. Seconds later the ship rolled over onto its side and then sank without a trace. There was no indication that there had been a vessel there at all.

Here I'd sat down to a simple foolish game, and as a result was stranded in the middle of nowhere on a plank, all thanks to Ronnell McDonnell.

"I deserve a break today," I muttered.

Chapter 3

Bored on Board

I've spent a considerable portion of my life drifting, essentially. Never before, however, had I found myself in a position where I was doing so literally rather than figuratively. It was somewhat ironic, really, although I've noticed that irony is something better appreciated from a great distance of either miles or years, or both, and best appreciated when it's happening to someone else.

In this instance, it was happening to me. Then again, why not? Everything seemed to happen to me.

Except as I floated under the night sky, calling as loudly as I could to see if any voices responded and hearing none, I had to admit that for all I mourned my unceasing hideous luck, I also possessed the most uncanny streak of good fortune that any fool had ever been "blessed" with.

Over and over again, I would be thrust, all unwilling, into the mouth of danger. Once again for no damned good reason, I'd survived it. The former incident was bad luck, the latter, good. Which led me to decide that I was the luckiest bastard on the face of the planet, since my luck ran so extremely in both directions.

It was now simply a matter of finding out which aspect

of my luck was going to be holding sway for the duration of my decidedly disturbing ocean voyage.

I clutched tightly to the table, skimming over the choppy waves as best I could. Every so often I would be completely submerged, and I would wait to be dragged down to the bottom. A nameless watery grave: how fitting for one whose greatest boast throughout his life was that he had nothing.

But gods or fate or what-have-you were not interested in letting me off that easily, no. As many times as I was pulled down, I bobbed back to the surface moments later. I was drenched, I was miserable, I was cursing the fates (since at that point I wasn't taking the long view of being grateful to be alive), and overall it was one of the most miserable nights I'd spent in my life. And considering some of the nights I'd spent, that's saying something.

I didn't think I was going to be able to sleep at all, because I was concerned that as soon as I dozed off, I'd lose my grip on the table and slip off into the water. Apparently my survival instinct was more powerful than even I realized, however. One moment I was flat on my back, staring up at the moon, and the next I was blinking against the morning sun. Spray was misting in my face, and the salt water caused my eyes to tear. Slowly I sat up, being careful not to dislodge my rather precarious perch, and looked around.

Nothing.

Just vast, vast stretches of emptiness. Water as far as I could see, stretching to the horizon, stretching away.

It had not been all that long ago that I had been "adrift" in a similar situation that was simultaneously the exact opposite. I had been in the middle of a fearsome desert with nothing but sand and dirt all around me. Water was a distant and fanciful dream. Now here I was with more water than any sane person could hope to want to see, but just as helpless. Worse off, really. At least I couldn't drown in sand. Also, at least Sharee was with me the last time. If you're going to die alone, it's always nice to have someone along for the ride.

I pulled my feet up to make sure they were clear of the water, and checked that my sword and staff were still with me. I also had a skin of water attached to my belt. After my experience in the Tragic Waste, it had just become force of habit. Out of curiosity, I cupped my hand and dipped it into the ocean, then tried to drink it. It tasted salty, as one might have expected, and not especially palatable. So I took a judicious sip from my water skin, even though my impulse was to suck it dry.

Then I waited.

What I was waiting for, I hadn't the faintest idea. I had no reason to expect a ship to come along and rescue me. I had no real means of paddling. I could use my sheathed sword as a makeshift oar, I supposed, but what direction would I head? The ship had been going east. . . .

I looked up at the sun. It was still low to the horizon, so I knew the approximate direction that east was. But so what? Miles upon miles of empty ocean stretched before me, and even if I did manage to gain a little ground with my sword as an oar, so what? Better, I reasoned, to save my strength and dedicate it to a useful pursuit such as not falling off.

I prayed no storms would arise, because if they did, I was a goner. I had no protection from the elements, and any truly fierce waves would likely sweep me off the wood and away to the aforementioned watery grave.

And so I lay there.

And lay there.

And lay there.

I watched the sun track across the sky and wondered if the old stories about it being pulled through the air by a vast being on a great chariot had any basis in fact. I somehow doubted it. If I were a creature with as much power as that, I'd certainly find some pursuit more worthwhile and interesting than doing the exact same thing day in, day out. I reasoned that one of the benefits of omnipotence was the right to be spared mind-numbing boredom and repetition. Otherwise what was the point of infinite power in the first place?

The sun finished its arc and night fell once more. The silence was deafening. Just the steady lapping of water against the table and my labored breathing, that was it. I fell asleep and dreamt of Sharee, and of Mordant. I dreamt of the Princess Entipy, and the court of King Runcible. They were pleasant dreams, which was surprising considering I didn't usually have pleasant dreams. In the taunting night vision, I was back at Runcible's court, except this time everything had worked out. I was respected, loved, admired. I was dancing with Entipy, and people were bowing and smiling whene'er I passed.

And my mother was alive. She was standing to one side, grinning at how much her great and glorious son Apropos had accomplished. "Your destiny," she mouthed, and Mordant was on her shoulder.

I woke up. It was night, but I could sense that the sun would soon be rising.

It did.

It crossed the sky. More tedium. More of the same. I supposed I should be grateful as there was still no sign of anything to break the tedium, such as a storm. I remained judicious about the water, even though my lips and throat were begging for more. My stomach was thick with pain from lack of food. It had been a day and a half since I'd had anything to eat, and I had no clue how much longer it would be, if ever. Why, oh why hadn't I thought to keep some sort of nonperishable food items upon me? Wouldn't that have made some degree of sense?

I castigated myself for that, and soon I was chiding myself for everything else in my life that I had done wrong or foolishly. It was a considerable list. What was interesting was that in virtually every instance, I found someone else to blame. This person or that person had done me wrong, had ill-used me, had found some way to exploit me. Poor, poor Apropos, never to blame for any foul deeds or unfortunate happenstance that befell him, for they were always the fault of someone else.

This was certainly not a new mind-set. Nevertheless, for the first time, with no one else around to voice my frustrations to or commiserate with, it seemed rather . . . I don't know . . . hollow.

The problem with any boring situation is that sooner or later you tend to become bored with yourself. With only yourself to talk to, it's easy to realize just how little you have to offer for intelligent conversation.

It wasn't as if I had always been my own greatest enthusiast. My loathing for the world was generally superseded only by my self-loathing. But when you're adrift on a piece of wood, even self-loathing will take you only so far. Sooner or later, you begin to wonder . . . why?

Why?

If life is so terrible, why not *do* something about it? Find options, look for new ways to approach it. If there was one thing I knew, it was that I was a rather ingenious individual for searching out alternatives to dealing with assorted predicaments. It had gotten me this far, hadn't it? Granted, where it had gotten me was a piece of wood in an ocean in the middle of nowhere, but still, the point was that less inventive people would have been dead long before this.

Most of my approach to life was filled with a desire to be left alone. Beyond a steady appetite for vengeance on those who had made my existence a living hell, I really didn't aspire to anything other than to let others get on with the business of adventuring, fighting, and killing one another. Leave me be. Don't drag me into it. Don't look at me.

But was that reasonable?

I had become the physical embodiment, the epitome of that philosophy. I had achieved the perfect state of isolation. There was certainly the downside of having no food and a very limited water supply. But let us say that I had both in abundance, through whatever means—mystical or natural—you could devise. Let us say that the constant concern over inclement weather and the resultant speedy death were not a consideration. Let us say, in short, that pure survival was not a concern.

It left me looking upon an endless vista and saying, *Is this all there is?*

I was an island unto myself. I was my own best friend, my own beginning and my own end. I was the ultimate in isolation, and the humanity for which I held such contempt was a distant and irrelevant consideration to my life.

It was the perfect existence for one who disliked so much.

I had to say . . . it wasn't much fun.

I stared down into the watery depths, hoping perhaps that some stray fish would pass by and I could snare it. Once I managed that feat, I had no clue what I would do with the damned thing. It wasn't as if I could cook it. I could certainly eat it raw; I'd consumed raw or nearly raw animals before when making a fire wasn't feasible. It didn't sound particularly appetizing. Then again, the way my stomach was feeling, just about anything should have been appetizing.

By the time of the third morning, I was ready to eat plankton.

By the time of the fourth morning, I was ready to eat plank. Specifically, the board of wood I was floating on.

I had never been so hungry in my life. The temptation to gulp down the entirety of the skin's contents was becoming overwhelming. I was going to die. I had no doubts on that score. What purpose, then, to dying thirsty as well as hungry? How would I be served by it?

I drifted in and out of sleep, regardless of time of day. The dream about the party at King Runcible's court was becoming more and more expansive. By this point, everyone was there. Everyone who had ever tried to kill me— and that alone was enough to fill a fairly sizable hall. Everyone who hadn't tried to kill me was there as well, although they took up a considerably smaller portion of the room.

Even within the context of my dream, I was impressed by the staggering number of people who had, at some point or another, desired to see my life terminated. It was quite an accomplishment, in a depressing sort of way, to find the means of annoying so many people.

This time around, however, they were all dressed in black. They were smiling, though. It seemed to be some sort of bizarre combination of funeral and banquet.

I wandered through the crowded hall, drawing no looks or conversation. It was as if I wasn't there. That figured somehow. To be a nonentity even in a figment of one's own imagination.

People were crowding in around a table and I pushed through to see what they were looking at.

I saw myself lying on the table, done up like a prize pig for the slaughter. I was on my stomach, my eyes dead and glazed. For that matter, the rest of me was glazed as well, cooked to perfection. I had an apple in my mouth. Sharee was standing there with a large fork and carving knife, preparing to slice me up. Others were leaning in with plates and eager expressions.

I awoke into daylight and realized I no longer knew for a certainty how long I'd been floating out there.

I wondered how long it took for the human body to turn on itself, to start devouring itself when there was no other means of sustenance around. I thought I'd heard somewhere that two weeks was the maximum.

I brought the water skin to my lips, not without effort, to eke out my meager rationing.

There was nothing in it.

Delicacy gave way to franticness, and I shook the skin desperately, trying to obtain a few more drops of moisture. Nothing. Bone dry. I'd finished it. I was finished. However long one could survive without food, I knew that continued existence without water was an impossibility.

Water, water everywhere, but none to quench the thirst of Apropos. More irony. I was getting well and truly sick of irony.

I twisted around, bringing myself to a sitting position, ready to toss the water skin into the ocean and myself along with it.

Then I saw it.

I stared long and hard, thinking that perhaps this was an illusion of some sort. Then I rubbed my eyes and looked again.

It was land. Far distant, and not directly to the east, but more to the northeast. It was large, whatever it was. Not a simple, small island, but something more substantial.

With newfound strength invigorating my exhausted limbs, I grabbed my sheathed sword and started paddling with it. I held on to it with all the feeble strength that remained to me. The last thing I wanted was to lose my grip on the weapon and watch it slide away into the depths.

I paddled and paddled until my muscles were so sore that I had to put the sword down upon the board lest I lose it.

The land seemed no closer. I couldn't even be sure if it wasn't farther away.

I choked in frustration. To be within sight of possible salvation and not be able to do anything about it other than stare at it from afar . . . it was almost more than I could bear.

Then I heard some sort of curious splashing from behind me, as if something was moving through the water in a very direct manner. I shifted myself around on the table and looked behind me. At that moment, my thirst and hunger were forgotten, replaced by an overwhelming sense of blind panic.

Something was definitely heading toward me at a significant speed. The only part of it that I could see was the exceedingly large, triangular curved gray dorsal fin bearing down upon me.

I had never seen a shark in my life, but I certainly knew of the creatures. I'd heard stories of sea beasts bearing a dorsal fin that knifed through the water toward you, grabbed you in their powerful jaws, and bit you in half. If you were on a sailing vessel, you had a modicum of protection. If you were just swimming or adrift, you were more or less screwed.

In my case, I was leaning closer to "more" than "less."

My limbs shook with terror as I envisioned that monstrous mouth sinking its teeth into me. Judging from the size of it, the meager defense the board would provide me wouldn't even slow it down. It would simply slam into it, upend it, send me tumbling into the drink. And then devour me whole, or perhaps bite my head off. And those were the best case scenarios.

Well, I was determined I wasn't going to go that easily. I may not have had any great love of my life, but dammit, it was the only thing that I truly possessed, and I was not going to lay it down cheaply.

I ceased my vain attempts to use my sword as a paddle and instead pulled the blade from its sheath. The sword seemed to glitter in the sun, eager to be pressed into service. For all I knew, it was going to be the last time I endeavored to use it. The creature sporting that fin might loom out of the water with a maw wide enough to swallow me whole, or drag me down and just hold on to me as I thrashed about helplessly and my lungs exploded. But I was not going to go down without a fight.

I watched carefully, my arm trembling from the strain of waiting, waiting, waiting for just the right moment. I sensed I would have only one shot at the beast. And I could only guess just how tough its hide might be. It was possible I'd have no chance at penetrating it. But if I was going to do it, it was going to require every ounce of my strength and every fragment of what I laughingly referred to as my luck.

Closer it drew, and closer still. It seemed to be coming faster and faster, probably sensing its prey. If it was possible for the creature to do so, it might well have been licking its lips in anticipation. I started counting out loud, trying to time out my thrust based upon the speed of its approach.

"One," I said, "two, three," and as I watched it draw toward me, I readied my sword, realizing that the velocity of the creature would bring it within range when I got to "ten." I continued to count, and suddenly I decided to bring my sword back and try for a sweeping slash, rather than a thrust with the point. I figured I had more chance of striking something vital that way. I drew back my arm with such nervous force that I almost capsized my fragile craft, but I never lost count.

"Seven," I said, my parched voice becoming thick in my throat, "eight . . . nine . . . *ten!*" I shouted the number in order to focus my energy and power my attacking cut and I swung the sword around and down as hard as I could, anticipating the creature's lunge.

It came up out of the water, and its face was pale and gray and quite human-looking, as was its torso. And it had human arms as well. It most definitely was not human, however, but rather some bizarre kind of mer-creature presenting itself to me, its arms wide as if greeting a long-lost friend.

All of that took a second to register on me. Unfortunately, in half a second less than that, my blade cut through him like kelp.

He was looking at me in unbridled joy with eyes as black as the ocean depths and then, startled, he looked down. Whatever pain he must have felt didn't dawn on him at first, because he appeared quite puzzled to see the gaping wound in his chest, and the black blood seeping out of it in copious amounts.

He looked back up at me, and there was a rattling in his voice that sounded as if his lungs, if such he had, were already filling with blood. "I . . . I came . . . to worship you . . ." he managed to say.

"All right, now, to be fair," I said, desperately trying to sound reasonable when all I felt was sinking horror. "I thought you were attacking . . ."

"I was swimming!"

"Yes, but . . . you were swimming very menacingly," I told him, not sounding convincing even to myself. "Look, I . . . I admit I might have been a bit hasty . . ."

"You . . . you have no idea what I . . ." The water was getting thick with his blood. "I . . . I've been on a quest . . . through a hundred hundred tides, I have searched . . ."

"Oh gods," I moaned, flopping back on the board. "Not someone else's damned adventure again."

He didn't hear me. He seemed totally absorbed with the sound of his own voice. His eyes were starting to glaze over. ". . . through untold menaces, searching for . . . for the one who was foretold . . ."

"Please, stop," I begged, "you're giving me a headache." The mortification at my haste in slaughtering what was clearly not a predatory creature but, instead, my potential salvation was bad enough. But now he was prattling on about quests and menaces and such, and it was just making matters worse. As guilty as I felt, I was starting to regret I hadn't decapitated him. Then again, the day was young.

"The foretold one . . . the drifter with the pale skin," he continued, "whom I would bring back to our island home . . . and we would worship and serve his every whim, provide him every luxury until the end of his days . . ."

"Okay, well . . . we can still do that," I told him. "There's no need for this quest of yours to end on a down note. . . ."

He fixed his fading gaze upon me. He was starting to sink, but with his last dregs of strength he held on to the edge of the board. "Now . . . now I realize. The prophecies played me . . . false . . . you are, in fact . . . evil incarnate . . ."

"What, just because I accidentally killed you?" I protested. "As if that's never happened to anyone?"

"My people will know you . . . for the destroyer that you

are . . . and they . . ." His voice was fading. "They will . . . attend to you. . . ."

"Look, I would really like to go back to the worshipping and island thing, if that's okay with—"

And then he let out a series of high-pitched whistles that near to liquefied my brain. I clamped my hands to my ears, rolled over, tried not to scream in pain, and failed miserably. *"Shut up! You'll deafen me!"* I shouted, grabbed my staff, and rapped him soundly on the top of his skull with it.

It didn't take much more than that, since he seemed barely alive anyway. He lost his grip on the board and slipped beneath the surface. I watched him sink but lost sight of him almost immediately.

"All right, this really *wasn't* my fault," I said to no one in particular. And indeed, I was reasonably sure that it was fair to say that. Yes, in my lifetime, I had stolen, and lied, and cheated. I had taken advantage of women, slaughtered men, behaved in a consistently cowardly manner. But for once, I felt I really had an excuse for the misfortune I had brought upon the poor bastard. He'd been on a quest and it ended badly. 'Tis to weep. He should have done more to announce himself before drawing within range of my blade, that was all there was to it, and if anyone asked, that was exactly what I would say.

That was when the water began to churn beneath me.

I sheathed my sword, secured my staff, and held on as the waves surged. I imagined it to be some sort of current that would, in short order, pass. I could not have been more wrong. Instead it grew in intensity and force, and the ocean began to buck fiercely as if it was trying to expel me from it. The waves became so choppy that they literally flipped me into the air. I landed hard, the water "splatting" beneath me. My clothes immediately became soaked through, my eyes stinging from the salt.

I squeezed them tightly shut, opened them, and gasped.

In the distance, but coming toward me quickly, was a series of gigantic waves. And silhouetted in the waves were gargantuan beings who bore a resemblance to the one I'd just killed, but much, much larger. Twenty, maybe thirty times bigger. The dead creature had obviously summoned them with his series of whistles, which had carried considerably well through the air, and I had a sneaking suspicion he had not painted a favorable picture of me.

They were barreling straight toward me. Because of their vast size, they were churning up waves that were bigger than some castles I'd stayed in. They were huge, capable of swamping me in a heartbeat if they caught up with me.

Cupping my hands to either side of my mouth, I bellowed, *"He should have done more to announce himself before drawing within range of my blade!"* They seemed unimpressed by my explanation as they continued to bear down on me.

I threw myself flat on the board, facing away from them, and started paddling madly with my arms toward the distant shoreline.

My progress remained depressingly slow, and then suddenly I realized I was starting to speed up. The water was surging, carrying me faster, higher. The water threw the board to one side and the other, and I realized that by remaining flat, I wasn't going to be able to control it. I got to my knees, remained that way, my arms paddling even faster. My speed increased, no thanks to me and every thanks to my briny pursuers, who were descending upon me.

I did the only thing I could. I clambered to my feet, even though my right leg was lame. But at least I was able to use my left to manipulate the board, steady it, prevent it from flipping over. The waves blasted toward me and I continued to ride on the crest, being carried at higher and higher speed toward the land. The water was a deafening roar around me, which would have been more severe if my ears still hadn't been ringing from that desperation scream the dying creature had emitted earlier.

And then the waves caught up with me. I kept the toes of my lame right leg resting gently, using it for steering and guidance, counting upon the strength of my other leg to provide the sheer muscle of balance. The waves tried to push me sideways, to drive me away from the land. But I saw a cresting wave that was going where I wanted, shifted my body weight, and sent the board skipping through a virtual tunnel formed by the water. I was down and through, and I tilted yet again, driving myself hard toward the land. I heard the outraged shrieks of whatever those creatures were hidden within the depths of the wave. They were howling for vengeance, for my blood. My blood. They hadn't even met me and they wanted to kill me. Usually people had to get to know me a little before they wanted to kill me.

For half a second I found my mind drifting, wondering if my mother—were she still alive—would have joined the ranks of those eager for my demise. I liked to think not. But I was probably kidding myself.

Then the creatures shrieked in chorus, and again my ears rang, and suddenly I was turned completely upside down. I couldn't keep my feet on the board, couldn't control it at all, and then the wood—my only salvation—skidded away from me. I flipped twice in midair, miraculously managed to keep a grip on my staff, and then crashed into the water.

Swimming was, to put it delicately, not my strength. So I

was reasonably sure that this was it. I was going to die. There was absolutely no way I was going to be able to survive splashing around in the ocean. Even left to my own devices, I wouldn't stay afloat for very long at all. And those creatures, whoever and whatever they were, weren't going to give me the luxury of time.

I sank and my feet hit bottom.

However, when they did, my head was still above water, as was everything above my waist.

I staggered forward, splashing, coughing. I tried to lean on my walking staff, but it sank into the sand and it was all I could do to pull it out. I looked around in bewilderment to discover that I was not more than eight feet from land. The combination of the pure power of the waves and my adeptness at using the board to navigate them had resulted in me winding up exactly where I'd wanted to: namely, anyplace except where I'd been.

Then I heard another earsplitting screech, and I realized the creatures were almost upon me. They had not remotely given up. I splashed desperately toward the shore, and then another wave of aquatic force hammered me, sending me tumbling. I went under, reminded myself that I was in relatively shallow water, hauled my head up, and pushed myself forward, slowed by exhaustion, spurred on by desperation. Exhaustion and desperation warred with each other for a moment and then, as it so often did with me, desperation won out.

I threw myself onto the shore, falling and rolling from the water as fast as I could. It surged onto the sand as I rolled frantically away. I crab-walked backward up the shore, watching the way I'd come, looking for some sign of the waterlogged monsters that had driven me hither.

Nothing. Whoever, whatever they were, they seemed to want to have no truck with the surface world. I couldn't entirely blame them. Many was the day when I likewise wanted to have no truck with the surface world. As much as they might have allowed their silhouettes to be seen in the huge waves, when it came down to it they preferred to remain hidden.

I gulped in air greedily. I still needed something to eat and, even more, something to drink. At that moment, though, all I really wanted to do was rest.

Which is what I did. Once I pulled myself securely out of range of the tides, I flopped onto my back and fell into a dreamless sleep.

Chapter 4

Leading with the Chin

*T*he roaring of the ocean was far more muted by the time I awoke again. I was astounded to see that night had passed into morning. Apparently I had been just that tired and filled with relief upon making landfall. Miraculously, no one had disturbed me in my slumber. Then again, I'd been lying flat on my back, so no one could have reached my sword. And I didn't see why anyone would want my staff, particularly if they weren't aware of the special weaponry built in. Other than that and the clothes on my back, and an empty water skin, I had nothing.

Now that I'd landed, the first thing on my agenda was water. I hauled myself to my feet, all my joints registering an aching protest. My clothes were still a bit damp, but the temperature in this place—wherever that might be—was quite warm. So my vestments would likely be dried off in very short order.

I looked around, trying to assess just where the hell I was.

It was not some small, puny island, that was for sure. It stretched as far as I could see. Not only that, but even from a distance, I could see that there were signs of civilization. Small wafts of smoke drifted in the breeze from what I was reasonably sure were home fires. I took some measure of comfort that there were fires burning and I didn't have to worry whether I was responsible for setting them. There was a grove of trees obscuring my view, however, so I couldn't see what type of villages or residences lay in the distance, or even how near they were.

Then I stopped and stared at the trees in wonderment. They were unlike any I'd ever seen. I drew closer to make certain that I was viewing them properly. It was as if a grove of walking staffs had sprung up. Tall and supple they were, more than a hundred feet high by my guess, with great green sprouts coming out the top. The trunks were jointed every foot or two along their length. I wasn't even sure if "trunks" was the right word for them. "Shafts" would have been more accurate. I could wrap my entire hand around even the largest of them. They were swaying gently in the breeze, rustling softly, and if I had not been sure before that I was in some strange, alien land, this was more than enough to convince me.

I pulled on one of the trunks experimentally. It moved with my tug, swung right and left, but did not break. I pulled again, harder this time, and was deeply impressed with the strength and resilience of the wood, if wood it was. As slender as it appeared, I could see that it was remarkably durable and did not break easily. I pulled it toward me with as much strength as I could and all it did was bend. Finally I released it. It snapped in the opposite direction, swung back with remarkable force, and smacked me in the face. I stumbled back, almost fell, but caught myself at the last second. Then I rubbed my nose and, despite the fact that I was bone-weary, still smiled at the mental picture of how ludicrous I must have looked at that moment.

Then I heard something. My hearing remained sharp as always, and I was reasonably certain I detected the faint trickle of water. My mouth was too dry to salivate, and I was so excited by the prospect of quenching my thirst that I nearly passed out from excitement.

I made my way briskly in the direction that my ears told me water lay. Every so often I would glance up once more, marveling at the walking-staff forest surrounding me. The trees were not particularly close together, so maneuvering was a fairly easy chore, even for me.

Eventually, just over a rise, I heard water rushing, even stronger than before. I clambered over it and, sure enough, there it was: a narrow river, the most glorious thing I'd ever seen. The water looked crystal clear and pure, and I almost broke my good leg in scrambling down to it, finally falling flat on my stomach and shoving my whole head into it. I made the mistake of laughing underwater and got a noseful of water for my troubles, but I didn't care. The river was quite shallow by the shore, and I rolled myself into it so that I was facing in the direction from which the river was flowing. Keeping my head elevated, I simply allowed the water to cascade into my mouth, and I swallowed it in great, eager gulps. I coughed some up at one point, then brought my head back down and drank some more.

I had been so parched that I wouldn't have thought it possible I could ever drink my fill. But finally I was indeed sated. Just to play it safe, I took my water skin and held it underneath until it was filled as well.

And then I noticed something drifting toward me from upstream. It was a little ways out in the water. I waded out a few steps and then used my staff to snag it and bring it in close for me to pick up and study.

It was a boat. A small wooden boat, as a child would have made. Nothing fancy. It looked like a miniature canoe. I looked in the direction from whence it had come. I wasn't sure whether to go toward the origin point of the toy, or away. I finally decided that a meeting with the locals couldn't be forestalled forever. Sooner or later, I was going to have to deal with whoever it was that was residing hereabouts.

A pocket lined the inner folds of my cloak, so I tucked the boat in there and started following the shoreline.

The day continued to be warm, and I was actually beginning to feel relatively good about myself. Such a frame of mind was always dangerous for me, for it was usually when I was in good spirits that huge storms of shite would rain down upon me courtesy of the gods on high. It was easier and safer for me to remain a pessimist. Nevertheless, there was a spring in my limping step that wasn't usually there.

My thoughts were continuing in the direction they'd been heading earlier. Here I was, still alive. The number of incidents threatening my life that I'd survived was starting to border on the epic. It was almost enough to make me wonder if I really was intended for something great. Then again, for me, just surviving from one day to the next was something of an accomplishment.

Although the sky was clear, a thin mist of rain began to fall. I pulled my hood up to keep myself dry . . . a ridiculous goal, I admit, considering I'd spent practically the last week being soaked. Before too long, however, the rain was letting up.

The walking-staff trees started to thin out and I soon found myself on the edge of some sort of field, a stiff but gentle breeze to my back, helping to dry me off. The field was filled with stalks of something that came to just over my head, thickening at the top. They were thin and white, and waving, and sure smelled sweet when the wind came right behind the rain, but I had no clue what they might be. I continued on my path, and soon I was starting to detect sounds of humanity. Mostly female. That sounded promising.

The river rounded a bend, and I came around it and saw

an assortment of women, all young from the look and sound of them, standing knee deep or near the shore. They appeared to be washing clothes. The outfits they themselves wore were almost entirely white. White, wide-sleeved robes, it seemed, with the bottoms hiked up and tucked into wide sashes or belts wrapped around their waists. Beneath those they sported loose white leggings that came down to the knees. Furthermore, on their heads they wore extremely curious, wide-brimmed hats that were so flat they looked like large plates that came to a point. I couldn't be sure, but it seemed that the hats were constructed from that same material that the staff trees were made of.

There were a few children there as well, dressed in simple one-piece knee-length white tunics, splashing about or playing quietly as their elders tended to their wash and chatted amongst themselves in a language I couldn't even begin to comprehend. It was rapid-fire and extremely guttural. I had no idea what to make of it, but knew that if that was all they spoke around here, I was going to have some problems. I was able to pick up languages fairly quickly, but I was a stranger in a strange land, and it would have been nice to be able to communicate with *someone*. I tried to tell myself that it wasn't necessarily a disaster, even as I noted that their skin color was slightly different from mine. More of an odd tint. Slightly yellow, it seemed. I reasoned that perhaps they had some sort of vitamin deficiency that caused their skin to retain such a curious hue.

Then one of the women happened to glance in my direction, and she gasped, as did I. The poor creature was deformed. Something was disastrously wrong with her eyes, or perhaps her eyelids. They looked almost slitted, although they opened wide enough upon spotting me. Certainly, I reasoned, it was some strange and unfortunate birth defect that had caused this to come to pass. My heart immediately went out to her in a way that only someone who was born deformed could possibly feel.

She cried out something in her native tongue, and the others turned and looked at me as well.

They all looked like her. So did the children.

I stepped back, gasping, horrified. It was far worse than I had thought. I had wandered into something akin to a leper colony. Someplace where people who had been born with this disfiguring condition had been sequestered so others wouldn't have to look upon them and be as thoroughly disconcerted as I.

They were all shouting by that point. They looked no less stunned to see me than I was to see them. The children were calling to their mothers and pointing to me and to their own eyes in obvious bewilderment. The women were shaking their heads, gesturing helplessly, having no answer to give their inquisitive youngsters.

That's when it finally dawned upon me. I wasn't in some area where deformed people had been cast out from a more round-eyed society. *Everyone* in this land looked that way. As far as they were concerned, *I* was the freak. They were probably more right than I was. After all, I had never seen anyone who looked the way they did, but they had apparently never seen anyone like me, and there were a lot more of them than there were of me.

Then I heard more voices, deeper, rougher, male. They were coming from the field all around me, and I felt the situation was deteriorating rapidly. I started to turn with the intent of heading back down the river, and suddenly my retreat was cut off, because the males of whatever-they-were had emerged with stunning silence from the fields behind me. There were five of them, of varying ages, and they seemed no happier to see me than I was to see them.

They were obviously warriors, holding some sort of

weapons that were totally alien to me. They were gleaming steel, held by handles not unlike daggers. They were longer than daggers, though, but shorter than short swords. They looked somewhat like miniature tridents, but the prongs weren't of equal length. A spike protruded from the middle, and the guard consisted of two smaller, upturned twists of metal, one on either side.

Everyone was talking at once, and naturally I didn't understand a damned word any of them was saying. On the other hand, I knew an attack when I saw one. They were advancing slowly, babbling to one another, moving in a tight formation. I didn't like the odds I was facing. Generally any odds greater than one against one, with my opponent having his back to me and being oblivious of my presence, was more than I liked to handle. In this instance, although I was at a distinct numerical disadvantage, they were all smaller than I was. But I wasn't ruling out the possibility—with their uncannily different faces—that they might actually be magic-based creatures, capable of doing who-knew-what to me.

I reached around to my back and yanked free my sword. They jumped back, startled, as the blade whipped around, and I held it in a guard position. "Just keep your distance!" I shouted, shoving my cloak over one shoulder to clear my sword arm.

As I did that, the little boat I'd picked up downstream fell out of the inner lining of my cloak. It clattered to the shore and lay there.

I heard an exclamation of joy and turned just in time to see a small girl dash toward me, oblivious to any chance of danger that might be presenting itself. Obviously it was her boat. Her mother cried out to her, grabbing for her, but she easily eluded her grasp and darted over toward me. Everyone was shouting, and I kept hearing "Jun!," which was either her name or "Get the hell away from the man with the huge sword!" in their tongue. Whichever it was, she blissfully ignored it, indicating that either she was an independent thinker or else stone deaf.

She ran right up to the boat, not more than a foot or so away from me. If I'd been of a mind to, I could have whacked her head off with one blow. Instead I simply stood there, sword still poised, but making no move toward her. Why in the world would I have done so? I was no slaughterer of innocents. All right, technically, I *was* a slaughterer of innocents, but I'd had a bad year.

The child picked up her boat and smiled, clearly happy to have recovered her toy, which had apparently gone sailing away from her. Then she turned and looked up at me and grinned. I suppose I should have grinned back, but instead I just stared at her, not quite knowing what to make of her and the whole situation.

Then she startled me as she briskly slapped her arms to either side of her body and bowed stiffly at the waist.

I wasn't about to lower my sword. This still didn't have the makings of a friendly encounter. Nevertheless, while keeping my weapon in a guard position, I stiffly mimicked her bow. She bowed once more. I bowed once more. Seemingly satisfied with that, she splashed back across the shallow river to the woman whom I assumed to be either her mother or elder sister.

By that point all the cross-talking and incomprehensible chitchat had ceased. Instead silence hung in the air, as the people were clearly uncertain of what I wanted, and I didn't have a clue what they wanted. And we didn't have the language skills to bridge that gap, or so I thought.

Then one of the men took a step or two toward me. *"Hunh,"* he said, not so much a comment of general bewilderment as it was a sort of noise to get my attention. To

announce that an attempt at communication was about to
be made.

He indicated the sword in my hand, mimed stabbing
with it, and then shook his head in a firm negative manner.
One of the women I remembered had likewise shaken her
head. It was comforting to know that there were some universal constants, and shaking one's head to indicate a negative was apparently one of them.

His meaning was clear: They were off-put by my sword.
They wanted me to put it down or sheathe it. They considered it a potential means of attack.

Which it bloody well was, of course. They were armed as
well, remember, with their pointy steel sticks of death. I
wasn't about to leave myself vulnerable to assault. So I
shook my head vigorously and said for emphasis, even
though I know they didn't understand the words, "I'm not
lowering my guard. You have weapons, too, you know,"
and I pointed at the lethal objects they were carrying.

There were bewildered expressions for a moment as they
exchanged looks. Then one of the men, an older fellow
whose hair was as straight black as the others, seemed to
"understand" something. I doubted he suddenly spoke my
language, so I waited.

He held up his "lethal fork" and I raised my blade in
automatic defense. "*Hunh,*" he said once more. Then he
said something in his language that I couldn't hope to comprehend while pointing at his own weapon. I shook my
head to indicate I had no idea what he was saying. For
some reason he spoke louder and more slowly as if addressing one who was either deaf or stupid or both. Again I
shook my head.

Everyone was watching the fellow, apparently waiting for
him to get across to me whatever it was he was trying to say.
Then he went down to one knee upon the shore and slowly

drew the points of his weapon along the ground, churning up the dirt. Watching me intently as he did so, he then took the weapon and stabbed the longest prong straight down, making a small hole. Then he held his hand over the hole and waggled his fingers, as if he were sprinkling something into it.

I watched him blankly for a long moment.

He pointed at the hole in the dirt and then at the white stalks that stood upright nearby.

And damn me if I didn't suddenly, in a burst of comprehension, understand what he was saying.

Those things they were carrying weren't weapons. They were farming implements. They used them as miniature hoes to turn the ground and dig holes, into which they would then drop seeds, from which these stalks had grown.

Warriors, my ass. These weren't warriors. These were farmers.

"Hunh!" I said, as much as in an amused laugh as anything else. Very slowly, hoping I wasn't making a disastrous mistake, I sheathed my sword. Watching me put my weapon away, they visibly relaxed. There was still tension in the air, but it seemed as if the immediate threat had passed.

The same man who had so deftly mimed the planting of seeds then spoke to me once again. He gestured widely, pointing in various directions, looking at me and shrugging in bewilderment. But it was an "artsy" sort of bewilderment, meant to put across a mind-set. Clearly he was inquiring from whereabouts I had come, since I was so obviously foreign to their land.

My mind raced, and then I suddenly turned to the girl who had so fearlessly approached me earlier. I snapped my fingers to gain her attention and gestured that she should come back toward me. She automatically started to do so, but her mother briefly restrained her. The man said something though in a soothing tone, his hands palm down, apparently putting across to her that everything was going to be all right. Clearly as a matter of trust—perhaps the man was her husband or some other relation—she released the girl.

The child came toward me and I went down to one knee at the water's edge. I put out my hand and pointed at the girl's boat. She hesitated only a moment, then handed it over to me. I held it upon the water's surface, pointed at the boat, then pointed at me. The man's face clouded for a moment, but then cleared and he nodded in understanding: I had been a passenger on a sailing vessel.

Obviously I wasn't about to go into detail as to specifically what had transpired to shipwreck me. Even if I spoke their language, I doubt I could have made them understand it. *I* barely understood it. Instead I simply indicated the ship cruising along, and then suddenly angled it sharply downward and pushed it under the water, conveying the notion that my vessel had gone down. He nodded excitedly to show his comprehension. I then mimed swimming gestures, gasped deeply to indicate exhaustion, and then walked two fingers in a staggering fashion up onto the riverbank to put across that I had made it to shore.

The man spoke in a loud tone, not to me but to his people. Obviously he was explaining to them, for any who might be mime-impaired, the short version of my ordeal. There were oohs and aahs and gasps of comprehension and—could it even be?—pity for what I had gone through. A foreigner with a strange face, surviving a disastrous voyage and managing to make it to shore of an unknown land. It was a dramatic notion, certainly, and one that served to make me a most sympathetic figure.

The most pleasant aspect of the whole thing was that it wasn't a lie. That was a nice change of pace. Many were the times I'd had to come up with some sort of fabrication to gain the sympathy of someone new I'd encountered. In this instance, the truth of what I'd endured was terrible enough.

The man shoved his farming implement into his belt and came toward me. His movements were not the least bit tentative, but instead open and welcoming. He stopped a few feet shy of me and I watched carefully, not wanting to make any sudden moves. My impulse was to stick out a hand to shake his, but for all I knew such a gesture would be perceived as a threat of some sort. It would be just my luck to frighten or insult these people when I was on the cusp of finessing my way through the situation.

He brought his hands around and placed them palm to palm, fingers straight up in front of him. Then he bowed in a manner similar to the way the girl had done. Slowly I got to my feet with the aid of my staff, having been down on one knee all this time, and handed the toy boat back to the child. I imitated the bowing gesture. Then, deciding to take the chance, I slowly extended my right hand, palm sideways. He stared at it, then mimicked the gesture with his hand so that it paralleled my own. We stood there for a moment, both our hands sticking out, looking rather ridiculous. So I brought my hand over to his, wrapped it around his gently but firmly, and slowly shook it up and down in the traditional gesture of "my people" to show that neither of us had weapons in our hands.

His expression was one of utter befuddlement, and then several women laughed at the really rather humorous look on his face. This prompted him to laugh as well, and he started to shake my own hand more emphatically. So emphatically, in fact, that our hands jerked up and down in a far greater arc than was standard for a handshake. I didn't let it concern me, though, since the primary intent was clear.

And so it was that I fell in with a village of farmers in a

foreign land. People who knew nothing of my checkered past. Who didn't know me as a bastard, or a knight of dubious reputation, or a vicious warlord who had laid waste to more cities than he could possibly count. A man who had ruined hundreds of lives and cut a swath of destruction through the world, leaving misery and unhappiness in his wake. A man who had been desired dead by just about everyone he'd ever met in his life.

Here I was just a stranger, a refugee, a man who had survived a terrible mishap when his ship had foundered, and yet had managed to endure. They appreciated my stubborn determination to cling to life in a way that only those who work the land and try to grow things can possibly do.

As odd as it seemed, apparently I'd found a home, however temporary, among people who were not my own and were happier to see me than those who *were* my own.

The cynic within me knew that it could not possibly last. Worse, that I'd probably do something to make a total mangle of it. At that moment, though, I didn't care.

It felt good. And I hadn't felt good in a very, very long time.

And so it was that I came to reside in the land that I eventually determined was called Chinpan. A land of mystery and rituals and a way of life totally unfamiliar to me, practiced by people whose very physiognomy was alien. Then again, I'm sure that I didn't exactly look normal to them either. That was all right, though. With my irregular features and pronounced limp, I was used to looking not normal.

Chapter 5

Through Chinpan Ali

My facility for languages served me well over the next months as the villagers made a priority of teaching me how to speak their language of Chinpanese. Some of them showed some mild interest in my own tongue, but overall a concerted effort was made to work with me so that I could learn to communicate with them. It certainly made sense for me to learn their language rather than they learning mine. There were, after all, far more of them.

The name of the village, I later learned, was Hosbiyu, and the population couldn't have been more than seventy-five, if that. They brought me back amidst much chattering, talking to me as if—now that I'd been accepted and my peculiar circumstances understood—I would magically be able to comprehend what they were saying. Naturally that wasn't the case, but I was determined to be polite. So I smiled and nodded, and this only seemed to encourage them even more.

The village was situated at the intersection of two man-made dirt roads, with well-worn grooves in them as a result of frequent passages with ox-drawn cart. Several of the beasts grazed in a field nearby, along with a couple of cows that probably fulfilled the milk needs of the populace. All the structures were simple huts or slightly larger buildings that served as barns, and the exteriors appeared familiar. Then I realized they were constructed of wood from the tall, flexible trees I'd seen earlier. It was one of the first words of their language that I managed to learn: "bamboo," it was called, and it was an extremely ubiquitous material. In addition to having used it to fashion their buildings, they'd also built fences with it to hem in the cattle, thinner shoots of the plant had been used to make those strange flat hats, some of the women wore shoes made of bamboo, and I even saw some of the young men sparring with one another with bamboo as quarterstaves.

I took great interest in the material, thinking of the myriad uses it could have been put to back in my native land. By the same token, they were intrigued by the solid oak from which my own staff had been carved. They marveled even more when I demonstrated some of the little tricks built into it, such as the blade that snapped from the dragon's open mouth, or the fact that the staff could be separated into two smaller staves.

The man who had worked so mightily to establish communication with me brought me to his hut, where his wife eyed me warily even as they hastened to prepare a meal for me. It was very touching. They didn't have much, but what they had, they were willing to share, even if all they were sharing was a bowl of rice. I'd never been particularly fond of rice, but considering I'd thought I was going to die of starvation on a plank in the middle of nowhere, it could not have tasted better had it been manna from heaven.

Through a combination of more pantomime, drawing primitive pictures in the dirt floor, and the like, my host managed to inquire as to what my plans were. The truth was, I had no plans. I had no overwhelming urge to return home. To what home, precisely, would I have returned? In my native state of Isteria, I was persona non grata. I certainly couldn't return to Wuin. I had no loved ones to be concerned about an extended absence. And the number of people I knew in Chinpan was limited to those whom I'd met that day.

So I managed to get across to him that I had nowhere else to go and nothing else to do. If I did have some sort of "great destiny," it was going to have to seek me out in Hosbiyu, because I didn't have the slightest idea where to go to look for it.

The man nodded, apparently comprehending. He and his wife left the hut after a while, and when I went to the door some minutes later, I looked out and saw what seemed to be the entirety of the village gathered in the middle of the place, where the two roads intersected. They were talking in low, thoughtful tones, and then someone pointed at me. They all stopped and looked in my direction. I didn't know why they'd ceased conversation. It wasn't as if I could understand them. Still, it was obvious that I was the topic of discussion. They were trying to figure out what the hell to do with me. I withdrew into the hut, having no wish to disturb them. Certainly annoying them would be counterproductive to my best interests.

I had no doubt that I could fend for myself if I had to. Still, not speaking the language was going to be a major handicap. I hadn't survived as long as I had through dazzling fighting skills, that was for certain. My strength was the quickness with which I could come up with the right lie to spin for any given situation. If I couldn't make myself understood, all the quick thinking in the world wasn't going to do me a fragment of good. I wasn't completely inept when it came to physical self-defense, but robbed of my ability to obfuscate and bewilder, the likelihood of my longevity was greatly curtailed.

So it was with a certain degree of nervousness that I waited to see what the village consensus about my fate would be. An interminable amount of time later, although in reality it probably wasn't all that long, my host returned to the hut and looked at me contemplatively for a moment. A group of his fellow villagers was standing behind him.

I said nothing. What would I have said?

He put out a hand and one of his neighbors handed him one of the pronged farming implements that I'd originally thought was a weapon. His expression was very serious and for a moment I thought I'd misjudged the situation horribly, and they were about to charge me and try to drive the weapon through my chest. My sword was on the ground a couple of feet away, but I resisted the impulse to lunge for it.

My host walked toward me, turned the tool around so the hilt was facing me, and proffered it. I hesitated and then reached for it. Taking it gingerly from his hand, I hefted it slightly. It was surprisingly light.

With gestures, he indicated that I should tuck the tool in my belt. I did so. Then, collectively, they placed their hands face-to-face and bowed.

The message was clear. If I was willing to pull my own weight, to work their fields by their sides, I was welcome to stay for as long as I wished.

My heart swelled. Never had I experienced such unbridled generosity. The closest I had come was when Queen Bea and King Runcible had extended an invitation to be a squire in his court. But even in that instance, a squire was one of the lowest of the low, and the other squires never missed an opportunity to make me feel like the titleless, unlanded peasant that I was.

This was a totally different circumstance. I was being

invited to join a community as an equal, no questions asked (even if questions could be posed). For an inveterate cynic such as myself, it was almost too much to cope with.

I contained my roiling emotions and instead simply returned the bow. They smiled and then walked out of the hut. My host's wife paused long enough to offer a genuine smile. Even she had overcome her hesitancy and seemed willing to welcome me if the others were.

Those who have been following my adventures know me well enough to be fully aware of exactly what started preying upon my mind:

What was going to go wrong?

It was too perfect, too wonderful. Despite my tendency to be thrust into adventures, I really had no overwhelming compulsion to embark on them. Yet they always seemed to overtake me, always.

Part of me wondered whether I didn't bring it upon myself somewhat. The closest I'd known to peace in some years was when I was an innkeeper at a place called Bugger Hall. My tenure there had ended rather disastrously (and, of course, thrust me into yet another escapade), but even before that happened, I had found myself growing bored with the quiet existence I was leading. In retrospect, I couldn't help but believe that on some level, I had brought it upon myself.

Which, of course, made me immediately start worrying about what disaster I would bring upon myself in this new environment.

Have you ever found yourself in a situation where you are desperately endeavoring not to dwell upon something? Naturally, it becomes uppermost in your thoughts. Every attempt to cease thinking about it only causes you to think about it all the more.

That was where I found myself mentally, having been

taken in by the good citizens of Hosbiyu. It was nerve-racking. I was fully prepared to settle into an environment that would ask nothing of me except the sweat of my brow and whatever effort lay in my arms to provide. Even as I did so, however, I started wondering how and when it would come to an end.

And in this case, it wasn't just myself that I had concern for. The people of Hosbiyu were unstinting in their generosity, and total in their acceptance of me, despite my obviously different appearance. Wherever I go, disaster tends to dog my steps. Typically, I'm the only one who suffers . . . or, at most, a "loved one" who had the poor fortune to be in proximity to me at the time. But this was an entire village, filled with good people.

All of whom seemed to be named "Chin."

At first I thought everyone was related in some manner. That was hardly a heartening notion: that all the villagers were siblings or cousins lying with one another and producing more spawn to engage in further incestuous relationships. I was assured, however, that it was merely coincidence. That "Chin" was just an exceedingly common name, with "Chen" a very close second, and "Wang" coming up in the rear.

Over time, I learned their first names, even as I learned their language. It was a challenging tongue to master, particularly since they had many words that sounded the same, but had different meanings depending upon inflection. And their names could be stunningly similar as well. Yes, over a period of months, I could readily distinguish "Nobuharu" from "Nobuhisa" from "Nobuhito," "Yoshitaka" from "Yositake" from "Yoshitoki," because I had faces to associate with the names. You, the reader, might have far greater difficulties keeping everyone sorted out through the narrative. I don't say this because I think you are somehow mentally deficient, or less clever than I. Although, to be candid, the very fact that you continue to exhibit such morbid interest in my life and waste precious time reading about it when you could be doing something of more importance, such as . . . well, anything, really . . . does indeed call your intelligence into question. For that matter, you very likely *are* less clever than I. Forgive the immodesty, but I like to think my having survived to old age is a testament to the fact that I've raised cleverness to the level of an art form.

Nevertheless, in order to simplify your following of my humble narrative, I will spare you the sound-alike names of the villagers and instead refer to them in the way that I first thought of them. You see, for my own amusement, until I memorized their real names, I tended to refer to them by various appropriate nicknames that stemmed from the universal "Chin" surname. I would even occasionally address them as such, and naturally they never comprehended the shadings of meanings.

For instance, my host, to whom I've referred before, was somewhat jowly. So I dubbed him "Double Chin." His wife, who seemed to enjoy the noontime meal the most, I called "Lun Chin."

Lun Chin's sister was the woman who had tried to control her daughter during my first encounter with them, to little avail. She was even more obsessed with the details of food preparation than her sister. She became Kit Chin. Her daughter, the one whose boat I had found, I naturally called Kit Chinette.

The town's nominal leader, a belligerent gentleman with graying hair and a perpetually suspicious air, I called Take On Chin. His undersized, constantly complaining wife? As you can surmise: Bit Chin.

Then there were other villagers such as Fet Chin, In

Chin, Cleft Chin . . . you get the idea. What can I say? It amused me, it didn't appear to bother them in the slightest, and it helped me feel at home.

And I came to like them.

You have to understand what a major development that was for me. I tended to dislike people. Intensely. All people. I would look upon them and try to imagine the darkness in their souls, and conceive of the ways they would turn upon me given the slightest opportunity.

The people of Hosbiyu defied such preconceptions. Their openness of manner was indisputable, and left no room for shadings or negative interpretations. I was not known in this land, so it wasn't as if I was concerned there was some sort of bounty upon my head and they were trying to keep me there so they could collect upon it. They were simple people of the land, extending their hospitality and making me one of them.

And if something happened to me, the chances were it would happen to them.

Which put me in a unique position: that of worrying about someone other than myself. As can happen with any new concept, it became overwhelming. I could think of nothing else.

Weeks passed into months, season rolling over into season. I would lie awake at night in the bamboo hut I had built with their aid. I would envision flames consuming their village, some horrific attack being brought down upon them by me. It would be inadvertent, to be sure. Who could possibly know from what direction it might come? I might offend some great warlord. Or perhaps the gods would take an interest in my relative peace and feel that some new tumult must be unleashed upon me. Perhaps the disaster would come from below, in the form of fearsome, supernatural beasts, or even destructive quakes.

Anything was possible when it came to my unerring ability to snatch defeat from the jaws of victory.

And during those sleepless nights, I would tell myself the same thing: *Leave. Leave now. Don't wait for daylight. Fade into the night with no explanation. Get out while there's still time, while these people still have bamboo roofs above their heads.* On a couple of occasions I even went so far as to pack a bag with the meager belongings the good farmers had provided me. *Just go, just go,* the voice would keep telling me.

Yet the rising of the sun would see me still in residence in Hosbiyu.

Because there was some small part of me—and I hang my cynical head in shame even to admit it—that held out hope for a happy ending. That I would live out my days in peace and contentment as a simple farmer. That this agricultural life of planting and tilling and cutting down the wheat would last. That I would find a young woman in the village to marry, and we would have little red-haired, narrow-eyed children. There was a chance that the gods had finally taken pity on me and brought me to this place to reside quietly and harmlessly, until I finally took the long sleep and perhaps my body would be laid in the fields to provide fertilizer for the next season's crops.

If that was the case, then sneaking away, fleeing the village, would be tossing a gift from the gods back in their faces. I could not imagine that doing such a thing could remotely be considered a prudent maneuver. Considering what vindictive bastards gods could be, I could easily see them venting their ire upon the village after I'd gone. Which would mean that the very act of running away to spare the people of Hosbiyu would guarantee their complete and utter doom.

Not a pretty picture.

And so I stayed, the time continuing apace. Every so often strangers would pass through, either on foot or on horseback. Whenever they did so, I would hide in my hut and worry that this was it. This was the disaster that was going to cost these poor bastards their livelihoods and homes, all because they had shown me kindness. But that was never the case. Sometimes the strangers were merchants. Other times they were just weary travelers, seeking a respite before going on their way. The people of Hosbiyu never failed, in such cases, to provide what accommodation they could.

Inevitably, they would depart, leaving the village unharmed. When they did, I would let out a great sigh and relax, feeling as if the people and I had narrowly escaped a killing blow.

There was one night . . . well, a day and a night, actually . . . that stirred up that feeling more than any other time. A day during which the sun never emerged, not once, from behind a solid blanket of black clouds. No work got done that day, as the farmers stood about and looked to the skies. There was much mumbling about the gods, and the end of times, and the sense of the unnatural in the air.

There was a steady rumbling of thunder so relentless I thought it was going to drive me mad. Lightning flashed across the skies at random intervals, throughout the day and all through the night. But it was pale blue lightning, giving it an even more ensorcelled and otherworldly feel.

I, along with many of the farmers, was up much of the night, staring at the night skies, which looked much as they had during the day. I felt as if I was one of those people who had been severely struck upon the head and was endeavoring to stay awake, since to go to sleep could well mean death. It was the same sensation here: the feeling that if I went to sleep, there would be no world for me to wake up to.

Toward the wee morning hours, however, I did doze, and the next thing I knew, it was approaching noon. The sky had cleared, the clouds had dissolved, and it was a glorious day. Everything smelled new, and the feelings of gloom and disaster that had pervaded the previous day were already distant memories.

Oddly, I couldn't help but feel that I—that all of us—had gotten some sort of reprieve.

It was a sensation that began to haunt me. The feeling that there was more going on than what I knew about. This was most disconcerting to me, for that which I did not know about and did not understand would be the most likely source of trouble in the future. Expect nothing, anticipate everything. That was my motto. If there were things occurring that I could not anticipate, it left me vulnerable. Worse, it left me discouraged.

Double Chin sensed my mood. "What troubles you, Po?" he asked me one night, "Po" being much easier for him to say than "Apropos." I was dining with them, and Lun Chin was busy cleaning up after our meal.

I spoke slowly and cautiously in those days, determined not to make a muddle of their language. "I feel . . . worry," I told him.

"About what?" inquired Double Chin.

I shrugged. "About . . . what will come. About the life I lead. About many things, my friend."

He and Lun Chin exchanged looks. Lun Chin initially had disliked me, but she had come to, at the very least, willingly tolerate me. So if Double Chin was concerned about me, his spouse felt likewise. "You lack balance, Po," said Double Chin after a time.

"Perhaps."

He waggled his finger as he shook his head. "No 'perhaps.' You lack balance. You have no inner peace."

I laughed bitterly. "Well, that much I'd have to concede. Inner peace and I are not ideal companions. Believe me, I would like nothing better."

"You can find it," Lun Chin told me. Double Chin nodded in confirmation.

"All right," I said gamely. "Where, exactly, would I find it?"

"Chinpan Ali," they said together, then looked at each other and smiled gently. The people of Hosbiyu rarely laughed, I'd noticed. If they found something humorous, they tended to laugh "inwardly." In this instance, the middle-aged couple clearly thought it amusing that they'd spoken simultaneously.

As for me, I didn't think it all that funny simply because I didn't know to what they were referring. I stared at them blankly.

They saw my bewilderment, and they once again exchanged glances, as if to mutely decide who was going to explain what they were talking about. Clearly Double Chin was mutually elected. "Certainly you have seen the hut on the outskirts of the village?" he asked.

I nodded. It was a decent-sized hut. But I never saw anyone go in or out, and had just figured it was some sort of storage facility. I told Double Chin and Lun Chin as much. Their response? More quiet-but-obvious amusement.

Then Double Chin shook his head. "No. In that place dwells Chinpan Ali. The wisest of us all."

"He's your village elder?"

"Actually," said Lun Chin, leaning forward and speaking in a confidential manner, "it is said he is older than the village. Older than everyone."

"And how has he achieved such extreme old age?" I asked.

"Through his studies and discipline," said Double Chin. "And most importantly—and I believe this will be the most pertinent aspect as far as you are concerned—through peace of mind. His calm is legendary. It is said it is impossible to cause anger within the breast of Chinpan Ali."

Lun Chin reached out and, rather sweetly, laid her hand upon mine. "All living creatures should have inner peace. They should understand the way of nature. The way of the water."

"The water?"

"We are as the water, Po," said Double Chin. "That which ripples our surface, sooner or later disappears without a trace. And we have but to wait and allow it to happen. If you can be as calm and still as the water, your worries would likewise vanish, never to be seen again."

"That would be nice," I said sincerely.

"Chinpan Ali can help you in this," Double Chin assured me. "I cannot guarantee that he would teach you, for none can predict the actions of Chinpan Ali or the direction they will take. But . . ."

"Truth to tell, my friends, I'm not looking for a teacher," I told them. "I'm afraid that I'm a bit set in my ways."

They shook their heads vigorously, almost in synch. "The wise man knows his lack of wisdom, and will learn from whomever he can, wherever he can," said Double Chin. "You are never too old, Po. Never. And learning is not confined to one's youth. It's the practice of a lifetime."

"I'll consider it," I said.

That clearly wasn't sufficient. "Do not consider," Lun Chin told me firmly. "It is to be done."

"Yes, ma'am," I said, properly cowed.

So it was that, the next morning, I found myself standing outside the hut of Chinpan Ali.

My hand hovered over the exterior of the hut for a heartbeat or ten, and then I knocked. There was no answer. "Ali?" I called. "Chinpan Ali?"

The door was not a typical door. Instead it was a series of

beaded strings, hanging together so densely they provided privacy. I heard some stirring from within, and then the beads separated.

An old man stared out at me, and he was the most elderly person I had ever encountered. He was a head shorter than I, and I wasn't all that tall to begin with. His skin was incredibly wrinkled. It is said that in order to know the age of a tree, you cut it open and count the number of rings on the stump. This always seemed a pointless exercise to me, because in order to determine the tree's age, you kill it and effectively render it moot. It doesn't matter how old it was; it's not going to be getting any older. But Chinpan Ali's face had so many folds that I couldn't help but think counting them would enable me to divine his age.

He had no hair atop his head, and the thinnest sliver of white beard clinging to his chin. He also had thick white eyebrows that tailed upward, giving him a perpetually quizzical appearance.

His eyes, however, were captivating. They were very dark, and intense, and when he stared at me it was as if he were boring a hole right through my head.

He said nothing. Just gazed at me as if he simultaneously was expecting me and also had no desire to see me.

"I'm . . ." I paused, licked my lips. "My name is Apropos." The pronunciation of my name in Chinpanese was an unusual agglomeration of syllables for them, but I felt constrained to give my full name rather than the simple "Po" they'd been using to refer to me. "I was told I should come to you."

He said nothing. His brow furrowed slightly, and his eyes glittered, although I couldn't tell if they did so in amusement or annoyance.

The problem when one person doesn't speak is that the other often feels the need to fill the air with words. "I . . .

haven't been sleeping well," I told him. "I worry. All the time. About the people here. Which, if you knew me, you would know is somewhat unusual for me, and I . . . well . . . you see, it . . ."

My greatest asset had always been my silver-tongued nature. I had thoroughly mastered Chinpanese, so I had no ready excuse as to why I couldn't string syllables together. I felt like a right fool. What in the world was it about this wizened man that made it difficult for me to communicate?

And before I could mangle this first meeting any further, Ali suddenly spoke. His lips hardly seemed to move, yet his voice was surprisingly firm, if a bit reedy.

"What do you seek?" he asked.

At last, something I could understand. "I seek peace of mind. Knowledge. I'm tired of feeling miserable all the time. Of being cynical. It's exhausting, always expecting the worst of any given situation. I'm tired of self-loathing, tired of being afraid to be happy. I seek a way of coping with the day-to-day stress of being me. I . . ."

He put up a hand in a peremptory fashion. I ceased talking and waited.

"Go away," he said. And he turned and started to walk back into his hut.

"Go away?" I couldn't quite believe it. "*Go away?* You don't understand. I was practically bullied into coming here. I was told that you could help make things better for me. It took a hell of a lot for me to come up to you and ask for your help, because I don't generally seek out help from anybody. I . . ."

He paused, halfway through the beaded curtains, and looked at me once more. "Go. Away."

I grabbed his shoulder. I could feel the bones beneath his simple clothing. "Now wait just one min—"

He turned and his eyes opened wide and fixed upon me

with such a fearsome gaze that I felt as if someone had just put the evil eye upon me. Then he looked at my hand, and I had the sudden distinct feeling that if he was so inclined, he could break it off at the wrist.

I had no reason to fear him. None. And if there was ever an expert in fearing things, it was a fundamental coward such as myself. Nevertheless I immediately removed my hand from his shoulder.

Slowly his eyes returned to their almost lazy look, and then he entered his hut, the curtains noisily swinging together and hiding him from view.

And then the words floated from his hut: "Return when you know what you seek."

I stood there for a long moment, then became aware that someone was watching me. It was Lun Chin, standing next to Double Chin.

Then Lun Chin nodded approvingly. "That went much better than I thought it would."

Astoundingly, Double Chin bobbed his head in agreement. "Clearly, he likes you. That went very well indeed."

Then they turned and made their slow way back to their hut.

"Wonderful," I muttered.

I assure you, by that point I would have been more than happy never to have any contact with Chinpan Ali again. Fate, however, had other plans, as it so often does.

Visitors to Hosbiyu were not all that common, but not all that infrequent either. So on one particular day, when the air was a bit crisper than usual, I thought nothing of it at first when I noticed three horsemen approaching from a distance.

At that moment, I was busy working with some of the young boys in the village. Several of them possessed small practice swords created from bamboo. Granted, I was hardly the greatest swordsman who ever lived, but I knew the basics.

I'd done a long day's work in the fields, and my leg was throbbing. Nevertheless, when I limped back to the village, there were some of the youngsters, waving their bamboo swords and looking to me hopefully. I had made quite an impression on the youngsters when I'd first arrived, or rather the sword strapped to my back had. Clearly they'd never seen anything quite like it. They knew of swords, but claimed that swords of Chinpan were very different from what I carried with me. I took their word for it, considering no one else in Hosbiyu appeared to own a weapon.

I had learned that the type of digging tool they carried was called a "sai." When I had eventually learned their language, I had spoken with Double Chin about the misunderstanding involving their wielding of their farm implements upon meeting me.

"I thought your sai was a weapon," I told him. "You know . . . it could be used as such."

Double Chin had simply looked at me skeptically. "A weapon? A tool designed to create life from the dirt, used instead to take life and place people beneath the dirt? Not possible."

"Very possible," I had countered. "Why, if used properly—as a means of extending one's reach—it could be as devastating as a sword."

"No, my friend," said Double Chin, resting a hand on my shoulder and smiling sadly at my lack of comprehension. "A sword is just a sword, while a sai is just a sai."

And that was where we had left it.

The youth of Hosbiyu, however, had their imaginations fired by my sword, and had taken to asking me for pointers as to how to wield one. This had earned me a great deal of scowling and disapproval from Take On Chin and Cleft

Chin, but the enthusiasm of the young men could not be denied. And so it was that the village was occasionally filled with the sounds of bamboo swords clattering against one another.

The boys were quick studies. I was able to teach them a number of basic blocks and guards in very short order, and within a month or so their wielding of the bamboo practice swords was so deft that I was hard-pressed to touch some of the more able students at all. Granted, there were limits as to what I could do thanks to my lame leg. But that didn't take away from their basic ability, and I liked to think that I had some facility as a teacher.

So there we were, in the village, sparring as was our wont, when the riders appeared.

The boys grew very quiet as the horsemen approached. They did not seem particularly concerned, but the banter and sense of fun we'd been having dissipated. I quickly saw why.

The horsemen were armed.

All the visitors who had passed through carried with them, at most, walking sticks, or small daggers tucked in their belts that could just as easily be used for carving up food as for anything offensive. These horsemen, however, all had swords with them. None of them, strangely enough, had scabbards dangling from belts. Instead they had very wide cloth belts around their waists, and the swords were shoved through the belts and held in place against their bodies.

Even though the swords were sheathed, I could tell they were very different from my own bastard sword. They were very slender, for one thing. It seemed to me that made their swords vulnerable to breaking should they come into contact with my own. On the other hand, if they were smaller and lighter, the wielders might be able to deftly maneuver past my own larger and slower blade, cutting me to pieces while I was still trying to bring my weapon around for a blow.

Not that I was either expecting or anticipating a battle. True, I had developed a most uncharacteristic affection for these people, but I had not lost sight of the fact that I was still Apropos. My safety came above concern for the safety of others, and I had no intention of laying my life upon the line for anyone. If a fight erupted, I would be more than happy to take refuge in my hut and wait until the screaming died down. I only fought when cornered, and preferred to try and prevent such a cornering from taking place.

Still, occasionally I did indeed find myself in do-or-die situations. In such instances, I always elected to do. The problem was, my actual blade—not the practice sword I was using in jousting with the lads—lay in my hut, out of reach. My staff was at hand as always, and was a ubiquitous weapon, but still not quite as devastating as my sword.

And I had the sai in my belt. My conversations with Double Chin came back to me at that moment, and I was damned glad that I had conceived of ways to use the implement as a weapon if need be. Because if these sword-bearing new arrivals sought to make trouble quickly, and I couldn't avoid it, I wanted as many means as possible of defending myself right at hand.

Others of the village were emerging from their huts as the beats of the horses' hooves grew ever louder. They started calling to one another, and in short order the entirety of the village was gathering in its small dirt streets. They were speaking rapidly to one another. My problem was that my comprehension of their lingo depended upon slow, careful enunciation. If they were addressing one another with any sort of genuine speed, I was hopelessly lost. I could pick out words here and there, perhaps even parse a sentence or two. Nothing beyond that, however. I knew in time I would comprehend more. Unfortunately, I had the uneasy feeling that these horsemen were bound and determined to provide us as little time as possible.

They reined up, looking upon the gathering throng with unveiled contempt. By that point I was wearing one of their own hats, those very wide-brimmed bamboo head coverings that served to obscure much of my face if I had it angled forward.

Their clothing bore no resemblance to that of the farmers. They sported robes with large, flowing sleeves, and intricate woven designs of red and gold. Their breeches were likewise loose and flowing, gathered in at the waist through that huge belt, and tapering down into black boots. Dragons seemed to be the predominant visual image upon their clothes, stitched in a variety of manners.

They had stylized haircuts, their hair pulled back tightly into topknots, leaving them with very high foreheads that glistened in the sun.

The centermost one bellowed in a strident voice, "Attention, people of—"

Then he stopped. And stared at me.

I lowered my head a bit, hoping to divert his scrutiny. It didn't work. "What," he demanded finally, "is wrong with your face?"

I said nothing. I didn't see where responding was going to be of much benefit. Instead I just shrugged in a vague manner.

Unfortunately, Kit Chinette chose that exact time to wander past, and she had apparently been taught always to respond when asked a question by one's elders. "That's Po. He's not from around here," she said. I fired her my fiercest look. She smiled back innocently. What a sweet child. Would that she had been within range so that I could have hugged her, or even better, staved in her head with my staff.

"Oh really." The horseman swung his leg over his mount and dropped to the ground. He swaggered toward me, his thumbs hooked into his sash. It gave me a chance to inspect his sword closer up. The hilt was white, ivory unless I missed my guess. It was ornately carved with images of dragons upon it. "And whereabouts might you be from?"

"Here and there," I said, still keeping my gaze fixed firmly upon the ground.

"I see." His voice was deep and guttural and had the familiar aspect of the bully that I had encountered on any number of occasions. "And where . . . precisely . . . is there?"

When I didn't respond, he swung his arm in a wide arc and knocked the hat from my head. Then he gripped my chin and turned my face this way and that, inspecting me as he would a horse. His face clouded with increasing suspicion. "I have never seen anything like you," he said.

Unfortunately, I had seen his type all too many times in my life. I refrained from saying so, however.

It was interesting. I felt as if part of me was stepping outside of myself. Once upon a time, my fundamental cravenness and weakness of spirit would have filled me with fear over what was going to happen next. But something was different this time. Perhaps it was all the time that I'd spent as the "peacelord" of Wuin, seeing people bowing and scraping before me. Instead of fear, I was feeling mounting anger.

And I quickly realized why. It was because, all this time, I had been wondering and dreading when something would go terribly wrong with the bucolic turn my life had taken. And now that it was here, now that the possible destruction of my newfound existence was upon me, all I could feel was slowly building fury that I had been right. The cynic in me rejoiced, but a budding, optimistic side hadn't wanted me to be right.

"What do you want?" It was Take on Chin who had spoken, with Cleft Chin right next to him, and Double Chin nearby. Cleft Chin was no more a fighter than anyone else in the village, but he was burlier than the others, and cut an imposing figure when he simply stood still and glowered. He had exceptional glowering skills. Unfortunately, his fighting skills were almost nonexistent. I'd watched him spar with the boys on a couple of occasions, and felt confident in saying that Kit Chinette could have disposed of him with alacrity.

I had to admit, though, Take On Chin—for all that he annoyed me with his perpetual scowls—wasn't backing down in the face of the newcomer's swaggering attitude.

The newcomer looked him up and down. "Do you know who I am?" he demanded.

"Should I?" asked Take On Chin mildly.

He thumped his chest and said, "I am Kaybi, of the Skang Kei family." He paused for dramatic effect. "You know the Skang Kei, I take it?"

"I know *of* them," replied Take on Chin. "They are reputed to be a business concern, are they not?"

"Do not toy with me," said Kaybi. "You know the power and influence wielded by Skang Kei."

"They are criminals," blurted out Cleft Chin. "You all are."

"An honest man," Kaybi said with mock approval.

"We are all honest men here, you will find," Double Chin told him. "We live in peace. If you come in peace, you will be received as such."

"I come in earnest, is what I come in," said Kaybi. He began to walk in a wide circle, hands behind his back, a distinct swagger to his stride that was typical of the thuggish mind-set such creatures possessed. "Thus far, the Skang Kei family has limited its influence to the major cities. We have decided, however, to branch out. For the solidarity and good of all, it seems the reasonable thing to do. And it will be to your benefit as well."

"Our benefit?" Take On Chin looked skeptical. "How is the interest of the Skang Kei to our benefit? We are simple farmers here," and there was a silent chorus of nodding heads. "We have no involvement in the activities of the Skang Kei, or their influence in cities, major or minor."

"That will change." He paused to let that sink in, and then continued, "Your village will offer up tribute to the Skang Kei family. Half of what you harvest will become property of the Skang Kei, to do with as we wish."

There arose an immediate babble of confused and astonished responses from the villagers, so much and so simultaneously that I was unable to make out what anyone was saying. In response, Kaybi spread wide his arms and repeatedly shouted, *"Silence! Silence!"* When absolute quiet had been achieved, he permitted a small smile as he went back to his swaggering. "Obviously you believe that you will be getting nothing for your contribution to the Skang Kei. That is not at all the case. You will be receiving protection."

"Protection?" Take On Chin looked bewildered. "From what?"

"From them," I said, unable to contain myself. "If you do what they say, you won't wake up one morning to discover the burning of your crops, or your homes, or yourselves."

"You have a firm understanding of business," Kaybi said mockingly.

"We won't stand for it!" Cleft Chin cried out.

"I see." Quiet menace radiated from Kaybi. "And do you speak for all in this village? All the men? The women?" His gaze settled on Kit Chinette, who was watching him with rapt fascination. He smiled. "The children?"

In a flash, his sword was in his hand, and I could see

instantly that the edge was lean and razor sharp. So sharp, in fact, that it would likely make short work of my staff.

Even as he brought the sword whipping around toward Kit Chinette, even as the people cried out as one, even as my mind screamed *What the hell do you think you're doing?!*, I stepped into the path of the blade with the sai yanked from my belt. I brought it up as I would a dagger, thrusting outward in desperation as much as anything else. But sheer, dumb luck was on my side, fortune favoring the foolish, and I intercepted the blade between the middle prong and one of the upraised sides with a resounding clang. I stepped forward, bringing me chest-to-chest with Kaybi, twisting my wrist so the sword was angled to one side, away from us, locked into the hold of the simple farming implement.

"Sometimes," I grated, "a sai isn't just a sai." And I twisted my wrist as hard as I could.

The blade was remarkably flexible, I'll give it that. But the pressure was unexpected and at an extremely odd angle, and the sword simply wasn't built to endure it. There was a satisfyingly loud snap and the stunned Kaybi was abruptly standing there holding a hilt with about half an inch of steel extending from it. The rest was lying on the ground, looking like a severed head lonesome for its body.

He spat out a word the meaning of which I did not know, probably because the residents of Hosbiyu were far too polite to have taught it to me. I had no time to rejoice in my minor victory, however, because Kaybi shoved me square in the chest, catching me off balance, and I tumbled to the ground. I came up quickly, though, still gripping my staff as he advanced on me, discarding the hilt and whipping out a dagger from hiding. More of what I presumed to be invective tumbled from his mouth, but I didn't wait for him to draw near. Instead I thrust the base of my staff forward, catching him squarely in the pit of his stomach.

Would that I'd had the other end in position, because I could have popped out my blade and disemboweled the bastard. As it was he staggered back, holding his gut and looking distinctly pale.

But matters were rapidly spiraling out of control, for the other two men had vaulted from their horses, and they had their own swords out. *Idiot. This is what you get for taking chances on the behalf of others,* my inner voice informed me with obvious contempt. *I'm quit of you. You're on your own, for the few seconds of life you have left.*

I had the sai still poised in one hand, the staff ready in the other as I hauled myself to my feet. Would that I'd had my sword. It probably wouldn't have done me much good. My lame leg severely limited my maneuverability, and anyway, it would have been far too cumbersome in comparison with the swords they were using. They'd have carved me up while I was still trying to get into a guard position. And I had a very strong feeling I wasn't going to get lucky with the sai once again so quickly.

That was when a strong voice abruptly called out, *"Stop!"*

You'd have thought that a single voice wouldn't have any impact on such as those outlaws, but something about it absolutely commanded attention.

Chinpan Ali had emerged from his hut. He was eyeing them thoughtfully, and he wore his calm like a comfortable cloak. He gestured toward his hut and said, "Come. Let us talk."

"This one must die!" said an angry Kaybi, pointing a quivering finger at me.

"And he will, as all men must," Ali assured him. "There is no need for you to hasten it."

"Oh, but there's very much a need," said Kaybi, wiping sweat from his brow.

"Then kill him later," suggested Ali, which hardly served

to mollify my concerns. "He is not going anywhere. Share the hospitality of my hut. We will discuss matters and come to an understanding."

"Are you in charge of this rat trap?" Kaybi demanded. He wasn't taking his eye off me, but he did take a sidelong glance in Ali's direction.

Take On Chin looked as if he was about to respond, but then thought better of it. Instead he simply folded his arms across his body, into the sleeves of his garment, and remained silent.

"I am the village elder," said Ali. "That has always been sufficient. Now come. Please. Humor an old man."

Kaybi hesitated, then smiled evilly. "Very well. Let this one," and he stabbed a finger at me, "dwell for a time on the fate that awaits him. Fitting punishment." He turned on his heel and headed for the hut. His companions fell into step behind him.

The villagers started to crowd toward me, obviously to thank me for my bravery and daring in the face of adversity. I quickly shook them off, saying, "It was nothing. Nothing," as I headed for my hut as fast as I could.

Why? To get the hell out of town was why.

I had no intention of hanging about and waiting for those brutes to saunter out of Ali's hut so they could continue where they had left off and lay waste to me. It was one thing to foolishly defend myself or even, gods help me, Kit Chinette, in the heat of the moment. But the moment had cooled, and so had my enthusiasm for remaining in Hosbiyu. The faster I could get out of there, the better.

What was problematic, of course, was determining how best to avoid my would-be killers. I couldn't just hit the road. They'd catch up with me in short order. I contemplated stealing their horses, but I couldn't be sure that would work. The animals might be too well trained to allow a stranger to ride them, and I certainly didn't need to have them hear a bucking and whinnying horse tossing me off its back so they could run out and dispatch me quickly.

My mind racing, I decided the best thing to do would be to head for the wheat fields. The stalks were tall and concealing, the fields fairly vast, and the odds of them managing to locate me if I didn't crash around in them too much were relatively slim. At least that's what I told myself.

Granted, there was every possibility that—upon finding me gone—the brigands would take out their hostility upon the villagers. I felt badly about that, which was something of an accomplishment for me. It wasn't all that long ago that I wouldn't have given a flying damn. In this case, I took a moment to mourn the likely unpleasant fate of these peaceful farmers. It slowed down my packing for about a second, and then I doubled my efforts to make up for the lost time.

There were footsteps at my door and my shoulders tensed in anticipation of a sword blade winging toward me, but before I could yank my blade from its scabbard in a last-ditch attempt to save my life, I heard Double Chin say, "That was very brave of you."

"Thanks," I said.

He studied my actions coolly. "What are you doing?"

"Reorganizing."

"Odd. To the dispassionate observer, it would appear that you are preparing to make a hasty departure." He cocked his head slightly. "Is that so?"

"I'm thinking a change of scenery might be in order."

"That is not necessary, Po. All will be well."

"With all respect," I told him, shoving the last of my clothes into a burlap sack, "you're not the one those butchers will be coming after."

"If you were to depart, I very likely would be, yes," he

said mildly. I said nothing in response to that, since he was correct. "Do you see me looking concerned?"

"No," I replied. "Then again, that could simply be because you don't realize the gravity of the situation."

"Or perhaps you do not realize the situation is under control."

"Look," I said, slinging the sack over my shoulder, "three criminal henchmen are out there who would just as soon kill me as look at me, and they'll probably do both in short order. The only thing standing between me and a very imminent death is one fairly small old man, and somehow I'm seriously doubting—"

That was when I heard the scream.

I'd heard people scream before. I'd been present at some truly ghastly dealings of death. I'd heard and seen people go to their graves consumed by soul-sucking depression as they realized—instants before their demise—that no beatific afterlife awaited them, but rather only blackness and oblivion. That can be a most disheartening experience when you've been living your life in self-delusion as to what occurred at the end of it.

But those screams were nothing like this.

It was three voices I heard, and for an instant I thought the brigands had stormed out of Chinpan Ali's hut and begun slaughtering random villagers just to show they were not to be trifled with. Just as quickly, I realized that it was in fact the voices of those selfsame brutes, filled with screeching horror such as I'd never encountered. And considering I'd seen people die at the hands of everything from male Harpies to evil shadow representations of myself, I had a fairly wide range of experience to choose from.

And Double Chin's expression remained cool and

inscrutable. The only change was the slightest twinge from the edges of his mouth. Otherwise . . . nothing.

Then the screams tapered off, and I could have sworn I heard a slight gurgling noise. Then . . . silence.

"What the hell was that?" I asked, and was surprised to realize my voice was barely above a hush.

Double Chin said nothing.

My consuming curiosity overwhelmed my normal sense of caution, and I hurried out of my hut. The villagers were standing about, and they bore that same, distant, faintly amused expression that Double Chin had. Even the children looked that way, and on Kit Chinette I can assure you it was a truly spooky sight. Whatever had just happened, it clearly came as no surprise to these people.

All eyes were upon Ali's hut. Perhaps they were content to simply stand there, but I was not. I hurried toward the hut as fast as my weak leg would allow me. I got to the beaded curtain entrance and pushed it aside, not caring about the clatter it made. Honestly, I didn't have the faintest idea what to expect.

The bodies of all three of the bravos who'd attempted to blackmail the village were strewn about the dirt floor. Their blood was seeping into the ground. Their torsos were in several neatly sliced sections. A butcher slaughtering oxen could not have done a more thorough job. Their heads were situated in various parts of the hut.

Chinpan Ali was squarely in the middle of the hut. He seemed to have more possessions than anyone else in the village, including a couple of trunks, some wicker furniture, some wall hangings. Nothing elaborate, but just an indicator that he'd been around long enough to accrue a few items. At that moment, he was sheathing a sword. I had never seen a sword quite like it. It was somewhat

straighter than the swords wielded by the other men, back
when they were in a condition to be a threat. But the handle was unique. Tinted light red, it was a carved representation of a bird, its head and beak forming the pommel while
its wings and feathered body insinuated itself through the
rest of the handle.

Eerily, it reminded me of the phoenix. I had once
encountered one of those gloriously mythic creatures, and
been subjected to a rather wild ride and the beginning of
another unwanted adventure. Here it was again, looking at
me like a silent, carved reminder of achievement—or
sins—long past.

The sword clacked into the scabbard with the finality of
a lid being slammed on a coffin. Ali didn't appear to notice
I was there at first. Instead he gently stroked the hilt, which
I had to admit was a disturbing enough image in and of
itself. Then, slowly, he turned and stared in my direction.
He said nothing, merely tilted his head slightly.

I backed out of the hut, turned, and saw the villagers
slowly moving toward the hut. Only the men. The women
and children were hanging back. In the uncanny silence, it
was like watching ghosts of people moving through the real
world without realization that they were dead. Except they
were very much alive, and they were carrying burlap bags in
assorted sizes. A handful smiled at me, as if we were having
a chance encounter at the local market.

"Do not dawdle," Take On Chin told his people, and
they hastened to do his bidding. One by one, the men filed
into the hut, and when each emerged he would be carrying
a sack that was bulging with what was obviously some body
part of the former representatives of the Skang Kei crime
family. On several of them, I saw large red patches forming
from the pooling blood.

They carried the sections off in the direction of the

wheat fields, which I quickly surmised would serve as their burial place. These were resourceful people, accustomed to making the most use of whatever they happened to have on hand. And decaying body parts would certainly provide as many nutrients to the soil as anything else they might choose to put down there.

I don't remember going back to my hut. All I knew is that eventually I found myself there, seated on the ground, staring off into space. I could not believe what I had seen. It was like some bizarre horror tale.

There was a noise at the entrance and I looked up. Chinpan Ali was standing there, looking very unassuming and frail and not at all capable of carving three men into fertilizer. He nodded to me in greeting. I said nothing. What was there to say?

"You were brave," he said. "Defending that girl. She might have died if not for you."

I shrugged.

"What do you seek?" he asked.

I couldn't believe he was asking this again. What did I seek? I sought normality in a world that had no stomach for it. I had thought I'd found a nice, simple village filled with nice, simple people. People who were incapable of inflicting harm upon anyone. People whom I had believed to be so innocent, so naïve, that they were in deadly danger simply because I was among them.

And yet here was a village elder who was quite possibly the most deadly fighter I had ever encountered. Here was a populace who did not fear intruders, because they knew they'd wind up burying potential enemies out in the fields to make their crops grow. How many body parts were already there that I had trod upon without knowing? What else was there about these villagers, with whom I had lived all these many months, that I didn't know?

My mind was whirling. Why was no one ever what I thought they were? Women whom I had loved betrayed me. Men would put forward public faces of chivalry while carrying out beastly deeds in the dark of night. And now these peaceful villagers, who calmly tidied up after a slaughter that would have made the most barbaric of barbarians envious for its efficiency and totality.

What did I seek? What was there *to* seek? Whatever I found, it would invariably, at some point, rebound to my detriment. I just didn't see the point of it, or the point of anything really.

"Nothing," I said with a heavy sigh. "I seek nothing. I'm empty."

Chinpan Ali nodded once, and then said, "Good. Then you are ready to learn. Come to my hut tomorrow morning. You will learn the way of total destruction through inner peace." And with that, he turned and walked out of the hut.

I stared after him for a good long time.

"Oookay," I said to the empty hut.

Chapter 6

Zennihilation and the Art of Water Cycle Maintenance

When I entered Ali's hut the next morning, he was seated in the middle in a cross-legged position. His eyes were closed. He said nothing to me. With a mental shrug, I walked across the hut, eased myself onto the ground, and sat opposite him.

"Why did you do that?" he abruptly asked.

"Sit down, you mean?" I blinked. "Well . . . because you were seated."

"Do you imitate all others?"

"No."

"Then why imitate me?"

"Because . . ." I cast about for an answer. "Because you were here. It's your hut. You establish how one is to behave within it. So I . . . thought it was what you wanted."

"And what did *you* want?"

"Truthfully?" I sighed. "I want to know what I'm doing here. I don't understand it at all. I don't understand my life at all."

"You think I can provide you understanding?"

"No, I think only I can provide that. I'm hoping that maybe you can tell me what I'm looking for."

"You are looking for that," said Chinpan Ali, "which you are not looking for."

I stared at him. "Thank you," I said tonelessly. "That was very helpful."

"No. It was not. Do you know why I said it?"

"No."

"Would you like to?"

"Not especially, no."

He nodded in approval. "You are a natural at this."

"At what?"

"Ahhhh," he said, raising a finger and pointing at the sky. Then he lowered it and folded his hands into his lap.

I was about ready to give up at that point, when suddenly he said, "What question would you most like the answer to."

That actually had some promise to it. I leaned forward and said, "How did you dispatch those men yesterday? Three of them against the one of you. Bigger, stronger, two swords to your one. And the way in which you did it . . . no matter how sharp your blade, there still has to be strength behind the thrusts. You cut through muscle, through bone, as if it were cheese. Yet you look . . ."

"Unassuming?"

"Yes."

"Helpless?"

"That's right."

He nodded, his eyelids half shut. "But looks can be deceiving. You appear to be a lame fool. Have you not used that to your benefit in the past?"

"Yes," I admitted. "I've played to that. Put people off guard. But playacting is one thing. You . . . you killed those men. You . . . how? I mean . . . how? You reduced them to . . ."

"To nothing. They are now nothing."

I bobbed my head. "Yes."

"You walked here and made yourself as I was. Seated. Waiting. In order to reduce men to nothing, you must first be nothing yourself. When you have emptied yourself of all that you are, you can project that nothingness upon your opponent."

"Well . . . won't that just result in both of us being dead?"

"No," said Chinpan Ali sagely, "because while you may be nothing, your opponent will be less than nothing. That is the essence of Zennihilation: creating the total absence of your enemy by creating a total absence of self. Do you understand?"

I nodded, then said, "No."

"Excellent. Stand."

I stood.

"Hop on one foot."

I raised my right leg and proceeded to hop on the left one. Up and down, down and up, for what seemed an hour. He simply sat there and watched. I felt like a complete fool and was only glad that no one else was around to witness this absurdity.

"Stop," he said. "Now switch."

"Switch?" He nodded. "But . . . I can't. My right leg . . . it's lame. You see it."

"The weakness," and he tapped his skull, "is in your mind."

"No," I said patiently. "The weakness is in my leg. It has been since birth."

"And you would let yourself be limited by your body? Do you think I am limited by the body that you perceive?"

"I . . . suppose not," I said, feeling less certain of this by the minute. Then again, I supposed it was that lack of certainty I was supposed to be endeavoring to overcome. "No, obviously you're not limited."

"Then hop on your right leg."

Taking a deep breath, holding on firmly to my staff, I switched in midhop from left leg to right, and was actually thrilled to discover that my lame leg supported my body weight . . . for perhaps two seconds. Then I collapsed like a puppet severed of its strings. My staff fell to the ground a moment after I did.

"What have you learned?" said Chinpan Ali.

"That you know nothing!" I snapped in mortification.

To my shock, he nodded approvingly. "Excellent. You are an even faster student than I first believed. Sit. Cross your legs."

I wanted to knock his head off with my staff. Instead, still steaming, I did as he said while wondering whether there was any point to it at all.

"A riddle," he said abruptly. "I never was, am always to be. No one ever saw me, nor ever will. And yet I am the confidence of all, to live and breathe on this terrestrial ball. What am I?"

I had always disliked riddles. They seemed a waste of time to me, providing the interrogator the chance to sit there and look smug while you struggled to come up with some sort of interpretation that fit all the clues.

"You are thinking too much," Ali said abruptly as if he'd read my mind. "You must meditate. You must relax and ponder the riddle. That is the fundamental concept of Zennihilation."

"I thought we were going to train. That you would teach me how you handled those men so easily. How—"

"Master."

I stared at him. "Pardon?"

"You will address me as 'master.' That is the proper respect a student gives to his teacher."

I didn't like the sound of that at all. It was not a word that would come easily off my tongue.

But I was hooked, you see. Desperately consumed by curiosity and desire. Here was this frail old man, far more frail than I. Yet he obviously knew techniques, secrets that made him virtually invincible.

Once upon a time, I had been invincible. No one was able to defeat me in combat, and I was feared wherever I went. It was a good feeling. No. No, it was a great feeling. Granted, I did a lot of horrific and barbarous things during that time, and I regretted much of it. But I had spent my entire life up until that point feeling endlessly vulnerable to a world that was—for the most part—bigger and faster and stronger than I. I, Apropos, limping along while the rest of humanity sprinted past. It was galling to live that way, and the exhilaration I felt during the time that I was the peacelord of Wuin was unequaled in my existence.

The problem was, it was puissance that came with too high a price, and I'd had to divest myself of it. In fact, I still carried scars on my chest from when I had done so. Since then I had gone back to my previous, and current, form. And if it was frustrating before when I'd had to deal with my assortment of fragilities, how much more so was it having tasted indestructibility only to have lost it once more?

But this man, this shriveled little man . . . he knew something. Something that could make me, if not omnipotent once more, capable of defending myself with far greater confidence than I had before. And if I wanted that knowledge, I was going to have to play along.

"Very well . . . master," I grunted. "But . . ."

"And you will not question me. The student never questions the master."

My patience was beyond wearing thin. It was becoming so threadbare as to let chill winds through without obstruction.

This was getting ridiculous. As much as I wanted to be able to dispatch opponents the way he had, I did still have my pride. It was a tattered and pathetic thing, my pride, and really not all that fit for human company. But I had it nonetheless. It was at that point I decided that this was simply not going to work. I was just going to give up, that was all. Give up, forget that I'd wasted my time in this worthless attempt to find mental balance and a means of self-defense. I would just go back to my hut, or perhaps out into the fields to work—trying not to step upon freshly dug graves—and at the end of the day, go to sleep and hope that some clearer answer revealed itself on the morrow . . .

And then I stopped. I blinked, my expression going slack.

"Tomorrow," I said.

"Yes?" said Chinpan Ali calmly.

"Tomorrow," I told him with growing excitement. " 'I never was, am always to be. No one ever saw me, nor ever will. And yet I am the confidence of all, to live and breathe on this terrestrial ball.' The answer to the riddle is 'tomorrow.' "

"The answer to the riddle is tomorrow . . . what?" he prompted.

I paused, and then smiled broadly. "Tomorrow . . . master."

"Yes," and this time a genuine smile crept across his face. "You see? Meditation leads you to be able to accomplish that which you did not know you could accomplish. To be able to rid yourself of all concerns. Once you find your core of inner peace, nothing can disturb you. All mistakes in combat stem from disruption of the spirit. With your spirit intact, you can be invincible."

"Invincible. Well, I like the sound of that . . . master," I added.

I look back on that exchange now and am, frankly, somewhat mortified by it. That I would have so quickly, so willingly given myself over to Ali and his teachings would seem to fly in the face of the inveterate skeptic that I have always painted myself to be.

I can offer you but one reasonable explanation, and indeed it is one that I have had to ponder long and hard to intuit.

The most fundamental impulse of a man is to please his father. But for all of my early years, I had no father. Just an unknown bastard of a knight who had produced a bastard of a son. While I was growing up, the significant adult male in my life was an abusive tavern owner who employed my mother as a prostitute. Eventually I did learn my father's identity, and during our fleeting time together, all I wanted to do was kill him. Hardly an ideal situation for male bonding.

In short, I had never had a significant, stable, fatherlike individual in my life. And although Chinpan Ali at first exuded a gruffness and emotional distance, I also believed that he wanted me to succeed. That he was looking for someone to whom he could pass on his techniques and knowledge, and considered me to be that person.

. . . I wanted more than I had. I wanted to be more than I was. My constant gnawing dissatisfaction was eating away at me like a cancer, and I believed that Ali might well be the cure.

I got to my feet with my usual clumsiness, and Ali said, "Another riddle to consider until tomorrow: Why is a raven like a writing desk?"

"Because they both require quills to truly take wing," I replied.

He stared at me. "Oh" was all he said, and then quickly he added, "All right. Come back tomorrow and I'll have another one for you."

"I'll be here," I said.

When I returned the next day, Chinpan Ali presented me with two handheld blocks, each of which had a rough, gritty texture on one side. They had straps on the back to make them easy to place on my hands. I held them up, studying them curiously. "What are they?" I asked.

"For sanding," he replied. "Smoothing down of surface."

"All right," I said gamely. "So . . . what am I supposed to do with them."

"Sand the floor."

I blinked. "Pardon?"

He pointed down. "Sand the floor. Make motions like this," and he swept his arms around in two semicircles. "You understand?"

"Well . . . yes, I understand the motions. But . . ."

"No but. No question," he said sternly. "Show me sand-the-floor."

"But . . . it's a dirt floor," I pointed out.

"No matter."

"Master, I'm not exactly a carpenter, but even I know that sanding something usually involves wood."

He folded his arms and gave me that same intense look that he had the first day we'd met. "Who is master here, and who is student? Show me sand-the-floor."

"It's a dirt floor!" I wailed.

"Show!"

So I sanded the dirt floor.

It worked out about as well as you might expect. Dirt flew everywhere. I got it in my eyes, my lungs. To this day, I think I still have some dirt beneath my fingernails. By the end of the day, the only parts of me that weren't covered in dirt were the parts where little channels of sweat had trickled down my skin. The only area of the floor I didn't touch was near his personal effects. I prepared to move some of them, such as his trunk, but he told me to leave them where they were. So I simply sanded around them.

And all during that time, Ali—standing just outside the

door so that none of the clouds of dirt could bother him—
spoke of the various philosophies of Zennihilation. He
spoke of the two different techniques of meditation, Rinsai
and Soako. He talked about containers, and how I should
envision myself as an empty cup, because only then could I
be filled with knowledge. He discussed the beginnings of
Zennihilation, which apparently had their start with temple priests who allowed themselves to be subjected to inces-
sant taunts and torments by soldiers, specifically so they
could allow their focused rage to build to a point where
they would be unstoppable.

He spoke of many things. Fools and kings. Ultimately,
though, it all came back to the fact that I was sanding a
goddamn dirt floor until every muscle in my body was
aching and crying out for rest.

Finally he strode into the hut and stared at the floor,
filled with hundreds upon hundreds of swirl marks. "All
right. Stand up," he said, gesturing for me to rise.

Slowly, my body screaming in pain, I got to my feet,
favoring my right leg even more than I usually did. I stared
woefully at my dirt-encrusted clothes. All I could think
about was throwing myself in the river to cleanse myself
and, if I was really, really lucky, drown.

"Now," he said, "you will instinctively be able to use the
sand-the-floor technique to defend yourself against an
attack."

"I will?" I asked.

"Yes."

And then he was glaring at me, and a low growl was
coming from his throat like that of an angry mongrel.

That was when he let out an earsplitting howl and drew
back his fist, clearly ready to hit me.

I did the first thing that came to mind: I brought the two
sand blocks up, both still in my hands, and started smack-

ing them together repeatedly. Naturally this caused a huge cloud of dirt to rise from between my hands. Chinpan Ali staggered back, coughing violently, trying to ward it off and not succeeding. He lurched out into the open air, leaned against the hut, and continued to cough until his lungs were clear.

"Is that what you had in mind, master?" I called to him.

There was a pause, and then he said, "Yes. Exactly. Very good."

I couldn't have been happier. All right, yes, I could have been. I could have been not covered with soil and not aching in every joint. Aside from that, though, I was in relatively good spirits.

Once more we sat and meditated. This time he said to me, "What is greater than the gods, more evil than the devil. The poor have it. The rich need it. And if you eat it, you'll die."

I thought about that one a good long time. I drifted deeper and deeper into my musings, letting my thoughts wander far afield, hoping that sooner or later they would drift back to the question at hand and I would eventually know it. Nothing seemed to be coming, however, nothing at all, nothing at . . .

My eyes snapped open.

"Nothing," I said. "Nothing is greater than the gods or more evil than the devil. The poor have nothing, as well I know, and the rich need nothing. And if you eat nothing, you will die."

"Come back tomorrow," he told me as he nodded in approval.

And so it went, day after day.

Every day riddles, and lessons, and various tasks and exercises he set me to. Unfortunately, none of them ever seemed to make any damned sense. He had me spend an entire day counting individual stalks of wheat. An entire night counting stars. One afternoon was passed quacking like a duck. A morning was consumed with seeing how many grains of rice I could fit in my navel.

Once he had me water an entire field of brown grass by taking one mouthful at a time from a bucket and spitting it out upon the grass. Then he had me sit and watch the water as the sun baked it out of the ground and it dissipated. "You must understand the transient nature of the water cycle if you are to understand the transient nature of man," he said. Fortunately I didn't understand either, so I had achieved some degree of consistency.

And on and on it went, each task or challenge seemingly more nonsensical than the one before. And while these went on, he would continue to talk to me about Zennihilation. How I could take down entire armies if properly trained. I would be able to break trees in half with one sweep of my hand. True Zennihilation masters, I was told, could levitate. I asked Ali if he could do so, and he said that he indeed could, but only when no one was watching. He assured me, though, that if I was a good and devoted student, at some point in the future I could not watch him do it.

There was one time in particular when I felt as if I was simply not getting it. That the teachings of Ali were beyond my ability to grasp. I confessed to my teacher, while in his hut, that I could almost sense comprehension and enlightenment, as if they were hiding just around a corner, tantalizing me.

"You cannot obtain nothing if you strive for something," he intoned.

"But how can one achieve absolute nothingness?" I asked him. "If one sets aside all concerns, all possessions, all self-awareness, all of it . . . then how can there be motivation to do anything? Rather than being able to harness nothing-ness, if someone achieved the level of no level at all, why would anyone care about anything enough to do anything about anything? Instead of saying, 'I will fight,' it would be just as easy to say, 'I don't c—' "

But immediately he put a finger to my lips. "You were going to speak of not caring," he said. I nodded. "Do not do so. You are not ready."

"I'm . . . I'm not?"

He shook his head. "That is the ultimate level. You have not come close to achieving it. When you do . . . then you will be able to master Zennihilation. Now . . . I want you to stick this wheat up your nose . . ."

I know it sounds like madness. And yet, for the first time in my life, I had faith. Faith that it would all make sense. Faith that the pieces would come together for me sooner or later, and I would comprehend how it all related.

Because Chinpan Ali really was a good man. A good, decent man. A little strange, gods knew, but certainly there had to be some allowances made for the oddities that invariably accompanied advanced age.

And here was the other thing: As I spent time day after day in training and learning and exploring the various ram-ifications of Zennihilation, it left me precious little time to dwell on all the negatives that were so routine for me. My lameness of leg, my assorted failures, my burning frustra-tions, all faded into a sort of distant haze of obscurity.

There was always in the back of my mind the concern that more swordsmen would come. It might well have been that the Skang Kei representatives had gone around to assorted villages at random, leaving no schedule of their visitations behind. If that was the case, then quite possibly no one would realize that the tiny village of Hosbiyu was the last known whereabouts of the Skang Kei strongmen. And even if someone suspected it . . . what then? Without bodies or any sort of evidence, nothing could be done.

I began to relax more and more. My confidence grew. Inner peace beckoned me and I greeted it with open arms. I finally began to hope that everything was going to be all right.

I should have known better. Particularly the night when, after a long day of training, Chinpan Ali put a hand on my shoulder and said, with a winning smile, "You have endured much, Po. In many ways, you are the son I never had."

Even as I grinned in appreciation, my inner voice—which had not been speaking to me for quite some time owing to tremendous annoyance with my recent actions—piped up and said, *Well, that's it for him, you realize.*

I hate my inner voice.

Chapter 7

The Shadow Worriers

*T*he night that I had dreaded for some time, and then was foolish enough to stop dreading (which naturally was more than enough to bring it upon us), was an inclement affair. A storm had been brewing for the last few days, and now the rain was coming down, splattering on the rooftop. But the hut was well constructed and no water was leaking in.

As the rain fell, I tried to imagine myself years from now, in exactly this same place. Would such a thing be possible? Could I truly wind up spending my life in this one small village? Certainly the villagers didn't seem averse to my continued residence there. Perhaps, at some point in the distant future, I might actually come to think of the place as "our village" instead of "their village."

In the twilight moments before I fell asleep, I habitually flashed upon images in my life that were typically distressing. Cities burning, or people being stabbed, or beheaded, or riddled with arrows, or falling, or being torn to bits.

This night, though, I saw myself, quite old. Perhaps as old as Ali himself. Children were ringed around me, listening intently to my every word as I imparted wisdom to them. They were smiling, and I couldn't help but smile in return.

It was a charming image, and one that sent me gliding peacefully into slumber.

I didn't know what time it was when I awoke. All I knew was there was trouble afoot.

There were soft footfalls outside. So soft, so delicate, that under ordinary circumstances even I, with my keen hearing, might have missed them entirely. But the rain was falling, turning the dirt road to mud, and I detected a quick splashing about. Faster than a heartbeat, gentle as a falling feather, but it was enough to reach my oversized ears.

I am not someone who wakens by degrees. I come to immediate and total awareness. It is a trait that had saved my life on more than one occasion. In the world that I live, if one does not develop a talent for waking up instantly, one can chance waking up dead.

It was a cool evening thanks to the rain, so I was dressed in loose-fitting breeches and a robelike shirt that came to just below my hips. Even in the darkness, I knew where my staff was. I never left it more than arm's length away. Next to it was my sword. It was sitting out of the scabbard, for I had freshly oiled it earlier that evening. I was glad for that, lest the pulling of metal from its casing alert whoever might be out there.

It was intruders. I was sure of it. I knew the comings and goings and schedules of the townspeople as well as I knew my own breathing patterns. This time of night, none of them were going to be out and about. Which meant that someone who wasn't supposed to be here . . . was here.

Naturally my first assumption was that more burly representatives of the Skang Kei family had arrived. That they would come looking for their missing fellow, and not leave until they had found him. Which quite possibly meant they weren't going to be leaving ever, if Ali had to end up doing to them what he'd already done to their predecessors.

My first impulse was to hide. This was quickly followed by my second and third impulses, which were also to hide. Unfortunately, my hut was somewhat sparse in its furnishings, as were just about all of the huts except Ali's. There was nowhere handy that I could secret myself. So I settled for simply lying as still as I could upon my sleeping mat. However, I angled myself so that I was facing the door, rather than being turned away as I had been. I closed my eyes to narrow slits, hoping I might be able to make out any intruders who entered. My hand rested lightly upon the hilt of my sword, just in case.

The slight sounds of splashing had tapered off, as if the intruders—realizing they were making noise—had ceased doing so. Had they stopped moving altogether? Or were they so superbly trained that they were able to walk about lightly enough on sodden ground without giving themselves away? I was quite accomplished in techniques of forest craft, particularly considering the physical limitations I had to bear. But even I couldn't proceed noiselessly given the ground conditions.

At that moment, the loosely hanging door of my hut opened. It did so noiselessly, which was amazing considering the damned thing always made a racket whenever I opened it.

A figure peered in.

Since it was dark outside, and clouded over to boot, light was not plentiful. And the intruder's method of attire did not help matters. I was reasonably sure it was a female, based on the stunningly graceful way in which she moved. But she was dressed entirely in black, head to toe. I thought, although I could not be sure, that there was a sliver of open area around her eyes, giving her unobstructed sight. Other than that, though, not a square inch of her flesh was visible.

She was of medium height and slender, and she eased herself into my room as intrusively as a ghost. The door closed behind her, still making no noise. Just before it did so, however, I caught the briefest glimpse of similarly clad figures moving about outside. Obviously she wasn't alone.

She had the hilt of a sword protruding from over her shoulder, indicating she had a sword strapped to her back. Of even more concern was that I was able to make out what appeared to be a dagger in her right hand. If she was coming toward me with that, I wasn't about to simply lie there and let her gut me in my "sleep."

She paused several feet away, afforded me a brief glance, looked around, and obviously didn't find what she was seeking. I remained still. With any luck, she'd be gone in no time.

But then she took another look at me, and stared more fixedly. Naturally she would. The odds were that she'd never seen anyone (or anything, for that matter) quite like me before. Silently she approached. She then crouched down, tilting her head. Clearly she was trying to get an even better look at me. It was really quite remarkable. Were I not looking right at her, albeit with a very narrow field of vision, I would not have known she was there at all. Her stealth was masterly, and I found myself more interested in knowing where she'd learned to move like this than in discovering why she was here.

And then, to my utter astonishment, she came in behind me and began to run her fingers along my body. I thought she was searching me for weapons at first, but no. She was probing my muscles, my flesh. She was panting softly, as if receiving increasing sexual gratification from doing so. And she murmured to herself. Even though her voice was muffled by her mask, I could still discern what she was saying.

"His face, effulgent, glowing, shining, unique in all the world in its singularity. I look upon it and my breast heaves, a soaring, crashing wave like the floating zephyr of an evening star. A woman's head upon a woman's breast is a woman placing her head upon her own breast, to be one with herself, and to know the soaring rapture of orgasmic release. But to look upon him is to look upon myself, and see the strangeness and wonder that is within me, within all women, in all the secret places above and below the world, locked within our wombs, like ripe, bursting—"

"What the hell are you talking about?"

It was not, in retrospect, the brightest way I could have handled the moment. Certainly I won no major points for subtlety. The woman was clearly a loon, and I might have learned more had I simply lain there and let her babble. But I could feel my brain beginning to dissolve within my skull just from thirty seconds of listening to her. If she'd gone on much longer, my gray matter would have begun leaking out my ears.

Curiously, she didn't seem to care that I'd just revealed that I was awake, or that I'd had an impatient outburst thanks to her blather. Instead she shoved me onto my back, straddled me, and began running her hands under my shirt. One would have thought I was still sporting the magic ring upon my member that had given me unparalleled control over the libidos of all females.

"He speaks to me, his words like great waves crashing against the oozing sandiness of my shores. I feel in my breasts the current of liquid fire . . ."

"Right! That's enough of that!" I snapped, having no desire whatsoever to have her breasts oozing anything on me, much less liquid fire. I shoved her off me as hard as I could, knocking her knife away. She landed on her back and then, to my amazement, scissored her legs about in a rapid circular motion that brought her immediately to her feet. I never even saw her hand move, but suddenly she was holding the sword she had pulled from the scabbard on her back.

"Now . . . hold on," I said, regretting I hadn't kept my big mouth shut and just let her have her way with me. I had gotten to my feet, favoring my right leg as always. I had my sword in a defensive posture, but I didn't fancy going up against the whip-fast blade she was holding. "This isn't really necessary. I'm sure it's a misunderstanding . . ."

"His voice sings to me like a heavenly choir as my heart thuds, fair to bursting against the milky softness of my skin," she said. Even as she spoke, she brought her sword slicing back and forth in the air in front of me. "I hear him and the death of my beloved goldfish no longer tortures me. To the birds! To the birds!"

Well, that more or less settled it: She was completely demented. Unfortunately, she was a demented woman with a blade, and she charged at me with the grace of a shadow. The speed of her sword made it so impossible to follow that I did the only thing I could: I threw myself backward, hitting the ground flat on my back as her sword hissed through the air where I'd just been standing.

I remembered the lessons of Chinpan Ali at that moment, grabbed up a handful of dirt from the floor, and threw it as hard as I could.

Fortune was with me. The dirt took her square in the eyes just as she leaned in toward me to try and cut my throat. She staggered back and I was on my feet, bringing my sword about.

How in the world she parried my thrusts, I hadn't the faintest idea. She was blinded, desperately trying to get the dirt out of her eyes, and yet no matter how quickly I tried to strike home with my sword, she deflected it.

Quickly I backed up. As I did so I bent and scooped up my staff. She was blinking furiously, still trying to clear her eyes, still unable to see a damned thing, and I threw my sword against the bamboo wall. It clattered against it and the sound was enough to distract her. She turned, sweeping her sword around, cutting at where she imagined I was, and I lunged forward with my staff even as she turned away from me. The sound of the blade *snik*ing out from the carved dragon head snapped her attention back, but even she wasn't able to calculate quickly enough what angle I was coming in at, or what the sound portended. So it was that even as she brought her sword up high, I thrust my walking staff from a safe distance and slashed across her torso.

She let out an alarmed shriek and reflexively bent over to clutch at the blood welling from around her shoulder, and I swung the staff around again. It cut high across her face, barely missing the skin but shredding some of the cloth on her mask, and she stumbled back. Even as she did so, more insanely poetic words about passion, lust, throbbing bosoms, and heaving sighs of glorious ecstasy spilled from her lips, splashing about like loose stool. None of it made any sense. One moment she was talking about her emotions, the next she was painting grand pictures of nature and stars and skies and internal organs and penetrating gazes and gazing penetrations. It was madness, like the rantings of an overheated madwoman who hadn't had sexual congress in decades.

"My love, my hate, my sexual mate of fiery passion and passionate fire, I shall remember you even as I forget you!" she called out, grabbed up her knife, and turned and crashed through the door, silence apparently a thing of the past. I was about to follow her, and suddenly realized that probably wouldn't be the brightest idea. She had friends with her. But then I just as quickly realized that she might well come back with them to finish me off. If I stayed where I was, I was in danger, and if I left, I was in danger.

Better to be a running chicken than a sitting duck.

I shoved my sword into my scabbard and strapped it across my back. Holding on to my walking staff, I slid sideways out the door and into the rain. The ground was thick with mud, the rain still coming down. Immediately I lay flat on the muddy ground and rolled about in it as quietly as I could. It took almost no time at all for me to be covered head to toe in mud. I even smeared my face with the stuff. Then, keeping flat to the ground, I flattened myself against the ground on the far side of my hut, keeping a view as to what this lunatic woman and her associates were up to.

There was no movement. Nothing. All was silent. Silent as death.

Then I heard the sounds. An outcry, something breaking, a struggle, all coming from Chinpan Ali's hut.

My master, my teacher, the man who had befriended me and tried to bring me a measure of inner peace—even if he had chosen to do so in a rather bizarre manner—was in trouble. These black-clad women had singled him out. They were attacking him.

And I lay there. Unmoving. Unwilling to push my luck against the women. I kept telling myself that my master did not need my help. He had, after all, disposed of the brigands handily enough. These women, silent and deadly as they were, certainly could not prove a real threat against . . .

"Where is it?" I heard a female voice call from within his hut, and more crashing, and suddenly the sound of a sword yanked from a scabbard, and a slash of metal cutting through air, and a noise of finality that I'd come to know all too well. The sound of a death rattle. *"Where is the tachi?"*

"What is happening?!" I heard a voice call. It sounded like

that of Cleft Chin, and he emerged from his hut, and shouted out, "What is going on out here?"

I took the chance. From my place of concealment, I cried out as loudly as I could, *"Chinpan Ali is under attack!"*

This immediately caused all manner of ruckus as more voices called out from other huts, and within moments the entire village was roused. The black-clad women did not wait about to be discovered, however. They quickly emerged, a half-dozen of them it seemed, although it was hard to be certain. They were looking about, clearly trying to figure out from which direction had come the shouted alarm that they were in Ali's hut. One of them, it seemed, looked directly at me. I didn't move, didn't breathe. Flat in the muck as I was, I was not easily discernible under the best of circumstances, and these were certainly not those.

Then they obviously decided that they had stayed as long as they dared. The problem was that these black-clad bitches would have no trouble laying waste to the entire population of the village if they were so inclined. But luckily for all concerned, they didn't have the stomach for it. They melted away into the shadows, although one of them was clutching her shoulder. I knew she was the one whom I had stabbed, and she was the last one to disappear into the darkness. She stared hard right in my direction, and I was certain she had spotted me. She made no motion of discovery, however, and within moments she, too, was gone as if never there.

People were emerging from their huts and heading straight toward Ali's. With the attacking women departed, there was no reason for me to continue to hide other than my own natural cowardice . . . a strong incentive, I'll grant you, but moot by that point. I got to my feet, slipped once, righted myself, and moved toward Ali's hut with the rest of them.

I heard cries and wails of lamentation and knew even before I got there what I was going to see. Villagers gave me confused glances, not recognizing me at first. I must have looked like a monster of muck having risen from the grave.

The body of my mentor, my teacher . . . my friend . . . lay prostrate on the dirt floor that I had so meticulously sanded weeks earlier. His eyes were staring at nothing.

I should have known.

I should have been used to it.

I should have expected it. I did expect it.

It may sound like the height of selfishness that I looked upon the death of another and could only dwell upon how it affected me. Then again, I never claimed to be anything other than a selfish bastard, so what other reaction could reasonably be anticipated from me?

The burning rage did not consume me immediately. It flared into existence deep in the pit of my stomach, but it did not come to instant, full fruition. Instead it nestled there, eating at me, stoking the already burning fires of my discontent.

"Everyone get back," I said, my voice choked. "Get back."

"Now, see here!" Take On Chin said, choosing that moment to act his most belligerent. "As leader of this—"

I whirled on him, my temper flaring, and with a look that could have incinerated him where he stood, I snapped, *"I said get back! I'm paying respects, dammit!"*

They got back.

I was alone in the hut. Well, alone except for a corpse.

I simply stared at him for a good long time, wondering what it would be like to be able to bring him back to life through force of will. Then I noticed that his left hand was outstretched, as if he was reaching for something. Mentally

I followed the path from the tip of his hand toward where it was pointing.

It seemed as if he'd been reaching for his trunk.

The problem was, if there was something within he sought, it was pointless to have tried to obtain it, for the trunk was empty. The women in black had been thorough about that. Various of Ali's personal effects were scattered throughout the hut, and the trunk he was reaching toward with his dying grasp had been gone over more meticulously than just about anything else there. The contents were strewn all over. But the valuables tossed about weren't all that valuable. Old clothes, scrolls with writing upon them I couldn't begin to decipher, for though I had learned to speak their language well enough, I had not had the opportunity to learn how to write it. The alphabet was completely different from my own, and to add confusion, they wrote vertically instead of horizontally. I'd picked up a few letters, a word here and there, but that was pretty much it.

Nothing else of value seemed to be anywhere about.

Then I realized what was missing: The sword. That strange, bird-headed sword he'd used. The one that he'd employed so handily to dispatch the thugs a seeming eternity ago. There was no sign of it. Was it possible the women had taken it with them? But I hadn't spotted it. They'd seemed empty-handed when they'd left.

I called out to Double Chin, and he stuck his head in tentatively, as if afraid this was some sort of trick and I was about to decapitate him because he had not left me in solitude. I was remembering a word one of the women had said. "What is a 'tachi'?" I asked.

"It is a type of koshirae," Double Chin said promptly. "A blade. About this big, generally," and he displayed his hands in a way that indicated a blade about the length of the one I'd seen Ali use, a little over two feet in length.

"Single-edged. Very sharp. Very deadly, when wielded properly. Usually associated with high-ranking warriors and officials . . ."

"Fine, thank you. That's all I need to know." I gestured for him to depart, and he promptly did so. That was definitely the word I'd heard the women bandying about: "Tachi." "Where is the tachi?" they had demanded. They'd been looking for the sword, and Ali had died rather than give it over. Or perhaps had died while trying to get to it.

He'd been reaching for the trunk. Certainly the women must have seen it. Which was why they concentrated so heavily upon the trunk in their search. A search that had been aborted thanks to the awakening of the village and the assortment of witnesses they obviously desired to avoid.

But the trunk was empty.

I went to it, studied it carefully. Yes. Definitely an empty trunk. I felt around the bottom, hoping to discover some sort of place of concealment. Perhaps a false bottom, something along those lines. Still nothing.

Then I remembered that, when I'd been sanding the floor, Ali had told me to steer clear of the trunk. Not just the trunk itself, but the general area of the trunk.

I stepped back, yanked hard on the trunk, and pulled it away from the floor where it had rested. At first all I saw was more dirt, but there seemed to be a variance in coverage . . . and then I noticed what appeared to be a piece of bamboo stuck in the ground.

I knelt, brushed it away, and quickly uncovered exactly what I thought I was going to find: a small trapdoor. Years ago, I had kept prized possessions of mine beneath the ground, underneath floorboards in an old barn. In the end, it had done me little good: a traitorous woman had robbed me of it all anyway. But the idea of burying one's valuables was certainly nothing new to me, and for some reason it even made me feel a little proud that my teacher adopted some of the same habits that I possessed.

I lifted the bamboo trapdoor aside and instantly saw, there beneath the ground, a bundle wrapped in oilcloth. I reached down, gripped it firmly, and extracted it. I knew the moment I saw it that it was the tachi sword. Delicately, almost reverently, I unwound the cloth until the blade was revealed. The sheath was next to it, both of them protected by the careful wrapping. I saw there was something else down in the small hole as well, and pulled it out. It was tethers to attach the scabbard to a belt.

It was certainly a different manner of scabbard than I was accustomed to. Where I came from, the typical blade hung straight down at one's hip (if not being sported on the back). In this case, it was obvious that the sword was designed to hang in a horizontal manner. I saw the superiority in terms of style. It meant one could instantly pull out the sword in a sweeping, sideways motion that was an offensive and defensive maneuver combined with the mere act of unsheathing the blade. As opposed to pulling out a broadsword, in which you were leaving yourself fully exposed and vulnerable for a direct-on attack while you were still getting ready to bring your weapon into play. In such instances, you counted on your opponent's fundamentally chivalrous nature to allow you to prepare your weapon. In other words, you lived in a fool's paradise until such time as someone killed you for doing so.

I held up the sword, snapped it through the air. It had a wonderful heft to it. So much lighter than my own sword. My bastard sword was designed to be utilized with one hand or two, but the one-hand approach was still a bit of a challenge just because of the sword's weight. The tachi, by contrast, was so relatively weightless that it felt less like a weapon than it did a long, sharp extension of my own arm.

"Po!" called Take On Chin, and I realized my time was minimal. I slid the sword into the sheath, rewrapped the entire thing in the oilcloth, and then shoved the bundle under my loose-robed shirt. I managed to obscure most of it from direct view. Then I bent over and made my way out of the hut into the rain as the others looked upon me in various forms of bewilderment. What a sight I must have seemed to them, covered with mud and muck and doubled over as I staggered from the hut that had, until recently, housed my teacher.

I returned to my own hut, pulled off my mud-covered clothes, laid the sword flat near the far edge of the hut, and tossed the filthy vestments atop them to obscure them from casual view. I'm not entirely certain why I took such pains to hide the sword from the villagers. I suppose, in my perpetual feeling of suspicion, I was concerned that the villagers would want to take it from me. That they would feel it should be given to someone worthier than myself, or of greater importance. I did not want to let that happen. I didn't know why; all I knew was that I wanted the blade. I wanted it to be mine, so I could feel a continued connection to Ali. So I could wield a blade that was capable of cutting down several men where they stood. Besides, those black-clad hell bitches had wanted it. Had been willing to kill for it. That alone was enough for me to want to possess it.

Which, when one thinks upon it in the cold light of years later, was a demented attitude for me to have. If something was that dangerous, traditionally I would want to separate myself from it. Put as much distance—preferably the width of a continent—between myself and something so desirable that there were those eager to kill the one who had it.

But I was not thinking clearly at the time, for the aforementioned burning anger was beginning to swell ever hotter.

I took a deep breath, let it out, and steadied myself. Minutes later, with water gathered from the rain, I had washed myself off as best I could and was seated in clean clothes, cross-legged upon the floor. I had a small fire burning in the dug-hole fireplace in the middle of the hut, and was warming my hands in front of it. My thoughts were spinning.

There came a gentle tap at my door. "Yes, what?" I said brusquely.

Double Chin entered, Lun Chin beside him. Both were soaked from the rain, but neither seemed to notice or care. They bowed upon entering. From where I was seated, I gave a halfhearted bow in return. They settled to their knees opposite me. Nothing was said at first.

"Ali would have wanted you to celebrate his life," Double Chin ventured finally, "rather than to mourn his passing."

"I tend to think Ali would have wanted to live, and the rest of it is speculation designed to make us feel better," I replied. I leaned forward, probably looking an eerie sight as the light from the flame danced across my face. "I saw one of his killers. A woman."

"A woman?" echoed Lun Chin. She looked apprehensively at her husband. It was purely a guess on my part, but I felt as if she suspected something already.

"Yes. Dressed in black. She came in here while looking for Ali, and she . . ."

I stopped. I suddenly felt rather uncomfortable with the notion of trying to explain what had happened. I wasn't entirely sure that even I understood it, and I had been there for it.

To my astonishment, Double Chin said, "Did she try to take advantage of you sexually?"

"Yes. That's correct . . ."

"And as she did so," asked Lun Chin, "did she speak in an overwrought, emotionally driven manner involving similes and metaphors that made little to no sense? In an almost superreal fashion?"

"Yes!" I couldn't believe it. "How did you know? Do you know who these women are? You must. You couldn't have just guessed all that . . ."

The older couple exchanged significant glances. Then Double Chin took a deep breath and let it out slowly. "One hundred and fifty years ago," he said, "a group of monks fell out of favor with the Imperior . . . himself a rather dyspeptic and vicious man who abused his power terribly. Women, in particular, suffered his wrath, some in the most vicious and unthinkable of ways.

"The Imperior feared the fighting skills of the monks, and came to believe court advisors who told him the monks posed a threat. So the Imperior set his deadliest and fiercest warriors upon them, and hounded them out of the heart of Chinpan. Eventually they founded a monastery, high in the mountain range known as the Anaïs. And there, in hiding, they became a place where women who feared the Imperior went to study, to learn self-defense. To become something other than victims."

"Eventually, the monks died off," Lun Chin spoke up, "but more and more women came to the monastery, there to study and learn from those who had absorbed all the monks had to teach them. They expanded their studies beyond anything the monks could have dreamt of. They learned to draw strength from their passions, to use their sexuality as a source of power, and to celebrate that sexuality in a variety of ways."

"And they became a warrior caste," said Double Chin. "Shadow warriors bursting with lust, and tormentedly twisted ways of expressing it. They meld with the darkness,

wives of the moon, sisters of the silhouettes. They are . . ."
And he paused and glanced around as if making certain no
one else was listening, and said in a lowered voice, ". . . the
Anaïs Ninjas."

"And why would these Anaïs Ninjas have an interest in
killing my teacher?" I demanded.

I didn't truly expect them to have the answer and, as it
turned out, I wasn't disappointed. They shrugged, shook
their heads. "The important thing to remember," Double
Chin told me, "is that Ali is with the ancestors now. He is
truly honored."

"He is truly dead, and the Anaïs Ninjas will pay."

Double and Lun Chin looked saddened. "There is no
point to vengeance."

"There doesn't have to be a point," I replied. "It's an end
in itself. It's just . . . it's too much."

"Too much?" His eyebrows knit.

"You don't know. You can't know!" I said, my voice getting louder, and it was with tremendous effort that I reined
it in. More softly, but speaking with a tremor that I couldn't
quite control, I repeated, "You can't know."

"Can't know what, Po?" asked Lun Chin.

"Me. What I've been through. The things . . ."

I was accustomed to lying. So accustomed to it, in fact,
that it was almost painful for me to speak the truth, as if I
was paying the price for flexing long-unused muscles. But
for once, I wanted to tell the complete, unvarnished truth.
I had to say it aloud, lest I explode, and I had to say it to
someone, lest I go insane.

"You have no idea of the life I've led," I said. "Every person I've ever loved has either been taken from me or
betrayed me or tried to use me in some way for personal
gain. Everything I've ever owned of any real value, ranging
from treasure to friendship, has been lost to me."

"Have you brought it on yourself?" Double Chin inquired.

It was a softly phrased question, but it cut through with the precision of a hot needle. I was fond of seeing myself as the perpetual victim. As fortune's fool, the favorite object of godly torment. I lowered my head and said softly, "Sometimes. Sometimes, yes. I have betrayed others. I have betrayed friends, and let them down. I was responsible for the death of my best friend, after stealing his fate. As much as I cry out over the misfortunes that fall like shite-filled raindrops upon me, the truth is that I've brought it on myself, more often than not. Payment in full for the misdeeds I have done to others."

I raised my gaze, looking up at them, not quite believing that I had been so candid with them. They were staring at me blankly. Then Double Chin said, "We didn't understand a word you just said. You spoke in your native tongue."

I blinked owlishly, and then laughed in self-deprecation. How typical. One of the few times in my life I'd ever been honest, and my basic nature kicked in and made sure they wouldn't comprehend what I'd said.

Well, who was I to argue with my basic nature?

"No. I've never brought it on myself, except that I've tried to live a good and decent life, and the world and the gods themselves have allied to prevent it," I said.

They nodded sympathetically. "There are some who are made to suffer," said Double Chin sagely.

"I know. And I'm tired of being one of them."

There had been times in my life in which I was struck by what I considered to be moments of clarity. Instants where I saw beyond where I had been, and was able to have a clear vision of where I should be going. They had been few and far between, but had always had a catastrophic impact on my existence, and sent my life into unexpected and unorthodox directions.

This was one of those instances.

The anger that I had mentioned earlier, burning within me, was stoked to new heights.

"Yes. Tired of being one of them. Tired of loss. Tired of . . ." I stared at them, but my mind was years agone and thousands of miles away. "My mother was killed. The only creature on this planet who never betrayed me, and she was murdered by a heartless brute. And do you know what I wanted to do in retaliation? I wanted to hunt down, not the murderer . . . but the murderer's mother, and kill her."

"As an act of vengeance, it has a certain poetic justice to it," Double Chin said judiciously.

"It was cowardice! Cowardice on my part!"

"It . . . could be seen in that way . . ."

I got to my feet, suddenly sensing that I was at a crossroads. But for once, it was a crossroads that I was not being propelled toward by outside forces, but instead striding toward myself. "Everything that I ever have is taken away from me! Everyone I ever loved has been killed or left me! And I let it happen! Every damned time, I let it happen, and I never do a damned thing about it. That's why it keeps happening!"

Lun Chin looked confused. "I . . . I don't understan—"

"It keeps happening because the gods look down upon me and say, 'Oh, look there! There's Apropos!' " I was pacing back and forth as fast as my right leg would allow. " 'We can do anything we want to him, and he'll just keep taking it and taking it!' Well, no more! No more! I was on the verge of something with Ali. I'm not sure what it was, and now I'll never know. That's the real killer of it. I'll never know! And I'm sick of it! Sick of not knowing what could have been! Sick of a life full of . . . of might-haves and just-missed-its! Those women, those Anaïs Ninjas, took Ali from me, and they didn't just do it at random. They did it for someone.

"But they didn't just do it to Ali. They did it to me. And I'm not taking it anymore. Do you understand? *It ends here and now! It ends today!*"

I'd gotten myself so worked up that I was shouting at the top of my lungs. My head was pounding, and the veins were sticking out on the side of my head. But I didn't care, because it felt good. It felt good to care about something so passionately that I could get myself so exercised.

"What . . . will you do, though, Po?" asked Double Chin. "You are but one man. What can you possibly do?"

"Find them," I said intently. "Find them . . . and kill them all."

Chapter 8

Dragon My Tail

$\mathcal{B}$y morning, naturally, I had come to my senses.

It was interesting to learn that I was still capable of such passion, of such fire, of such a staggeringly naïve belief in ephemera like justice and fairness, that I was capable of feeling—even for a few moments—as if I wanted to do something personally to maintain such things.

Except I wasn't.

It wasn't that I was afraid of dying. Once I had very much been, so much so that it had informed every single thing I did. But during my experiences in Wuin, I had come to something of an "understanding," for want of a better term, in dealing with my own mortality. My innate cowardice had caused me to grab on to life so desperately that it had placed a stranglehold on every other aspect of my existence. Wuin had loosened that stranglehold somewhat.

However, there was still enough of the stubborn bastard in me that I was not prepared to simply throw my life away. That was the province of heroes. Heroes, as near as I could determine, fell into two categories. Either they had so little regard for their own lives that they didn't care if they died, so long as it was in some heroic fashion. Or else they were

so convinced of their own superiority and innate righteousness that they were certain they would overcome whatever
challenge lay before them and live to laugh over the corpses
of their enemies.

For my part, I had seen far too many heroes come to
unfortunate ends, usually with very surprised expressions
on their dying faces. So I had no interest in rushing headlong into a potential lethal situation simply for something
as pointless as vengeance.

Still, I had been utterly sincere when I'd spoken of seeking
revenge in the name of Ali. One of the ways I had survived as
long as I had was that I was something of a master of deception. The number of people I had fooled, lied to, outfoxed,
outwitted, flimflammed, and cheated was practically legion.
Apparently, not being satisfied with fooling others, I had
taken up the ultimate challenge: fooling myself.

And temporarily, I had succeeded. I had convinced myself
that I was ready to go charging into the fray, to seek out the
bitches who had killed my teacher and make them pay.

That resolve had lasted for as long as it had taken me to
stare long and hard at the ceiling of my hut as the rain-
storm, with renewed energy, splattered away on the roof,
and realize just how close I had come to being killed by that
one woman. And that was just one of them. And I'd been
damned lucky. If I went after the Anaïs Ninjas, I would not
only be pressing my luck, I would practically be shoving it
through the ground.

Depression swept over me. Depression over my innate
weakness, depression over my inability to overcome it. I
really, truly wanted to do something to avenge myself
upon Ali's assailants. But simple vengeance had never been
sufficient motivation for me to embark on any endeavor,
especially if it required putting my own meager existence
on the line.

The problem was, I had just made a great show of talking about vengeance to two of the Chins. I had valiantly declared that I was going to dispose of the Anaïs Ninjas. I had spoken great words. The problem with great words is that they have a habit of spreading. That night, mine spread faster than syphilis at a prostitute convention. Despite the increasing lateness of the hour, despite the foul weather, various members of the village kept showing up the entire night. Each time, the ritual was exactly the same. They would politely knock, come in upon my permission, smile, and bow deeply. Then they'd leave. One after another, sometimes in groups of threes and fours.

They didn't need to say anything. I knew why they were coming by, and they knew I knew. They were mutely thanking me for taking it upon myself to defend the honor of the village and achieve vengeance for the demise of Chinpan Ali.

Which left me wondering what the hell I was supposed to do next.

I couldn't just pretend that I hadn't said anything about it. I couldn't back out. They would all think me a coward. Not that I was normally especially worried over what people thought about me, but I couldn't quite bring myself to be dismissive of what the good people of Hosbiyu considered me. I liked them too much. They'd been too good to me.

I had spent my life letting myself down. I was used to it. The thought of letting them down, however, was too much.

Besides, they might be so annoyed that they'd turn against me and I'd wake up one morning to find myself buried out in the wheat field.

By the time the rain stopped and the morning sun rose, I knew I had to leave the village.

I had, however, already hit upon a plan. It was not one of my more elaborate schemes, but that was perfectly fine. In this situation, simpler was probably superior.

Hosbiyu was a small, isolated village. In all the time I had been there, such a thing as "news" was nonexistent. None of the villagers ever left town, except for Cleft Chin, who would, every so often, haul the excess wheat to a larger city and exchange it for supplies that were not readily handy. Other than that, the people of Hosbiyu were more or less self-sufficient and knew nothing of what transpired beyond their boundaries.

Which meant that they'd have no idea if I was successful in my quest or not beyond what I told them.

Faced with a problematic situation, I realized upon further consideration that instead I had a win/win scenario on my hands.

I would pack my few belongings and depart. Granted, smuggling out Chinpan Ali's sword was going to be a bit of a challenge, but I was up to it. Once I left, I would simply wander about for as long as seemed a reasonable time. Who knew? Perhaps I would happen upon a situation that was superior to the one I'd initially stumbled into. But if I didn't, then when enough time had passed, I would return to Hosbiyu and simply tell the people that I'd done exactly what I'd set out to do. I'd certainly have more than enough time to come up with a good story as to how I'd accomplished it.

I'd make sure it was filled with much derring-do, adventure, and even a bit of tragedy. I'd give myself a sweet young thing who would die pitifully at the eleventh hour trying to save her great love—me, of course. And I'd include an evil villainess who wasn't at all what she appeared. Gods knew I had enough experience with that. And at the end, I would survive all the challenges and leave everyone else in the dust, annihilated. Chinpan Ali would be avenged, and honor would be right.

Even as I mentally congratulated myself, I was appalled at the glee I found in devising a way to bamboozle these people.

It made me wonder how anyone ever felt good about themselves.

I mean, I certainly never did. Oh, on rare occasions there were brief moments of happiness and a sense of self-worth, but such times usually meant that someone was suffering and I was benefiting from it. At which point, I would loathe myself all the more.

Was I really that different from everyone else in the world? Did they truly toddle through life, filled with good thoughts and an innate sense of their own wonderfulness, and never stare directly into their dark side and recoil from it? Was anyone truly happy? Or were they simply more skilled than I at putting a false face upon their own self-contempt and misery?

After all, virtually everyone I'd ever encountered until coming to Chinpan had been something of a right bastard. Were they happier than I?

Was anyone? And if so, how did they manage it? Was it that I was entirely too self-aware, or that they were simply oblivious?

I mean, as much as I despised myself, there were so many, so damned many who were so much worse. At least, I liked to tell myself that. Were they eaten up with the same self-doubts, frustration, and loathing as I? Was the concept of human happiness mere myth? Was the only difference between me and the rest of those I'd encountered that I was the one-eyed man in the proverbial land of the blind? And if so, when the hell did I get to be king?

Well . . . what about the people of Hosbiyu, I wondered. They were decent people. They felt consistently good about themselves. What were they doing differently? Was it something in the food? Something in the air? Philosophies, religion?

Or was it that they weren't actually all that superior after all? There was always that possibility.

Consider the joy with which they had greeted the news that I was going to seek vengeance for the death of Ali. Perhaps they were so cheered because they burned with as much dark need for retribution as anyone else.

Yes. That was probably it. Despite their outer trappings of righteousness and goodness, deep down they were as scummy as anyone else, including me. And cowardly. They were cowardly, too, hanging back and letting me attend to the job of vengeance.

The thought should have made me happy. Instead it made me more depressed and more filled with self-loathing than ever before.

It was nice to know there were some things on which I could count.

There was a knock at the door and I looked up. Cleft Chin was standing there, scowling at me, as he was wont to do. I realized he was the only member of the village who had not come by to bow to me and mutely express appreciation for my self-inflicted adventure of vengeance.

He wasn't bowing.

He continued to scowl.

I got to my feet. "Problem?" I inquired.

He didn't step in. It was as if he thought he would be contaminated if he set foot into the place. Instead his face darkened and he growled, "I know you."

"Yessss," I said slowly. "Yes, I should think you . . ."

"I have been watching you," continued Cleft Chin. "I know your type. I know how you think."

"Oh, do you?" I was on my guard. "And how do I think, precisely?"

"You think beyond matters of mere vengeance. You do nothing unless there is some personal gain for you."

Well, I had to admit, the fellow was rather savvy for a farmer in the middle of no damned place at all. He'd certainly read me well enough. Still, I wasn't about to say, Well done you, fellow, you've got me pegged. Instead I simply replied, "Really. And what personal gain would I derive from seeking out Ali's murderers?"

I was ready for him to say, *None, you poseur.*

"You want the reward," he said.

That stopped me cold. "Reward," I said. "The reward . . . for the destruction of the Anaïs Ninjas?"

"And for the Forked Tong," said Chin.

"And how would I know of these things," I said, "considering I am still relatively new to your land?"

He sniffed disdainfully. "The others would have told you. These things are generally known to all our people. No doubt you saw this as an opportunity to enrich yourself, while cloaking yourself in the righteousness of an honorable quest of vengeance."

"No doubt."

It is said that ignorance and arrogance are a devastating combination. The ignorant man you can outthink. The arrogant man you can trip up using his overconfidence against him. The man who is both ignorant and arrogant, however, can be most problematic if not handled properly.

Cleft Chin, fortunately, was simply arrogant. His "reading" of me was so dead on that it never occurred to him that any other conclusions he might draw could be in error.

He simply assumed that since something was common knowledge to the others in the village, it had to be known to me as well.

Except, of course, it wasn't.

I was, however, quite good when it came to guessing at things. That intuition had served me well on any number of occasions, and I suspected I was going to be able to have it serve me again in this case.

"So how do you plan to do it?" asked Cleft Chin, watching me carefully.

I casually circled the interior of the hut. "Why would I tell you that? Why would I tell you how I intend to bring down," and this was where I began my conjectures, "that notorious criminal organization, the Forked Tong . . . and their foot soldiers, the Anaïs Ninjas?" All he did was scowl more at my lack of being forthcoming, which led me to conclude that my guess was accurate. Thus emboldened, I continued, "Granted, the reward being offered by . . . the . . ." My mind raced as I tried to figure who would most benefit from the destruction of a major group of criminals. Well, obviously, it would be the person or persons who would most like to see a source of competing power go away. Which meant that it was likely the person or persons in power in Chinpan . . . except I'd never heard the names of any such individuals bandied about. For these isolated farmers, such matters as rulers were of the vaguest import. Double Chin had mentioned some ruling sort, but I couldn't recall the title.

So little time had passed, that it could barely be discerned as a hesitation in my speech as I completed the sentence, ". . . the . . . supreme ruler of his land . . . the honorable . . . the divine . . . the lordly presence over all—"

"The Imperior, yes, yes," Cleft Chin snapped impatiently. "If there is one habit I cannot tolerate, it is this tendency to place endless honorifics before his title. Just say 'the Imperior' and be done with it."

"The Imperior has set out a reward for the destruction of the Anaïs Ninjas and, presumably, the Forked Tong as well."

"I know that!" said Cleft Chin in frustration. "You're telling me things I already know! What I want to know is, to earn the ten million yeng, what are you going to do? How are you going to go about it?"

I had no idea what a yeng was, or how much it was worth, and whether ten million was truly a significant amount, although it certainly sounded impressive to me. The one thing I did know, however, was someone trying to mooch their way into an ideal situation. "You still haven't explained to me why I should possibly cut you in."

"You've no reason to," Cleft Chin told me. "I do not seek riches. I find my wealth in the simple things. In the shining of the sun. In the—"

"Spare me," I sighed, raising a hand. "You must want something. Somebody always wants something. What sort of deal are you endeavoring to cut with me here?"

He entered the hut with visible effort. Before I could say or do anything, his hand lashed out and encompassed my throat.

"These are a good and gentle people," he informed me, and I was hardly in a position to argue the point. "They neither want nor deserve trouble. If you are indeed intent to embark on this course of action, then for their sakes . . . for all our sakes . . . you had best succeed. That is all I have to say to you."

He held me that way a moment longer, as if he was going to add something to his pronouncement. But then, true to his word, he released me, adding a shove for good measure.

Gasping, leaning against the wall, with my hand to my

throat, I managed to say, "Did you give a lecture like this to Ali? Before he brought down upon himself whatever doom he did? Were you concerned his activities, whatever they were, would rebound to the detriment of your people?"

His eyes narrowing further so the whites were visible as little more than slits, he said, "Yes. Almost exactly the same lecture. And look how it turned out for him." And with that emphatic, if melodramatic, pronouncement, he departed.

I stood there, rubbing my throat. That had been wholly unexpected and somewhat painful.

It was also informative and wildly tempting.

There had been any number of times I had allowed my innate greed and love of fortune get me into some sort of dire predicament. One would have thought that I'd learned by that point that such endeavors never came to a good end. Unfortunately, such was not the case. Given the opportunity, would I turn around and make the exact same mistake?

Absolutely.

"A reward," I murmured.

"Ten million yeng," I muttered, without having a clue what a yeng was, remember.

"The Imperior," I continued, as I prepared for my departure with renewed vigor.

Matters of vengeance were of little interest to me. Matters of honor were of even less moment. But matters of personal aggrandizement and benefit were definitely more than enough to intrigue me.

I wasn't committing myself to anything, surely. I could contemplate an action without necessarily seeing it through. I could explore this concept, find out as much as I could about this Forked Tong, learn how their organization was set up, and perhaps discover a weak point that I could exploit. I was, after all, an outsider. And sometimes a particular situation that mystified or frustrated those who were close to it could be easily resolved by a fresh outlook.

But I had to find this "Imperior," this ruler of all Chinpan. As it turned out, that wasn't so much of a chore at all. Child's play, in fact. To be specific, I asked the children who were playing out in the center of the village, "Where would one find the Imperior?"

The response was immediate and uniform: "Taikyo," they said, "in the great palace."

Well, that seemed reasonably straightforward. A small bit of further probing divined, from the older children, the fact that Taikyo was fairly easy to get to, at least from a directional point of view. One went to the main intersection of the small path out of town with the main road, and then went due west. Simple enough. Keep my back to the sun during the day, ride toward it as the day waned.

As it turned out, I wasn't going to have to walk. Kit Chin's family, with great pomp and display, provided me with a horse. It was one of the beasts that the thugs who had come to our village and wound up as fertilizer had been riding. I knew there was a small element of risk, since the animal might be recognized by the people who had dispatched those musclemen in the first place. But the horse itself was fairly nondescript, with no markings or brands upon it that I could see, so it was worth the minimal gamble in order to spare me limping all the way to Taikyo.

And so that very morning, I set out. I had transformed Ali's unique sword into the center staff of a bindle, keeping it wrapped in its concealing cloth and attaching a sack at the end that contained my belongings. I slung it over my shoulder, and for all anyone knew, the long support for the sack might have been made from bamboo.

The people of Hosbiyu lined the street to see me off. It was quite an overt demonstration for a group of people that generally tended to remain low key. It made my heart swell with pride, so much so that it was an effort for me to remind myself that my initial impulse had been to fool them completely. For that matter, it remained my backup plan.

Still, as I set out, I could feel the smoldering gaze of Cleft Chin burning upon me for the entirety of my departure, and for much of the time thereafter.

The first few days of my sojourn passed rather unremarkably.

I encountered a few travelers who were heading in the direction opposite to mine. They stared at me as they approached, and continued to watch me silently as we passed one another. It was natural for them to have that sort of reaction. I was, after all, like nothing they'd seen: a round-eyed individual wearing the apparel of local farmers, with one of those wide, flat hats upon my head to ward off the sun. No doubt they thought me to be exactly what I had first erroneously concluded about the residents of Hosbiyu: the result of a freakish birth, a poor unfortunate bastard whom the gods had gifted with a uniquely bizarre and quite disgusting visage.

Whatever pleased them. So long as they didn't see it as cause to attack me, it was of little consequence.

The road ran roughly parallel to the river. This was a very clever bit of design, for it simplified the journey tremendously. If my water skins were getting low, I would get off the road, walk over to the river, and refill them. The villagers had provided me with various simple foodstuffs that traveled well. Rice, mostly. Lots of rice. *Lots* of rice. When I wanted something else, I would settle in at the river's edge and fish. I had neither string nor hook, but I had become extremely adept with the sai that I had brought with me, tucked into my belt. I was actually fast enough of hand and sharp enough of eye that I could skewer passing unwary fish without too much difficulty.

I couldn't recall a time when I had been better or more thoroughly armed, which was an impressive achievement considering I was someone who tried to avoid combat whenever humanly possible. The two sai, when not in use, were tucked into the wide sash I wore as a belt. My bastard sword was strapped to my back, as always, and my walking staff was lashed to the right side of the horse's saddle. The bird's-head sword hung on the saddle's left side.

I shied away from the occasional inns I passed, having no idea of the reception I would receive along the way. Other travelers might have settled for simply gawking at me, but I didn't want to count on being able to sleep safely in a road-side establishment where, for all I knew, foreigners were not kindly looked upon. Instead, when night approached, I would hie myself over to the nearby forest, which also seemed to run the length of my sojourn. And there, amidst the bamboo trees, I would find rest and an uneasy form of peace. Fortunately, I was always a light sleeper, so if anyone should happen upon me in the night with the intent of mischief, I would most certainly awaken fast enough to deal with them.

Occasionally I would have dreams. Dreams made me nervous, for sometimes they bordered on the prophetic. I didn't know why. A result of the traces of magic that dogged my being, no doubt.

On the road to Taikyo, I had one recurring dream that was particularly troublesome for me. I would see the bird's-head sword that I was carrying with me. It was whirling through the air at formidable speed, like a spinning scythe.

And there was light, blinding, brilliant. I saw myself, trying to shield my eyes, and everything was silent around me. There was ash, ash everywhere, and some sort of outline against a wall, but I couldn't make out what it was. And Mordant was there, shaking his head sadly, and looking at me in a most pitying manner.

I would wake up sweating, gasping for breath, looking around in confusion. The dream would dissolve like paper on water, and try as I might to retrieve it and divine what it was trying to tell me, I was unable to do so.

And so the time would pass. A couple of times along the way, I came upon places where the road split or branched off. There was signage, but as I mentioned earlier, I had not taken the time to learn how to read the local language, so it was all meaningless. If nothing else, I should have learned how to read the word "Taikyo," but I hadn't even done that. For someone who prided himself on his intelligence and wit, I could be exceedingly shortsighted sometimes.

Luck was with me, though, for I continued to use the sun as my guide to the west, and inquiries to other travelers affirmed that I was staying on the right track.

The weather remained warm, and the skies clear. The longer the traveling conditions held, the more I wondered when something was going to go wrong. I was starting to wonder whether it was ever possible for me to simply appreciate good fortune for what it was, rather than perceive it as a setup for inevitable disaster.

I was another day or two's ride from Taikyo (according to one of the passersby with whom I'd checked) and had settled into the forest for the evening. The forest was thinning out, and I wasn't sure how much longer I was going to be able to avail myself of its friendly shelters. The unfortunate problem was that I wasn't entirely sure what I was going to do once I reached my destination. I couldn't very well just wander about the city trying to find the Anaïs Ninjas or the Forked Tong. I knew very little about the former and virtually nothing about the latter. They, on the other hand, might well have eyes and ears on every street corner of the city, and unguarded queries about them could cause me to have an arrow in my chest or a dagger slipped between my ribs without warning.

The key to my quandary might well lie with this "Imperior" that Cleft Chin had mentioned. But if this fellow were truly the leader of the entire country, what possible reason would he have to see me?

As I lay on my back, staring at the sky, a plan began to bubble within my brain. Until this point, I'd considered my obvious foreign appearance as a handicap. Now I was starting to realize that it could, in fact, be a benefit.

During my stay in the court of King Runcible, there had been any number of occasions where ambassadors had shown up, representing some damned king or monarch or warlord or other. They would come bearing greetings and say nice words of alliance or obedience, and would be in turn treated with deference and as honored guests.

There was no reason in the world I couldn't be dealt with in a like manner. Considering the stares I was continuing to get, and from what the people of Hosbiyu had told me, foreigners in this land were more or less unknown. So if I said that I was representing a far-off king who wanted to establish ties with the Imperior of Chinpan, who was there to say nay?

It wasn't as if I was showing up to declare war. Such messengers occasionally came to bad ends, with their heads on pikes while their hands, genitals, and entrails were shipped back from whence they came with a note that said "You want war? You've got war" or something to that effect. But me, I was simply an arriving visitor showing due deference.

Granted, if the Imperior was a complete madman, he might have me gutted just because he didn't like my eyes. So there was a calculated risk involved, but it was one I was willing to take, for the reward seemed promising . . .

. . . and also, as much as I wanted to deny it, I really did want to try and find a way to avenge Ali's death. During my travels, the more I dwelt upon it, the more I thought of all the things he might have been able to teach me. I wasn't just thinking of combat, although that was certainly a consideration. There was also the matter of my state of mind. If he could have shown me a way to ease the constant frustration and sense of gloom from my being, he would have earned my eternal gratitude and devotion. And those who had deprived me of him were going to pay.

Somehow.

As I lay there in the bamboo forest, pondering the imponderables of my life and dozing as I did so, I heard some curious noises out by the road. There were shouts, people yelling at one another, the squeaks of laden carts grinding to a halt on their wheels.

And another sound as well, one that instantly snapped me to full wakefulness. It was a high-pitched, angered, challenging screech, and I had heard it months and months ago during a frightening battle in the heights of Mount Aerie.

"Mordant?" I whispered, scarcely able to believe it.

It didn't seem possible. I'd seen him in my dreams, and knew all too well the chance that they gave hints of things to come. But the notion that he was really, truly here? And if that was the case . . . could Sharee be with him?

I realized at that moment that in many ways, my heart had not been beating for quite some time. But the merest chance that Sharee might be around caused it to jump and flutter and pound with newfound vigor against my ribs.

Gods. Embarking upon missions of vengeance (albeit with the added incentive of reward). Feeling such passion for a woman who had abandoned me that I was almost giddy at the prospect of seeing her again.

What had happened to me? What mad land had I entered? It was as if I'd entered a land that was trying to make me less than I was.

Less . . . or perhaps more.

Opting for stealth over speed, I quickly made my way through the forest to the edge, which came right up to the road. It was a moonless night and I managed to keep myself adroitly concealed within the shadowed bamboo woods as I peered out and saw something exceedingly strange.

There was an assortment of about half a dozen carts lined up, having come to a halt upon the road. Each was being pulled by a broken-down-looking horse. A more pathetic collection of nags I had never seen.

The cages had barred sides, and I could see that each had some sort of animal pacing back and forth. They were a bizarre assortment. One appeared to be some sort of bear, but it was large and round, with black-and-white fur, looking more like an oversized raccoon than anything truly ursine. There was another creature that I thought could be something I'd once seen drawings of, called a "monkey." It was making loud chittering noises, bouncing around like an insane two-year-old child, and was covered with a thick coat of golden fur. A most curious creature; in many ways, it seemed almost human. Another odd animal was curled up almost into a ball, and its entire skin seemed to be composed of overlapping scales. There was also a large bird—an eagle, I was reasonably sure—which was dark brown, with a patch of golden feathers on its back. It was on a perch, stretching its wings and cawing.

There was also the largest cat I had ever seen. In my life,

I had encountered occasional oversized felines wandering the forests, but this was as nothing I had ever experienced. It appeared to be at least six feet from fearsome maw to whipping tail, perhaps longer. Even in the dimness of the night, I could see its fur was orange with black stripes winding around its body.

The most important cage, however, was the one occupied by Mordant.

Presuming it was Mordant, of course. It could simply have been any drabit, although it certainly bore a striking resemblance to him. He was on a perch similar to the one the eagle was on, the difference being that there was a thin but sturdy chain anchoring him to it. His neck was fully extended, and he was screeching loudly in the way that I'd heard him from deep in the forest.

The reason for his upset, beyond the fact that he was imprisoned, was immediately evident. There was a slim young man there, in the process of trying to free Mordant from his cage. He was crouched on the side of the cage, perched on it batlike, and he'd been clearly trying to pry a thick padlock off the gate with a curved bar. The caravan had been moving and he'd clambered aboard the cage, trying to bust open the lock and free Mordant with no one the wiser. But obviously someone had noticed him.

The young man had his black hair tied up in the customary topknot. He was dressed entirely in black, wearing a loose-fitting jacket and equally loose pantaloons. His face was round and looked to be gentle by nature, but now it was twisted in a fierce and defiant expression, shouting rapidly at the men who were advancing on him.

And there were quite a few men. Close to a dozen, and they were coming in from all sides, looking and sounding well and truly pissed off.

It was all painfully clear what was transpiring. This was

some sort of traveling circus, and the young fellow had—
for reasons of his own—been endeavoring to free Mordant
from it.

Presuming it was Mordant.

My natural instinct, of course, was to refrain from risking myself. I saw no sign of Sharee, and if this truly wasn't
Mordant, then there was no point in putting my own life
on the line by trying to intercede. It was not, after all, as if
I were some great brawny barbarian who could go sweeping
into the middle of the situation and lay them low with my
terrible swift sword. I was who I was, and who I was wasn't
about to hurl himself into the midst of danger unless
absolutely necessary.

Suddenly the small dragon's head whipped around, and
even from the distance I was standing, I could see his nostrils flaring. He was sniffing the air as the young man continued to exchange angry words with the circus folk. And
then the diminutive winged creature screeched out
"Apropos!" in such a way that it might well have sounded
like some curious anomaly of an animal cry to the casual
listener. But to me, it was my name clear as day, and I could
even see that he was now looking straight at me in my place
of concealment.

It was Mordant all right, and if I was going to find out
how in the world he had come to be in Chinpan—and
where Sharee might be—I was going to have to do something to get him out of there myself.

Despite the lameness of my leg, I was capable of moving
with a good degree of stealth when the situation warranted
it. This seemed to be one of those times. Sticking to the
lengthy shadows, keeping low, I moved toward the halted
caravan even as the angry circus men surged forward and
grabbed the young man off the cage holding Mordant
prisoner.

The young man, however, was not prepared to go quietly. Somehow he managed to shake free, and was standing several feet away from the circus men. The assortment of fearsome, burly men advanced on him, and suddenly he was in motion. His hands and feet moved with such speed that it was impossible for me to follow. As they grabbed for him, he deftly dodged between each thrust, finding key points such as the crotch or throat to strike with devastating kicks or powerful forward thrusts of his fingers.

It was amazing how quickly opponents were going down. Some, however, were able to meet his attacks with deft defenses and thrusts of their own. He was doing well, but there were too many of them. Sooner or later, they were going to bring him down and, very likely, beat him to a bloody pulp.

His fate didn't concern me too much, but Mordant's was definitely of interest. While the athletic young man kept everyone else busy, I made my way around to the rear of the carts.

The big cat looked at me with interest as I approached his cage. He raised his head, and I slid open one of the hidden compartments in my staff. Studying the padlock, I was immediately able to withdraw the proper lock pick for the job from the assortment I maintained in there for just such situations. I slid the wire in, made some deft movements, and the lock snapped open.

I yanked it clear of the cage, the door swung open, and the huge cat completely changed its attitude. It leaped out of the cage and hit the ground, landing lightly despite its bulk. It fixed its gaze on me, its yellow eyes narrowing, and then it opened its maw and bared a set of teeth that could have torn me to bits. A full-throated roar ripped from its throat, and at that moment I suddenly concluded this might not have been one of my brightest ideas. I had thought of the beast as primarily a means of a large distraction. Because it had looked so placid, I didn't consider it a serious danger. Seeing it out, I realized I'd woefully miscalculated.

I backed up, starting to reach for my sword, and realized with sinking heart that I would not be able to pull it clear from the scabbard before the cat was upon me. Then abruptly there were alarmed cries from some of the circus folks, and the shouts instantly captured the great beast's attention. Whatever the animal's opinion of me, I was far too recent an acquaintance to sustain its full interest. Instead its fierce brain remembered its captors, the ones who had captured it and kept it prisoner for who knew how long. There was obviously no love lost in that relationship. It might even have been that its keepers were abusive to it during its captivity.

If that was the case, "forgive and forget" was most definitely not in the beast's philosophy.

The cat voiced another roar, twice as loud as the previous one, and sprang. There had to be a distance of twenty feet between us and the cat's prey, and the animal covered it in one powerful leap. It landed squarely on the back of one of its keepers, who was standing there rooted to the spot by the cat's fearsome battle cry. The most he was able to accomplish in terms of self-defense was to bring up his arms and try to ward the animal off. This worked not at all as the great cat drove him to the ground. It sank its huge teeth into the man's face and pulled, growling with satisfaction deep inside its throat as blood jetted all over.

There was more shouting and confusion, and although most of the circus men were running as fast as they could, several noticed me and advanced, shouting and drawing daggers, which they brandished fearsomely. The time for subtlety was over. I yanked out my bastard sword, turned, and smashed open the nearest padlock.

The men froze as the huge black-and-white bear lumbered to freedom. I waited for it, like its formidable cousins, to rear to its feet and launch an unstoppable attack. The creature's bulk was gargantuan. It could probably flatten anyone there.

The bear glanced left and right, then promptly waddled off toward the forest.

That was all the men needed in the way of incentive to charge at me. I swung the heavy blade at another lock, breaking this one off as well. The monkey leaped out of its cage, chattered and squawked, and then bounded toward its erstwhile captors with the clear intent of killing them.

One wouldn't have thought a monkey to be all that much of a threat. But between the surprising strength it displayed, and the limberness of its moves as it scrambled all over its victims, it was a holy terror, screeching and tearing with its teeth and breaking body parts with its small but powerful fists.

Within minutes I had all the beasts but Mordant free, which was nicely ironic considering he was the only one I was genuinely interested in. Throughout the rest of the caravan, people were running about like lunatics, trying to stay ahead of the great cat or in a vain endeavor to recapture some of the animals. Neither goal was being achieved. The prime concern seemed to be the great cat, whom the men were trying to surround, using what appeared to be pitchforks, while simultaneously endeavoring to stay clear of the sweeping talons that had already eviscerated two of them. The eagle was hanging about, calmly picking apart one of the corpses, and was in the midst of devouring a small, dainty bit of internal organ.

The bizarre scaled thing had unfurled itself, tumbled out of the cage, and promptly curled back up in a ball again. The monkey had taken up station atop one of the wagons and was defiantly throwing its own feces at whoever was coming near, a dazzling trick that I filed away for future use in a particularly dire situation.

Ever the pragmatist and never losing sight of an opportunity, I saw that a few of the corpses had upon them small leather purses dangling from their belts. How comforting to see that, in Chinpan as well as anywhere else, money was carried by the same easily recognizable means. It was the work of mere moments to divest the bodies of their assets, and I did so with clear conscience. After all, I'd thought nothing of robbing people while they were alive when I was in times of need. So why should I hesitate to take from those who clearly were never going to be using their funds for future purchases?

The young man and Mordant had been forgotten as the larger creatures were being dealt with. I made my way over there quickly to see the young man with a dagger jammed into the padlock, trying in futility to pick it. I gave him high marks for effort, but he clearly had no idea what he was doing.

He saw me coming, yanked the dagger out of the lock, and struck a defensive pose. At the same time, his brow furrowed as he studied my face, obviously unsure what to make of me.

"Mitsu! It's all right! He's a friend . . . in a very broad sense of the word," Mordant snapped at him. If there had been any doubt remaining that this was the talking mini-dragon of my acquaintance, that certainly put it to rest.

"Back away," I said sharply, and the one called Mitsu did as instructed. I swung my sword. It knocked away the lock in a heartbeat, sending it clattering to the ground, and Mitsu yanked open the door.

I heard an outraged shout from behind me and whirled in time to see two of the circus men charging us, waving knives. I readied my sword, not eager for a fight, but not in a position to back away from it.

I needn't have concerned myself. Mitsu somersaulted through the air as if he were being hoisted on strings, and landed squarely with one foot in each of the men's faces. They went down and Mitsu ricocheted off them . . .

. . . and found himself face-to-face with the great cat.

Obviously the animal was being indiscriminate in its destruction. It was a short distance away, even shorter than the space I'd seen it clear with one simple thrust of its mighty limbs. I knew it would take no effort on its part to leap upon Mitsu, and whatever self-defense tricks Mitsu obviously had at his disposal, they weren't going to do much good against a beast of such power.

Suddenly Mordant swept forward, perching upon Mitsu's shoulder. His head was extended all the way forward on his slim neck, and he screeched at the great cat in a series of guttural noises that sounded impressively like communication. The cat's tail twitched, then pointed straight outward, its gaze never leaving Mordant. Then, slowly, the tail drooped down, relaxing, and the orange striped cat made a noise that could have been taken as something akin to acquiescence. It turned its back to us and went off in search of other prey.

"Let's get out of here," said Mordant. "It may change its mind."

"What did you say to it?"

"It doesn't translate," Mordant informed me.

I had a hundred questions, but they could all wait until

we made it back into the woods. Behind us we left a symphony of roaring and chittering and squawking and screaming, a most pleasant agglomeration considering that none of the noises involved—the screaming in particular—were originating with us.

A short distance ahead of us, I heard crashing and my horse whinnying. I didn't like the sound of that at all. There was every possibility that the great cat had doubled back ahead of us somehow, and was in the process of devouring my steed. It wasn't as if I'd grown particularly attached to the animal, but I wasn't looking forward to walking the rest of the way to Taikyo. But when we drew near, I almost had to smile upon discovering the black-and-white bear seated contentedly on the ground, chewing on a bamboo tree, leaves, wood, and all. My horse was standing nearby, watching with obvious confusion. The bear had startled it; however, once it was clearly established as being no threat, the horse was content to watch it devour the tree at a leisurely clip.

Then the horse saw Mordant and immediately began to make more sounds of alarm. I crossed as quickly as my lame leg would allow me over to the startled animal and soothed it with soft, clucking noises. Eventually the poor creature calmed, which was an achievement. Between the bamboo-eating bear and the small dragon, this poor horse was having one hell of a night.

"I think we'd best get out of here," I said, glancing around. I hadn't been doing much traveling at night, and since I didn't dare head back down to the road for guidance, I wasn't entirely certain which way to go.

"Where are you headed?" Mordant asked.

"Taikyo," I replied.

"It's that way. Come. We'll bring you."

"No, we won't," Mitsu said abruptly. It was the first time

I'd heard him speak in something vaguely approaching normal conversational tone . . . that was to say, not shouting challenges or curses. His voice was light but strong, as if he had undercurrents of untapped strength.

Mordant was positioned on Mitsu's shoulder. Now he hopped off and landed on a branch so he could face Mitsu more easily. "We've discussed this, Mitsu," Mordant said firmly. For a creature who was once reticent, he'd certainly become quite chatty.

"Listening to you telling me what I should do isn't a discussion," retorted Mitsu.

"Excuse me," I said, "I would love to hear the continuation of this discussion, provided it wasn't boring me to death. I'd like to get going before those fools come after us and make our lives more difficult than they need to be. Mordant, you said you knew the way."

"Yes," said Mordant, and then he turned and leveled his gaze upon Mitsu. "Are you coming?"

"No," Mitsu said.

"Fine. Apropos, this way." He bounced off the branch, his wings beating the air, and landed some feet away.

I climbed astride my horse and we started off, and then from behind Mitsu called in obvious annoyance, "You're not just going to leave me here?"

"I can't force you to come," Mordant said, sounding quite reasonable about it. "Stay if you want, come along if you want, head off in a different direction entirely. It's up to you."

Once more we started in the direction of Taikyo, or at least the direction as claimed by Mordant. I heard an impatient stomping behind us, and then Mitsu started following us. "Friend of yours?" I asked, indicating the trailing Mitsu with a tilt of my head.

"Not exactly."

"Don't take this wrong, but he reminds me a bit of a certain princess I used to know, insofar as his attitudes. Is he a prince?"

"No," sighed Mordant.

"Well, too bad. With that kind of attitude, being royalty was his best bet for not getting the shite kicked out of him. But enough of him. Where is Sharee? Is she with you?" I was trying to maintain a neutral, even casual tone. I was doing my best to keep excitement out of my voice.

Unfortunately I don't think I was all that successful, because Mordant looked at me with a bit of a smirk. "You miss her, don't you."

"No, I don't miss her. I'm just intensely curious to know. For gods' sake, drabit," I insisted, "I did experience some adventures with the woman. Naturally I'm interested to know how things turned out. This quest you went on with her. Has she come here because of it? Is she at Taikyo? How much of a coincidence would that be, eh?" I wasn't quite able to keep the growing excitement from my tone, and I was beginning not to care. "Sometimes . . . sometimes things come together, Mordant. You don't think they will, but they do. It almost makes you believe in—"

"She's not here, Apropos. The quest is over."

"Over? Well . . . how went it, then? Successful?"

I wanted to hear that it wasn't, of course. I wanted to hear that that fool weaver, Rex Reggis, had led them to disaster and humiliation. Wouldn't that be glorious?

"We . . ." Mordant cleared his throat as he continued to hop from tree to tree. He could have simply flown alongside, but I think he appreciated the exercise after being cooped up in that cage. "We, uhm . . . well, not to sound immodest, but . . . we saved the world."

"How now?" I couldn't quite credit what I was hearing. "You did what? Saved the what?"

"The world. In its entirety. Surely you must have noticed."

"Noticed? How would I have noticed?" I asked with growing incredulity.

"Well, the final battle, Apropos. It was grand, on an epic scale. Or epic on a grand scale, take your pick. I won't bore you with the details . . ."

"Thus earning my undying gratitude," I assured him.

". . . but the bottom line is that Rex, Sharee, the others, and I faced odds beyond imagining. We didn't all make it, but those of us who did will be able to tell our grandchildren about the day and night of great darkness, when living lightning nearly consumed the planet . . ."

As he described it, memories flooded back to me. "I . . . I remember that night," I said slowly. "That day and that night. It seemed endless. Are you . . . are you saying that you were somehow responsible for that . . . ?"

"Responsible for the storms themselves? No. Responsible for stopping them, though. You see, a dark magic user employed ancient tomes to—" He stopped and smirked once more. "I forgot. You don't care about such things."

"Not when there are other things to care about. You said you didn't all make it." I could barely form the words. "Does . . . does that mean . . . Sharee . . . ?"

He clearly didn't realize what I was asking at first, but then realization dawned. "Oh! Sharee, dead? No, no. More lives than a cat, that one. No, she and Rex made it through, as did I. Not that I bonded in the same way with Rex as Sharee did, I'm rather relieved to say. He would probably be relieved as well . . ."

"What are you going on about now?" I demanded. "What 'bonded'? What are—"

"Well . . . Apropos . . ." He stopped and clung to a tree trunk, wrapping himself around it and actually looking slightly chagrined. "Ohhhh. Do you not comprehend, then? About Rex and Sharee . . . ?"

"I have no idea what you're . . ." Then my voice trailed off, and it registered upon me at last. "They're . . . together. Is what you're saying."

His triangular faced bobbed. "That is what I'm saying, yes."

"How together?"

For a moment, Mordant obviously was seeking a way to inform me gently, but ultimately discarded it for the straightforward approach. "They are wedded, Apropos. I was there for the ceremony."

I felt a slow numbness spreading through me, but fortunately I was on horseback and so it was less apparent. Outwardly my demeanor did not change at all, or at least I was trying to make sure it stayed that way. "I see. Wedded. Well . . ." I paused, taking it in, making sure my pose upon the horse was firm and steady, and then continued, ". . . that is . . . probably for the best."

"Apropos . . . are you quite all right?" inquired Mordant. He was being far more solicitous than usual. I found it off-putting.

"Yes, I'm fine. This is not unexpected, Mordant," I assured him, even as I felt my heart crumbling. Foolish, foolish heart. As if I'd ever had a chance with her. As if I'd ever let her know I had the slightest interest in her. "It is most usual for people who share remarkably dangerous adventures to form strong, even unassailable bonds. Their marriage is simply a natural outgrowth of that bonding."

"You and Sharee shared remarkably dangerous adventures," Mordant pointed out. "Are you saying that you two—?"

"Obviously not," I said. "Let us keep in mind, the

adventures we shared, neither of us entered willingly. I was dragooned into them, and she wanted to kill me much of the time. Hardly any sort of foundation upon which to build a long-term relationship. Besides, you should know by now that I am not exactly like other men. What serves the purposes of other, lesser mortals cannot hope to stand up to my requirements."

He didn't appear to have the faintest idea what I was talking about. That was quite all right. I shared the same sense of quandary. Shaking it off, I immediately said, "But how did you happen to come here? And wind up in a cage in that . . . that traveling circus?"

"The circumstances were . . . curious," said Mordant, and he glanced at Mitsu. Perhaps he thought I didn't notice the look, but it's difficult to hide body language when one's head is designed to unconsciously have one's tongue flick in the direction one is contemplating. Then, in a slightly posturing tone, he added, "And none of your business, really. Frankly, given your repeated disdain for hearing other people's tales, I'm almost surprised you'd even ask."

"I'm a surprising individual," I said archly. Then I gestured toward Mitsu. "What about him? Can he be trusted?"

"Him? Oh . . ." and Mordant seemed to smile, as much as he was able given the construction of his face. "Yes. He can be annoying at times, but he is on the whole trustworthy."

"Is that the case?" I reined up and turned to look at Mitsu, who had been following us in that sullen manner that only young boys can possess.

"Do you not trust Mordant?" asked Mitsu icily.

"When you get to know me better, you will come to understand that I don't trust anyone," I said.

"I have no interest in getting to know you better."

"Really." I smirked at him. "Perhaps you haven't been

paying attention, but if it weren't for me, those circus folk would have torn you apart. I'm the one who released the animals to distract them. I'm the one who got Mordant out of his cell. Considering all of that, I'd show a bit more gratitude if I were you."

He looked about to reply, but then exchanged a silent look with Mordant. Then he drew himself up stiffly, slapped his hands to either side of his legs, and bowed deeply at the waist. "I am in your debt. You shall not find me stinting in my endeavors to acknowledge and honor that debt."

I inclined my head slightly in acknowledgment. "Thank you. That means a great deal."

"Does it?" asked Mordant.

"Of course not." I snapped the reins and brought the horse back around. "Now then . . . let's be on our way."

There were many more things I could have asked Mordant. Press him on the question of how he'd wound up in Chinpan, or attracted the attention of this Mitsu person. But asking about Sharee and discovering the direction her life had gone somehow left me with little interest, or even less interest than I would usually have in such matters.

I realized I just hadn't been prepared for that aspect of my life to be ended so completely. Sharee had come into my life when I was quite young, when my childhood friend Tacit and I had rescued her from some angry villagers intent on burning her to cinders. Since then, even when she had not been with me physically, she had been in my dreams, in the periphery of my existence in some way, shape, or form.

But she hadn't been in my dreams lately. Indeed, not for quite some time. And now I was understanding why. It was because she was, for good and all, a thing of my past. And I apparently wasn't quite ready for that. Nevertheless, it had happened whether I was ready or not.

"Why are you going to Taikyo?" asked Mordant abruptly, flapping along next to me. "You never said."

"There was a man I knew. A good man. He was killed. I go to seek justice for him," I said.

"Really. Have you ever sought justice for someone before?"

"Once," I said. "For my mother. It didn't work out particularly well, and underscored for me the futility of such endeavors."

"And yet you do it anyway."

"Yes."

"Why?"

"Because," I said, "there is no idea that exists that is so foolish that it can't be embarked upon twice. Sharee . . ."

"What?" His head snapped around and he looked at me curiously. "Did you just say . . . ?"

"I was just wondering if she is . . . happy. In your opinion."

"Yes," said Mordant. "I don't think I've ever seen an individual quite as happy as she was."

"Ah. Happy then."

"Very much so."

I considered that and then said, "I wonder what that's like. Being happy."

Mordant became silent once more.

BOOK TWO

Caveat Imperior

Chapter 1

Bright Lies, Big City

I'll say this for Taikyo: It wasn't made of bamboo.

It was easily the largest city I had ever been in, bigger than anything I might have imagined. Here I had thought that I had encountered some sort of primitive culture, and instead the construction of the city indicated a civilization far older than any I had known.

For starters, all the roads were paved. All of them. Every city I'd ever been to had some, if not most or even all, of the roads made from nothing more than dirt and—more frequently—mud. Such was not the case here. The roads through Taikyo were hardened, made from some sort of . . . of black tarred substance or pitch, near as I could tell, rather than the cobblestone with which I was familiar. I was accustomed to seeing such things used for bathing some miscreant in and attaching feathers, or perhaps dumping in large flaming quantities upon attacking enemies. But walking upon it? It was a bizarre sensation.

Many of the buildings, however, were raised above the ground on platforms of rammed earth, brick, or dirt. According to Mitsu—who was obviously familiar with the city, but reluctant to discuss it in detail—it was from a time before the roads were paved, in order to keep the buildings above the mud and dirt.

I marveled at the architecture, with many ornately curved roofs on the larger buildings, supported by structures of wooden beams . . . to provide bracing in the event of an earthquake, I was told. That was a bit of news I could have done without.

Taikyo was also divided in terms of economic strata. The domiciles of the richer, more elite citizens were all clustered in one section, and had the aforementioned remarkably lavish style of design. But as we moved through the city, we found other sections that were far less so. The fish market, for example. It was easily the busiest and most thriving area of the city, understandably since the majority of the populace reputedly subsisted almost entirely on a diet of fish.

The fish market was situated on either side of a massive river that carved straight through the middle of the city. Large curved bridges traversed the river, and they were quite crowded with people coming and going from the market. This made the bridges no different from the rest of the city, which seemed to be packed from one end to the other with humanity. There were more people there than I'd ever seen in one place in my life, and that included the royal jousts back in Isteria.

Fortunately enough, everyone seemed far too caught up in their own interests to pay much attention to us. That was something of a feat, considering the odd little group we were. Drabits were still not exactly commonplace creatures to see, and certainly my features marked me as something completely out of the ordinary. I still had my cloak, though, and I had pulled it out of my bundle before we'd entered the city. I draped it around my shoulders and brought my hood up, deftly serving to obscure my face. Mordant then took up position beneath the cloak, clinging onto my bag and flattening himself so that, at the most, I looked as if I had a small humpback. Humpbacks were also not common, but I suspected one saw them more frequently than tiny dragons or men with round eyes in these parts.

By this point I had dismounted and was simply walking through the streets, holding the horse firmly by the reins and guiding it through the crowds. At least people got out of our way, which was a plus, although many of them gave us slightly annoyed looks at having to step aside. I wasn't certain what alternative I could present. It wasn't as if I could fold the horse up lengthwise and slip it into my pack.

In the marketplace, I found a fellow who was selling sword belts, the kind that had the latches that would support the sword that Ali had wielded. I was getting uncomfortable with the notion of keeping it attached to the horse. So I purchased a belt, lashed it around me, pulled the sword out of its place on the horse, and attached it.

It was the first time that Mitsu had seen the weapon, and his eyes widened upon spying it. "That is . . . an impressive-looking weapon," he said. It was the closest thing to a compliment he'd ever tossed in my direction.

"Thank you," I replied. "It's an heirloom." I pulled my walking staff from its place on the other side of the horse. Despite the fact that it was a necessary device to compensate for my lameness, by that point in my life I actually found that I derived a measure of comfort, even security from it. Thus outfitted, we continued on our way.

The domiciles in the fishing district, as opposed to the richer sections of town, were packed in almost one atop the other. Mitsu informed me that conditions were so crowded that Taikyo families lived as many as seven or eight in a single room. I found this appalling, and couldn't help but wonder at the conditions of the city which required so many people to live so close together.

But then I began to understand. For as we glided through the fish market, I saw in the distance the single largest structure in the entirety of Taikyo. Hell, for all I knew, it was the single largest structure in the entirety of the world.

It was a sprawling castle sitting atop what I could only describe as a small mountain. Great stone pillars rose up, supporting the sprawling curved roof composed of overlapping tiles and, ironically, a series of twisting, sinewy statues of dragons that bore a passing resemblance to the creature hitching a ride on my back. The palace was separated from the rest of the city by a series of moats. It loomed there, sending out a sense of majesty and superiority.

"That," I said, "I take to be the residence of the Imperior?"

No answer. I turned to discover that Mitsu was gone.

"Now what the hell . . . ?"

"Problem?" came Mordant's muffled voice from beneath my cloak.

"Your fool friend is gone. Mitsu!" I called, cupping my hands to my mouth.

"Odd. That's not like . . . him, to wander off."

"Well, he did it anyway. *Mitsu!*"

"Yes," came Mitsu's voice, practically at my elbow. I turned to find him standing there, looking quite calm.

"Where did you get off to?"

"Nowhere. You're the one who wandered away from me."

I started to protest that I had wandered nowhere, but quickly decided it wasn't worth the effort. "That castle," I said, pointing in the direction of the looming fortress. "That is where the Imperior resides?"

Mitsu nodded, not appearing too forthcoming with details.

We had come to a halt in the midst of the fish market and no doubt looked like a couple of tourists as we stared at the palace in the distance. Anxious to get off the street, I noticed what appeared to be a small eatery. We headed over and within minutes were seated at a small table near the ground. To be specific, there were no chairs. We simply knelt on either side of the table with small pillows under our rumps to provide minimal support. There were not many other people around at that moment, which was something of a blessing. I had no idea how much the tea that was served to us was, but I dropped one of the coins I'd taken off the dead men into the hand of the serving wench, and she seemed perfectly satisfied with the amount.

We sipped tea from simple cups and did not speak for some moments.

"All right, then," I said finally. "I'll just have to present myself to the Imperior and we'll see what I can learn from . . ."

"Wait," Mitsu said, looking at me in amused contempt. "Do you seriously think you're going to be able to just walk up to the Imperior? It's impossible."

"Why impossible?"

Mitsu placed his cup down. "To begin with," he said, keeping his voice low as if concerned we might be over-heard, "the Imperior only sees the public two days a year."

"Two days?" And here I had thought that King Runcible was out of touch owing to lack of frequent interaction with the residents of Isteria. Compared to this Imperior fellow, Runcible was virtually a man of the people. "And what two days would those be?"

"The New Year, and his birthday. Neither of which is anytime soon," he added, obviously anticipating my next question.

"All right," I said thoughtfully. "That may well be how he treats his citizens. But I'm not a citizen. I will be presenting myself as a representative of a far-off, unknown land."

"Are you?" He looked amused.

"Prove that I am not."

He shrugged his slim shoulders. "It does not matter. All that your 'status' would guarantee you is a quick death."

I felt the blood draining from my face. "A quick death? Why?"

"You don't understand," he told me. "The Imperior is not simply a mortal man."

"He's not?"

"Well, he thinks he's not. The Imperior is designated by the gods. He is divine. He is holy. He is all-knowing. And I am quite, quite sure that your race and the land from which you come is completely unknown to him."

"So?" I still wasn't following.

"So?" It was Mordant's voice, speaking softly from beneath my cloak. Anyone nearby would have thought themselves mad with voices apparently wafting out of thin air. "Are you not paying attention? One cannot be all-knowing and be faced with the unknown both at the same time."

"Ah," I said slowly.

"Now you understand?"

"Yes," I admitted. "If there is physical proof of someone or something that the Imperior doesn't know about, then his divine, all-knowing status is challenged. He cannot tolerate any such challenge. So what he would be obliged to do is eliminate that which is challenging him. But," and I shook my head, "wouldn't he be interested in finding out about that which is new to him?"

"Of course not. Because, by definition—"

"He already knows about it," I sighed. "And if he doesn't know about it, then it must not exist. So if it does exist, it behooves him to make certain it stops existing."

"Precisely," said Mitsu. He looked at me with curiosity.

"Why was it so necessary for you to speak directly with the Imperior, anyway?"

"Because I want to help find a way to destroy the Forked Tong."

"Ahhh. The Forked Tong," Mitsu said, nodding. "You are familiar with them, are you?"

"Not really," I admitted. I could feel Mordant on my back, settling himself back down to rest. "But I know enough."

"And what do you know?"

"That they are some sort of criminal organization. And they work in tandem with a group calling itself the Anaïs Ninjas. The group that was responsible for killing my teacher."

"I see." He held his cup delicately and took another sip. "And how do you propose to destroy this Forked Tong and the Anaïs Ninjas?"

"I'm not sure yet. I need more information about them." My eyes narrowed thoughtfully as I stared at Mitsu. "You seem a knowledgeable sort."

"Do I?" His voice was neutral.

"What can you tell me?"

"That if you meddle with organizations such as those whose names you are so unwisely bandying about, you will die."

Trying my best to sound nonchalant, I replied, "Sooner or later, I'll die anyway. So what difference does it make?"

"All the difference in the world if you desire sooner to become later."

"Trouble."

Once again it was Mordant who had spoken from concealment. But his tone had changed. There was tension in both it and his body. I could tell because suddenly his

talons were digging into the flesh of my back. I gasped in
pain and growled, "Ease up on the claws, if you don't
mind." I felt a slight lessening. "What 'trouble'? What are
you talking about?"

"Not sure. I just smell it. Let's go."

"This is ridic—"

"Let's go!" There was a definite hiss in his voice, and I
could feel the claws pricking at my skin once more.

Having been given sufficient incentive, I used my staff
to hoist myself to my feet. Mitsu, impressively, went
directly from cross-legged to standing in a bit of muscle
control that I could only envy. As we quickly gathered our
meager belongings, I glanced around the eatery in search
of what looked like a plausible menace. Nothing presented itself.

Quickly we made our way out into the streets. How in
the world Mordant could possibly smell trouble, I hadn't a
clue. All I could smell was fish.

"There," Mitsu suddenly said. He didn't point, obviously not wanting to draw attention, but I followed the
young man's glance and saw what he was indicating.

I recognized them instantly.

Not them specifically, but their mode of dress, the colors
they wore, which was identical to that of the three thugs who
had ridden into the small village of Hosbiyu with the intention of causing problems . . . right before Chinpan Ali had
caused them more problems than they could ever have imagined. There were two of them, and they were not taking their
eyes off us as we made our way through the market.

We wove our way through the crowd, trying to get to the
horse, and then I stopped so abruptly that Mitsu bumped
into me. "We have a problem," I said.

Two more of them were directly between us and the
horse.

It seemed as if the people in the crowd sensed that these men meant trouble, and tried to get out of their way as quickly as they could.

"You know them?" asked Mitsu.

"They work for the Skang Kei crime family," I told him.

"Well, if you're interested in finding out about the Forked Tong, they would certainly be the ones who tell you what you wish to know."

"*They're* with the Forked Tong as well?"

"You don't seem to understand," said Mitsu. "Everyone of criminal intent in this city is part of the Forked Tong. Why do you think the Imperior despises them so? Because they're organized. Enemies who are splintered are far more easily handled than enemies who are united."

"Words of wisdom. I shall carry them with me for many years, provided we manage to survive the next few minutes."

"Why are they coming after you?"

"I don't know," I replied. "For all I know, they're coming after you."

"Me? What did I ever do to the Skang Kei family?"

"Since I really don't have any clue as to who you are, I'd have no way of answering that, would I. For all I know, you raped and murdered a favored daughter." Even as I spoke, I glanced around desperately to see if there was a way out. "Come," I said, and headed off to the left.

They were coming from that direction as well. I turned and saw that a fourth possible means of retreat had also been cut off.

"What's happening?" demanded Mordant from hiding.

"We have a problem," I said again.

The advancing men, as if by unspoken cue, suddenly unsheathed their swords.

"We have a *major* problem," I amended.

"Do you need me to intercede?"

"No, I need you to grow about twenty feet in length and be able to blast fire out your mouth."

"I'll work on it," said Mordant from beneath my cloak.

The crowd was melting away around us, and I suddenly felt extremely vulnerable as a space cleared in every direction. No one wanted to interfere or get involved. On one level, I couldn't blame them. Had I been in the crowd and perceived that someone else was being pursued by a group of criminal strongmen, I would have gotten myself so far out of the way that I'd have wound up in a different county. However, as the targeted individual, I felt more inclined to curse the cravenness of the throng.

"Gentlemen!" I called out. "May I be of some assistance?"

They came in quickly, their swords swinging. I didn't know where to look first. I was totally paralyzed, no clue what to do.

Mitsu, on the other hand, did not hesitate. He leaped forward, angling his body as he went, and slid between the legs of the foremost of the attackers. He brought his legs up fast and slammed them into the crotch of his opponent. The man gasped, doubling over, losing his grip on his sword as he did so. Mitsu arched his back and snapped up to his feet, plucking the sword out of the air as it fell. He whipped it back and forth with amazing speed, judging its heft, and instantly deflected the thrust of the next attacker.

And then he was gone.

Just like that. He darted between two of the attackers and vanished from the scene, leaving me on my own.

I had to give him credit. I hadn't expected actions quite that craven. It was almost worthy of me. If I weren't seized with the desire to cut Mitsu into shreds at that moment, I'd actually have admired him for his self-centeredness.

Whatever vain hope I had that perhaps these bullies were

after Mitsu evaporated because none of them went after him. Instead their full attention was still focused upon me.

I backed up and suddenly found myself up against a wall. There was a muffled grunt from Mordant, and I muttered, "Any time now would be useful."

Mordant erupted from beneath my cloak with a warning screech, and the men froze where they were. Their eyes widened, their faces turning ashen, and Mordant angled toward them. They swept at him with their swords, but Mordant danced between the flashing blades with dazzling agility, and then there were glorious screams as his claws raked across their faces.

Suddenly I felt a tug at my hip. I turned just in time to get an elbow in the face, and saw that one of the behemoths had gotten close enough to try and yank the bird's-head sword from its scabbard. Apparently it wasn't coming out easily, and the pull was sufficient to get my attention. Unfortunately my attention in turn had gotten me the aforementioned elbow.

I sagged against the wall even as I snapped out the blade at the end of my staff and swung it. He wasn't expecting it, and the blade cut across his chest, glancing off the rib cage, leaving a trail of torn cloth and blood in its wake. He staggered, cursing, and I gripped the tachi sword and yanked. It came free of the scabbard, and my attacker's eyes widened as he stepped back, bringing his own blade to bear but not looking as if he was happy to do so.

It was the first time I'd wielded the blade in combat. I continued to be amazed by the lack of weight. If I hadn't known better, I'd have thought I was holding nothing at all. I brought the sword back, prepared to defend myself as best I could.

"I know you're with the Skang Kei family," I snapped out, hoping to stall for time until something other than a very likely death presented itself. "But what the hell do you want?"

"We operate under the orders of the great Ho," said the thug, with what sounded like a touch of pride. "The Ho gives us orders, and we obey. It is not for you to ask, or for us to explain ourselves to you. It is for you to lay down your life without question."

"Oh really. Well, if you think I'm just going to roll over at the say-so of some Skang Kei Ho, you can just forget it."

Obviously that wasn't the thing to say to placate them. They came in fast, watching the sword warily.

Which was why, naturally, I used my walking staff.

Whipping the sword to one side, I lunged to my left, my strong side, and used the staff as a cudgel to bat the nearest sword out of the way. For about a second, I was in the clear. There was no way, with my lack of footspeed, that I'd be able to get away, but I could even the odds in terms of balance.

My lunge had taken me right next to a stand filled with some sort of fish. Dozens of small, gray, scaled bodies lying in a massive pile. With a quick thrust, I overturned the stand, and the fish spilled out everywhere onto the ground.

The Skang Kei musclemen were barreling toward me far too quickly to stop. They hit the fish, their feet going out from under them, and with outraged shouts they skidded to the ground.

I slammed the walking staff into the ground and hopped forward, keeping my right leg tucked under and relying on my left foot and the staff for balance. With my free hand I brought the sword around, about to start slicing them up while demanding answers.

And that was when I heard lusty bellows of *"One side!"* and *"Make way!"*

Just like that, the men of the Skang Kei family were gone. They bolted in all directions, leaving me standing there with my sword in my hand and a bewildered expression on my face.

I gaped as I saw what were clearly several burly warriors shoving Mitsu forward. They were wearing long, sweeping black robes—the type that I had learned were called "kimonos"—of far finer cloth than the rough-hewn material sported by the others. The black was accentuated by inner lines of white against the V neck. Each warrior wore an additional garment atop the kimono, gray with straps across the chest and shoulder pieces that flared out, making the shoulders seem even wider than they were. The garments were belted at the middle, and would have looked like skirts in the lower half save they were split at the legs.

Mitsu was struggling mightily in their grasp, but this was a very different cut of opponent from what we'd been facing before. You could see it in their eyes. They were strong, well trained, and likely capable of handling anything thrown their way. And "anything" certainly included a young man, no matter how much resistance he was putting up.

"In the name of the Imperior," shouted one of them, "surrender! Surrender immediately! Surrender completely! Surr "

"Yes, I get it, there's a degree of surrendering involved. We surrender. Don't *we*," I said pointedly to Mitsu, conveying that I was somewhat irked over the desertion.

One of them strode forward, kicking the fish to one side to get them out of his way, and shoved my hood back to get a better look at me. There was a collective gasp, from him and all the onlookers, that gave me a sense of what it must be like for lepers. All I needed was to have little bells to jingle to announce my presence and I'd be all set.

"What are *you*?" he demanded. "What are you that speaks with such an odd accent and has such abnormal features?"

"Abnormal features?" I frowned, feigning uncertainty of what he was talking about. I reached up, touched my face, and gasped. *"Oh . . . gods!"* I cried out. "What has happened to me?! What perverse enchantment?! My face! My beautiful *face!* Not as beautiful as yours, of course," I assured him, "but fair to look upon nonetheless! What dark magic has inflicted itself upon me? It must have been . . . him!"

"Him?" He clearly didn't know what I was talking about.

"That man who claimed to be a magic user! Who said he would put a curse upon me because he misliked the way I looked at his daughter! I never touched her, I swear! You have to believe me!" I pawed at him and he shoved me back. Indeed, if I had been a leper, he couldn't have been more repulsed. "I must . . . I must go and find him immediately! Thank you for drawing this horrific matter to my attention!"

I turned and started to bolt, and then one of his meaty hands clamped upon my shoulder, immobilizing me. "Problem, Officer?" I inquired.

"You have been brawling! In the streets!"

"Now, what gives you that idea?" I asked.

"Witnesses. And this," and he pointed to blood spattered upon my shirt.

I looked down at it. "I cut myself," I said.

"I see no cut."

"It happened days ago."

"This blood," he said, "is fresh."

"I'm a slow bleeder."

He didn't seem impressed. I couldn't blame him. As lies went, it wasn't one of my better ones.

"All right," I said abruptly. "Do you want the truth?" It wasn't my normal style, but I figured I didn't have much to lose. "The truth is, we were attacked by members of the Skang Kei family. I don't know why."

"Who does?" demanded the soldier.

"Ho does," I told him.

"Your accent remains strange," he rumbled. "I'm asking you, who knows why you were attacked."

"And I am telling you, Ho knows why."

"Who knows why?"

"Ho."

"Who?"

"No, Ho."

"Who who?"

"Ho is who."

"Who is who?"

"No, Ho is who."

He swung a gloved fist and knocked me flat. In retrospect, all things considered, I suppose I couldn't blame him. My lousy luck that in Chinpanese the word for "who" was the same as in my language.

I lay on the ground, the sword still in my hand but nearly forgotten as I tried to stop the world from spinning. Then I yelped as a heavy pressure settled on my right forearm, immobilizing the hand holding the sword.

"Did you not know there was an edict from the Imperior that there is to be no public brawling!" he demanded.

"No, I didn't," I said with a grunt, "but thank you so much for bringing it to my attention. The problem is, it wasn't my fault! We were the ones attacked!"

"Then you should have let yourselves be killed rather than disobey the edict!"

Remember earlier how I spoke of the unassailability of someone who possesses both ignorance and arrogance? Such was the situation I was now faced with. I couldn't think of any response to the kind of thinking that encouraged being slaughtered instead of fighting back just to accommodate a rule I didn't know existed, made by a man I'd never met.

"Sorry" was all I could think of to say.

"Do you know what the penalty is for disobeying an edict of the Imperior?"

"A severe scolding?"

"Death!"

"Clearly," I said desperately, "you haven't considered the full ramifications of a severe scolding. The mental scarring it can leave is far more damaging to—"

He appeared unimpressed. Instead he gestured for Mitsu to be brought forward. Protesting, the young man was shoved in my direction and tumbled to the street next to me, the man standing on my arm giving way to make room for him. "Thanks for the support," I muttered.

"You would have done the same," Mitsu snapped.

"You don't know that."

"You deny it?"

"No," I said, seeing no point to lying given the situation. "I'm just saying you don't know it."

The soldiers converged, each of them with his sword out. The blades glistened in the sun. I gripped the tachi sword, knowing there was no place to go. My mind raced, trying to come up with anything, some brilliant lie, that would buy us some time. The emissary-from-the-foreign-land routine would probably be a dead end, literally, if Mitsu's earlier comments were true, but it might be worth a try. Mitsu, for his part, was looking wildly right and left. As deft as he was with his hands and feet, there was no place for him to go that two or three sword blades wouldn't come at him from several different directions. He was fast, but he wasn't superhuman.

And at that moment, I heard Mordant's voice cry out. Naturally, since no one else was expecting an animal to speak, no one knew that he was the source of it. It came from above. He was doubtless perched upon a roof, keeping out of sight. And what he called out was:

"Don't kill her, you fools! She's the princess!"

The huge soldiers froze in position, looking around for both the origin of the voice and also the alleged princess. Then the one who was gripping Mitsu firmly and painfully by the elbow looked down at him as if seeing him for the first time, and let out a cry of alarm. He released Mitsu's arm as if it were on fire and immediately prostrated himself upon the ground. *"Highness!"* he cried out.

The others promptly followed suit, and Mitsu, with an annoyed snarl, reached up and released his hair from the topknot. The black hair cascaded down to shoulder length, long and luxurious, and suddenly there was no doubt at all that this was a female and, from the arrogant look to her, a royal one at that.

In a heartbeat, everyone in the fish market was on the ground, except for me; I was gaping at her.

The soldier who had been manhandling her cried out, with his face practically flat against the ground, "Divinity, in failing to recognize you and treating you in such a fashion, I have disgraced my good offices, my family, and my ancestors going back five generations."

"Yes. You have. You should kill yourself immediately," said Mitsu.

In a heartbeat, the soldier pulled out a small dagger, jammed it into his stomach, and ripped it up and then to the side.

"I was *joking*," Mitsu told him, looking profoundly annoyed.

"My mistake," grunted the soldier before he keeled over. He lay there in a rapidly spreading pool of his own blood.

"Divinity," said another, even larger soldier, who was on the ground along with the others, keeping his eyes fixedly down. "We are under the strictest orders imaginable. Your absence from the palace has been of great concern to your godly father, and he has commanded us that if we are to come upon you, we are to return you to the palace immediately, whether it is what you desire or not."

"Oh, very well," she said, rolling her eyes, and then she called out, "This is all *your* fault! I didn't want to come back here! But no, *you* insisted we had to come! Let it be on your scaly head, then!"

I, of course, was the only person in the place who knew whom she was addressing.

Then she looked at me and noticed I was making eye contact with her. "You realize I could have you executed on the spot for gazing upon my godly countenance."

"It's a bit late in the game for that. I've been staring at it for quite some time," I pointed out.

She shrugged. "Yes. You're probably right. Fine, then," she said with a dismissive wave. "You have enough trouble walking anyway, without having to concern yourself about not being able to watch where you're going."

"You're too considerate, 'Divinity,' " I said.

"Yes, I know," she replied, oblivious of the sarcasm. I found that annoying. Generally my sarcasm was more obvious than that. I might well have been losing my edge. "Get your horse. Let's go to the palace."

"Us?" inquired the largest soldier. He looked up, but in my direction rather than hers. "You would bring this . . . individual . . . to the palace?"

"This individual brought me safely back to the city and fought to protect me from assassins," she replied. "He is deserving of the highest honors we can provide him. He comes with us, and his person is to be considered sacrosanct."

"Divinity, I . . ."

"Sacro. Sanct. Do you all understand?"

"Yes, Divinity!" they chorused as one.

Her comments caught me off guard, and she looked at

me with a raised eyebrow and an imperious manner that seemed to say, *See? It would serve you better to be my friend than my enemy.* "Go get your horse and let's go. We might as well get this over with. I'm sure my father just cannot wait to see me."

Then she took a couple of delicate steps toward the dead soldier, said disdainfully, "Idiot," and strode over him.

When I'd been a younger man, I'd spent an inordinate amount of time with a borderline insane princess named Entipy.

The princess Mitsu clearly could have given her a run for her money. The best thing I could say about her was that she hadn't tried to set fire to anything.

Then again, the day was young.

Chapter 2

Royal Pain

*A*s insane as Princess Entipy had been, her father, King Runcible, had been a fairly harmless individual. His main sins were those of omission rather than commission . . . unless, of course, one counted his throwing me in a dungeon. Then again, considering that doing so had been a mercy, as compared with the endeavors to kill me that so many others had undertaken, Runcible's actions were positively benign.

I was hoping that the Imperior would fall into that same category.

That hope lasted for exactly as long as it took to meet him.

The soldiers were apparently members of some sort of warrior caste collectively called the "Hamunri." They had been around for a few hundred years, rising up from an elite group of seven and becoming one of the single most powerful classes in all of Chinpan. After a series of civil wars that had threatened to shred the entire class structure, the Hamunri had wound up swearing fealty to the Imperior, and so it had been for five generations.

All this was imparted to me by Mitsu in a very offhanded way as we strolled side by side to the palace. As we walked,

the people of Chinpan would automatically flatten themselves and avert their eyes lest they look upon Mitsu
and . . . well, I wasn't sure what was supposed to happen to
them if they did. Probably they'd have to kill themselves the
same way that poor bastard back in the fish market had.

There were more Hamunri standing guard upon the ele-
gant curved bridge that led to the palace. They began to
reach for their swords as we approached, and then saw me,
and then the princess, and they didn't know whether to
bow or stare. They settled for looking down while casting
quick, sidelong glances as we walked past.

Nowhere did I see Mordant, but I very much suspected
that he was following somewhere. I could have strangled
the little bastard. Here I had made the observation that
Mitsu had the attitude of a princess, but then I'd asked if
Mitsu—whom I naturally assumed to be a male—was a
prince. "No, not a prince," Mordant had said in his
damned smirking manner. He could have bloody well told
me at that point, but no, he had to play his little games.
Granted, his well-timed shout out had resulted in my
winding up very much not dead, but even so, I reserved the
right to be exceedingly annoyed with him.

Once we got over the bridge, the first thing we were confronted with was stairs. I wasn't ecstatic about that; stairs
were, and are, a problem for me. But there wasn't anything
else for it, really. They were incredibly wide, wide enough
to accommodate fifty men walking side by side.
Nevertheless, I wasn't about to look feeble by climbing
back on the horse to ride up so I made my slow way up
what seemed to be a hundred steps to the main courtyard.

Mitsu, to her credit, made no effort to get ahead of me,
even though I knew she could easily sprint to the top of the
stairs with no difficulty. Perhaps she was being polite. Or it
could have been that she wasn't in any hurry to get there.

Once we passed through the main gate, we walked upon dragons etched in bold relief in pavement blocks of carved marble. The palace was not simply a single building, but rather a series of buildings of varying sizes, contained within a walled-in area. With the Hamunri keeping a wary eye upon us, as if afraid the princess might suddenly snap her fingers and vanish into thin air, we passed through the main court area and into a smaller court on the farther side. There was perfectly trimmed vegetation everywhere—ornate trees carefully sculpted, and other trees with delicate fruits dangling from the branches.

The interior of the palace, the main hall, was breathtaking, and as different from Runcible's castle as the sun from the moon. In addition to the marbled floor, the ceilings were deeply paneled and there were vast, elaborate carvings on everything. First and foremost in all the ornamental designs were images of dragons. Winged, unwinged, legs and no legs. Mordant would have been worshipped there as a god if he'd chosen to show himself. I couldn't quite understand his reluctance.

There were incense urns and figures of bronze, gorgeous tapestries, statues of great warriors from throughout the history of Chinpan. And there were courtiers beginning to emerge, bowing and scraping to the princess and obviously being bewildered over my presence. I wasn't sure what the hell I was doing there, either.

Several of the courtiers came forward and extended their hands for my horse's reins. "Don't worry," said Mitsu. "Your animal will be well groomed and attended to."

Reluctantly—reluctant because I didn't want to deprive myself of the option of a fast getaway—I handed the reins over to the closest courtier, and they led the horse away.

Ahead of us was a vast archway, and Mitsu glanced at me

in a manner that could almost be described as impish. "Are you ready?" she asked.

"I somehow doubt it," I said. I turned to face her, and heard a few stray gasps from onlookers. I flinched slightly, partly concerned that some outraged Hamunri would charge forward and behead me for my forwardness. "What am I doing here, Mitsu?"

"Not 'Divinity'?" she inquired with a faintly mocking tone. "Not 'Princess'?"

"Titles mean very little to me. I tend to judge the person by his or her qualities as an individual, rather than the pretentiousness of a designation."

"And who are you to judge?" There was a challenge to her tone.

"No one and nothing, which makes me the ideal judge."

She actually laughed at that. She had a nice laugh.

At which point I nearly pulled out my sword and ran myself through with it. The absolute last thing I needed was to become enamored with another princess.

"Come then," she said and, with an inclination of her head, walked in through the archway. I followed her.

The room we entered was as ornate as any of the others we'd been through, but there was a large throne positioned at the far end of it. The armrests of the throne were dragons carved from what appeared to be gold and silver intertwined. It was accessed by three small steps that led up to it, and seated upon the throne was an old man with a long, wispy, white beard.

Slowly the man—whom I took to be the fabled Imperior—rose from his dragon throne. He was clothed in elaborate robes of red and purple, which seemed to envelop and even dwarf his body. He did not have enough hair on his head for a standard topknot, but instead his silvery hair hung short at the sides.

"Down. Now," Mitsu said softly, and I realized that proper respect was going to have to be shown, presuming I wanted to continue breathing. I noticed interwoven mats upon the floor directly in front of the throne, and immediately knelt on the closest one. Mitsu's description of her father's reactions to anything unknown weighed heavily upon me, but I had to hope that she wouldn't have brought me here if she didn't have some sort of plan to make certain I wasn't going to be killed.

Then I remembered how casual she had been over the demise of that one idiot guard, and had to face the possibility that my confidence might have been misplaced.

The Imperior stood at the top of the stairs for what seemed an eternity. Then he spoke, in a voice that was thin and reedy, but filled with strength. "So."

"So," said Mitsu.

"You have returned."

She nodded.

"You departed the Forbidding City without my permission," and his voice became louder. There was no anger to it. It sounded almost singsong. "Against my wishes, in fact."

"Yes." She nodded again.

"If they are my wishes, they are the wishes of the gods. Do you defy the gods?"

"It was not my desire to defy anyone," Mitsu told him, "but simply to live my life. The life you would deny me."

"The life it is my right to deny you." He sounded rather reasonable about it, even though his words were daunting. "Do you deny that?"

Mitsu looked as if she was about to say something far more defiant, but then changed her mind. Instead she simply stared resolutely ahead.

"You have acted in a manner that is disgraceful. That

brings dishonor to your name, and to the dragon throne. Honor must be restored."

I felt a chill gripping my spine. I didn't know where this was going, but I couldn't say I liked the drift of it.

The Imperior clapped his hands briskly three times. In a moment, three young women dressed in silk kimonos ran in quickly. They moved lightly, almost as if they were dancing upon their toes. With their hair done up identically and the same sort of makeup, they were almost impossible to distinguish one from the other.

"Your handmaids. They have missed you," said the Imperior. "Choose one."

"Choose . . . ?"

"One. To die in your stead and so preserve your honor."

I couldn't believe what I was hearing. It was madness. Madness. Certainly she would say something to intercede, come up with some way to save the life of an innocent young woman who had done nothing to deserve . . .

Mitsu pointed at the one in the middle. "That one," she said carelessly, as if she were randomly picking out a frock to wear.

But . . . surely the handmaiden would protest. Cry. Plead for her life. Put forward her sense of betrayal, or . . .

The handmaiden promptly dropped to her knees, pulled out a small dagger, and plunged it into her perfect breast. "It is an honor," she said, and then fell forward so softly I never even heard her hit the floor.

At which point I knew I was definitely in an asylum that had been taken over by madmen.

I had gone through my life encountering people who had no sense of honor, or else possessed honor in a way that was personally convenient. Here in Chinpan, honor had been taken to the opposite degree. It had been elevated to a point where it superseded compassion or wisdom or even basic humanity. Life itself had no meaning other than to lay it down at the most capricious of whims.

The Imperior didn't even glance at the handmaiden who had taken her own life on behalf of his daughter. Instead, to my gnawing horror, he turned his attention to me. "And this?"

I waited for her to provide an explanation for me. To come up with some way of finessing a way around the obvious fact that I was like nothing her father had ever seen . . . which would inherently be fatal.

Silence.

"Well?" he prompted.

More silence. I risked a glance in her direction, surreptitiously under one of my arms. Her lips were thinned, her face impassive.

She wasn't going to say a damned thing.

My mouth was suddenly very dry as I realized I was about a sentence or two away from death. Fortunately enough, it was when I was at my most desperate that I was usually at my best.

Keeping my eyes resolutely upon the floor, I ventured, "She does not answer, O Divine One, because she is aware that you already know the answer."

There was a pause during which—not for the first time—my life flashed before my eyes. I couldn't say I was any prouder of it this go-around than before.

"Indeed," he said.

"Well . . . of course. How could you not?" Gaining confidence, however misplaced it might have been, I said, "After all, you are the . . ."

Blood from the fallen handmaiden was trickling toward me. I moved my feet carefully, trying not to be ill. "You are the chosen of the gods," I continued, my voice not shaking only through great effort. "Naturally it would be unthinkable that you would not know who I am and from where I hail."

"Yes. It would be unthinkable." He paused. "So tell me . . . what you think I know."

"I . . . think you know that my name is Po. That I am an ambassador from the state of Isteria, from the ruler known as Runcible."

"And you have, of course, brought me an offering from your king."

I froze for a moment, but then reached into the hidden compartment on my staff and extracted several Isterian coins. "These are exceptionally valuable. Very limited in number. He wanted you to have them." Without looking up at him, I extended the coins. It was just a couple of sovs, nothing special. But they had the king's features imprinted upon them.

The Imperior took them and studied them thoughtfully. "Very generous," he said. "And, of course . . . you are able to guess how your king knew of our land."

My brain froze. I cursed myself for a fool. That simple notion had not occurred to me. I didn't have the slightest inkling how King Runcible—or, in point of fact, any monarch I might have served back in my homeland— could possibly have come to have knowledge of the land of Chinpan.

But then I calmed as I realized I didn't have to know. The whole point of this wasn't to cover my knowledge; it was to cover the Imperior's lack of same.

"I could not guess that, Imperior," I told him with a carefully manufactured hint of embarrassment, and a generous helping of subservience to boot. "I am but a humble messenger. When I am told to go, I go. It is not for me to question my ruler, or to ask how he came by certain knowledge. Certainly it is enough that he know, you know, and the gods know. What matter if a humble creature such as I am aware of the truth of the matter? As long as those whom I obey know the true nature of things, that is more than sufficient."

"As it should be," said the Imperior judiciously. "Rise. Rise, messenger Po."

I was afraid to relax as I did so. For all I knew, I was being asked to stand up in order to make a simpler target for a large man with a large sword.

"My understanding," said the Imperior, his hands folded within the sleeves of his garment, "is that you were in the fish market with my daughter. That you were attacked."

"That is right, Imperior."

"By members of the Skang Kei family . . . they themselves allies of the Forked Tong."

"That is correct again, Imperior," I assured him. I sounded utterly subservient, and was perfectly comfortable doing so. He seemed to prefer it that way, and if it was going to enable me to keep myself alive, I was happy to do it.

Slowly the Imperior shook his head, his long white beard waggling from side to side, making him look like a human-shaped goat. "It is obvious why they were there," he said. "They sought to attack my daughter. To take her from me and make her a prisoner in hopes that I would bow to their will."

"Bastards," I whispered in indignation.

"Indeed," agreed the Imperior, his whiskered eyebrows furrowing. "Indeed they are."

I wasn't about to correct him, of course. The fact was that the Forked Tong or Skang Kei family didn't have the slightest clue about Mitsu being there with me. Which is not to say they wouldn't have acted upon it if they had known. But they hadn't. In fact, when Mitsu ran off, they ignored her utterly and continued assailing me.

Which meant that they wanted something from me, not her.

Except I wasn't about to tell the Imperior that. Because he was reputed to be all-knowing, and one simply didn't correct all-knowing people, particularly when such corrections could cost you your life.

"Something," he continued, "must be done."

Speaking very delicately, for one never wanted to be too aggressive when dealing with a homicidal loon, I said, "Well . . . perhaps I was misinformed, your illustriousness, but I have heard tell that you have issued a reward for any who are able to help bring an end to the Forked Tong and their associates . . . including the Anaïs Ninjas. Is that correct?"

"Yes. Yes, you have heard truly," said the Imperior. He stepped down from his throne, and I was amused to see that he came up barely to shoulder level on me. Since I was hardly a giant of a man, it certainly cut down on his regalness, at least for me. He looked me up and down. "I am an excellent judge of character, Po. And I . . ." He glanced down. "What is this doing here?"

He was looking at the corpse of the handmaiden.

"She took her life, Father, in order to please you." There was no anger, no edge to Mitsu's comment. To her it was simply by way of explanation. She was so matter-of-fact about it that it prompted me to wonder just how many times this scene had been played out in similar fashion on other occasions.

"I know that," he said. "Why isn't it cleaned up?"

Immediately a squad of servants charged forward. Two of them were carrying a large piece of cloth, and they used it to roll up the body. The rest of them used cleaning materials to wipe up the spilled blood as best they could. My guess was that they would come back later with washing fluids to try and get up the remainder of the mess. My further guess was that they had a good deal of experience with it.

The message was obvious: Life here was cheap.

"I am an excellent judge of character, Po," he repeated, "and it is my belief that you would do well to serve on my council."

"What?" The decision caught me off guard. At that moment my major concern was trying to figure out what to do if he started demanding I eviscerate myself because he didn't like my haircut or thought that I'd looked at him cross-eyed. An advisory position was the furthest thing from my mind.

"Yes. There has been a place open on my council ever since the departure of my sick younger brother."

"Oh. Well, I . . . I hope he recovers soon."

"I doubt he will," said the Imperior, in a tone that implied to me that the brother might not have gotten sick all on his own. That his older brother might have given him some help on that score. I suspected the less I knew of that, the better.

"But Your Graciousness," I reminded him, "I am simply a humble messenger . . ."

"It is the wise man who knows his own humility. It is settled." He clapped his hands briskly and more retainers rushed forward. I couldn't blame them for rushing. Around this place, the slightest hesitation could result in personal disaster. "Bring Po to a guest suite. See that he is bathed. He smells distinctly like fish. Make certain he is provided with proper garments. I shall receive him first thing in the morning." Almost as an afterthought, he turned to me and said, "Would you like to have sex?"

I felt as if I'd been struck in the head with a mallet. The old man was looking at me expectantly. "Your . . . Greatness, I . . . I don't know what to say . . ."

"Either 'yes' or 'no' would be acceptable answers."

"I . . . of course, I'm . . . I'm just . . . wondering whether I'm . . . I'm worthy of such an honor . . ."

Mitsu, smirking, said, "He means with a female bathing attendant. Not with him."

I felt a great weight unclench from my chest. "Oh. Uhm . . . very generous, Your Worship, but . . . I'm not interested right now . . ."

"Males are also available," suggested Mitsu.

"I'm not in the mood, all right?" I said frostily to Mitsu.

"As you wish," said the Imperior, and clapped his hands.

The last sight I had of the throne room was the attendants trying to mop up the blood of the fallen handmaiden.

Chapter 3

Tub Thumping

*B*athing was a curious proposition, particularly since there was another man in the tub.

As much as I had no idea of what to expect in the royal palace, the notion that there was a man in the tub when I arrived at the bathing area was another level of lack of expectation entirely.

I was wearing a white linen robe upon my arrival, accompanied by a young woman who kept refusing to make eye contact with me no matter how much I encouraged her to do so. I stopped when I saw the scowling, bare-chested man lounging in a very large wooden tub in the center of the room. There was also a large drain to one side, which allowed any water splashing upon the floor to run off.

"I'm sorry," I said slowly. "I . . . didn't know this was occupied. We can come back later . . ."

"Bathe," he said brusquely. His face was long and square-jawed, and his eyes were slate gray and hard, hard as granite. His gravelly voice rumbled from deep within his chest. This was someone who could probably break me in half with his bare hands.

I was so distracted that I was barely paying attention

when the serving girl pulled the robe off me, leaving me standing there stark naked and rather self-conscious about the whole thing. Gods knew I'd been sexually active in my life . . . particularly during one time when a magic ring lodged on my privates had brought me more female companionship than most men experienced in five lifetimes. Yet I still felt embarrassed about standing nude in front of this young girl who was a total stranger . . . not to mention being subjected to the withering glance of the man in the tub. And I do mean withering.

She then proceeded to wash me down with warm cloths. It was relaxing, but I was a bit puzzled. "What are you doing?" I asked, trying to separate my mind from the fact that this attractive young woman was busily scrubbing my buttocks.

"Cleaning you, sir," she said.

"Then . . . what's the point of the bath?"

The man in the tub replied, as if speaking to a fool, "Bring a filthy body into the bath? The water will become dirty and unusable."

I was about to toss off a retort before realizing that he had a valid point. So I simply stood there and allowed her to wash me off, which was probably the best thing that had happened to me that day, or even in the past month. Once she'd cleaned me to her satisfaction, she gestured toward the tub. I looked at the man warily. He didn't seem to be going anywhere. The tub was wide enough, however, that there was ample room for two. In fact, half a dozen people could have fit in there with little to no difficulty.

So I eased myself into the tub, forcing a smile, and making sure that no part of me came into contact with the other man. He continued to scowl. I was starting to think it was the only expression at his command.

There was a small wooden ridge extending from beneath

the water which appeared to run the circumference of the tub. Obviously it was there to sit on, and I did so. The wood was smooth, for which I was grateful. I wasn't interested in getting splinters in delicate areas.

There was a long silence then. Finally I told him, "I am called Po."

He stared at me for some time. I couldn't begin to imagine what he was thinking, his face was such a deadpan. Finally he said, "I am Go Nogo."

"I see."

"What are you doing here?"

"Well . . ." I wasn't sure where to begin. "I . . . was told I should bathe, and after having my things put in my room, I was brought here to—"

"What are you doing here, in the Forbidding City?" he interrupted.

"Oh. That. Well . . . I was sent here by a great king as an emissary . . ."

"No."

"No?"

"A king is one who operates from a level of strength," said Go Nogo. "He would choose as his emissary one who reflects that strength. He would not choose one who is lame of leg, for that would send a message to all who saw him that the king is weak as well."

"Really," I said, my mouth drawn tight. "And yet the Imperior, who draws his inspiration from the gods, accepts me at my word. Are you saying that the Divine One is wrong and you are right? I would hate to think you would try to elevate yourself above him. Seems rather insulting. Even dishonorable. You might be asked to apologize by gutting yourself like a trout."

His face darkened even more than it had been, and I

knew I had him then. "I would gladly lay down my life in the service of the Imperior."

"If laying down your life is what you're interested in doing, then judging by what I've seen, you're working for the right fellow. By the way, if I may ask, what do you do here? What's your function, I mean."

And suddenly I was submerged.

Go Nogo had reached across the tub underwater, quick as a swamp snake, and grabbed my ankle. Considering my relative vulnerability at that moment, I suppose I should have been grateful that my ankle was all he was grabbing. But I was hardly in a position to express gratitude for anything, considering he had pulled me sharply toward him. I slid right off the seat and it was only by a miracle that I didn't strike the back of my head upon it as I went under.

I tried to sit up, but was unable to as his hand shoved down on my chest, pushing all the air out of my lungs. I grabbed at his forearm, tried to push him away, but wasn't at all successful. I might as well have been trying to uproot an oak tree. *Assassin! He's an assassin! An assassin from the Forked Tong! I'm going to die. Underwater, in a damned bathtub, at the hands of a stranger, I'm going to die. Well . . . at least I didn't have to have sex with the Imperior . . .*

Suddenly the pressure was gone. Instantly I splashed upward, and when my head broke the surface, great geysers of water blasted out of my lungs. I thought I was going to accomplish the singular feat of drowning while above the surface of the water, but thirty seconds of violent coughing, spasming, and heaving later, I had managed to get all the water out of my chest.

The bathing wench was kneeling nearby, her hands daintily placed upon her thighs. Go Nogo was seated on the opposite side of the tub, his face as inscrutable as it had been before. And standing nearby, her hands on her hips, was Mitsu. She was wearing a plain white kimono and was looking far more like a female than when I'd first met her.

"Are you quite through, Go?" she demanded.

"What the hell did you do that for?" I said. Actually, "said" may be too generous. I managed to get the sentence out one or two words at a time in between gasps.

"A warning."

"Doesn't anyone around here believe in just *saying* what's on their mind instead of trying to kill somebody or making sure they kill themselves?! Why is everything life-and-death with you people?"

"Life and death are intertwined," said Go Nogo. "To accept the way of one is to accept the inevitability of the other. It does not matter when death comes. Only how one dies is of consequence."

"All right, well, I'm casting a vote right now for in my bed of old age!"

He snorted disdainfully at that, and then rose from the tub, at which point I was able to see for myself just why he would hold me—and probably a good deal of the rest of mankind—in disdain.

Mitsu barely afforded him a glance. These people were amazingly blasé about nudity, which was interesting considering I hadn't seen any such attitudes among the farmers back in Hosbiyu. And considering the attractive figures of some of those farm girls, they couldn't have gotten me to leave in any manner short of swordpoint if they'd had such customs.

Go Nogo picked up a robe from a peg where it was hanging nearby, and draped it around himself. "Remember my warning," he said. Then he turned, bowed once to the princess, and walked out with a swagger that was almost as impressive as the rest of him.

"He's an assassin!" I said the moment he was out of earshot. "He would have killed me if you hadn't—"

My voice caught. Princess Mitsu had divested herself of her robe and was now standing naked as her birthday. Her breasts were quite small, almost childlike. The rest of her figure, though, belied the notion that she was in any way immature. The only thing that managed to draw my attention away from the more traditional eye-catching parts of her body was the fascinating tattoo she had on her right arm which stretched to her upper shoulder. It was a dragon (no shock there), its tail encircling down to her elbow and its head coming up and over her shoulder. Its mouth was open and it had a long, fierce, red tongue extended angling down toward her . . .

Quickly I looked away again.

Several bathing maidens had entered and were washing her down with cloths. She looked rather bored. "He wouldn't have killed you. He simply becomes overenthusiastic sometimes." Then I heard her chuckle from behind me. "You know, this is the first time you've lowered your gaze from me. Do you have a problem with naked women where you come from?"

"Not under certain circumstances. But these are not those."

"Ahhh. You associate the naked body of the opposite sex with intercourse, yes?"

"And you don't?"

She shook her head as she gestured for the maidens to step aside, and she approached the tub. My mind flew back to the last time I was in a tub with a naked woman. It had been the Lady Kate, back when I was peacelord, and a good time was had by all. Then I suddenly began to feel a certain degree of urgency in my loins, stemming from both my recollection of times past and what was occurring now. I came to the realization that if I didn't get the hell out of the tub at that moment, my condition would reach the point where exiting the tub and displaying my "enthusiasm" would simply prove far too embarrassing.

And I did not want to take any chance of anything happening with Mitsu in the tub. The circumstances were very different from what had transpired between Princess Entipy and myself, but there were enough similarities that I wanted to steer very clear of any possible repetition. To say nothing of the fact that her father was a crazy man who thought that requiring people to kill themselves was a perfectly acceptable way to conduct one's daily routine. I had no desire to be added to that rapidly expanding list of corpses.

I lurched to my feet, moving quickly, turning my back to Mitsu. My back, admittedly, was also naked, but it was less inflammatory. I splashed out onto the floor and my slick feet went out from under me, causing me to fall flat. This was one occasion I didn't mind, however, since it helped conceal that which I far preferred to keep to myself.

There was amused laughter from Mitsu and the other women, but I didn't care. I quickly got my robe around me, and draped a towel around my middle for good measure. With a sigh of relief, I got to my feet and leaned against the tub.

Mitsu was in the middle of the tub, looking very relaxed. She was regarding me with a raised eyebrow. "Are you quite all right?" she inquired.

"As right as I can be considering someone was trying to kill me less than a minute ago."

"I told you, he was just warning you. Go Nogo takes his position very seriously."

"And what position is that?" I demanded, grabbing another towel and drying my hair. "Lord high executioner?"

"No. Head of security."

"Wonderful." I stared at her more openly considering she was submerged from the neck down. "So you wandered about and your father objected."

"He objects to anything I do that would be akin to what a man does," she replied airily. "He believes females should know their place. Do you?" she asked.

I shrugged. "I don't even know what *my* place is. I wouldn't presume to tell someone else to know theirs. And how did you get together with Mordant?"

"Mordant?" She raised the other eyebrow, both of them meeting somewhat near the top of her forehead.

"The drabit. You know . . . the small dragon . . ."

"Oh. Yes." She made a casual, dismissive gesture. "He caught my fancy in the circus cage. I decided it was unfair such a creature should be imprisoned. So I decided to free him. Simple as that."

I knew perfectly well it wasn't that simple. The princess may have been many things, but a skilled liar was not among them. But there was no point in pressing her on it.

"I am very impressed, by the way," she said.

"Oh. Well," I cleared my throat, not knowing whether to feel pride or self-conscious. "I mean, the water was just a little bit cold, but I'm flattered that you would—"

"With the way you handled my father," said Mitsu.

"Oh."

"Earlier. The manner in which you manipulated my father's beliefs, played to his sense of godly superiority. That was very deft. You might fit in here after all."

"I'm just a visitor," I said, shaking my head vigorously. "And, considering what transpired here minutes ago, not even all that welcome a visitor at that."

"You should not sell yourself short, Apropos . . . all evidence to the contrary." When she saw my face fall upon that comment, she laughed lightly. "You are a very serious individual. You need to become more relaxed. Do you see that table?"

She pointed to a table standing nearby. I nodded. "Go lie down flat upon it. Remove your robe. Keep the towel around your middle if you wish."

"I really don't see how . . ."

"Do as I say," she said firmly.

Deciding it wouldn't be wise to press matters with her, I limped over to the table, removed my robe (but maintained the towel, as per her suggestion), and lay flat.

I had no idea what to expect. Then I heard the quick movements of bare running feet, and one of the bath maidens landed feetfirst upon my back. I gasped in surprise. She weighed almost nothing; her bones must have been hollow. "Now . . . now just a minute," I started to say.

Then she started to move across my back, digging her toes in, loosening the muscles. I couldn't believe it as the tension began to seep out of me.

"Feeling a bit more at ease, Apropos?" inquired the princess.

I tried to reply, but all I was able to manage was an inarticulate "ggrrcchh."

"There are many techniques, many aspects of Chinpan of which you can avail yourself. If you do not do so, it would be a great tragedy."

I should have just lain flat and enjoyed it. Instead I forced myself to look over in her direction as she soaked in the tub. "And if I fail to do so . . . will I be required to kill myself?"

She looked puzzled. "No. Why would you?"

"Why was that young woman?"

"Oh." She seemed to have forgotten about her. "Yes. Well . . . she was required to take my place. The Imperior can't very well be executing, or demanding ritual suicide of, his only daughter, now, can he?"

"Doesn't it bother you that your actions cause others to suffer?"

"Does that never happen where you come from?"

"*No!*" Then I paused and amended, "Well . . . royal families do have whipping boys. When young princes misbehave, the whipping boys are flogged since the persons of royalty are sacrosanct. But . . . that's different . . . and they don't kill the poor bastard . . ."

The girl on my back placed her toes on the back of my neck, and started to manipulate something within between her toes. I felt a jolt of energy that seemed to originate at the bottom of my brain and ran through all the way to my feet.

"And if two kings are not able to get along? If they have disputes over borders or some such, and declare war upon each other?" asked Mitsu. "Are not soldiers summoned to serve as proxies, to fight and die in the name of a dispute that the rulers simply couldn't be bothered to settle in a less terminal way?"

"You're distorting it, Princess . . ."

"Am I? Seems to me I'm putting things perfectly accurately, and you simply don't wish to acknowledge that."

"It is pointless to continue this discussion, Mitsu. I do not wish to offend you, but fear if we keep on talking about it, then sooner or later I will."

"As you wish," she said diplomatically.

Truthfully, I really didn't want to risk angering her. But even more important, I didn't want any more distractions from the astounding things the incredibly light woman was doing to my back. I allowed myself to succumb to the pure pleasure of it. The next thing I knew, the bathing maiden was shaking me gently.

I had fallen asleep, and was feeling tremendously rested.

I looked around. The princess was gone. The other maidens were gone. Only this one remained. I had half turned over and the towel had fallen away. She was regarding me with interest, and then she said very politely, "Sex now?"

"What's your name?"

"Timtup."

"You know what, Timtup? Life's too short not to be polite," I said, and accommodated her.

When I returned to my quarters some time later, I almost jumped twenty feet in the air when a soft voice said from overhead, "I wouldn't leave my weapons alone next time."

I spun in a circle, nearly falling over, and then looked up. Hanging in the rafters overhead, dangling by his tail, was Mordant.

"Where the hell have you been?!" I demanded. Even as I spoke, I glanced in the direction of where I had laid down my weapons. They were exactly as I had left them. "And what have you gotten me into?"

"Gotten *you* into?" retorted Mordant, dropping onto my bed. His tail whipped back and forth lazily as he curled up upon the pillow. "May I remind you that you're the one who wanted to come to Taikyo."

"And you're the one who knew we were traveling with a damned princess."

"What, you don't like her?" He sounded faintly sarcastic.

"Oh, I like her just fine for someone who stands there and lets her servants be butchered and then walks around ass-naked, prepared to climb into a bath with any stranger she happens to encounter. She's just wonderful."

He cocked his head and said, "You don't understand this culture, Apropos. Until you do, don't presume to pass judgment on it."

"I'll pass judgment on anything I damned please,

Mordant, thank you very much. You could have told me she was a princess, you know."

"And if I had?"

I sat down on the far edge of the bed, studying him carefully. "I don't want to get into 'if you had.' What I want to know is why you didn't."

"She was traveling incognito. I decided to respect her privacy." He dropped his head onto his forepaws, which were crisscrossed one atop the other.

"I see. And is there anything else you're neglecting to tell me? Any other major piece of information I'd benefit from having?"

He yawned widely, his long tongue flicking in and out repeatedly as he did so. "None that springs readily to mind. Other than that the Skang Kei family have obviously targeted you for some reason."

"Obviously," I said, "but why?"

"I don't know. Can you think of anything you might have done to offend them? Or the Forked Tong?"

"Possibly," I admitted, thinking of the events that had occurred back in Hosbiyu. "But they'd have to know the village I'd come from, and things that had occurred there that they couldn't possibly know."

"Never underestimate what the Forked Tong might and might not know," warned Mordant. "They have eyes and ears everywhere. You never know who might be feeding them information."

The thought chilled me. Everyone in the village was well aware of all that had transpired. They knew that Ali had slain the representatives of the Skang Kei. They knew of my altercation with the Anaïs Ninjas. If one of them had some sort of secret ties to the Forked Tong, then word would have been out about me. And how difficult would it have been to make certain I was found? I could just see the message: "Look for the man with red hair who bears a resemblance to absolutely no one else in the entire country."

"Wonderful," I muttered. I looked at him warily. "How do I know I can trust you?"

"Because there's no such thing as a talking dragon," Mordant reminded me. "Any fool would tell you that. So who would possibly want to ally themselves with something that cannot possibly exist?"

The argument had a pleasantly perverse, twisted logic to it. I liked it.

"So you will be watching my back while I'm in residence here, is that it?"

Mordant yawned once more. "If you'd like," he said casually. "But don't let that allow you to get lazy."

"You needn't worry about that," I assured him. "Trying to keep an eye out for people who might be trying to kill me is something of a full-time occupation for me. In fact, I met a brand-new one just today. His name is—"

"Go Nogo?"

"Right. You know him?"

"Only that he is one of the deadliest warriors in the city, and one of the most highly decorated and respected captains of the Hamunri there is. If he wants you dead, then you are pretty much dead."

"Wonderful," I said. "Comforting to know that, no matter how far I go in my life, I always seem to wind up exactly in the same place as before. Why is that, Mordant? Why do people take an instant dislike to me?"

"It saves time."

I frowned at him. "That is a very old joke, Mordant."

"The reason jokes become old is because they're true."

Unfortunately, I couldn't think of a response to that.

Chapter 4

Pillow Talk

*W*alking was never my strong suit even under the best of conditions. Considering how relaxed I was by the next morning, however, I was damned lucky to be able to move at all.

I was escorted from my rather sumptuous quarters to the council chamber of the Imperior. There I found the Imperior with half a dozen other men, one of whom was the glowering Go Nogo. They were seated in a semicircle, the Imperior in the middle. They were not on chairs, but rather reclining against oversized pillows.

Feeling it appropriate, I bowed to him and he nodded in acknowledgment. "Did you sleep well, Po?" he inquired solicitously.

"Yes, thank you, Your Eminence."

"And the bath? Was it likewise restful?"

I looked straight at Go Nogo, who said nothing. "It was . . . more exciting than I could possibly have anticipated, Your Marvelousness."

"Good," he said. "Sit down. You know everyone here?"

"No," I told him, easing myself down onto an oversized pillow, decorated with strange pictures of long-limbed birds standing upon one leg.

"Good," he said again. "Then we can begin."

Which was the closest I came to getting an introduction to the members of his inner cabinet. Aside from Go Nogo, the only other name I caught was that of his chief advisor, Itso Esi, a squat fellow with a scowl that went even deeper than that of Go Nogo. The others made no effort to introduce themselves. I couldn't blame them. For all I knew, doing so would instantly require sacrificing one's life in order to placate the Imperior.

Such a situation was not conducive to my desiring to stay where I was. Obviously the other members of this court served the Imperior for reasons that were deeply ingrained into their society, into their very being. I was not so inculcated, and was perfectly willing to depart from this curious and off-putting place whenever it seemed necessary. Indeed, I couldn't help but feel that I was risking my life with every passing moment that I remained.

Still, I hadn't forgotten those things which had brought me there in the first place. Considering that the Skang Kei family, and this mysterious Ho they served, had targeted me specifically, my simply departing Taikyo without protection from the Imperior might be problematic.

I felt naked without my weapons, but I'd been informed early on that none were to be armed in the presence of the Imperior during closed council, presumably so he didn't have to worry about assassination attempts. It seemed a reasonable enough concern. Still, I was glad that Mordant was in my room, keeping an eye on them. I never knew when I might need them, and he'd be there protecting them in case someone tried to relieve me of them. I was particularly concerned about Go Nogo, who might take it upon himself as head of security to make sure that I was as helpless as possible.

"The Forked Tong," said the Imperior, "must be done

away with. It is bad enough that their criminal activities throughout Chinpan have created an embarrassment and inconvenience for me. But now they have targeted my daughter. The princess Mitsu would be in their hands right now if it had not been for our visitor," and he indicated me. He turned and glowered at Go Nogo. "How could you have allowed that to occur, Captain?"

"Personally, I'm shocked you haven't offered to kill yourself just from the sheer disgrace of it," I said helpfully.

If he could have spit knives at me at that moment, he very likely would have. He spoke to the Imperior while watching me the entire time. "I had men searching for the princess everywhere, Divine One," he said slowly. "There are always challenges involved when it comes to protecting one who desires protection. When the situation involves one who has no desire to be protected, it becomes even more difficult."

The Imperior considered that a moment, and then said to me, "Would your king accept such an excuse, most honorable Po?"

Part of me wanted to say no, absolutely not. But there was no second-guessing what the Imperior might do with any given reply. Opting for neutrality, I simply said, "It is not for a humble messenger to speculate on the inner workings of my liege lord's mind. It is possible he might accept it. It is equally possible he might not. He is a man of many moods and many mysteries . . . as are you yourself."

"Yes," said the Imperior. "I would like to meet this ruler of yours at some point, Po. If and when you depart our land, it will be with the instruction to bring him here so we may talk."

Those were daunting words from the Imperior. I could not, of course, produce King Runcible, or any other king for that matter. But the most chilling aspect of his state-

ment was the "if and when" part . . . specifically, the "if." I
didn't take to the notion of my future being that much up
in the air.

Fortunately the Imperior seemed incapable of holding a
thought in his mind for more than a minute or so. Before I
could formulate a reply, he was already back talking about
the Forked Tong.

"You have offered reward after reward," observed Itso Esi,
"and still information about them remains scarce. It might
be time to take a new direction in dealing with them."

"Such as?"

"An all-out assault," said Itso Esi. "Seek them out
throughout the countryside. Root them out, wherever they
may be hiding. Make that the number-one priority of the
Hamunri."

"With all respect, Divine One," Go Nogo said carefully,
"the forces of the Hamunri are not endless. Ours is an elite
group. Your first, best line of defense. We have enemies
within and without. Devoting too much of the Hamunri
to any one opponent can be . . . difficult."

Deciding to take the chance of holding Nogo's feet to the
fire, I said, "I am a mere stranger to these shores. But it
seems to me that your job would be to accomplish what
His Splendidness asked you to do, rather than listing the
reasons why you cannot do so."

"I did not say I could not do so," came the icy reply. "I
merely was endeavoring to explain . . ."

"I did not ask for explanations, Captain," said the
Imperior, and although there was no anger in his voice,
there was clearly a lack of patience. "Simply results."

It was all I could do not to pump the air in triumph with
my fist. Looking back, it was a fairly insane thing for me to
do, to bait Nogo in that way. But I was already convinced
that Go Nogo had it in for me. So I really felt as if I had

very little to lose, and everything to gain. If they all felt compelled to disembowel themselves every time their ruler became impatient with them, I might be looking at Nogo's spilled innards before noon.

"Yes, Imperior" was all Nogo said, this time looking directly at the floor in deference. "If that is what you wish, the full attention of the Hamunri will be turned to it."

"See that it is," the Imperior replied.

"I would be most interested, however," Go Nogo continued unexpectedly, "to know precisely why members of the Skang Kei family were attacking our esteemed visitor in the streets of the fish market."

"Yes, that is puzzling," said Itso Esi, and the others were nodding as well. It didn't seem to me that Esi had any personal agenda in the way that Nogo obviously did. He just appeared curious.

"They said they were working for someone called Ho," I said after a moment. "Does the name mean anything to any of you?"

"A legend," Itso Esi said immediately. "The reputed leader of the Skang Kei family. If the Ho even exists, virtually nothing is known about him. Or her. It's uncertain even if the Ho is a man or a woman."

"If this Ho does exist, naturally it's a man," Go Nogo said with obvious impatience. "The idea of a woman running an organization dedicated to death and destruction? Why, it is absurd. Ridiculous."

"Don't be so certain," I said. "Some of the deadliest creatures I've ever known have been female."

But the Imperior was shaking his head. "Go Nogo is correct. No mere woman could ever achieve such an exalted rank."

"As you say, O Illustrious One," I said promptly, not wanting to take any chances.

"Discussing a fictional leader is of no relevance, Po," Go Nogo said intently and fixed his gaze upon me. "What matters is, why were you singled out?"

"What are you implying?"

"Nothing, honorable Po," was his gruff response. "I am merely asking."

"Well, I thought we had been over that," I said quietly. "They were attacking the princess, and I simply happened to be there to defend her."

"I see," said Nogo. "And you had no business dealings with them?"

"I am not in the habit of engaging in dealings with criminals. Why, honorable Nogo? Are you? I'm not implying anything, you understand. Just asking."

"What are you saying?" asked the Imperior.

"He challenges my honor, Divine One," said Go Nogo.

Sensing a trap, I shook my head. "I did not mean to imply wrongdoing on the part of your head of security, O Gargantuan One. I hope you did not think I meant to do so."

"I think nothing of the sort," the Imperior said. "I just couldn't hear you. I'm an old man and my hearing isn't what it was. So I was asking what you were saying."

Nogo and I exchanged looks and, for a heartbeat, there was a moment of shared amusement between us. Then we immediately remembered that we were supposed to be in opposition to each other.

"I was merely pointing out," I said, "that one should make sure one's own house is in order before embarking on major forays against enemies."

"Yes! Exactly!" said the Imperior with far more enthusiasm than I would have thought such a casual remark warranted. "Who told you about my house?"

That stopped me cold. I looked in bewilderment at the others.

"The Imperior is speaking of the new house he desires to build," Itso Esi explained.

"A new house? May I ask what is wrong with this one?"

"Nothing," said the Imperior. "It is divine perfection, as are all things associated with me. But I require a house at the outer provinces. In fact," and his eyes widened in eagerness, "I am calling upon you, Po, to design it!"

"Wh-what?" I was getting that familiar sinking feeling I typically had when I found myself in a situation that was going to be overwhelming. "Design . . . what? A house?"

"Yes," he said, clearly pleased with the idea. "A new palace, to provide shelter when I visit the outer provinces."

This was a situation that called for the greatest of tact. As judiciously as I humanly could, I leaned forward and said, "That is . . . a great honor, O Resplendent One, but I have no experience as an architect or designer of buildings. As anxious as I am to serve you, I must wonder why you would—"

"Because you know of designs of other lands," the Imperior said with growing excitement. "You would be able to bring a fresh eye and different perspective."

"Again, Imperior, I am . . . honored, but certainly I think there would be others who could do a far superior job . . ."

"There had been," said Itso Esi with just the slightest hint of annoyance on his face. "However, their designs had not been up to the Imperior's high standards."

Which told me all I needed to know: The previous holders of this illustrious position had all been asked to remove themselves from this plane of existence due to dishonor.

"I . . . see," I said, not liking the direction this was going.

"Of course," continued the Imperior, "I would not ask you to undertake such an endeavor without appropriate compensation."

"Oh?"

"Shall we say . . . a million yeng?"

I could see from the expressions of the others that this was an unexpected development, and no doubt a fairly healthy outlay of funds to serve as an incentive bonus. Considering the reward for the destruction of the Forked Tong was ten million yeng, this had suddenly turned from a no-win scenario to one that was rife with possibilities.

Granted, yes, I had no experience whatsoever as an architect. But I had advantages over my predecessors. For one thing, my mandate would be to design a building that looked like nothing the Imperior had seen. That should not prove difficult at all. And I was confident enough in my ability to manipulate discussions that I was certain I could handle the Imperior. That might have been foolish pride talking rather than a reasonable perspective, but my ability to deceive others was pretty much the only aspect of my personality that I genuinely did take pride in, so I suppose I could be forgiven the flash of arrogance.

A healthy reward for drawing pictures of buildings, while the destruction of the Forked Tong and their criminal associates who had killed Ali was being handled by armed soldiers with no risk whatsoever to myself. Yes indeed, matters were shaping up rather nicely at that.

I bowed deeply, so deeply that I almost tumbled forward off the pillow. When I righted myself, I said carefully, "Imperior, it would be an honor to serve you in this manner."

Go Nogo looked at me very suspiciously. I could intuit why. He wanted to be pleased over this development. To convince himself that I had just willingly shoved my head into a noose and invited it to be drawn closed around my neck. But my confidence was disconcerting to the point where he no doubt wondered just what it was I had up my sleeve. That was fine by me. The more I could do to keep adversaries off balance, the better I liked it.

"Have you considered taking advantage of my daughter?"

I had been in the midst of drinking tea when the Imperior asked me the question, and my rather ungenteel response was to blow a good part of it out my nose.

Several weeks had passed since the initial discussion in the council chamber which had led to my rather curious installation as chief architect . . . curious since I had no experience at it.

And yet the entire process had gone remarkably smoothly. Fortunately enough, I had lived in the castle of King Runcible for more than enough time to memorize every nook and cranny of the place. So all I really had to do was draw a reasonable representation of Runcible's castle and I was set.

I quickly realized I would have to do multiple drawings, since otherwise there would be an overlap of the images and it would be impossible to distinguish one from the other. So I did half a dozen different designs, beginning with one that laid out the castle's outer garrison wall, followed by the interior towers, the courtyard, and other accouterments. I worked closely with Itso Esi, who, for all his officiousness, was an efficient enough fellow. He seemed genuinely interested in the designs, and kept saying he wanted to do everything he could to make certain my "vision" was realized. He even simplified my life by providing me with cleverly designed paper with clearly delineated grids upon it. I could use them to indicate scale. I was told that each grid equaled "ten feet," and that was a relief as well. I wasn't anxious to learn an entirely new method of measurement, so it was convenient that the Chinpanese used the same calibrations as I was accustomed to.

Of even greater relief to me was the Imperior's enthusiasm for the designs. I felt I was walking a tightrope with a shark-filled moat for a net when I first presented the drawings to the Imperior. Despite Esi's claims that he thought them dazzling, I was not fooling myself. The moment the Imperior said he disliked them, I knew I'd be on my own.

Fortunately enough, that didn't happen. Instead the Imperior looked over the drawings with growing excitement, his aged head bobbing up and down as if threatening to tumble off his shoulders. "Yes," he kept saying, "yes, exactly, yes." He clearly could not have been happier, and if that's how he felt about it, naturally I did as well.

During that time, Go Nogo was hardly around. On the occasions when I did see him, he was deep in discussion with members of his elite Hamunri guards, and I would constantly hear words like "Tong" and "Skang Kei" bandied about. Clearly he was doing everything within his power to act upon the Imperior's wishes. I wished him all the luck that I would normally wish upon someone who had tried to drown me.

Meanwhile, I was feeling growing excitement with my current assignment. Believe it or not, as I contemplated the reward, I was thinking about the impact it would have— not on my life, but on the lives of the villagers of Hosbiyu.

Yes, I was actually dwelling upon improving not my own life, but the lives of others. For the longer I was away from the simple folk of Hosbiyu, the more I came to realize that I had really, truly enjoyed my time there. Indeed, I had been more purely happy in Hosbiyu for a longer period than any other segment of my life. The more I thought about it, the more I became convinced that my return there was not only likely, but a certainty.

In a strange sort of way, it was the classic tale. The young man from the farming village embarks upon a journey of discovery, has some adventures, and then returns to his village wiser in the ways of the world, with rewards for the people of the village that would enrich their lives.

Granted, there were some significant differences in my case. First and foremost, I was not a young man. By that point in my life, I had reached my mid-twenties. Astonishing to consider, really. When one took into account the number of times people had tried to kill me, it would have seemed rather unlikely I would make it out of my teens. Second, my "adventures" mostly entailed trying to stay the hell out of trouble rather than throwing myself into the thick of the fray, as most such mythic heroes did.

On the other hand, what I found most attractive about the notion was that it made me the center of the story.

It was a view that seemed peculiar to me, but I had a singular awareness of the world that no one else appeared to possess.

Everyone liked to believe that they were the center of their own little universe. But only I seemed blessed—or, more correctly, cursed—with the awareness that my own existence was of so little consequence, that it was never important enough to be the center of anything, including my own life. Instead I excelled at being germane to other people's adventures. I was a sidekick, a supporting character, or—most discouraging of all—an obstacle to be overcome while the hero went on to some great accomplishment.

You, of course, might think me mad. Who considers the world in that way? In terms of fiction and romance and novel concepts instead of the true, factual way of things?

In answer to the question: I do. I had an epiphany one day, you see, and it is really quite impossible to convince others who have not had an epiphany of the truth of things. So those of you who would consider me mad, I would in turn consider you to be poor, unfortunate souls who likely don't even enjoy the rank of being a secondary or supporting player in a grand epic. The vast majority of you are very likely relegated to being mere faces in the crowd or—worst of all—spear fodder. Corpses on legs, walking about until the next great war or unleashed disease or act of barbaric brutality occurs, at which point you will simply be one of the many bodies heaped into a pile to help underscore the tragic seriousness of the predicament. You won't even survive to see how it all turns out.

As much as you might feel sorry for me in thinking me demented, I likewise feel sorry for you. I understand the way of things while you are simply destined to live and die as a mere shadow being in an epic that you didn't even know was being spun. As much as I despised the being I was, I wouldn't want to be you for all the tea in Chinpan.

So . . .

My plans for the Imperior's new estate were met with great enthusiasm by the ruler of Chinpan, and they were immediately shipped out to the outer province where a vast army of workers had apparently been sitting idle for quite some time. The Imperior was most pleased to be able to set them to work. And if the Imperior was happy, then I was happy, bordering on ecstatic.

In the evenings I would chat with Mordant, who seemed to have an almost supernatural ability to keep himself out of sight. Then again, he was a talking dragon, so perhaps "supernatural" was not out of the realm of possibility.

That left the princess Mitsu who, to be honest, I kept hoping would run away again.

It wasn't that she was all that much of a difficulty for me. After our rather stimulating encounter in the bath, I had hardly run into her at all. Considering the size of the palace, it really wasn't that odd that I did not encounter her.

One day, however, I was invited to a private tea with the Imperior. This, of course, made me nervous. A small table sat between us as tea steeped in the center, and serving girls poured out for us as the Imperior nodded in approval. I was just taking the initial sip of the beverage when he brought up the notion of "taking advantage" of his daughter, at which point I lost control of both myself and the tea. I could only be grateful that, when the liquid sprayed, it did so primarily over myself rather than the Imperior. I could only imagine what the penalty was for blasting tea out one's nose all over the divine personage of the ruler of Chinpan. Actually, I didn't have to imagine all that hard. I could readily guess what it was.

"Take . . . advantage, Imperior?" I managed to cough out as the serving girl helped dab me clean. "I . . . I don't—"

"She is an intelligent female . . . for a female, that is," he added. "She has been trained by the finest self-defense teachers in Chinpan. She might be of use in teaching you fighting techniques."

"Ah," I said, calming somewhat. "Well, that is . . . that's an intriguing notion, Great One. Very intriguing. And generous." The serving girl had poured another cup and I started to drink from it.

"Plus you might want to have sex with her."

This time the tea did not exit explosively. Instead I choked on it. It took me a few moments to pull myself together as the Imperior simply stared at me, his eyes peaceful and relaxed.

"Your, uh . . . your people's approach to sexual union . . . is a bit more straightforward than mine, Your Stupendousness," I said.

"Is it?" He looked politely surprised.

"Yes. We . . . tend not to discuss it so blatantly. Nor, in

my culture, would a father offer intimacy with his daughter in so matter-of-fact a fashion. Unless, of course, she were a—"

"A what?"

I had been prepared to say "prostitute," but I realized an instant before the words escaped my lips that it probably wouldn't be the wisest thing to say. Quickly I substituted, "—princess. Of course. If she were a princess, and her father a king, well then naturally, different rules of conduct apply. Because when one is royalty and divinely inspired, there are no rules save that which the royalty makes up."

The Imperior nodded approvingly. "And that is as it should be," he said contentedly. Then, warming to the topic of his daughter's carnality, he said, "My daughter is very wise in the ways of pleasuring a man."

"Is she?" My voice was suddenly constricted.

"Oh yes. She has read many texts on the subject."

"Well . . . that's how I hear you get experience."

"It is possible you could learn much from her."

"I . . . have no doubt," I said. "But I . . . well, Imperior, you see . . . I am but a lowly messenger. Understand, I take great pride in the fact that you have treated me with such honor and respect. In here, however," and I touched my heart, "I cannot help but feel that I would not be worthy of such a . . . a treasure."

"Not worthy . . . ?" His face clouded, but then brightened. "Ah. I comprehend. And you are concerned that because of that feeling, you would be unable to perform as a man should."

"What? Now . . . wait. I didn't . . ."

"It is all right," he assured me, nodding and looking sympathetic. "You should not think the less of yourself simply because you are impotent."

"Imperior, I didn't say—"

"It happens to all men. Well . . . not to me. Never to me. But I am more than a man, so it is understandable. But do not worry, Po. Your secret is safe with me."

"Imperior, I am not impotent! I can function perfectly well! As well as the next man! Better than the next man!" I said with growing frustration. "Why, I could take your daughter right now and—"

"Very well," he said, and clapped his hands together briskly.

At which point I realized I'd well and truly screwed myself . . . appropriate, I suppose.

"Tell my daughter that the honorable Po will be coming to her chamber shortly, and she is to tend to him in the manner that a woman is supposed to tend to a man." He nodded gravely at me. "I will appreciate an excellent performance on your part, Po. It will help to take her mind off that foolish peasant boy."

"Peasant boy?" My mind was whirling. I felt as if I'd missed an entire part of the conversation.

"Yes. A pathetic young beggar who caught her fancy one day when she was out and about in the marketplace several years ago. She became obsessed with him. For a long time, she spoke of nothing else. Then one day he disappeared, as such creatures tend to do. She blamed me for that." He shook his head, looking aggrieved. "As if I am responsible for the comings and goings of gutter rats."

"It sounds most unfair," I agreed.

"Oh, it is," sighed the Imperior. "Even after all this time, she still brings him up. Take her mind off him, noble Po. If you are a man, you can accomplish this."

I gulped deeply.

Interesting thing about the doors in the palace, which I had not mentioned earlier: They were made of some sort of rice paper, stretched across wooden frames. Rather than opening like normal doors, they would slide from one side to the other, and you could see through them to some degree.

I stood outside the door that led into the princess's chamber and cleared my throat loudly. "Princess," I called, and was annoyed because my voice broke slightly. I cleared it again and said, "Mitsu?"

I heard movement from within and soft footsteps approaching the door. Then I saw the outline of her figure through the door. She was standing there like a shadow come to life. She stretched her arms luxuriously over her head, and I could tell—even though she was in shadow—that she was either unclothed, or wearing nothing to speak of.

"My father told me you would be coming here," she said.

"Yes, well . . . that's open to debate."

"Will you be entering?"

I suddenly felt the need to throw myself into a tub of ice water. "I . . . do not think that would be wise. At this time."

"My father desires it."

"Do you?"

"My father desires it."

"Ah." Well, that certainly answered that question, even though it wasn't being directly answered at all. "And what about your desires?"

"My desires?" There was a sharp, bitter laugh from the other side. "My desires are of no consequence, honorable Po. That has been made abundantly clear by my divine father. By everyone, really."

"And what about the boy? The boy in the marketplace?"

There was a brief silence, and I saw her "shadow" stiffen. "What of him?"

"Does he feel that way as well? That what you think is of no consequence?"

She said nothing in response.

"Mitsu?" I prompted.

"He was so beautiful," Mitsu said softly. From the way she spoke, it was as if I wasn't even there. As if she was talking to herself. "The moment I looked at him, I knew. I just knew. Have you ever looked at someone and just . . . known?"

"No," I admitted.

"It is as if you've been together in a previous life, and recognize each other from that earlier incarnation. The connection is just there, and you instantly know that you would do anything for that person. That they are more important to you than anything in the world, including yourself. Such is the power of that connection."

"I envy you that," and I meant it. "I'm not sure whether a cynic such as myself could ever feel that way."

"In any event . . . he's gone. And my father is responsible."

"You don't know that."

"I do." There should have been anger and ferocity in her tone, but instead she simply sounded resigned. "I do know it. And he knows I know it."

Unwillingly, my mind spun back to Entipy. She, too, had been in love with a young man who had earned the disapproval of those who "knew best." Her great love had been Tacit, my greatest friend in youth . . . and my greatest enemy in life. I had been consumed with jealousy upon learning of her feelings for Tacit, even though I had no particular affection for the princess. In truth, I actually disliked her intensely. But the mere fact of her devotion to Tacit was enough for me to use every means in my power to sunder their bond. And I had succeeded beyond my wildest dreams.

Odd. I'd never felt guilty about it until that moment.

"You are silent, Po," said Mitsu. "Why?"

"As . . . you are thinking of friends long gone, so am I," I said.

"Are we to have intimacy with each other, then?"

I took in a deep breath and then let it out unsteadily. "I would feel it . . . trespassing, Princess. And . . . dishonorable." It was quite possibly the first time I'd used the word and actually meant it.

"But my father wishes it."

I glanced around. There was no one about. "What your father does not know cannot hurt him. Or us."

"You would lie to my divine father?"

"That would not be possible, would it. Since he is divine, he would know the truth of things. So if he asks . . . we will smile. And look knowingly at him. And say nothing beyond that. If that is acceptable to you."

She rested one hand gently upon the paper door. I reached up and placed my palm flat against hers. "You are a decent and caring man, Apropos."

"No. But . . . I am trying," I said.

"Thank you for trying."

"Have no fear," I assured her. "I am quite certain that, sooner or later, somehow or other, I will wind up being punished for it."

As I've mentioned in the past, I despise my knack for being correct all the time.

Chapter 5

Scaling the Heights

Over the next six months, I conducted the most torrid non-affair I had ever engaged in.

As I expected, nothing more than looks and smiles and even the occasional polite chuckle was required to satisfy the Imperior that his daughter was performing her designated duties in terms of keeping me sexually challenged. Meantime, a couple of times a week I would go during the evening to the chambers of the princess. After our first "non-encounter," I actually entered her rooms on all my subsequent visits. We would always make sure to extinguish the lights so our shadows would not betray our activities against the door.

And we would talk.

Just.

Talk.

It wasn't as if I'd never spent time talking to a female before. During a long hard winter, I'd been forced to share close quarters with Entipy, and we had discussed various things back then. But most of them centered around how poorly treated she'd been by her parents, and how everyone thought her insane, which wasn't really fair, even though if one asked me, I would have been the first to say she was half a dozen arrows short of a quiver.

It was different with Mitsu.

To start with, there was no question of sex.

It wasn't that she wasn't attractive. For that matter, it wasn't that I wasn't intrigued. And she certainly seemed accommodating enough. There was every possibility that, had I expressed interest, she would have been willing.

But I didn't. Because, despite the casual way in which the Chinpanese seemed to treat it, for me sex would have changed things. And I didn't want to change them, because I was becoming quite taken with getting to know a woman as simply a woman.

As the weeks passed and we carried on our sustained non-affair, I found Mitsu to be by turns acerbic, funny, melancholy, wise, foolish . . . the entire gamut of human emotions. There seemed to be nothing missing from her. She was a whole person, with no one aspect of her personality—such as, say, a delight in seeing things burn—consuming the rest of her.

We spoke about a vast array of topics, and I slowly began to realize just how long it was since I had had a friend. A nice, simple friend. Someone who had never wanted to kill me. Someone I had never screwed, in any sense of the word. Even the decent villagers of Hosbiyu, I had never really thought of them as "friends." I had been friendly toward them, but I had never been able to escape the knowledge that, in so many ways, I was different from them.

With Mitsu, I didn't feel that difference. We established a relaxed rapport. Far too relaxed to risk it with anything as potentially complicated as intercourse.

Besides, it was quite obvious to me that, even though he was gone from her life, Mitsu still had strong feelings for the nameless boy from the marketplace. "You know what?"

I said to her at one point. "Judging by the way things usually seem to transpire in my life, your missing love is off on some great quest even as we speak. He is embarking upon wondrous challenges and ordeals and will, eventually, return with great wealth to claim your hand in marriage."

"You spin lovely fantasies, Apropos," she told me.

"I have no time for fantasies," I replied. "My real life is bizarre enough."

Although Mitsu didn't teach me a damned thing about sex, she did teach me other things, such as some of the various hand-to-hand combat techniques I'd seen her display. Naturally I couldn't hope to match her agility, or even come close to it. But she started showing me what she called "forms" in which I would make various movements again and again and again, swinging my arms, sweeping my hands into blocking positions, repeating other gestures which all seemed almost random and more like dance than anything resembling self-defense.

Still, once she would show me the basics of the forms themselves, she would then challenge me to try and strike her. It was not a task I undertook lightly. I wasn't in the habit of hitting people I liked. Then again, I hadn't liked all that many people in my life, so I was very much exploring new territory. I needn't have concerned myself, however. For every time I did try to connect with her, she would brush my fist away and counterstrike using one of the techniques I had been practicing. In this way, I slowly began to see how these "forms" were clever means of perfecting ways of defending oneself.

I couldn't help but think that these were some of the techniques that Chinpan Ali was in the process of showing me. Unfortunately, he had died in the midst of endeavoring to do so, so I would never know the specifics of what he'd wanted to show me. Mitsu, however, was a perfectly decent teacher. I certainly hoped that she wouldn't wind up being killed as well.

I did not see much of Go Nogo during that time. I didn't feel that to be much of a hardship. No doubt he was out there endeavoring to destroy the Forked Tong. More power to him. I was busy spending my evenings with a charming princess while learning new and interesting ways to not die.

Still, there was one image, one moment that I was not able to erase from my mind. An instance of heartlessness that didn't seem in keeping with the caring, thoughtful young woman I'd gotten to know. One night Mitsu was even able to tell that it was preying upon me, and asked me what I was thinking about.

"That young woman," I said. She looked at me blankly, and I elaborated, "The one who killed herself. The one you singled out . . ."

"Oh. Her," said Mitsu, obviously recalling. "What about her?"

"Why her? Why did you pick out that girl? Had she done something to offend you? Angered you in some way?"

Mitsu was clearly surprised. "No, of course not. She was my favorite handmaiden."

"Your favorite?" I couldn't comprehend it. "And yet you chose her to be the one to end her life?"

"Poor Apropos," sighed Mitsu, and she actually looked sorry for me. She reached over and ruffled my hair. "You truly still don't comprehend. I didn't sacrifice her. I venerated her. To die in order to maintain the integrity of your master's or mistress's honor . . . there is no greater reward for distinguished service than that."

"I don't understand."

"It is because," she said sadly, "you do not truly understand honor."

"No, I understand it. I just don't understand dying because of it."

She shrugged. "Perhaps," she told me, "someday you will."

Mordant showed only the most casual interest in what I was doing with my time. Most nights when I returned he either wasn't in the room at all, or else was hidden away in some convenient nook and sleeping. Truthfully, I couldn't figure out why he was hanging about. Mordant, however, didn't exactly have a history of being forthcoming under normal circumstances, and this was no exception.

Then, one day, the Imperior came to me. More than six months had passed, and he was anxious to see how his workers were doing. "We are going to go out ourselves to check their progress," he informed me.

This pronouncement didn't exactly sit well with me. "Imperior, it has only been six months. I doubt that they have managed to build all that much . . ."

The Imperior waggled a finger at me. "Are you questioning my word?" he inquired.

Well, I certainly knew better than to fall into that one. "Absolutely not, Imperior."

"That's excellent," he said, and appeared to be visibly relieved. Yes, a very strange one, the Imperior. With added cheer, he said, "How far do you think they've gotten?"

"I . . . don't know, Imperior. I'm sure they have accomplished as much as is humanly possible."

"That," he said, and here came the waggling finger once more, "is never enough. It is necessary for all creatures to do more than is humanly possible. Only then can we hope to become what the gods want us to be."

I did what I always did when I wasn't sure what the Imperior was talking about: I nodded. I tended to nod a lot.

That evening, I informed Mitsu that I would not be

around for the next few days, and explained why. Her brow clouded. "That," she said slowly, "is unfortunate."

"Why?" I didn't like the sound of that. "Why unfortunate?"

"Because anything can happen when it comes to my father. Just . . . be careful, Apropos." She rubbed my shoulders, drew my head forward, and placed her forehead against my own. "I would miss you if you died."

"As would I," I said cautiously.

The next day, we set out.

It was quite a procession that made its way across Chinpan. Myself and the Imperior, of course. Itso Esi was there as well. Apparently he considered this the ideal opportunity to converse with the Imperior about every damned thing under the sun. At first he clearly thought that I was going to try and horn in on his time. But when it quickly became evident to him that I was more than content to hang back and let him have the floor, he took it and held it with relish.

The Imperior appeared to listen to everything he had to say. Every so often he would nod, which pleased Itso Esi no end, and he would veer off on to another "incredibly important" topic.

We were certainly well protected. There was a handful of Hamunri there, but my assumption was that most of that upper echelon of warriors was off with Go Nogo, investigating the Forked Tong business. Granted, no reward for the demise of the Forked Tong would be forthcoming if Nogo's people disposed of them, but the bastards would be gone with no risk to myself. Plus I had my own rather handsome compensation awaiting me upon completion of the Imperior's new home. So I was satisfied with the situation as it stood.

Instead of the Hamunri, there was a large column of regular Chinpan soldiers on either side of us. They looked as if they'd been cut from a cookie cutter. Each one identical, marching in perfect, uniform stride or, in some cases, on horseback with their mounts also moving in precision. Their grim expressions were identical, the way they wore their swords, their weapons, absolutely indistinguishable one from the other. I had to shake my head in grudging admiration. All the times I'd seen knights riding out into battle or going on a journey, I was able to discern individuality. Not from this bunch. They moved with one mind and, presumably, with one purpose. I was relieved that we were all on the same side. I would have hated to have to face them in combat.

The journey took several days. We passed farm villages along the way, or groups of travelers standing to either side of the road to make way for the Imperior's procession. People would bow and scrape as the Imperior passed. I liked to entertain myself every so often by pretending they were responding to my presence rather than his. When one is on a long journey, one passes the time any way that one can.

On the fifth day of our journey, I knew we were drawing close. I could even hear the sounds of construction coming from the far side of a ridge. We would not be able to see the progress of the house until we achieved the top of the ridge, but that was perfectly fine as far as I was concerned. It would be more dramatic that way. To ride to the top of the ridge and look down upon the sprawling achievement that would (if my instructions were being followed) look remarkably like King Runcible's castle lifted stone by stone from Isteria and relocated to Chinpan.

I drew close, ignoring Itso Esi's chatter about some new and amazing weapon he was trying to convince the Imperior about called "gunpowder," and I said, "Prepare to be dazzled, Your Worship."

The columns of soldiers separated as we approached the ridge, allowing us access to the top. The Imperior's horse reached the top of the ridge first, which was of course as it should be. He paused there for a long moment, staring outward thoughtfully. Then slowly he turned toward me and said, "I am perceiving a severe lack of dazzlement."

Well, I certainly didn't like the sound of that. I snapped my horse's reins and urged the beast forward, carefully so that I didn't startle the Imperior's steed and cause an accident. I achieved the ridge and looked down, and couldn't believe what I was seeing.

Far below, like a swarm of ants, the builders were constructing what was clearly a wall. It was supposed to be one of the four sides of the exterior wall that would surround the castle.

There was not, however, a castle. Not even the beginnings of the foundation for the castle.

Instead there was simply a wall. The one wall. It stretched as far as the eye could see, miles in either direction, and was roughly twenty-five feet high. As near as I could determine, workers were continuing to labor to extend the wall farther and farther both ways.

"What the hell—?" I gasped out.

"There is a wall there," said the Imperior. He did not sound especially pleased.

"Yes, Imperior, I know there is a—"

"Where there is one wall, should there not be at least . . ." He paused, counted. ". . . three others?"

"I would think so, yes."

"To form a sort of square?"

"Most definitely." I was starting to feel faint.

"And yet I count just the one," the Imperior noted. "One very long wall, running—it would seem—the length of my country's border. I do not pretend to understand it. But I cannot say I like it."

"I fully understand, Great One, and we shall immediately investigate the cause of this . . ." I searched for the right word. ". . . this anomaly."

"See that you do. Because I am quite sure I wanted to see a house. Or, minimally, the recognizable beginnings of a house. Not a single wall. And if a single wall is all you have to show me, honorable architect, then you will have a serious problem on your hands."

I noticed that he wasn't saying "we" would. I would.

Quickly we made our way down to the work site. The workers saw us coming, and word spread quickly throughout the camps. Within minutes all construction had halted, and everyone was on their knees, their eyes resolutely down.

It didn't take us long to find the foreman, an aggressive fellow named Kan Du, renowned for his attitude. He approached us, grim-faced and clearly determined to make a positive impression upon the Imperior. He had my plans for the construction of the residence tucked under his arm. They looked rather worn. I had the feeling he never put the damned things down.

But Kan Du wasn't stupid. He could see immediately that the Imperior did not appear happy. Nevertheless, he gamely bowed and said, "Greetings. Work continues apace on the wall."

"On *the* wall?" asked the Imperior. He turned and looked at me questioningly.

Kan Du was staring at me strangely as well. I should have realized that he was reacting to the clear fact that I was not from this country, but I had too much else on my mind at that moment. "What about the other walls?"

"We do not have remotely sufficient building materials

for the other three," said Kan Du as if it was the most obvious thing in the world. "So we elected to accomplish as much as we could on the one wall and wait for more materials to arrive."

"More materials!" Itso Esi squealed out. "But what you had should have been sufficient to construct the entire palace! Instead you have placed it all into this . . . this . . ."

"Wall. Is it not great?" said a cheery Kan Du.

"A great wall is of no use to me," said the Imperior. He sounded angrier than I had ever heard him, and I couldn't entirely blame him. "How did this happen?"

"We simply followed the designs we'd been sent."

"Designs," and slowly the Imperior looked at me. "Designs crafted by you."

"But my designs didn't call for a miles-long wall!" I protested. I dismounted and limped over to Kan Du, practically ripping the designs out from under his arm. I eased myself onto the ground and spread the designs out. "Look! Look here!" I jabbed my finger repeatedly into the plans. "Each of these squares is supposed to be ten . . ."

I stopped.

Keep in mind, I didn't know how to write the language. But Itso Esi had volunteered to show me how to write "One square equals ten feet" and I had then meticulously copied what he'd written onto the plans. The thing was, I had stared at the designs for so long that I knew every square inch of them. So when I looked at the writing now where the scale was, I knew something was wrong. There was a variation in the letters. Minor variation, so small as to be almost unnoticable at casual glance. A line or two added. But it was enough to change it.

"What does this say?" I asked slowly.

Kan Du leaned in and said, "One square equals ten miles."

I shook my head. "No. No, that's not possible."

"Possible, not possible, no matter," Kan Du replied. "That is what it says. Our job is not to question documents. Our job is to build what documents say. We did our job."

Itso Esi looked at me in a most accusatory manner. "Honorable Po," he said in a voice reeking of stunned shock, "how could you possibly have made such an error?"

"Me?" I clambered to my feet. "You're the one who told me how to write the scale!"

"And I told you correctly. I can't be held responsible if you sent it out with a mistake."

"There was no mistake when I sent it out!"

"And yet there it is!" pointed out Itso Esi. "Do not attempt to shirk responsibility."

"But you looked at the plans as well!"

"And they were correct when I did," he said calmly.

"But now they're wrong!"

"And whose fault is that?" he inquired.

That, of course, was when I knew. When it became clear to me.

Itso Esi had set me up. He had deliberately tampered with the plans for the purpose of making me look bad to the Imperior. I didn't know when he'd done it, but he had. And I was being left twisting in the crow's cage because of it.

"You little bastard!" I snarled, and in an uncharacteristically aggressive move, I swung my walking staff at him. It slammed across his knees, taking his legs out from under him and sending him sprawling to the ground. In a heartbeat I was atop him, gripping my staff firmly and placing it crosswise across his throat. His eyes went wide as he tried to shove it off, but with no luck. *"Admit it! Admit what you did!"*

Even if he'd been inclined to admit to what I wanted him to, pressure from my staff was making it impossible for him to draw enough air to say anything. He struggled in futility, glorious terror reflected in his face, and suddenly I was being hauled off him. Hamunri were on either side of me, and I realized my feet weren't touching the ground. Esi lay on the ground, gasping, his hand to his throat.

"I am disappointed, Po," the Imperior said. "*Very* disappointed."

"This is not my fault, Imperior! I . . . I'm being set up! This man is trying to get rid of me! To dishonor me!"

"That is a very grave charge," said the Imperior. "Do you have any evidence?"

"*Evidence?!* There's a sodding *wall* there! A wall that exists because of what he did!"

Esi was managing to shake his head and protest his innocence. Everyone was looking at me suspiciously.

Part of me understood why. After all, who was the outsider? Who was the one who was unlike the others? Is it not always the unknown and unfamiliar who becomes the scapegoat? Itso Esi had obviously understood that all too well, and realized he could booby-trap me with impunity. And I, the booby, was indeed trapped.

"You have to be able to see through this, Imperior," I said urgently. My arms were already starting to go numb because I was being suspended on either side by the much larger Hamunri. "You have to realize that this is . . . is some sort of trick!"

"Are you claiming that one who has the divine sight could be tricked?" he demanded. Despite his outward appearance of a feeble man, there was nothing frail about his demeanor or tone.

"No, I'm . . . I'm not saying that . . ."

"Then how can you possibly claim that trickery is involved, when by definition, I could not be fooled no matter how clever the deception?"

I had no response to that. No matter what I said, I would only be burying myself deeper.

"It is your name that is signed upon the designs," he said. "It is your carelessness that has wasted the time and materials to create this pointless wall. I can see no other way to redeem yourself, Po, than to take your life immediately."

"Why?" I demanded. "Your honor hasn't been besmirched. I'm . . . I'm from out of town. Truly. I'm not part of your staff . . ."

"It was the Imperior who selected you for this task," Itso Esi said. His voice was raspy, and he looked unsteady on his feet, but deep anger burned in his eyes. He looked as if he'd be all too happy to take whatever measures were necessary to speed along my demise. "Since you botched it, naturally it reflects upon him . . ."

"I didn't botch it! I was made to look bad! By *you!*" I added angrily.

"That is a lie, and you only dishonor yourself further," Esi said.

"Oh, the horror of that notion," I said sarcastically. "What could the outcome of further dishonor be? Perhaps I'd have to kill myself a second time. Imperior, listen to me . . . I did nothing wrong. What kind of life is ended because of such unfair means?"

"Yours," the Imperior said. And frankly, considering what my life had been, I couldn't say he was entirely without foundation in his claim. If anyone was going to wind up losing their life over something as spectacularly absurd as this, it would very likely be me.

"You will have one hour," he continued, "to take your

life. You should know that I do not customarily provide so
much time. But you are from beyond our shores, and
therefore it is important that I be as generous as possible."

"If you were truly going to be generous, Imperior, you
could just let me live."

He appeared to give that some serious thought, and for
an instant my heart swelled with hope. But then all he
said was "I could use some tea. Itso Esi, would you like
some tea?"

"That would be excellent, yes."

The Imperior looked around. "Anyone else?"

There were nods of agreement from all around.
Naturally. When the man who is offering you tea can have
you kill yourself for refusing to join him, that's going to
create a powerful thirst for all concerned.

And as everyone ran about to prepare tea for the
Imperior, I was dragged off to end what I laughingly
referred to as my existence.

They had erected a small tent for me. Very considerate. I'd
hate to have to die while a large number of strangers were
looking on.

The only things in the tent, aside from myself, were my
weapons. My two swords, my walking staff, and the sai.
There was, however, nowhere for me to go. I couldn't possibly fight my way out. There were far too many guards. I'd
be cut to ribbons before I got ten feet.

I was kneeling, wondering just how best to proceed,
when I heard the sound of footfalls from just outside the
tent. I had no idea who was about to enter and yet, amazingly, I had a suspicion . . . which turned out to be exactly
right. The tent flaps drew aside and Go Nogo entered,
scowling as always.

"What are you doing here?" I asked. "I thought you were off dealing with the Forked Tong."

"I am," replied Go Nogo. "The Imperior had asked me to meet him here in order to give him an update. Every so often, the Imperior prefers to discuss matters as far away from the palace as possible."

"Commendably cautious." I frowned. "And how is the Forked Tong doing?"

"That is none of your concern."

There was something in his tone, something defensive. Something that alerted me that matters might be more than what they seemed. "Rather curious, Nogo. How you've had so long to dispense with the Forked Tong once and for all . . . and instead they're still operating. I wonder what could possibly be causing the delay."

Go Nogo didn't seem especially interested in engaging in small talk. His arms folded across his chest, he growled, "Your hour is nearly gone. I am here to oversee your taking of your life."

"And a fine show it would be," I assured him, "but let's talk about other matters for a moment . . ."

"There is nothing to talk about."

"Isn't there?" I thought I sounded rather crafty, the way I said that. "I'm not stupid, you know."

"You're not?" It appeared to be news to him.

"No. I'm able to figure things out. To put clues together. To perceive the truth of that which people are not discussing, or hoping to keep hidden."

"Are you planning to kill yourself anytime soon?" he asked. "Because I really have other things I must do."

I got to my feet. "You tried to kill me," I said, "because you know of the animosity I bear for the Forked Tong."

"I never tried to kill you," said Go Nogo. "If I had been

trying to kill you, you would have been dead. Which would have saved us some time now. If you require a short sword to begin the process . . ." He pulled a sharp blade from the folds of his kimono and offered it to me, hilt first.

I didn't touch it. "You don't have to pretend anymore."

"I don't?" he said, raising an eyebrow.

"I've figured it out. You are actually in league with the Forked Tong. Or with the Skang Kei family."

"Ah. You've figured that out, have you." He spoke with a sort of vague contempt.

"Yes. And the fact is, I'm very interested in joining them."

Now on the surface, that may have seemed a hell of a gamble. But keep in mind the circumstances. I was standing there face-to-face with one of the most formidable warriors in the Imperior's stable, who was making clear that either I was to kill myself or he would send me to the gods with one swipe of his blade. If I didn't have the guts, he would spill them for me. I was not being presented with a sizable number of options.

But if my vague suspicion was correct—if, in fact, Go Nogo was in league with the Forked Tong—then what I was saying might have an outside chance at saving my life.

"You wish to join the Forked Tong?"

"That has been my goal for some time," I assured him. "You see . . . the ruler I represent has already discerned who is the true future of Chinpan, and who we should form an alliance with. He's not interested in forging bonds with the Imperior because he knows that it will be the Forked Tong that will ultimately triumph . . ."

"Interesting. You wish to join the organization which attacked you in the marketplace."

"Ahhh." I felt I'd lucked into something from what he'd just said. "Now everyone else seems to believe that it was the princess who was the target. But you say that I was the one they were trying to kill. Why would you say that?"

"Because I can see why anyone would want to kill you."

And suddenly his hand was a blur, and the hilt of the blade slammed against the side of my head. I fell over, my skull throbbing, and blindly I reached for the nearest thing I could get my hands on: one of the sai. I yanked it from my belt.

"You wave a farming implement at me?" Go Nogo couldn't have been more amused at an offensive tactic if I had turned around and flashed my naked buttocks at him. Then all amusement vanished from his voice as he advanced on me. "My patience is running out, and your insults only elevate the depth of your dishonor—"

I lunged forward with the sai, hoping to get lucky. I didn't. Go Nogo was far too quick. He took a few steps back, bumping up against the side of the tent, and he yanked out his sword from its scabbard even as he moved. In one smooth motion he swung the sword, and it was only by a miracle that I moved my hand fast enough to save it from being severed at the wrist. As it was, I lost my grip on the sai and it skidded across the ground.

There was not a lot of room in the tent. All Go Nogo would have to do is take a step or two toward me, and he would easily be able to eviscerate me with one sweep. "You," he said, pointing the sword at me, "are a pathetic fool."

Suddenly I heard the sound of cloth tearing. He blinked, seemed rather puzzled, and then he looked down.

A sword blade was protruding from his chest, having penetrated from his back and through out to the front.

He looked back up at me, his face clouded with suspicion. "How did you do that?" he demanded. Then his body spasmed as the sword was yanked back out through the same means it had entered. He stood there for a

moment, swaying, a red splotch spreading rapidly across
his chest.

His gaze remained fixed on me, and he tried to bring his
sword up to finish the last job he would ever undertake for
the Imperior. But his arms had already gone numb from
shock, and his weapon fell from his hand.

"I have . . . failed . . . the Imperior," he managed to say,
blood bubbling up from between his lips. "I have . . . dishonored him . . . I must . . . kill myself . . . immediate—"

And then he toppled forward. I slid back as fast as I
could and he thudded to the ground, lying there with a
look of pained frustration on his dead face.

"Don't let *me* stop you," I told him.

Then I looked at the far side of the tent. I could just
barely see a figure standing there, outlined against the dark-
ening sky. Then there was another sound of tearing, and a
bloodstained blade sliced through the tent.

A black-clad figure was standing on the other side. I recognized her instantly. Well . . . not her specifically, but certainly the group to whom she owed allegiance.

"We meet, and are met, have never met, and will meet
again," said the Anaïs Ninja. I had no idea whether she was
the one whom I'd fought back in the village. All I knew
was, she was eyeing me hungrily. "My passion is a flame,
like a blazing star consuming the heavens."

I wasn't taking any chances this time, nor was I letting
myself get caught up in her endless, superreal rants. I
yanked out the bird's-head sword and brought the blade
between us. She froze, her eyes staring at the blade hungrily.

There was something about her. Something almost
familiar. Suspicion began to play at the outer edges of
my mind.

"Well?" I demanded. "This is it, isn't it? The blade your
people killed my teacher for? My guess, it's the real reason

some of your associates attacked me in the fish market. Why do you want this weapon, eh? What's its secret? Is there treasure hidden within it? Is it the key to something? Is it magic?" I advanced upon her. She didn't move. Her eyes, the only part of her face that I could see, remained with their gaze fixed upon the sword. She appeared to be coveting it. "Well? Come on! Speak! You couldn't natter on enough a moment ago. I've been through enough in my life to know when people are seeking a talisman. But this time—this time—I'm going to be firmly in control of things! If quests insist upon throwing themselves upon me, then for once I'm going to initiate it, I'm going to master it! I won't be running five steps behind while everyone else seeks—"

The Anaïs Ninja brought the tip of her own sword up to her face covering and cut a small hole half an inch under her nose. This permitted her to extend her tongue from behind the covering.

She laid her own sword carefully upon the floor, then approached the tachi blade and dropped to her knees beside it. "The ocean of my passion crashes within me, like a great wave of orgasmic serenity," she sighed. Her tongue flicked out and deftly licked the flat of the blade. Then she eased her head alongside it, running her tongue along it while saying, "I feel the heat awakening within me. My moon of ecstasy orbits the sphere of my desire, pulling one upon the other, as the stars burn with—"

"All right, that's enough of that!" I snapped as I pulled the sword away and shoved it in the sheath. Then I was appalled at how loud I'd let my voice get, and I looked around nervously. Something was wrong. This crazy woman had cut her way into the tent, which was surrounded by Hamunri and soldiers. Yet no alarm had been sounded. No people had responded to the sound of fighting.

The Anaïs Ninja coughed deeply, as if trying to pull herself together, and then she spoke in a voice that was husky with emotion, kept focused only through what was clearly a tremendous force of will. "Do you truly wish to join the Forked Tong?"

"No greater desire beats within me."

"Then come. Come. Come," and her voice began to rise, "come with blinding intensity of crashing blue waves upon a distant shore . . ."

"I *will* hit you if I have to," I warned her.

Beneath her mask, she smiled. "Promises," she said, and then moved out through the hole in the tent. As she did so, she called out, "I am reborn, moving through the opening like a newly spawned child, destined for woman, experiencing the—"

I wondered if it was too late to stab her with the sai.

Cautiously I stepped out through the rip in the tent and looked around in bewilderment.

There were bodies. Bodies everywhere. Hamunri, soldiers, Itso Esi, the Imperior, all slumped over.

"Did you . . ." I could barely get the words out. "Did you kill them?"

She shook her head. "Drugged the tea. They all drank of it. They all collapsed. I could have killed them all. I could have killed the Imperior," and she looked down at the unmoving form of the divine one. She kicked him sharply in his divine stomach. "But I did not."

"May I ask why?"

She looked at me and said, "Because it is not time yet, although my passion would certainly prompt me to."

And at that point, I knew. I knew beyond question, beyond doubt.

I took several fast steps toward her, or at least as fast as I was able. She looked up at me with luminous eyes.

"And because," I said triumphantly, *"he's your father! Isn't that right, Mitsu!"*

I reached up and yanked the mask away from her face.

I have to say, that was one damned ugly woman.

Gorgeous eyes, but flattened nose, scarred and twisted lips, and apparently twice as many teeth in her mouth as normally resided there.

"Or . . . not," I said. She just stared at me. I held up the blade. "Would you like to lick my sword some more?"

Okay, so I wasn't *always* right. I'd been wrong about the late Go Nogo, and who this odd Anaïs Ninja woman was. Everyone has an off day now and then.

Chapter 6

Love at First Wang

*T*he Anaïs Ninja had certainly come prepared. She led me a short distance from the camp, and my horse was waiting there, tethered to a small tree. Standing beside it was the animal I presumed my rescuer had arrived upon. It was truly a magnificent animal. Solid black, with a sleek coat and fiery eyes that bespoke intelligence. Then again, considering some of the fools I'd encountered in my life, it wasn't that difficult to find a horse with more brainpower than they.

Having affixed her mask back in place, whilst giving me strange looks as she did so, she vaulted onto the back of the horse so lightly that she seemed almost like a puppet yanked aloft by strings. I, naturally, took far longer to get atop my horse, but soon we were mounted up and riding away from the scene of the calamity. In the distance, I could hear the sounds of building continuing. The lunatics were still constructing the incredibly pointless wall, probably because no one had specifically said to them, "Stop doing that."

And we got the hell out of there.

Night had fallen, which meant we could ride only so

fast, lest the horses trip. But we pushed the limit as much as we could. We rode long and we rode hard, and the only thing that made me somewhat insane was that the Anaïs Ninja seemed to be getting tremendous sexual gratification from riding the horse. In fact, she appeared to be bouncing up and down upon the animal with far greater vigor than could remotely have been deemed necessary. *"Madam, stop that at once!!"* I kept hissing at her. I don't think she heard me over her constant low moans. On the other hand, I didn't have to worry about losing her in the darkness. I could have kept up with her if I was blind.

As we traveled, my mind was racing ahead of us. I kept toying with the notion of breaking off, trying to escape into the night. But to what end? To return to the Imperior? Perhaps even be rounded up by soldiers who might have awakened by this point from the drugged tea? That certainly seemed a less-than-intelligent strategy.

Yet look at the alternative. I was riding hell-bent-for-leather to keep up with a mysterious, vicious, lethal woman who was leading me to others who were probably just like her. I was willingly being led to the very people who were responsible for the death of the very fellow whose death I was out to avenge. The odds were sensational that they would endeavor to annihilate me the moment I set foot in their lair, wherever that was, take the tachi sword, and be done.

Why did they want the sword? I still had no idea.

However, one thing kept tumbling around in my mind, prompted by something that the late Go Nogo had said:

"If I wanted to kill you, you would be dead."

The fact was that these Anaïs Ninjas seemed to come and go as they pleased. The shadows were their second homes. They wafted through the air, as easy to capture as a passing breeze. This one had the Imperior at her mercy. The

Imperior, reputed to be their greatest enemy and opponent. But she did not dispatch him. And all that time that I was residing in the palace, how likely was it that the Anaïs Ninjas could not possibly have made their way in under cover of darkness, kill me, and take the sword for themselves?

They didn't just want the sword for some reason. They wanted the sword *and me* for some reason. I couldn't fathom why. It did, however, embolden me.

Once upon a time, I would never have embarked upon such a foolish avenue of endeavor for fear of my life. But, as noted, my experiences in Wuin had hardened me. I did not actively seek out death, but paralyzing dread of it no longer ruled my actions. I was willing to take a chance, to play along with the Forked Tong, to see who was in charge and what they wanted.

Besides, it wasn't as if the other side in this power struggle was any great delight to work with. The Imperior had tried to have me kill myself. That hardly engendered depths of loyalty.

But I was not about to forget they'd slain my teacher. Someone was going to pay for that. And if it meant playing along, outwitting the women in charge, playing them against one another while seeking out weaknesses I could exploit, well . . . I was fully confident that I had the mental tools to engage in such a battle of wits and ultimately triumph.

Such were the dangers of hubris.

It was some hours later that we departed the main road and headed off down a side path. We had gone only a few feet, however, when the Anaïs Ninja called a halt. As I reined up, she vaulted off her horse, went back to the road, pulled some brush from a nearby bush, and wiped away any trace on the dirt road that we had veered off. She slapped her sleek black horse on its rump, and the animal obediently charged back off onto the main road, vanishing moments later into the darkness. The reason why was obvious: to lead away any possible pursuers. The road was fairly well traveled. It would take even the most eagle-eyed of trackers some work to notice that the number of tracks they were following had gone from two to one.

She walked down the dirt road toward me, and I couldn't help but think she'd just created more work for herself. Then I looked beyond her and realized she was walking so lightly, she was leaving no tracks in the dirt. I didn't know how such a thing was possible, unless she was spectral. At that point I wasn't prepared to dismiss any notion out of hand.

Just as she'd leaped onto horseback with facility before, she vaulted this time onto the back of mine. Instantly she insinuated her body against me.

"Let's stay professional, shall we?" I insisted.

"Absolutely," she replied. And yet I noticed, as we continued on our way that apparently the only thing she could hold on to to maintain her balance was my bum.

The side road angled downward for a time, and I guided the horse through carefully, keeping an eye out for stray roots or logs overgrown by ivy and weeds. The entire business was becoming increasingly creepy for me. I felt animal eyes upon me from all directions, things moving through the forest. I heard a brief crack of a branch overhead, thought I saw something winged and menacing, and then it was gone. My forest-trained senses were running riot, although part of that might well have been fueled by my agitated state.

"Where are we going?" I said, trying not to sound nervous.

"There," she said, and pointed.

At first I couldn't see where she was indicating, but then I squinted and was able to make it out. There was what appeared to be some sort of temple or shrine ahead of us. A small building, overgrown and covered with weeds and vines. I reined up and dismounted, as the Anaïs Ninja lightly vaulted to the ground behind us.

"This had better not be a trap," I warned her.

Even in the darkness, I could see the grim amusement in her eyes. "Or else—?"

Naturally I had no fallback. But I simply looked intense, nodded, and said, "Yes."

That appeared to confuse her slightly, for which I was glad. My certainty that I was doing the right thing was starting to waver a bit, but it was too late to back out.

I waited a few moments for my eyes to adjust, and then I made my way into the temple. As soon as I was within, I saw there were candles burning just ahead. So someone was waiting for us.

This is it. You're not getting out of this, you idiot. You've stuck your head into the noose and they're going to snap it tight around your neck. Enjoy dancing in the air.

But I didn't believe it. As reliable as my inner voice usually was, there was just no feeling of . . . of completion. If I were to die here, now, there was too much left unanswered, too many questions hanging about. None of it made any sense.

Then again, life wasn't about making sense. Life was about existing for as long as you could until some thing or things brought you down, and there was no requirement for closure or an answer to all life's mysteries. In fact, the odds were that when you died, you'd die in ignorance at some level no matter what. It was hardly a comforting train of thought to engage in.

The shadows were long from the candles, and then they began to move.

I couldn't make out a lot in the darkness, but that much I could see. More of the Anaïs Ninjas, stepping out from the inky blackness, their eyes glittering. I heard them breathing heavily, and some of them were absently running their hands across their breasts.

This was one wild group of shadow warriors. They seemed as likely to embark upon an orgy as kill you. Although considering the overheated sentiments the ones I had encountered had been spouting up until now, I wasn't sure which would be the preferable fate to suffer.

(All right, that's obviously not true. But damn, it *sounded* good, didn't it?)

The one who had led me there stepped forward, placed her right fist into her left palm in front of her chest, and then mashed them against her breasts three times. The others promptly returned what was obviously their form of greeting.

And then, from beyond the candles, I heard a musical voice, filled with amusement and even vague interest. "So . . . this is he. The renowned Po."

"And you would be . . . ?"

A woman stepped from the shadows, although to call her a woman would be to understate it.

She was, quite simply, the most magnificent creature I'd ever encountered.

The Anaïs Ninja once again performed that bizarre little ritual of breast pushing, and the gorgeous woman who had taken center stage in this show of force and strangeness returned the gesture.

As for me, I had no idea how long I stood there, staring at her. Time seemed to freeze. No, not just freeze. To become utterly irrelevant. I could have remained there all day just gazing at her. The Anaïs Ninja had stepped forward and was speaking softly to this perfect creature, who was listening and nodding, glancing in my direction every so often as she took in the information. When she was done, the Anaïs Ninja stepped back and the woman straightened up, staring at me, giving not the slightest hint of what she was thinking.

Her fragile Chinpanese features gave her the look of a porcelain doll. Her face was pure white, her eyebrows and eyes delicately underlined and slightly exaggerated, adding to the exotic and erotic look of her. She was the most elaborately costumed individual I'd yet encountered. Her outermost garment was a wide-sleeved jacket, reaching to the waist, with a pattern of bird medallions brocaded in greens and yellows.

Attached to the waist of the jacket's back was a long, pleated train of sheer, white silk, decorated with a dragon design. This one actually looked surprisingly like Mordant. Beneath the jacket, she wore a purple kimono of what also seemed silk. It was abnormally large, the large skirt swirling out around her feet, since she was wearing more kimonos beneath.

Her hair was done up in an elaborate coiffure, and attached to her forehead were lacquered, gold-sprinkled combs overlaid with a gold lacquered chrysanthemum crest.

And her eyes . . . I could swim in her eyes. Drown in them, die in them, and go to a watery grave happier than I'd ever been in my entire miserable existence. She was as nothing I'd ever seen or could ever hope to see again.

All I could think of at that instant was what Mitsu had said to me about instantly falling in love. At looking into someone's eyes and seeing a reflection not only of yourself, but the life the two of you had spent together in some previous incarnation.

Madness. Insanity. I, Apropos the Cynic, Apropos the Realist, Apropos Who Knew Better Than Anyone Else. To even open myself up to the possibility of such an experience was to admit that there were far greater possibilities to life than I had ever dared imagine.

Romantics were fools. They were mold on bread, mushrooms upon trees. They grew upon the harsh reality of life and softened it and made it weak. They viewed the world through a wet prism of feebleness that bordered on the pathetic. I had always known this for a fact. To fall in love to any degree is to needlessly expose yourself to inevitable betrayal and falsehood and, ultimately, the object of that love not possibly being everything that you wanted them or needed them to be.

I knew all this. I knew it as surely as I knew my own name.

And yet, at that moment, I did not care. Seeing her there illuminated by the candles, it was as if light was being brought for the first time to the wretched and tortured thing I called my daily existence.

She was beautiful. She was soulful. And best of all . . .

She was evil.

Well, of course. Naturally. That had to be clear, wasn't it? She was evil. She was connected to this group of thieves and criminals and murderers. She was quite likely the leader, or one of the key figures, considering the deference they showed her. Perhaps she was even this mysterious "Ho" I'd heard tell of.

What did that mean to me?

No chance of being let down. No chance of betrayal. No chance of her turning out to be something other than she was.

If I did follow the call of my heart, I was going into it with my eyes wide open. Dazzled by her beauty, but wide open. Every woman that I had ever become romantically involved with had not only turned out to be something other than what I'd expected, but had wound up betraying my trust in the process. Here was a woman, though, whom I knew I could never trust. Ever.

Most romantics believe that true, great love must be

built upon a foundation of trust. This is patently untrue. True love is not built on trust. True love is built on knowledge. Trust is simply what you substitute for lack of knowledge, and then you hope for the best. But with this woman, with this goddess in a mortal world—and believe me, I know something of goddesses in mortal worlds—I knew that betrayal was not only a likelihood, but nigh unto a certainty. It removed all doubt. I would never have to worry *if* she would betray me; only *how*.

It was liberating. With the knowledge that she would betray me came the awareness that I could likewise betray her at some point when it suited my needs. All was fair, as the saying went. Love and war, gloriously intertwined.

Was any of this passing through her mind? I couldn't know for sure. She appeared to regard me with open curiosity. She arched a single eyebrow which, thanks to her makeup, was laced with a subtext that was practically erotic.

"I hear tell," she said, "that you occasionally have been known to speak."

I found my voice. To my surprise, it was huskier than it usually was. "I am . . . Apropos. That is my full name, actually."

"Apropos." Her tongue seemed to glide over each letter. "Ap-pro-pos." She said it several times, each time slightly different in her pronunciation. "A most unusual name."

"And to whom do I have the . . . honor . . . of speaking?" I asked. My left leg was trembling slightly and I steadied it. Since that was my good leg, I certainly didn't want it going out from under me. Falling flat on my face was not the best way to make a good first impression.

"I," she said slowly, "am Wang Ho. Veruh Wang Ho. Leader of the Skang Kei family. Founding member of the Forked Tong. I am who your Imperior has been searching for, for quite some time."

"He's hardly *my* Imperior," I said. "I'm just a visitor here."

"And yet, for a visitor, you have made quite an impression and have found yourself in the midst of some very troubled circumstances."

I shrugged, trying to sound casual in her presence. "Call it a knack."

"Oh, I call it far more than that. I call it . . . most interesting." She was standing, but perfectly still, like a statue. Only her small movements, such as reaching up and thoughtfully touching her chin with an outstretched finger, convinced me that she was actually flesh and blood. "So it is my understanding that you wish to join the Forked Tong. Why should we permit that?"

"The question could easily be turned around," I replied. I couldn't let my overwhelming attraction to her shake my resolve or unman me. I sensed that this was a woman who respected only strength. To display weakness would be fatal. "Why should I want to join? I have grievances against your organization."

"Do you."

"You killed my teacher. You killed my teacher, Ali."

"Ali. Yes." She nodded thoughtfully. "The previous owner of that sword," and she inclined her head toward the sword dangling from my hip. "He imparted knowledge and wisdom to you, did he?"

"What my teacher taught me remains between he and I," I said. "Just as the unbalanced scales for his death remain between you and I."

"I see. And what would you have, Apropos?" she asked with a faintly mocking smile. "Revenge? Revenge upon the sisters who killed him? Can you pick out which ones did it?" and she gestured sweepingly around the room.

"Perhaps I could just avenge myself upon you."

"You could. However, be aware that I did not order the

attack upon Ali. I do not direct every move the sisters make. In this instance, sisters were doing it for themselves. They have their own plans, their own priorities."

"So you do not condone what happened?"

"I did not say that." She laughed. She had a lustrous-yet-light laugh, like morning bells calling vespers. It was difficult for me to believe I was admiring the laugh of someone who was chuckling over the death of my teacher, and yet, so it was. "For reasons you do not yet fully comprehend, what happened to Ali was no tragedy."

"If I do not fully comprehend them, then perhaps it would be best for you to explain them to me."

She regarded me thoughtfully for a moment, and then stepped down toward me. It was only at that point I realized she was standing upon a slightly raised platform. She descended four steps so that she was almost at eye level with me; she remained taller than I, but not by much. "I would explain," she said, "to one who is part of the Forked Tong. Are you joining us?"

"I have already expressed my interest." It was getting difficult for me to remain focused. Since she was closer, I was able to detect the aroma of some sort of scent she was wearing. It smelled like honeysuckle and lilacs, and was nearly enough to make me light-headed. The most amazing thing of all was, I wasn't certain whether it was some sort of fragrance she added after a bath, or whether it was her own natural body scent.

"To join the Forked Tong requires far more than an expression of interest," she told me. "It requires a show of dedication."

"Dedication? To an organization whose representatives attacked me at the fish market?"

She shrugged slightly. "A mere test."

"Of what? Of me? Or of this?" and my hand went to the hilt of the tachi sword.

I wasn't sure, but it seemed to me the Anaïs Ninjas suddenly tensed, as if expecting trouble. Trouble from me? Or trouble from the sword itself? Pieces were falling into place in my mind.

"Our motivations will remain a closed book to you for now, Apropos," she told me. "Consider, though: The fact that we have not yet killed you should be enough to indicate that there is more to the Forked Tong than you suspect."

"Perhaps. Or perhaps it's simply an indication that you feel you can't kill me."

"Oh, we can," she assured me.

I took a step toward her. "Oh, can you?"

And she moved toward me in response. "Yes. We can."

My entire body was quivering. I had never wanted a woman so much before. And I could see it in her dark brown eyes: There was feeling for me there as well. She would never admit to it, of that I was sure. But it was there. We were having a powerful effect on each other.

With a superhuman exercise of willpower, I stepped back. "You know what I want," I managed to say. "Information. A balancing of the scales. Tell me what you want."

"Proof of your interest in the Forked Tong."

"The Imperior wants me dead and I am an outsider wherever else I go. What more proof would you require?"

"That is simply the nature of your personal predicament. That is not proof."

"What would you consider proof, then?"

"The princess."

I blinked. "You mean Mitsu?"

"Yes," said the Skang Kei Ho. "The very one."

"How would she be proof of anything?"

"Bring her to us."

I felt as if a fist were closing in my chest. "To you."

She nodded. "Deliver her to us, and we will know that

you are genuinely interested in joining the Forked Tong, and are deserving of the knowledge we can impart."

Now the truth was, I was so besotted with Veruh Wang Ho that I would have brought her the beaten and bloodied corpse of just about anyone it was within my power to obtain, if I knew it would put a smile upon her carefully painted face. But Mitsu? The thought of putting her into the hands of these . . . these criminals . . .

"Have no fear," Veruh assured me. "We will not harm her."

"And how would I know that?"

"Because," said Veruh, "she would be of no use to us dead. It is our intention to use her as a bargaining chip in dealing with her father."

"That might well be a dead end," I said. "There may not be much love lost between father and daughter. What if your intentions fail? If you insist on some sort of deal in exchange for Mitsu's life, and her father tells you all to go to hell. To do your worst. He is not someone who is concerned about the value of human life. You might have as much luck threatening his favorite tea service as his daughter."

"There is that possibility," she acknowledged. "Should that transpire, though, that will be our problem, not yours. And if it does occur, I repeat: She will not be harmed in any way. We do have boundaries, and depths to which we would not stoop."

"I see. So you would kill old men, but not young girls."

"Yes. That is exactly right," she said. "So . . . what is your answer?"

"If I refuse?"

She moved toward me once again, and the scent of her was so powerful that I leaned heavily upon my staff for support.

"If you are truly interested in the Forked Tong, you would have no reason to refuse, would you."

"That is true," I admitted. I hesitated, my mind racing, trying to come up with some other way. None presented itself. "Very well. I accept."

"Excellent. The means by which you obtain her is up to you."

"Damned generous of you," I said sarcastically. "Especially considering I'm not the most popular individual with the Imperior just now. Perhaps . . . perhaps," I mused aloud, "I can head straight back to the palace right now. It'll be hard riding for several straight days, but—"

"That will do you very little good," said the "sister" who had brought me here. "By this time, the little drug I put in the tea will have worn off. Even now, word is undoubtedly being sent to the palace by swiftest messenger. You'll never be able to overtake it before the palace is alert and ready for your return."

"Great. So the task is impossible."

"Think of it more as an opportunity to prove your ingenuity," said Veruh, and then added, "and your devotion."

The way she said that almost made my heart puddle around my feet, and it was all I could do to refocus. "And if, and when, I manage to obtain her . . . ?"

"Do you remember the bridge that leads into the fish market? Bring her to the top of that bridge and we will handle matters from there."

"All right," I said slowly. I stood there, uncertain as to what I should do next. I knew what I wanted to do. I wanted to pull Veruh to me, to lose myself in her. But these were hardly what I would call ideal circumstances for a first date.

She gestured in a leisurely fashion and said, "You may go. The sister will see you on your way. Oh, and Apropos . . . it is fortunate you agreed to our terms."

"Why?"

"Because if you had refused, you would not have left this shrine alive. And, having made a pledge to the Forked Tong, if you attempt to abandon it, you will not leave this country alive."

The woman with whom I was madly, deeply, passionately in love had just threatened to kill me.

It sounded so right.

Chapter 7

The Taking of Mitsu 1 2 3

*Y*ou will not leave this country alive . . .

The entire journey back to Taikyo, the words kept echoing in my mind. At the same time, the scent of Veruh Wang Ho lingered in my nostrils.

I kept trying to determine just exactly what had happened. Had I been deluding myself? Was she wearing some sort of perfume, perhaps, that was addling my mind? Or could it be that she had some deep hypnotic power? Perhaps it was something as simple as that she was a weaver. Why not? There was no reason to think that weavers were unique to my country. There was every chance that Veruh possessed some sort of mystic ability that was causing her to manipulate my perceptions.

On the other hand, it could be me rather than her. It could have been that my endeavors to explore new areas of my life, to push myself to new horizons, had prepared me for this moment. Mitsu's comments about love at first sight, about connections made in earlier lives, was still fresh in my mind, and the power of suggestion could be a powerful thing indeed.

What it really came down to, though, was: I didn't care.

All I cared about was the passion that Veruh raised within me. The hows and whys of it were of no interest. All I knew was that, just as Mitsu had so deftly predicted was possible, I had encountered a woman whom I knew, on a gut level, was my soul mate. So besotted was I that all I could think was, should she stab me in the back in the dark, at least I'd be dying at her hand.

In retrospect, separated by the events of that time through the relative serenity of the years, I would liken it to the fervency felt by a recent religious convert when he has just discovered some god or savior or some such. One is embracing not only the being or the concept, but an entire way of life that will fulfill some deep-seated need one may have. The amount of enthusiasm with which the new obsession takes hold is directly related to the amount of need.

With all that I had been going through as of late, it was no wonder that I became utterly obsessed with Veruh Wang Ho. Although, honestly, even as I think back upon it, it would be hard to believe that any mere mortal would have been anything except totally enamored with that high-priced Ho.

For Veruh Wang Ho and the Forked Tong came with a very high price indeed.

Princess Mitsu had never been anything but considerate to me. All right, yes, we had a significant difference of opinion when it came to such matters as the sanctity of human life and flatly expecting people to execute themselves in order to accommodate one's sense of honor. But other than that, our time together had been everything from relaxing to enlightening. So how was I supposed to take the first female that I had genuinely come to think of as a friend and turn her over to an organization composed of thieves, murderers, criminals, and oversexed shadow warriors who tended toward non sequiturs?

The answer was: Reluctantly.

But I was going to have to do it nevertheless.

Upon departing the shrine of Veruh Wang Ho, the Anaïs Ninja who had brought me there lent me her horse. The intelligence of the animal was beyond measure. Speaking in soft tones to it, she instructed it to take me "via the secret ways" back to Taikyo. Yes, you read that correctly: She spoke to it. The horse nodded, apparently in comprehension, and at that moment I would not have been surprised if the ebony equine had started chatting up a storm, not unlike Mordant.

Then she continued to talk to it, lowering her voice, whispering in the animal's ear. Even with her voice so hushed, I immediately recognized that dementedly erotic tone. She was running her hands up and down the horse's neck, and the poor creature was starting to look decidedly nervous.

"I think I'd better go," I said quickly, seeking to rescue the animal before it found itself with its mistress hanging upside down under it doing only gods knew what. "Unlike you and your 'sisters,' I can't blend with the shadows."

Reluctantly, she stepped away from the horse, and I mounted it quickly. "What do I do with the horse once I reach the city?"

"The horse will return to me at our arranged place of meeting."

"Oh." This was one hell of an impressive horse.

I urged the horse forward, but truthfully it needed little urging. I think it was as happy to get away from that over-heated harridan as I was.

To this day I've no idea how that horse made it through the woods with the efficiency and awareness that it did. I told myself that the Anaïs Ninja had taken the animal through this cleverly concealed route so many times that the beast knew precisely where it was supposed to go and what it should do. Even so, its sense of direction and ability to handle itself was astounding. We were certainly off the beaten track. There was a narrow road that wended its way through the forest, created no doubt by the Forked Tong over a period of years. It was so deep in the woods, however, that no one would have known it was there to travel it. Nor was the road always easy to see. Particularly at night, I could barely see my hand in front of my face.

But the horse kept moving. It was certainly operating on its own, because I had no idea where we were and couldn't have found my way back to Taikyo for any price. The horse knew the way. In this regard, it was smarter than I was. Hell, it was probably smarter than I in many regards.

Every so often, when both horse and rider were exhausted, I would rein up and we would rest, the horse grazing on grass and sometimes drinking from a convenient brook or stream. Then we would continue on our way. I never once heard the slightest sound of pursuit.

Eventually we made it to the outskirts of Taikyo. I still had my cloak, and fortune was with me in that the weather had turned inclement. There a steady drizzle was coming down, which meant that if I walked through the city with my hood up, it would attract no attention, since people would simply assume it was to keep my head dry. If the sun were out and the weather were balmy, I would have been even more noticeable than I already was.

The horse stopped with the city in sight, and I realized that my ride was done. I eased off the horse, patted it on the side of the head, and whispered, "I wish you were mine." The horse bobbed its head, perhaps coincidentally, or perhaps it just simply agreed wholeheartedly with the sentiment. Then, with a whinny and swish of its tail, it was gone, back into the forest.

I made my way into the city, glad for its size. I had money on me. The Imperior had been generous in a stipend he'd provided me while I was in the palace, and it wasn't as if I'd had anything to spend it on, so most of it was still with me. It meant that I would be able to get a room for the night, again without attracting attention.

Thanks to the weather, the streets were half as crowded as they'd been when I'd first arrived. Even so, they were still teeming with people, and losing myself in the throng was no difficulty.

I studied everyone I passed, always wondering if this person or that person was actually a member of the Forked Tong, watching me, spying upon me and ready at any time to relay word to Veruh as to what I was up to.

This exercise in uncertainty and fear was with me until I found myself a room at a small inn, situated right near—as luck and also design on my part would have it—the foot of the bridge that I was supposed to cross to summon Veruh Wang Ho and her Skang Kei associates.

Unfortunately, I saw something rather dire on my way to the inn.

I saw myself.

Specifically, pictures—drawings—of myself, adorning walls of assorted buildings. I was scowling in the drawing, and some of the details of the ears and nose were wrong. And the eyes were definitely not quite right. Apparently the artist had never been required to draw eyes such as mine, and so he produced something more in line with what he was familiar. As a result, I didn't look exactly Chinpanese, but I didn't look exactly like myself, either.

There was writing beneath the picture. I didn't have to be able to read it to guess what it said: Reward. For my capture. I didn't know whether it said "dead or alive," but I wouldn't have been surprised were that the case.

I felt ill as I registered at the inn, even as I kept my hood well over my face.

I was provided with a simple room with more of those paper sliding doors such as I'd seen at the palace. There was a rolled-up sleeping mat in the corner, and a small pot of hot water with tea nearby, freshly put out with the steam still rising. I undid my weapons and lined them up next to one another, determined to keep them no farther away than arm's reach lest I require them quickly. I sipped the tea and ate sparsely of some rice that my hosts later provided. Other than that I kept to myself, lying upon my back and staring up at the ceiling.

And wondering what in the world I was going to do.

I couldn't just wander about in Taikyo. My face made me problematic enough in terms of recognizability. But now it had been pasted all over town on a wanted poster. Which meant as soon as the weather became balmy, I'd have no excuse to wander around with my hood up, and I was in trouble. The four paper walls surrounding me might be my new permanent home.

I could just try and flee Taikyo. For that matter, flee Chinpan altogether. Running away. I could handle running away. Gods knew I had done it before, and was quite comfortable with the concept. It had the warmth of familiarity.

Three problems with that.

First, there was little doubt in my mind that somehow, somewhere, the Forked Tong or the Anaïs Ninjas or the Skang Kei family—in short, every deadly entity in Chinpan—was keeping an eye on my progress and was prepared to strike back with deadly force if I did not keep my part of the enforced bargain. Whatever else happened, it was perversely intriguing that I had maintained my knack for incensing deadly people.

Second, there was my fascination with Veruh. Even if,

through some miracle, I managed to elude all pursuers and find my way out of Chinpan—where to, I'd no idea, but out—that would mean that I would be leaving behind the woman who had awakened something within me I'd no idea was there in the first place. Was it odd, perverse, inexplicable that I was so attracted to an entity who could easily represent my destruction? Look no further than a moth's fascination with a flame to know the answer to that question.

And third . . . it would still leave dangling the murder of Ali. My great mission of vengeance, unfulfilled. But why? Why should that matter to me?

I lay there all the long night, staring up at the ceiling, and pondered it. I had always prided myself on knowing exactly why I did the things I did. Yes, granted, there had been some who claimed the contrary was true. That I in fact lived in a perpetual sense of denial, supposedly always doing "what was right," whatever that might be, while simultaneously "fabricating" reasons that were self-centered and self-serving. Pure tripe, in my opinion. I knew myself, and knew what the world was getting when it was dealing with me, even if the world chose to live in self-denial.

Yet in this instance, I found myself flummoxed. And inevitably, my thoughts kept turning back to my time in Wuin.

I had done bad things there. A *lot* of bad things. I had told myself that I had done so because I was not myself, but was instead under the control of something else, something sinister. However, truth be told, much of what I did, I took a dark and sinister pleasure in. Nearly sadistic, in fact. And that had disturbed me greatly, for I knew myself to be many things, but never once had I believed I was someone who enjoyed the pain of others. Yes, I had caused others pain, to be sure. But it had always been a by-product. Or they'd deserved it, or done me harm in some way and I was getting back at them. Hurting the helpless simply to enjoy the sensation of inflicting suffering . . . that wasn't me.

I have observed throughout my life that things rarely occur by themselves. That when one type of situation transpires, invariably and inevitably, something of the opposite sort occurs as well. For every action, some action of an antithetical type—but otherwise equal in every way—happens. This is so immutable that I would almost venture to say it's universal. There are a couple of other "laws" I've observed regarding how fate seems to move, but I'll save those for some other time.

How that applied to my situation in Chinpan was obvious. If, in Wuin, I had done terrible things—and I had—then I was now being compelled by the laws and forces of nature to do equal but opposite things.

The thought that those black-clad bitches had killed Ali with impunity was gnawing at my gut. So much so that I knew I had to do something.

The problem was, fetching Mitsu into the hands of the Forked Tong was an evil deed in and of itself. Which, if my theory was correct, meant that while I was busy trying to even the scales on one side, I was going to wind up tipping them against me at the same time. But as much as I turned it over and over in my mind, I was forced to the inevitable conclusion that there was no other way. And considering I was someone who excelled in finding another way when all seemed hopeless, that was a frustrating admission to make.

The only conclusion to which I could finally come was that, if 'twas to be done, then it would be best to do it quickly. With that in mind, I immediately turned my thoughts to pondering just how to go about getting Mitsu to the Forked Tong.

Truthfully, conceiving the mischief took me almost no time at all. Fairly impressive, I had to admit: My ability to cause difficulty for others remained undiminished even as trials were heaped upon my shoulders.

Having developed the plan, I then proceeded to get no further sleep that night. How was it that I was intending to atone, in any sense, for the evil I had done as the peacelord of Wuin, and yet the first step in that atonement was to put an innocent girl at risk?

I satisfied myself by saying repeatedly that she wasn't really going to be at risk. That the Forked Tong, just as Veruh Wang Ho had stated, would find her of far greater use alive than dead. Furthermore, it could always be said that in some ways, she was living on borrowed time. Had I not interceded when I'd first seen her being confronted by those angry circus folk, she would very possibly have been beaten to death right then and there. In that sense, she owed me her life, and really, I should be able to do with it as I saw fit.

Remarkably, at the time that made a twisted kind of sense. At least, I thought it did. This is further proof that people will say or do virtually anything to justify their own actions.

So it was that, very very early, several hours before the rising of the sun, I stepped out onto the deserted street. There was still a steady mist of rain coming in, and I kept my cloak tightly over me. There was a faint but steady wind from the south, the direction of the fish market, carrying with it a distinctly scaly aroma.

Then all I had to do was whistle. I knew how to whistle: I put my lips together and blew. The note was long and sustained and quite sharp. It carried high and far over the rooftops of Taikyo. I held it for as long as I could, stopped, drew in a deep breath, and did it again. Then one more time for good measure.

After that, I just stood there. I felt no need to keep whistling. Instead I waited. And waited.

At one point, the proprietor of the inn stuck his head out and gave me a very curious look. He had still not seen my face clearly, since I'd been careful to keep my hood up. He probably thought I was a loon. That was perfectly acceptable to me. As long as he didn't think I was a fugitive from the stained honor of the Imperior, we'd get along just perfectly.

He ducked back in without questioning why I was out there in such unfortunate weather, which was fine with me. I continued to stand there, watching, waiting, looking to the skies, depending on something that I really didn't fully understand.

Then, far in the distance, I saw a small, dark object, wings flapping smoothly in the air against the night sky. I didn't want to get too excited too quickly. It could be a large hawk or eagle or some other more traditional avian. But within moments the figure drew closer, and I knew my initial impression had been correct.

Part of the magic that was Mordant was his ability to hear my summoning him from, it seemed, anywhere. Back in Wuin, it didn't matter where I was. I would just let out with a piercing whistle and, lo and behold, he would show up before long. There were limits, of course. Were I trapped in a cell or somesuch, he wouldn't simply appear from thin air. He would, at most, show up outside the cell and offer the dubious aid of providing cutting observations over how foolish I was to have gotten myself into this situation in the first place.

But if I was anywhere outside, Mordant would somehow hear me and would come, no matter where he was.

I realized belatedly that it might have been a good idea to test the limits of that responsiveness when I'd been floating on a piece of wood in the middle of bloody nowhere. But it hadn't occurred to me. Besides, Mordant didn't just magically appear from one place to the next. Presuming he could have broken off from whatever he was doing to see why I was summoning him, it might have taken him days, even weeks, to fly the distance separating us. By that point I would have been fish food, so ultimately it didn't make any difference.

As he drew closer, I could hear the slightest flapping noise from his wings. I wound the trailing end of my cloak around my forearm several times to provide a cushion, and I extended my arm as he neared, providing him a perch. Making his final approach, he ceased his flapping and glided the rest of the way, nestling gently down upon my arm. I tried not to wince as his claws dug into my skin and was only partly successful.

"So," he said without preamble, "quite a situation you've gotten yourself into."

"You've heard?"

"It's all through the palace. The Imperior is incensed with you, and instead of doing the Imperior the courtesy of ending your life, you instead killed the leader of the Hamunri, the most formidable warriors in Chinpan. Every Hamunri with the slightest sense of honor—namely, all of them—wants to be the one to make your shoulders lonesome for your head. They're roaming the countryside looking for you."

"How flattering," I said. "What, they're not scouring the city as well?"

"I think they believe you would never be so stupid as to come here."

"Well, I try to make it a policy never to be underestimated when it comes to stupidity," I said sourly.

"Don't count on it to help you in the long run. They'll be looking here soon enough. So what do you want? I'll tell you right now, if you're looking for an airlift out of here, I don't think I'm going to be able to carry you."

"I need help, all right. But not from you."

He stared at me with his unblinking eyes for a moment. "The princess," he said with immediate understanding.

"Yes."

"What makes you think she can help you? If she were a son, perhaps. As it is, her father has little to no regard for her, or haven't you been paying attention?"

"I assure you, I have," I said. "Nevertheless, she's my best shot at trying to salvage this. To begin with, I didn't kill Go Nogo."

"Didn't you?"

"No! Why?" I asked in annoyance. "Did you think I did?"

"Well, he was stabbed in the back," Mordant said reasonably. "That certainly sounded like your style."

I was about to issue a scathing retort until I realized that, yes, that more or less *did* sound like my style. "Be that as it may, I was not responsible," I said. "But I know who was."

"Really? Who?"

"A member of the Anaïs Ninjas."

Mordant cocked his head slightly and looked at me askance. "Really. That might well be of interest to the Imperior."

"That, along with the fact that I was subsequently approached by the Forked Tong. They want me to join them. If the Imperior has any interest in burrowing into the organization and destroying them from within, the opportunity may well have presented itself. Provided the Imperior's people don't kill that opportunity before it has the chance to benefit them."

"For 'the opportunity,' read 'Apropos.' "

"That," I nodded, "is the way of it."

"And you believe that somehow the princess can fix all this."

"Yes. I need to meet with her."

"Meet with her?"

He paused, and it might have been my imagination, but he sounded suspicious.

"Yes. Meet with her."

"Why? I can relay whatever you want to say . . ."

"But you cannot guarantee that she will believe it," I told him. "For me to truly convince her of the truth of what I'm saying, I need to be able to look her in the eyes. To tell her with my own voice and convince her to aid me. Plus she may have questions, and time is far too much of the essence. While you are busy flying back and forth, some of the Imperior's soldiers may find me and make short work of me."

"She may not come."

"She'll come," I said with conviction, hoping that conviction was not misplaced. "I'm certain of it."

For the longest few moments of my life, Mordant pondered what I was saying. If he refused to cooperate, or smelled some sort of trap, then I was effectively buggered. The odds of my gaining entrance to the palace were negligible. On the off chance I was able to get in, I likely would not get out in one piece.

But if I did not produce the princess, the Forked Tong would put me at the top of their list for swift and sure execution. Furthermore, I would have disappointed the lovely Veruh Wang Ho, which really shouldn't have factored in, yet did.

"All right," Mordant said, startling me from my brief reverie. "Are you staying within this place?"

"Yes."

"Don't go anywhere."

Beneath my hood, I couldn't help but smile a humorless smile. "I can assure you there is very little likelihood of that."

With that, Mordant bounced off my arm like a diver bounding into a lake. He ricocheted skyward, bouncing off buildings to gain altitude, and moments later was angling away into the sky.

There was nothing for me to do but wait.

I returned to my room, taking care not to make any sort of eye contact with the innkeeper. He simply bowed slightly upon passing me. Very likely he gave me no further thought, having things of far more importance on his mind than the activities of some sleepless guest. Still, I was nervous enough about my situation to spend the entire morning in my room wondering if, at any moment, soldiers were going to come crashing in. Call me a fool, but somehow I didn't think the wafer-thin walls were going to afford much in the way of protection.

One would have thought that every hour that passed would have made me feel more and more secure that I had not been somehow betrayed by Mitsu, or even the innkeeper. Instead all I did was get increasingly nervous, figuring that since the attack had not come yet, it would probably come soon.

By noon the innkeeper, from outside my door, was politely asking me if I wanted anything for lunch. I muttered as gracious a refusal as I could manage, considering my stomach was one large knot. The more time passed, the more I dwelt on all sorts of possible outcomes, and none of them—not a single damned one—was a good one.

So I hardly think it should come as a surprise when the sound of footsteps at my door and a gentle rap were enough to have me let out an embarrassingly high-pitched scream.

The puzzled voice of Mitsu came from the other side. It was definitely her. I could see her shadow. There was no one with her. "Apropos?" she called softly.

I sighed heavily and tried to slow the pounding of my heart. Feeling it unwise to call out her name, I just said softly, "Yes."

"If this is a bad time . . ."

"No, no," I assured her.

"I just . . . I thought you had a woman in there with you."

I bit my lower lip in chagrin, but then had to allow a soft, self-contemptuous laugh. "No. No woman. Just me doing my best impression of a woman."

"Oh." Obviously she had no idea why I would do that. I could see her shrug. "Well, it's . . . it's very effective."

"Thanks."

"Shall I come in there?"

"No. No, that's . . . quite all right." I got to my feet, grabbed my staff, and slid open the door.

She was once again dressed in a manner similar to a boy. If I hadn't known it was her, I would have thought her a him. I shook my head in wonderment. Even though I knew her gender, I never would have been able to tell. "I see you're wearing your traveling clothes."

Mitsu bowed slightly. "I'd be a bit conspicuous if I endeavored to depart looking the way you've seen me back at the palace."

"You mean naked?"

She laughed in that light voice of hers. "That too, I suppose."

I looked into her face and the guilt I felt was almost overwhelming. It took genuine mental force to get my legs to move, since I knew I was leading her to betrayal and capture. "Where are we going?" she asked.

"Out of here for the time being. Who knows who's listening in."

She nodded and we headed out.

As we walked into the street, thoughts continued to tumble through my head. Would she hate me? The notion that she would come to hate me over this betrayal was remarkably painful. I couldn't blame her if she did, though.

Why wouldn't she? Who in the world doesn't hate someone who betrays their trust? Then again, I'd had my own trust betrayed so many times that I'd become used to it. Maybe I'd just forgotten how much it hurt.

I was so self-involved that I didn't realize she was talking to me at first.

"Pardon?" I asked.

She made a slightly impatient whistling noise. "I was saying that you could have thanked me for dropping everything, sneaking out of the palace—"

"Of course, of course. I'm sorry."

We were strolling along the riverbank. The bridge was not far away at all. It seemed more than just a man-made structure. It was a metaphorical bridge, daring me to cross it and, in doing so, cross over into depths of betrayal I once would never have thought possible.

"Mordant says you claim you did not kill Go Nogo," she said. The amusement had vanished from her voice. She was all business now. This was a princess faced with a supplicant who desperately needed her aid and mercy.

"That's right, I didn't," I assured her. "I had nothing to do with that, or with the drugging of the tea which rendered all the men unconscious."

"Drugging of the—" She sounded amused. "Is that how you got away from my father?"

"Well . . . yes." I was suddenly suspicious. "Why? What had you heard?"

"As the story has grown in the retelling, you were described as a fiercely demented warrior who hacked and slashed his way out past some of the best soldiers Chinpan has to offer."

I should have laughed, I suppose. But I was so used to the almost routine nonsense that passed for human interaction that all I could do was be mildly amused. "Would that it were so," I assured her. "No, I tiptoed quietly around them while they were lying insensate."

"And who," she inquired, "had drugged them?"

One of my rules of thumb when engaged in a series of lies was to keep matters simple. If one couldn't come up with a fabrication that would sound convincing, nothing was as easy to put across as ignorance. "I do not know," I said.

"And why would they have administered this drug? To what end?"

"Again, I don't know."

"If it was an enemy intent on performing mischief, why didn't they commit it while my father and his people lay helpless?"

"Perhaps we are dealing with a disordered mind. We can ponder it from now until the end of existence and still find no comprehensible reason for any of the actions taken."

"That is very true," she said, much to my relief.

We were drawing nearer and nearer to the bridge. I wanted to shout a warning, to keep walking, to do anything except what I was doing. And yet I kept us moving forward. The day remained overcast, although the rain had stopped falling.

I looked around and tried to figure out where the eyes of the Forked Tong were. Thanks to the weather, shadows seemed to crawl everywhere through the crowded buildings. At any moment, someone could come leaping out and grab Mitsu from my side.

"So what would you have me do now?" she asked.

"I'm not sure."

"Interesting, the position you find yourself in."

I laughed coarsely. "I wouldn't exactly call this fiasco 'interesting.' "

"Oh, I would."

We were at the edge of the bridge. All I had to do was

walk along and, presuming she followed, we would be at the midpoint within moments. At that point, I would have fulfilled my end of the bargain.

She saw my hesitation, and glanced at the bridge. "Do you wish to walk over to the fish market? I'd think you'd want to go nowhere near the place, considering the difficulties we've encountered there before."

One of the greatest strengths, the most consistent certainties in my life was that I was a superb liar. It had never presented a difficulty for me. Yet I sounded incredibly unconvincing to myself as I said, "What an opportunity, then, to explore it without people trying to kill us."

She'll never fall for that. Ever.

"By all means," said Mitsu.

I gulped deeply as we set foot on the bridge. I wanted to scream *Run! Run now! Run quickly and as far as you can! Leave me to my miserable fate!* And I did scream it. Screamed it so loud within my head that my brain was aching. Insane as it sounds, I was hoping that the shouting from within my skull would be heard by her. Unsurprisingly, it didn't work.

As we started across the bridge of no return, Mitsu said, "Remember, Apropos, when I willingly sacrificed my handmaiden in order to satisfy my father's sense of honor?"

"Of course I do."

"And you condemned me for it. Even when I explained it to you, you still never truly accepted it or appreciated my point of view."

"I appreciated it as best I could. I apologize if it was insufficient for you."

She looked at me thoughtfully. I tried to keep my gaze from wandering. My steps felt even more leaden than they usually did, my right leg so heavy I thought it was going to drag me right off the bridge, despite the high handrails.

"What if I told you there was a way out of our current predicament?"

"What sort of way out?"

"Well, let us say that I am able to convince my father of the truth of your story. That you were not responsible for the death of Go Nogo. Unfortunately it will do nothing to erase the stain of failure attached to your design for his other home. That mark still remains, and the scale would have to be balanced."

"Then . . . what would happen?"

"A life would have to be sacrificed. Fortunately, that could be solved without the loss of yours. All you need do is select a personal servant to lay down his or her life in order to redeem your honor. Then all will be well."

"But . . . but I didn't have any personal servants . . ."

"Have you forgotten?"

I stopped walking. We were about thirty feet shy of the middle of the bridge. "Forgotten . . . ?"

"Timtup?"

Believe it or not, I blanked on the name at first. But then I remembered. "The . . . the bathing maiden . . ."

"Yes. You had sex with her. She may not have been exclusively your servant, but being intimate with a palace servant would certainly qualify as 'personal' in matters of honor."

"Yes, I did have sex with her," I said, thinking fast. "But . . . but it wasn't really personal. It was . . . truthfully . . . it wasn't anything. It was . . . a diversion. A way to pass the time."

"Ahhh," she said. "I thought as much. You wanted . . . something else?"

That was absolutely true, yes. I wanted passion, depth of emotion. The bathing maiden had been efficient, interested in pleasuring me . . . but beyond that, there had been no connection. And I was finding that I wanted, needed that connection. Otherwise all it did was reinforce the emptiness within me.

In short, I wanted the intensity of feeling that I hadn't even known I was missing . . . until I had encountered Veruh Wang Ho.

"Yes. Exactly," I said.

"I thought that might be the case. Still . . . the physical act was undertaken. That is sufficient for our needs."

My heart clenched. "You're . . . you're telling me that all I have to do to get into the Imperior's good graces is to ask an innocent young woman to lay down her life. To die simply because we had sexual intercourse."

"It is slightly more complicated than that, but yes. That is essentially it."

"I . . . I can't . . . that would . . . that would . . ."

"That would make you as bad as me?" She said it with faint sarcasm, but she almost sounded genuinely interested.

My thoughts were swimming. I moved away from her, needing distance, trying to find grounding. Should I do that? Could I? Actually ask an innocent young woman to sacrifice her life for me? Was I that craven?

Or was it craven? If I kept in mind Mitsu's arguments over the past months, then to take her suggestion would simply be in keeping with the philosophies and the—

No.

Just that flatly, my inner voice rejected it. And when one considered that there was no greater advocate of my finding ways to live than my inner voice, then that had to be considered a thumpingly flat rejection.

There was only so far, and no further, that I would go to save my own miserable hide. This was, believe it or not, a bit of a revelation for me. I'd really thought there was nothing I would not stop at to keep breathing. But apparently that was not the case.

"No," I said, my tone flat. "No, I can't do that."

"Even if it provides a means of saving your life?"

"Even if. I have . . . other considerations," I said.

"Yet you would sacrifice me to prove your loyalty to the Forked Tong."

As much in disarray as my thoughts had been, that comment of hers suddenly penetrated the haze of confusion like an ice spear.

I turned to face her and realized we were standing right in the center of the bridge. Without even noticing it, since I had been so distracted by the torment and confusion in my mind, I had brought her to where I had promised.

My mouth was suddenly dry.

She was shaking her head, and there was a satisfied smirk playing upon her lips. "Ah, Apropos. Ever the contradiction. You would condemn me for sacrificing a handmaiden, and yet you think nothing of placing me in jeopardy when it suits your needs."

"Saying that I think nothing of it isn't remotely accurate. I've agonized over this more than any other decision I've made in my life, and how the hell do you know that's what I was doing?"

Except she didn't really have to provide me the answer, because I already knew it. Even as she stepped toward me, placed her right fist into her left palm and mashed them against her breasts three times, it was clear to me.

"I knew it," I muttered. "I *knew* you were one of them. Were you there in the shrine? Standing there, watching me sweat?"

"No," she said. "I was at the palace. But I learned of it quickly enough. We have eyes and ears everywhere. And a quick spy who relayed information to me with unmatched alacrity."

"Mordant," I said with growing comprehension. "I *thought*

I saw something winged in the trees of the forest. It was he."

"Yes." She patted my face. Reflexively I drew back slightly.
My thoughts were a strange mishmash of triumph that I had
fulfilled my end of the bargain, thus "proving" my loyalty,
and relief over the fact that Mitsu was in fact in no danger at
all since she was already a part of this insanity. But I had not
known that Mitsu was part of it when I'd willingly brought
her to this place to put her at the mercy of the Forked Tong.

As if she could read my mind, she smiled and, keeping
her hand on my cheek, said, "Don't be concerned,
Apropos. I'm very pleased matters have worked out this
way. Now you will never be able to feel morally superior to
me. After all, my handmaidens willingly and knowingly
make the sacrifices that are asked of them. You, on the
other hand, were going to take an 'innocent' girl and sacrifice her for the purely self-serving purpose of showing your
loyalty and desire to join our cause. So whose escutcheon is
the more stained? Yours? Or mine?"

"I have no escutcheon," I replied. "I have nothing. And
perhaps that's exactly what I deserve."

She drew my face to hers and kissed me lightly on the
forehead. "Do not feel that way. You are about to embark
on the most glorious adventure of your life. One that you
richly deserve."

I hated it when people told me that.

"Well," I said, "at least you had nothing to do with the
attack on my teacher."

She looked at me, amused. "You don't realize? I was the
one who fought you that night. You served to delay me so
that I wasn't in the hut when he . . ."

"You?" I couldn't believe it. "But . . . no . . . it . . ."

She nodded. "Yes. It was on my way back from that business that I came upon Mordant and recogniz—"

I wasn't listening. "I saw you naked!"

Mitsu blinked in confusion. "What?"

"I cut the woman I fought. Cut her badly! I would have seen a vicious, red wound on you . . ."

"Here, you mean?" she asked, touching her shoulder area. "A wound that might look like the tongue of a dragon?"

"Yes, just like . . ." I stopped, thunderstruck. "Gods . . . your tattoo . . ."

"One of the sisters obliged me. I consider my body a work of art, Apropos. You defaced it. I had to restore it. A job well done, don't you think. Is my body not a piece of art once more?"

"Yes. I'm especially impressed by your brushwork."

She swatted me on the back of the head.

Chapter 8

Divine Revelations

 he sun had come out, but you couldn't have told that from where we were.

Following Mitsu had been like following a flickering shadow during a moonless night as we made our way to a section of town far removed from any we'd been to. The streets grew narrower and narrower to the point where it seemed almost impossible to keep moving through them, and yet we did. I had gone back to the inn and gotten my belongings, and we had headed out almost immediately. Now I was starting to wish I'd stayed where I was. I was constantly checking my person every time I came near any of the denizens of this pit to make sure that no one had relieved me of any valuables. "That's probably a very wise thing for you to do," Mitsu had assured me. As assurances went, it wasn't very reassuring.

Because the buildings were so close together, the roofs overlapped. As a result, no sun was filtering through. I felt as if we were swimming in gloom. Just to try and distract myself from the sense of foreboding, I tried to engage Mitsu in conversation as to how she had wound up being part of an organization dedicated to removing her father from office.

She was not especially forthcoming, unfortunately, which was a bit of a change from the young woman I'd known who was happy to talk about practically anything. Then again, it seemed ridiculous to think of her as the young woman I'd known considering, obviously, I hadn't really known a damned thing about her.

All she would say was "You've no idea what my father's done. No idea what he's like. If you knew, you'd understand."

"I can't know unless you tell me."

"Not yet. When it's time, you'll know."

"Wonderful," I said, rolling my eyes. "But I still don't understand. If you lived in the palace with him, and you want him out of power, why not just—"

She stopped, turned, her eyes flashing. "Kill my father?"

"Well . . . yes. Except you make it sound so unpleasant when you say it that way."

Mitsu looked disappointed with me . . . which, considering the circumstances, was quite an achievement. "That is not an option. Eventually you will understand. But not now."

And again she had said I wouldn't be able to understand. I wasn't sure if she was just being patronizing, or whether she was one of these people who believed that fate and the gods dictated the timing of certain things, and it wasn't for her to do anything to muck with that timing. The one thing I knew for certain, though, was I was starting to get well and truly annoyed.

"Where are we going? Will I understand that?" I asked.

"Yes. Once we get there."

"Wonderful."

Nothing more was said. Eventually we reached a section of town so impenetrable that we were the only people on the narrow street. I felt as if the buildings were alive, moving toward us to hem us in so we'd have no possible means of escape.

Suddenly I collided with something, and realized belatedly it was Mitsu's back. At least I thought it was. It had gotten so dark that I could barely see her face. If she'd been dressed in her Anaïs Ninja black, she would have literally been invisible.

"Through here," she said.

I had no idea where she was pointing. I couldn't see a damned thing. "Where?" I said.

I felt her placing her hands upon my shoulders and guiding me slowly forward. I kept my walking staff extended, like a blind man with his cane, waiting for it to bump into a wall so I would know when to stop walking. But it encountered no obstruction. Instead I kept moving and, within moments, was off the street entirely. I was completely surrounded by blackness. No air currents were moving about me; I was in some sort of structure, but how big it was or what it looked like, I couldn't even begin to guess.

"Mitsu?" I called out softly.

No answer.

"Mit—?"

And then that scent wafted toward me. That singular, incredible scent. My skin tingled just from the slightest hint of it. I felt as if it was lifting me up, up off my feet, sending me soaring above the city. As if I could touch the heavens just buoyed by it.

"So . . . you've proven your loyalty."

It was she. Her voice was coming from just ahead of me. I moved in the direction of where I thought it was coming from and just ahead there was the gentle flickering of light. More candles. The Forked Tong apparently used more candles than everyone else in Chinpan put together.

I took several deep breaths to clear my mind. It was essential that I not let my infatuation—or was it obsession—with Veruh Wang Ho cloud my judgment. "You deduce that because Mitsu brought me here."

"Yes."

"Are more of the sisters here?"

"No. We are alone."

I listened carefully, my hearing as sharp as ever. I was reasonably sure she was telling the truth. I could detect no one else around.

The twinkling illumination made it easier for me to see the doorway of the room just ahead. One more deep breath, and then I entered the room.

Veruh Wang Ho was seated cross-legged upon the floor. As opposed to the far more elaborate garb she had sported when I had first encountered her, now she was outfitted in a simple white kimono. Her face was still delicately made-up, though, her hair elaborately piled atop her head.

That first rush of passion I felt for her paled in comparison to what I felt for her now. That same giddy, intoxicating rush of sensation.

There was a small table in front of her with the now-familiar sight of tea set up. Two cups were upon the table on opposite sides. The steeping tea was in the middle. She gestured for me to sit, and I did so. It was something of a relief. In her presence, I was literally becoming weak in the knees. It would hardly be the height of manliness to collapse in front of her.

"I confess," she said softly, "I am glad. Very . . . very glad."

"Really. Why would that be?"

The edges of her mouth upturned slightly, and there was amusement in her dark brown eyes. "Why do you think?"

"I couldn't begin to guess."

"To guess? Or to hope?"

The truth was the latter rather than the former, but I did

not trust myself to speak. For someone who had spent a lifetime being glib, I was atypically tongue-tied.

She poured the tea into my cup, then into hers. I reminded myself that the woman was evil—which, granted, was part of what I found so attractive—and did not make a move for my cup. She saw that I was allowing it to sit there, and appeared most amused by my caution. Without comment, she lifted her own cup and delicately sipped from it. I noticed a small bit of her bright red lipstick was rubbing off on the inside of the cup. I sipped from mine as well at that point.

"What would you know, Apropos?" she asked.

I lowered my glass. "Know?"

"Would you know the truth? Or would you know me?"

I quickly put the cup down, because I could feel my hands starting to tremble. "Know you . . . in what sense?"

She did not answer immediately, instead prolonging the delightful agony by simply sipping more tea. Then she held it a few inches from her face and the smile widened ever so slightly. "Apropos . . . we are aware, we two."

"Aware?" I asked guardedly.

"Yes." Her voice continued in its lyric grace. "There are very few people in this world who are aware of the truth of things. Who see the world for what it is, and what it isn't. People with true clarity of vision. And when two such encounter each other, there is an instant attraction. You must have felt it. Do not bother to deny it."

"I . . ." My voice felt thick and heavy, as if coated with tar. "I . . . don't deny it . . ."

She nodded slightly, apparently approving. "You want to know why events of recent vintage have happened. You also want to know me . . . in every sense of the word 'know.' You may have either or. Choose."

I wanted to scream. I wanted to burst out of my skin. I

wanted to clamber across the small table, knock her to her back, and take her right there on the floor of this darkened room.

But I could not allow myself to become totally at the mercy of lustful impulses, no matter how gratifying they might be if acted upon. As much as I wanted her, burned for her . . . there were priorities that needed attending to. Things that simply had to be done.

I wanted her. Desperately. But I, who was one of the most selfish bastards in the history of selfish bastards, couldn't do it. What I didn't know now could get me killed later.

"Why have these things happened?" I asked. It was the most difficult five words I'd ever uttered together.

Veruh Wang Ho looked truly surprised. I think there'd been no doubt in her mind that I would forgo all other concerns in favor of satisfying my carnal urges with the woman who might very likely be my true soul mate. Then the surprise gave way to . . . approval? Yes. She didn't seem upset at all. In fact, it appeared that she was regarding me with something akin to approval.

"Very well," she said. "Let us be specific, then. What do you wish to know?"

I decided to speak forcefully and, even more important, quickly. Who knew if she might change her mind and feel that I had somehow insulted her by making the choice that I had. "Mitsu resides within the palace," I said. "As does the most obvious enemy that the Forked Tong has. I understand Mitsu's rejection of the notion that she assassinate her own father. On the other hand, I suspect her loyalty to your organization would have prompted her to obey you if you ordered her to do it. Furthermore, with her there, she could very likely facilitate your getting your own agents and assassins within the palace walls. In short, if you wanted the

Imperior dead, then he would be dead. Yet he lives. What am I to conclude from that?"

"You seem to be under the impression that the Imperior would die as do other men."

That stopped me short. "Well . . . why would he not? Is he not like other men?"

"No. He is a shennong."

"A what?" The word was completely new to me. I didn't have the faintest idea to what she was referring.

"A shennong. A wielder of sorcerous powers."

"He's a *weaver?*" I mentally called up an image of the wrinkled little man and tried to comprehend how such a one would possibly be any sort of true magic user. "I don't believe it!"

"It does not matter whether you believe it or not," she said, sounding quite reasonable. Her tea was getting low in its cup and she refreshed it from the pot. She offered it to me and I politely waved her off. "It is true. Furthermore, he has knowledge that we need. Knowledge both general and specific, which precludes us from simply removing him from the equation . . . as much as we would like to."

"What 'specific knowledge' are you referring to?"

"Ah . . . that is not my story to tell." With that, she sipped more from her newly replenished cup. "The point is, if we were able to kill him by treachery, it still would not serve our needs. Plus the military might he wields is vast. Greater than we can readily combat on our own. So because of the nature of our opponent, and the magicks and might he wields, we had sought help in dealing with him. We thought we had found it. We had heard tell of a vastly powerful magician from a distant, foreign land. A round-eyed individual, similar to yourself. We had learned that he would be traveling by boat to a land some distance from here, known as 'Azure.' We sent an emissary to meet him there. It was our intention to enlist his aid and bring him here to defeat the Imperior. But the famed sorcerer never arrived in Azure. As of this point, the vessel he was coming aboard is so overdue that it is generally believed his ship was lost in the crossing."

"Uh . . . huh," I said slowly. "And this, uhm . . . this sorcerer. What would his, uh, his name be . . . just out of curiosity?"

"An odd name, actually. Almost as odd as yours. He was known as Ronnell McDonnell of—"

"—the Clan McDonnell," I finished.

With eyebrow arched, she said, "You've heard of him."

"In passing, yes. I, uhm . . ." I coughed loudly. "I think assuming him lost at sea by this point is probably a wise idea. It's, uh . . . been a long time."

"Yes. And so we have taken other measures."

"What other measures?"

She placed the cup of tea down gently and then smiled with grim satisfaction. "It has taken us years to reach a point of mutual trust and respect with them, but we have done so."

"Them?" I felt as if all I was doing was echoing what she was saying. Then again, I so adored every perfect word that came from those perfect lips, that it didn't bother me.

She nodded. " 'Them' being the Mingol hordes, a fierce tribe that lives to the west of our land, beyond the outer provinces. Very soon, they will come swarming over the hills of Chinpan, and overwhelm the Imperior's army."

"Are they of sufficient number to do so?"

"They are. With their help, we will be able to attend to the physical defenses. But we still require help against the Imperior himself . . . help that you can provide."

That did not seem terribly likely to me. "I can? What can I do?"

"What would you do for me if I asked?"

I didn't hesitate. "Anything. Anything you asked, any-thing you desired. Anything within my ability."

She leaned forward. Her breath was upon my face, and it had the same sweet honeysuckle smell as her skin.

"Do you trust me?" she whispered.

And once more, I didn't hesitate. "No," I said.

The word had popped out before I even realized it. My eyes were half-lidded, but they snapped open as I realized the unexpected, and potentially crushing, honesty of my answer. I looked into her face to see her response, which I was certain would be roiling fury.

Instead she laughed.

"Well said," she told me. "You know me well. Had you said 'yes,' I would have felt most sorry for you. Perhaps I might even have done away with you, in a fit of pique. One never knows what I might do." She reached over and ran a tapering finger along the line of my chin. I trembled at her gentle touch. "But you! You always know just what to say, don't you."

"It's how I've managed to survive," I replied.

"Yes. Yes, a survivor you are, and shall be. I see that in you. Just as I also see in you the potential mystic edge that we need to overcome the Imperior. It is that edge that has made you such a priority with us."

I knew it before she said it. "The sword," I said, my hand resting upon the bird-headed hilt of the weapon hanging at my waist. "The tachi sword."

She nodded. "You are the bearer of the demon sword."

The phrasing surprised me. "The what?"

"Kumagatu, the demon sword. You've no clue, Apropos, how long it had been sought. You hold there a blade of leg-end and mystery. A blade that has passed from owner to owner, leaving devastation and death in its wake. It is said that the blade was spat up one day centuries ago from the very bowels of hell, emerging from an active volcano. That it landed in the hands of a powerful shennong who was appalled by the amount of power it possessed, and managed to bind it and harness it."

To say I was extremely nervous by that point would be to understate it. Here I'd had this damned thing—this literally damned thing—hanging at my side all this time, and I was suddenly discovering that it was the deadliest weapon in the country. I had already figured out they were after the sword, and that it might even have had some sort of power of its own. But the level of what she was describing bordered on the terrifying. Demons? Volcanoes? Spat up from the bowels of hell? I knew a little something about mystical talismans, and that little something was that whatever power they possessed sooner or later turned around and bit you on the ass. Considering what she was describing, this one could rip off my entire backside with one chew.

My impulse was to rip it off my belt and shout, "Here! Take the bloody sword!" But I resisted it because, as I had just admitted, I didn't trust her. And as long as I had something she wanted, I figured I was safe . . . although "safe" was a very relative word under the circumstances.

My mouth moved, but no sound came out. I cleared my throat and this time managed to say, "Bind and . . . and harness it?"

"Yes. With potent magicks that remain to this day. Even so, the shennong yielded to the temptation to use it, and its power consumed him. Since that time, it had been lost for ages. But it was finally tracked down by the Anaïs Ninjas of the Skang Kei, in the possession of a madman named Ali."

I bristled upon hearing that. It didn't matter how enamored I was of her. I was not going to tolerate such words.

"He was no madman," I said heatedly. "He was my teacher, a great fighter . . ."

She laughed at that, and then she saw the anger in my face. Immediately she looked contrite, as if sorry that she was causing me pain. "Oh . . . oh, sweet Apropos," she said, and then she leaned forward and her lips brushed against mine.

I trembled upon the contact, but resisted the urge to lose myself, to give in to the pulsing urgency within me. Instead, with superhuman effort, I remained focused and insisted, "He was . . . a great man . . . a great fighter . . ."

"I do not say this to hurt you, because I understand your devotion to him, and in a way it is touching. But you must understand . . . he was no fighter. He was a senile lunatic. Everyone knew it, even the people of his own village. But it pleased them to delude themselves into thinking that he was a great and wise man. Furthermore, they knew that he wielded a devastating power. But they had no desire to bring that power down upon themselves, so it was within their interest to cater to it. That power, of course, being the sword. Ali stumbled upon the magic words which had bound the sword, and they enabled him to harness its might. Without those magic words, the sword is simply an ordinary sword."

"That's why you sent your shadow sisters. But if they needed to know these magic words in order to wield the sword, why did they kill him?"

"They didn't."

"Don't tell me that," I said angrily. "I saw with my own eyes . . ."

"What? His body?"

"Yes!"

"And the wounds?"

"I . . ."

I searched my memory, tried to recall where on his body

he had been stabbed. I couldn't recall. "He . . . was lying flat on his stomach. So he was probably stabbed through the chest or—"

"Did you see blood pooling beneath him?"

"Well . . . no. But . . ."

"Apropos," she said gently, "the sisters did not kill him. To become possessor of the blade was not enough. We needed those magic words. But when he was confronted by the sisters, Ali had some sort of attack. His heart, perhaps, or something within his brain . . . we do not know. All we know is that one moment he was facing the sisters, and the next, he had collapsed. When they checked his body, they found he was dead." Softly, she added, "If it is of any consolation, the sisters are reasonably sure he did not suffer. The end was . . . was very quick."

"That's . . . good to know."

"When our people recognized the sword in the marketplace, they attacked you in hopes that you would speak the magic words and activate it, so that we would learn it in that way. But you did not do so. It does not matter now, though," she said with a shrug, "for you have become our willing ally."

For a long moment, nothing was said. Then her lips were right against my ear, and her breath was hot against it as she whispered, "You were his student. The inheritor of the sword. And you are our willing ally. Do you know the words? The words that activate the magic of the sword."

"Of course I do," I said quickly. "But I've learned something about alliances: What makes them function is when they operate from mutual strength. You need me because of what I know. If you know it as well, you will no longer need me, and my worth as your ally will be greatly diminished."

"Perhaps. Or perhaps you are simply lying about knowing the magic phrase."

"Always a possibility," I said. "Either way, I've no intention of telling you what it is."

"Can you whisper it without my hearing it and bring the sword to life so I can see a demonstration?"

"Yes . . . if you have an overwhelming desire to die," I said, improvising as fast as I could. "You see, once the blade is brought to life, it will slaughter everyone around it, save the blade's wielder, until they are all dead. Now if you truly wish me to do this thing, then I can—"

"No," she said quickly. "That . . . will not be necessary."

"Would you like me to . . . ?"

"No."

I was very much enjoying the power I was wielding at that moment. Even without the magic words, I was suddenly in charge. Veruh was clearly daunted by the power of the blade and the implicit threat that I would use it. I felt as if it was shifting the balance of power over to me.

Thus emboldened, I put my hand behind her head and pulled her to me, even as she was still forming the word "No" in response to my previous question. The word was smothered against my lips. She stiffened slightly in surprise, but then became soft and pliant against me. She murmured against my mouth, made soft cooing noises, and when we parted she smiled and touched my face.

"You were the most exotic-looking person," she said.

"I have never met anyone like you," I told her. "I'm not sure if there is anyone like you."

"You may very well be right about that."

There were too many bits and pieces of information floating around in my brain. Too many things for me to assimilate, to comprehend. I chose instead to jettison them and focus on the one thing that was clear and pure and true, and that was my attraction to this incredible, phenomenal woman. All else was set aside, and the second

time our lips came into contact, it was more her kissing me
than the other way around. Her tongue darted into my
mouth, and energy seemed to dance between us. My body
trembled from it and when we came up for air, I managed
to say, "What . . . was . . . ?"

"My spirit. My 'shi.' I shared a bit of mine with you, and
took some of yours into me, since you don't yet know how
to focus it yourself. But I will teach you. Show you things
you haven't known."

I reached for her breasts, but she placed her hand atop
mine gently and whispered, "I will touch . . . and you will
feel."

Then she leaned over and blew out the candle.

She told me to lie down upon my back, and I did. And
then . . .

. . . then . . .

I cannot even begin to describe it. Clothes rustled and
fell away, and there were more scents that permeated my
very being, and her lips were everywhere, everywhere, and
her skin rubbed against mine, with more of that energy,
that "shi" seeming to leap off her into me. My body trembled beneath her ministrations, and then I slipped into
incredible moistness that sent my consciousness spiraling
away. I was outside and inside myself all at the same time,
and thoughts of Ali and the village and Mitsu and Mordant
and all of them, they were gone, just gone, of no importance whatsoever. The only thing that mattered was Veruh
and the things she was doing with me and to me, and the
heat built within me and built and built, and I was that
volcano that had spit up the sword, and when I erupted it
seemed to go on forever, and when I was sated and thought
nothing more could happen, she started over again, and
soon I was unable to distinguish reality from fantasy. The
real world, such as it was, had lost all meaning to me

because it paled in significance to the overwhelming glory that was Veruh Wang Ho.

Time passed.

How much time, I did not know. It might have been later in the day, it might have been days later. I wasn't hungry, I knew that. All sustenance was drawn from the incredible energies that Veruh had unleashed within me.

All I knew was that, eventually, an eternity later, I was lying in darkness.

My eyes had adjusted somewhat to the lack of light, and suddenly a full and true comprehension of my vulnerability flooded into me. I reached out, grabbing for where I thought the demon sword should be . . .

. . . and there it was. The sword, plus my other weapons, my staff, even my clothes, all in a tidy heap upon the floor.

She had taken nothing.

This evil woman, this woman from whom I had expected betrayal, had taken nothing of mine.

Of course, there was always the consideration that nothing of mine would have been of much benefit to her. She couldn't make use of the demon sword without the magic words that she thought I knew. The rest of my weapons were useless to her. She could have tried to torture me for the information, but considering the power I had ascribed to the sword, she might well have been bringing her own doom upon herself.

So she had loved me, or at least made love to me in ways that I had never experienced. Whatever connection I felt our souls had made, it had been solidified and grown through the physical contact.

Gods knew I was no virgin. But I had never, ever, encountered anything like the techniques that Veruh had used. Or perhaps . . . perhaps it was something as simple as that we had bonded on an emotional and spiritual level in a way that I never had with another woman.

Except . . .

. . . now what?

There, in the darkness, my mind began to wander. Wander toward a conclusion that I couldn't say I was enjoying drawing.

I had no idea whose side I was on anymore.

It had never been a question in my life before, because the answer had always been the same: I was on my side. I didn't give a damn about anyone else. There was me, my considerations, my concerns, and that was it. The rest of humanity could go hang.

That hadn't been happening in Chinpan, however. Instead, ever since I had come to this infernal country, I had wound up forming alliances with, or developing feelings for, just about everyone with whom I'd come into contact.

And every single alliance I'd formed and feeling I'd had had come a-cropper. Had been disastrous.

I should not have been surprised at this. Not a cynic like me. Not someone who always expected everything to turn to shite.

Yet I was indeed surprised.

There had been the people of Hosbiyu. The gentle, sweet, loving farm people . . . who, as it turned out, used the bodies of their departed enemies to help their crops grow.

There was my teacher, my mentor, Ali. The man who had me engage in involved exercises and lessons that I had convinced myself all led to some greater purpose. Except, if what I'd now learned was true he hadn't known a damned thing about self-defense. This entire "Zennihilation" thing was just rubbish. Something he'd developed to cover the fact that he was a fake and a charlatan, dependent upon a demon sword to dispatch any serious threats.

Then there was the princess. The one whom I had thought I had come to know, despite a rocky beginning, only to discover that she was part of an overly amorous cult of shadow warriors plotting to bring down her father. And as for her father . . . well, actually, he was the least disappointing of the lot of them. At least I'd known going in that he was something of a loony. Even when he was busy calling me his friend and expressing satisfaction, I knew that entire relationship could come apart at any time.

And Veruh . . .

My soul mate.

My lover.

My eventual betrayer.

That had to be the case. Sooner or later, somehow or other, she would betray me. Between the fact that she was already heading up a criminal organization and my own tendency to hook up with women who stabbed me in the back at the first opportunity, it was only a matter of time.

I had wanted to begin a new life in Chinpan. I had wanted things to be different here.

But they weren't.

Because of me.

As much as I enjoyed blaming the gods or the fates, or writing off the rest of humanity as base and pointless, I was being brought face-to-face with the realization that unhappiness followed me the way disease followed rats.

I had found myself in the midst of a life-and-death political struggle that would have immense consequences for all concerned—

And I simply didn't care. The princess was a shadow assassin, the Imperior wanted to kill me, the criminals were bleeding criminals, the innocents had dark secrets, my lover would probably betray me, my teacher was probably a sham and, if the evil and probable betrayer could be believed, had died of natural causes.

Oh, and I had in my possession a weapon of deeply

destructive power, except I didn't know how to use it. But people who would likely kill me as soon as look at me thought I did know how to use it, which was probably the only thing keeping me alive. And those were my allies.

What the hell was I doing there? What was the point of any of it? It was madness. Madness. Here I had endeavored to become more a part of the world, and instead I was more detached than ever before.

In Isteria, I had known the dark, unpleasant underbelly of the order of knights who were so revered. Because of my own foul conception, I knew that the principles of chivalry were a sham and a joke.

So here I had come to Chinpan, to a far-off land, handed a new and fresh start by the gods, and discovered a people who claim to elevate honor above everything. Yet not a single one of them appeared to be motivated by honor at all. Instead it was merely a pretext to do whatever the hell they felt like doing. Everyone here was just as self-absorbed and vicious as anyone else I'd ever met.

"I have to get out of here," I said aloud, and realized that it probably hadn't been especially bright for me to articulate that intention.

But then I listened very carefully for some indication of soft breathing in the darkness. Nothing.

Veruh was gone. Gone as if she was never there.

I whispered her name. No response. A creature of mystery was she, and obviously she liked to keep it that way. I supposed I couldn't blame her. She enjoyed her exotic makeup, her dalliances in the dark. It just helped to underscore the hopelessness of any sort of long-term relationship. Familiarity takes the exotic and reduces it to the mundane. And if Veruh Wang Ho became mundane, she would lose an important part of herself. Obviously she knew that, and I was just beginning to understand it.

So where did that leave me?

Depressed, naked, and in the dark.

I began to shiver, as if the shadows were permeating my skin. This was certainly alarming, considering that one time shadows really had permeated my skin. It was enough to motivate me to dress quickly and get the hell out of there. And by the time I was back out in the incredibly narrow street, I knew exactly what I was going to do.

With all the evils I was faced with . . . I was going to return to the least of them.

The people of Hosbiyu might not have been what I expected them to be . . . and Ali might well have been a fraud and a fool . . . but at least they weren't actively trying to kill me, which put them several notches above everyone else in this damned place.

I was going to go back to the farmers.

I would live as one of them for as long as I could . . . hopefully forever. With any luck at all, I would seek solace in the anonymity of the village.

Would the Forked Tong come after me there? There was always the possibility. Then again, there was the possibility they would come after me anywhere. On the other hand, perhaps there was something in Ali's personal effects that contained the words that would activate the demon sword. And if I wielded its power, why then . . .

Then I could defend the village.

I wouldn't use it to seek out power for myself. I wouldn't use it to conquer. It would simply be for defense, and ideally I would never have to use it. But if I did, then it was a necessary evil. And that would be a nice change of pace from all the unnecessary evil I had encountered in my life.

And then I heard Veruh's soft voice. It seemed to come from right beside me and everywhere, all at the same time.

"You want to leave?" she asked.

I was quiet for a long moment. I considered all the lies I could tell at that point.

But I was tired of lies. And for someone like me, for whom lies had been as mother's milk, that was a remarkable admission to make, even for myself.

"Yes," I said.

My shoulders tensed. I braced myself for . . . I wasn't sure what. A reaction. A torrent of rage. A blow to the back of the head. Something.

"Very well."

I blinked in the darkness. "Pardon?"

"Very well. You may go. We of the Forked Tong are patient. We do not require all our goals to be met immediately. When you leave this place, do you think you can find your way to the West Gate?"

"I . . . I think so. Yes."

"Go there. The forest is near. Enter it, go fifty paces. A horse will be waiting for you. Do what you need to do."

"And . . . what if I don't come back?"

There was silence. And then, sounding both amused and saddened, she said, "If there is something you love, you must be willing to release it. If it returns to you of its own volition, it will never leave you again."

"You're . . . saying you love me?"

"I'm saying go. All else can wait."

I was suspicious, of course. It was too perfect not to be suspicious of it. I started to make my way out through the darkness, hesitated, and then said, "How do you know when you truly love someone?"

"Have you never truly been in love?"

"I don't think I ever have, no."

"Ah. The way you know, Apropos . . . is that the welfare of your partner is more important than your own welfare.

You elevate their needs above your own. Are you capable of that?"

Another question which almost screamed for a lie. Yet once again, I spoke the truth:

"I don't know."

"Nor do I," she admitted. "So I suppose . . . this will be a chance for both of us to find out. Farewell, my love."

And with that, she was gone. Moments later, so was I.

Chapter 9

Chin Music

I had to say this for the Forked Tong: They were damned efficient.

I had only one mishap on my way to the West Gate. Considering that I had been . . . not exactly lying, but let us say overly confident in stating I could find my way to the West Gate, it was miraculous I did not encounter more problems than I did.

I actually found my way out of the twisting, turning darkened section of Taikyo and was heading over toward the West Gate . . . after asking directions merely four times from passersby and still managing to get myself lost repeatedly.

I was passing through a busy marketplace in which vendors were selling various wares, many of them assorted trinkets. For no particular reason, little Kit Chinette sprang to mind, and I thought of her face lighting up if I brought her something. I saw a small, black-and-white stuffed bear, identical to the one I'd last seen chewing happily away on bamboo. I envisioned Kit cuddling it. I picked it up. It was weighted nicely, filled as near as I could tell with small hardened beans. I purchased it from the grateful merchant, who apparently had had a slow day and was already preparing to close up as night was falling.

"Halt!"

I turned and saw a Hamunri soldier standing about ten feet away. His eyes narrowed. He was looking right at me. Even though my hood was up, obscuring my features, and my cloak was concealing my weapons. But it was possible he recognized the cloak itself, or the walking staff I was holding.

It wasn't immediately evident to others that I was the focus of his attention. I froze, trying to determine what to do. Talk to him? Run? Fight him? None of them seemed attractive options.

Suddenly I heard the distinctive high-pitched buzz of an arrow slicing the air, followed by a thud as it struck its target. The soldier looked confused for a moment, took a step forward on a shaking leg, and then went down like a felled tree.

A torrent of confused cries erupted from all around me. As for me, I didn't hesitate to haul myself out of there. If he had any associates, they'd be showing up in response to the tumult, and I wanted to distance myself from it as quickly as I could.

I wasn't puzzled over the arrow's origin. Obviously Veruh Wang Ho had made sure that I was watched by one of her people, to make certain I got on my way safely. I was genuinely touched. I'd never had a lover considerate enough to have arrows fired into my enemies. A special woman indeed.

I encountered no further problems as I headed out the West Gate. I did exactly as Veruh had told me and, sure enough, the horse was where she said it would be. It was not the impressive black-coated animal I'd ridden to Taikyo, nor did I expect it to have the same level of intelligence. But as long as it got me where I needed to go, we were going to get along just fine.

I mounted up, snapped the reins, and we moved out.

Never have I been more cautious in traveling.

As sharp as my senses usually were, I depended upon them now as never before. I had to be aware of everyone I might encounter upon the road, for there was every chance I might run into more Hamunri warriors. And if I did, I wasn't going to be able to count on some friendly archer watching my back.

I used every technique I had ever learned to hide my movements from any who might be searching for me. After all, I knew that supposedly there were Hamunri searching the area for me. And it wasn't as if I was going to be able to blend with the local populace.

At night I traveled upon the main road. It was the only time I considered it relatively safe. My features were more easily obscured, and there were fewer people about. Still, to play it safe, every so often I would stop, dismount, and put my ear to the ground. In that way, I was able to hear whether other riders were approaching from either direction. If I detected the slightest vibration, I would hie myself to hiding and wait for them to pass by. This happened a number of times during my journey, and I was never certain if any of the groups of travelers I allowed to pass in one direction or the other were pursuing me.

That's the problem with being on the run: You begin to suspect that everything is about you. A passing glance from the most humble of peddlers, and you instantly think he's a spy who will report you to the nearest authorities.

On the other hand, it was far easier to become severely dead from being not cautious enough rather than too cautious. I opted for the latter.

I kept wondering what I would do once I returned to

the village. How would they react to me? Would they accept me? What was I going to accomplish once I was there? None of these were questions to which I had any ready answers. If nothing else, returning to Hosbiyu would give me the opportunity to sit, think, meditate. And if my full plans came to fruition—if I was indeed able to activate the demon sword, master it, control it— then the people of Hosbiyu would never have to fear anything again.

I pondered what I would tell them about Ali. They had revered the old man in life. I just couldn't find it within myself to tell them that he was a fraud, presuming of course that was true. There was nothing to be served by it. Let them have Ali as they remembered him. Me, I would be striving to find the secret within the sword and benefit from it.

Naturally, Veruh Wang Ho was never far from my thoughts. The speed with which we had connected was well outside of my range of experience. And gods knew some of the things she had done with me, and to me, during that incredible endless time of passion, had also been outside my range of experience. Could I really leave my soul mate behind? If I remained in the village, that's what would happen.

The even more pertinent question was whether she would truly allow me to. I knew what she had said, and I had her word. But there was this little problem of her being evil. Because of that, it wasn't as if I could trust what she said. It all sounded nice to utter pretty words about letting go of that which you love. But a week or two might pass, at which point Veruh could say, "All right, then, that's enough of that," and send her people out searching for me. Between the Hamunri wandering the countryside and the combined forces of the Anaïs Ninjas, the Forked Tong, and the Skang Kei family, someone was going to find me. At that point, I was starting to wonder whether it wouldn't make more sense to just throw myself into the sea and try to swim back to Port Debras. I'd probably have about as much luck accomplishing that as I had virtually anything else these days.

Thanks to all my caution, my trip back took considerably longer. However, better to prolong the journey than to make a mistake that either lengthened my time indefinitely in jail, or worse, cut it short with the blade of the executioner.

At the point where it felt as if I would never get there, I saw familiar landmarks along the road that alerted me the village was nigh.

I also noticed something else, however. Something that I couldn't help but consider very, very odd.

Crows.

I had not seen many of the black-feathered creatures since I'd arrived, which was probably why I was noticing them at that point. It was broad daylight and thus I was staying off the main road when I spotted crows in flight. First it was singly. Then time passed and a group of five flew past. Then ten, then later twenty. It was almost eerie, watching them hurtle past. And what was even eerier was that they were heading in the same direction I was.

I took a chance and moved out onto the main road, reasoning that I might have a better view of what lay ahead.

What I saw bewildered me at first. Crows were coming in not just from behind me, but from other directions as well. And they were converging. Like a great, feathered funnel of ill wind, they swirled around one particular area some miles ahead of me.

My horse whinnied and bucked slightly, clearly unhappy

with my wanting it to head toward the area where the crows were gathering.

That was when I realized.

The area where the crows were gathering roughly corresponded to where I thought the village of Hosbiyu was situated.

And still I didn't fully comprehend.

Then it hit me. A horrifying, nauseating realization struck me in the gut with the force of a mallet blow. Suddenly I didn't give a damn whether I encountered the Imperior's own bloody army on the road. The only thing that concerned me was getting back to Hosbiyu as quickly as possible.

Ignoring the horse's protests, I snapped the reins and bellowed as loudly as I could to show the animal who precisely was in charge. To the horse's credit, he could have tried to buck me off. But he didn't. Instead, deferring to the wishes of his human rider, he thundered down the main road, his hooves chewing up dirt. I held on as tightly as I could. "Yah! Come on! Yah!" I kept shouting, having no idea whether my urging was serving to speed up the horse's gallop and not caring one way or the other. It was a beautiful day, the sun bright and cheery, not a single white cloud blocking the pure blue sky.

How could anything possibly be wrong on a day like this?

The answer lay ahead of me.

As I drew within a mile or two of the village, I could see that the skies above were black with crows. They were cawing and summoning to more of their kind, a huge indigo whirlpool, and I didn't think they could hear my shouts. So I shouted louder. I shouted and screamed and bellowed and howled, and the closer I drew, the more the crows took notice of me. I could see a number of them were down upon the ground already, but as I approached riding bent for leather, they turned from their activities and sought sanctuary in the air where I could not reach them. There was no incentive for them to behave in any other fashion. If creatures such as they had brains to reason, they would have thought, *What's the rush? We have all the time in the world. In fact, the longer we wait, the tastier our pickings.*

It was at that point that the wind shifted, and the smell was wafted to me. A smell I knew all too well.

I charged down from the small range of hills that stood between me and the village, and that was when I saw the first of the bodies.

It was Cleft Chin, of course. I could just imagine him standing there, fists on his hips, shouting defiance, demanding that they—whoever they were—leave this place at once.

They had cut him down right where he stood.

Then they had moved on.

There were more bodies. Bodies everywhere. Bodies of every shape, every size. Every age, every gender.

No one had made any effort to bury them or hide them. They'd left them there as a warning. As a boast.

It was at that point I heard screaming, which made my heart jump, because I thought that it might mean there were some people alive. I realized belatedly that it was my own screaming I was hearing. I wasn't aware when I had started it. I did know, however, when I stopped.

It was when I stumbled over Kit Chinette's body.

Oh, there had been others. Over there was Double Chin. Half in and out of her hut was his wife, Lun. And the others, so many others.

Cut up. Lacerated. Some had had their throats slit. Others were beheaded. Still more were stabbed to the heart.

All of them.

Every damned one.

Even as another name, another villager would occur to me, I would discover him within his hut, or behind a bush, or in a stable.

I was screaming that entire time. Screaming until my throat was raw, screaming because despite all my conviction that I was some harbinger of doom, there had been a piece of me—the tiniest piece—that hadn't really believed it. That had thought, *Oh, you, Apropos, always the pessimist, always the cynic, you have to believe that all is gloom and doom when it need not be that way.*

But when I came upon Kit Chinette, the screaming stopped.

My mind stopped.

Everything stopped.

The sweet child who had been my salvation when I first arrived was lying flat on her back upon the ground. A crow had just lit upon her forehead and was about to pluck out one of her eyes. Other crows were approaching, apparently considering Kit Chinette to be a particular delicacy.

Without thinking, I pulled out one of the sai from my belt and hurled it as hard and as fast as I could. I doubt I could ever have repeated the throw. The sai lanced straight through the crow, knocking him off Kit's head and pinning the thrashing bird to the ground. It managed a squawk in protest and then shuddered and died. The object lesson was not lost upon the other crows, which immediately took wing.

I didn't care about them. I wasn't even noticing they were gone. The crows above continued to circle, but wisely did not approach me.

I staggered toward Kit, and when I got within a few feet of her, my legs gave out completely. That didn't stop me. I tossed aside my walking staff and crawled the rest of the way to her. Right up until the moment I got to her, even though I'd seen that damned bird perched upon her forehead, I nurtured the idea that maybe, just maybe, she had survived.

But no. I could see the deadness in her eyes. I reached over, felt the cold skin. I noticed her mother lying ten feet away, her throat cut. That was when I realized there wasn't a mark upon the little girl. There were, however, tearstains. Her face was covered with them. So was the front of her clothes.

As Chinpan Ali had died of heart failure, so, too, had Kit Chinette. But it was a different sort. The child had seen death, carnage, dismemberment, saw the end of innocence, the end of her family and friends and childhood, and she had cried until she could cry no more, and then her spirit had simply departed her body. She had died of a broken heart.

Carefully I laid my pack down, reached into it, and withdrew the small stuffed bear that I had purchased for Kit. I laid it upon her lifeless chest. In my imaginings, it cuddled against her, waiting for a girlish hug that would never come.

Through all the shite I had experienced in my life, all the difficulties I had endured, I had always wondered . . . was it possible to discover a low point? To experience something so horrifying, so fraught with hopelessness, that one could simply go no lower?

In the village of Hosbiyu, filled with slaughtered farmers who were waiting to be food for crows, I found my answer.

I hit bottom.

My world blew apart.

I began to sob in total and abject despair. Despair in its purest form. The end of hope. The end of aspiration. The end of everything. I sat in that one spot, clutching the child's body to me, and I rocked gently back and forth and cried as I never had. Not when my mother died, not when I had suffered loss after loss.

There was no trace of manhood or manliness in me. Like an abjectly miserable woman did I cry. My body shook and heaved, and tighter still did I hold Kit to me. I tried to will her back to life, to infuse my soul into her. It was, of course, no use. She lay in my arms, body limp and cold and as dead as anyone else there, and I could not remember a time when I had not been crying.

In the plains of Wuin, I had reached a point where I did not care if I died. Here, in the remains of a farming village, I transcended that. Not only did I not care if I died . . . I didn't care if I lived.

I cried until I was exhausted, until I thought I could shed not another tear, and then new waves would come and it would start again.

How long I sobbed, I could not tell you. But then, very slowly, I became aware of something.

I turned my head and looked up at a far ridge.

Seven men on horseback were there. Even from that distance, I could see they were Hamunri.

They had come for me. They had found me.

I didn't give a damn.

Instead . . . I began to sing.

Many was the time I had heard the villagers in the wheat field, singing some light tune that would make the hours of grueling work pass in a bit more entertaining manner. I had even memorized some of the songs. Bouncy, airy songs about cloud shapes, or passing zephyrs, or great triumphs of past warriors. That sort of thing.

And Kit Chinette had been the most enthusiastic singer of all. Enthusiastic not as in "talented," but as in "loud." On any given day, I was able to hear her voice above the others, chorusing as if she thought the gods themselves were listening in on her and appreciating her talent (or, truthfully, lack thereof).

I sang to her now, that sweet music that had belonged to a now-extinct village. Continuing to rock her gently, as if she were an infant I was trying to lull to sleep, I sang one of her favorite songs. Something about a dancing cow or some such. I wasn't even familiar with all the words, but I knew enough of them to make her happy.

Make her happy.

I hadn't even accepted she was dead yet. I was in shock, unable to wrap myself around the concept. So I ignored it. My eyes red from tears, I held her so close, and I sang gentle songs to her.

The Hamunri thundered toward me, perhaps feeling that the way to prevent me from running once more was to be as screamingly loud as possible. I think they thought I was going to bolt. They were probably looking forward to the chase, and were just a tad disappointed that I was doing nothing except staying exactly where I was while rocking back and forth.

Their approach did have one benefit: The racket scared away the crows. The damned scavengers liked relative privacy in which to conduct their grisly work, and so distanced themselves from the scene in favor of a time when there would be fewer people around to disrupt the proceedings.

The Hamunri slowed a distance away and came to a halt about twenty feet shy of me. I continued to sing and ignore them. I must have looked quite the sight to them, seated on the ground, cradling a dead girl, cooing a tune to her. I didn't even look up at them, probably because they were of no relevance to me. At that point, even I was of no relevance to me.

They dismounted, thumping heavily to the ground, little bits of dust puffing up under their feet. I finally afforded them a glance. They were certainly fierce-looking, these seven Hamunri. Their scowls were like thunderheads, their wide shoulders swaying, their swords slapping against their thighs as they walked. Any one of them could have cut me in half with one sword thrust. Against the seven of them, I had no chance. That was all right, though. I wasn't seeking one.

They stopped several feet away. It was as if they didn't want to get too close to me, lest they catch the odd illness that had reduced me to a simpering, useless sack of meat and bone. The foremost one, whom I took to be the leader, growled, "You are Po?"

I nodded. No point in denying it. His asking me was just a formality. Who the hell else looked like me. I had stopped singing, and I asked, sounding like the haunting cry of a ghost, "Did you do this?"

"We questioned them," said the Hamunri soldier. "We demanded to know your whereabouts. They would not cooperate."

"What made you think they would know?"

"That one," and he pointed at the body of Cleft Chin, "spoke to others of the strange-faced one named Po. We traced him here."

That fool. That gossiping fool. Couldn't keep his mouth shut when he'd gone to market. Had to blab about what he knew. And look at what the result had been. Just look.

"And you . . . you just came here . . . and killed them all? For no reason?"

"They would not cooperate." He spoke gruffly, his back stiff. "We questioned them and they did not cooperate. They would not tell us where you were."

"They didn't know. I wasn't here. They couldn't have possibly known."

"They did not tell us that. They did not tell us anything. They said it would be dishonorable."

"Oh my gods." I held Kit tighter to me. "Oh my dear gods . . ."

"For what it is worth, they held you in very high esteem."

"It's worth nothing," I said between clenched teeth. "Nothing."

He shook his head, clearly put out. "You are correct. In seeking to honor you, they dishonored themselves. Their loyalty should be to their Imperior. Not to a strangely faced outsider who brought dishonor to the Imperior as well."

"And so you killed them. Killed them all."

"They brought their deaths upon themselves," said the Hamunri. "We were simply the instruments of those deaths."

"No," I told him, shaking my head. "I was. I brought this on them. This is on my head. Mine."

The Hamunri stared at me for a time. Then the leader turned to the others and gestured that they should gather around him. They held a hurried, whispered conference. What they were saying was of no consequence to me. I was stroking Kit's cheek. I wondered why I wasn't crying anymore. It was probably because I'd used up all my tears.

They broke ranks and turned to face me. "If you wish, you will be given one chance to do the honorable thing. It is, frankly, more than you deserve."

My mind should have been screaming at me to try and seek vengeance upon these cold-blooded bastards. Or desperately trying to find ways to run away.

But there was nothing. My inner voice, my first, best line of defense when it came to survival, was silent. Well, that was certainly a hint, wasn't it.

"Yes," I said slowly. "Yes . . . it is."

I eased Kit to the ground and stared at her. Then I gently arranged her hands so they were crisscrossing her chest.

Her eyes were still open, so I passed my hand over her lids and slid them closed.

I leaned back upon my knees then and gripped the tachi sword. The demon sword, they'd called it. And I thought, *Fine. Let it do the work of a demon. Let it send me to hell.*

I pulled the sword from its scabbard. I was surprised by how silent it was. No hiss of metal against the scabbard. It was as if I was drawing a phantom sword.

The entire moment had slowed to a crawl, as if the final moments of my life were going to be as painfully prolonged as possible. The sword seemed deliriously sharp. I knew it would be no effort at all to shove the blade into my heart and pierce it.

My life was over. As far as I was concerned, it was over the moment I set foot in the village and saw the first corpses.

The Hamunri seemed a bit surprised, as if anticipating some sort of trick. "You do not resist?"

"No," I said tonelessly.

I turned the sword around, placed the point against my chest. It was as if I was dreaming.

The faces floated before me, as they had in times past when death seemed imminent. My mother, and Tacit, and Sharee, and Entipy, and the men of the king's court, and the lady Kate, and the soldiers dedicatedly serving the rapacious ambitions of the peacelord of Wuin, and King Meander, and the faces of all those who had been made to suffer because of me . . . an endless list, it seemed. They paraded across my mind's eye, and they all looked as if they felt . . . sorry for me. As if they pitied me.

And why not? Was I not a pitiful, hopeless thing? Was I not mired in despair, beyond help, beyond redemption, beyond anything?

"Yet before, you fled rather than do honor to the

Imperior," growled the Hamunri. "Why do you not resist now?"

Apparently the successful completion of his mission was insufficient. He had to have every question answered, every dot connected.

"Because," I said, telling the truth for what I was certain would be the last time in my life, "I don't care."

Chapter 10

The Breaking Loose of Aulhel

*A*nd then, as I prepared to thrust the sword into my breast, it started to tremble in my grasp.

The Hamunri looked contemptuous. One of the others called out, "He shakes in fear! Do the job for him!"

I screamed, but it was not in fear. Instead it was in pain.

The hilt of the sword had suddenly become scalding hot. Waves of heat blasted through my hands, and I thought they were being incinerated. Yet I could not release the sword. My hands, in fact, gripped the hilt even more tightly than before. They were shaking, but not of their own accord. It was the sword that was shaking. All I was doing was hanging on.

A high-pitched screech cut through the air. My teeth were chattering violently, my head snapping back and forth. It was at that point that the Hamunri realized something was definitely wrong, and it had nothing to do with me and everything to do with the sword.

Obviously fearing a trick, seeking to end this before I pulled some sort of stunt, the leader of the Hamunri charged forward, yanking out his sword, intending to cut me down and end this.

He never even got close.

For the blade of my sword suddenly bent, twisted, distorted, and then came completely free of the hilt.

There was a blinding flash of light, a discharge of energy, that knocked me onto my back. I held on to the hilt as if my life depended on it, which I was beginning to suspect might be the case.

It was as if a star had descended from the heavens and exploded onto the ground in front of me. I blinked furiously, trying to clear the glare from my eyes, and I heard a horrific roaring. Louder than the great cat that I had released from its cage. Louder than the crash of the surf in a storm. Louder than anything.

And then I heard the screams. And the rending and tearing, the sounds of bones breaking and flesh being torn from bodies, and muscles being stretched and torn, and other sounds, horrifying noises that I hadn't known the human body was capable of producing.

My vision started to clear then, and what I saw . . .

. . . I couldn't believe what I saw.

There was a creature there. A being, a . . . a thing. It was hunched over and thus it was difficult to determine its height, but I would have guessed over seven feet tall. It was naked save for a tattered loincloth, its skin unearthly white, its arms long and dangling. It had four fingers on each hand rather than five, but each finger ended in a cruel, curved talon. The talons were dripping with blood and gore.

And its face.

It turned, glanced at me over its shoulder, and its face was the stuff of nightmares. Burning red eyes, a long and pointed chin and hooklike nose. It had no ears, but instead small holes on either side of its head, and its teeth were jagged and sharp. It clicked those teeth several times rapidly.

The Hamunri were scattered about the ground in various states of dismemberment. Some of them had had time to draw their weapons, some hadn't. It hadn't made much difference in the end. They were all equally as dead.

I braced myself, waiting for it to turn upon me and dispose of me the same way it had them.

Slowly it approached me, its knuckles dragging upon the ground.

And then it went to bended knee.

"All are dead," it rasped in a voice that sounded like metal scraping on stone. "I have fulfilled my function. Are you done with me, master."

"M-Master . . . ?"

It brought up one of its clawed hands and I reflexively flinched back, certain it was about to tear into me. "You hold the demon sword. You are master. Are you done with me?"

"I . . ." I licked my dried lips. Unfortunately there was no moisture in my tongue. "What . . . what are you?"

"I am Aulhel. I am the Slojinn of the demon sword. Destruction is mine to give. Merciless. All-consuming. Aulhel the Destroyer am I. You released me."

"How?"

"You spoke the words of power," he rasped. "Speak them again, that I may return and rest."

Frantically I ran through my head all that I had said.

And then I realized.

"I don't care," I told him.

In a flash of light and energy, he was gone once more. The hilt shook in my hand and I squinted against it lest I be blinded once more.

And then, just like that, it was over. The blade was intact once more. I no longer felt compelled to hold the hilt. I had been certain that the scorching heat had seared the flesh from my hands, but I looked at my palms and they were not even lightly blistered. For all the intensity of the heat that I had felt, I was undamaged.

"Aulhel the Destroyer," I muttered.

A Slojinn. I had never heard of such a creature. Obviously some sort of demon spat up from the netherworld, bound within this mystic sword.

This was the means by which Chinpan Ali had annihilated those thugs. He had spoken these words of power . . . the words that I had now uttered and that consequently caused the destruction of these soldiers.

My mind whirled back to when I had been training with him. I remembered how I had been about to say, "I don't care," and he had warned me away from doing so. Now I comprehended why. Even though I wasn't holding the sword at the time, he didn't want to take any chances that the words would trigger the unleashing of the demon.

I sat there for the longest time, just staring at the blade. I turned it this way and that, looking at my reflection in it, imagining that the creature within was looking back.

Veruh Wang Ho had told me that Ali was a fraud. That he knew nothing of true disciplines. That he had just been trying to cover up his own ignorance by wasting my time with pointless lessons.

There might well have been some truth in that. And yet I now realized that much of what he had told me had its basis in other truths. The exercises might well have been mere distractions in hopes that my interest would wane and the fact that he was a fraud would never come to light. But the basic precept he had taught me was completely true.

I had emptied myself of everything, and because of that emptiness, I had been able to annihilate my opponents. Granted, I had required a magic sword to do it, but hey . . . destruction was destruction, was it not?

Destruction . . .

"I don't care," I said, closing my eyes and looking away to avoid any sort of damage to my eyes. They were only just now starting to clear, and I had no desire to start the process all over again.

Even though I was braced for it, the force of the energy unleashed still knocked me over. I shook my head to clear it as the Slojinn stood over me, staring at me with fierce intensity. I thanked the gods I was the one holding the blade—or at least the hilt of the blade—because the prospect of the creature tearing into me was a horrifying one indeed.

"There are none to destroy," he growled, sounding rather irritated by it. "Why have you summoned me?"

"I do not desire to leave the bodies of these people," and I indicated the villagers, "for those." And I pointed to the crows.

"I don't do birds," the Slojinn snarled.

All right. The Slojinn wasn't the sharpest quill in the ink well. That was acceptable. "No. Not the birds. Can you burn the bodies? Reduce them to—"

The Slojinn's mouth opened wide, and I threw up my arms out of reflex as a huge jet of blue flame erupted from his mouth. He swept his head back and forth and within seconds there was nothing left of the villagers but small piles of ash.

He turned and looked at the bodies of the Hamunri. "What of them?"

"Leave them," I said grimly. "Let the birds pick them clean. And I hope they take their time doing so."

"May I leave?"

"I don't care."

And in a flash, he was gone again, the blade intact once more upon the hilt.

I stood there for a time, running the options through my mind. A tremendous change had just come over my world, a change I wouldn't have thought possible mere minutes ago.

I had been ready to die. I had wanted nothing but sweet, sweet oblivion. Because I had been convinced that in this world there could be no justice. No love without betrayal, no life that did not end in tragedy.

No hope.

Except I had found hope.

Hope . . . and a tool that gave me the potential for as many casualties as I cared to pile up.

That's what I was holding.

The ultimate weapon.

It was nothing less than that. Nothing could stand before it. Seven men, seven powerful, armed soldiers, part of the elite of this land, and the Slojinn had effortlessly torn them to pieces.

I had gone from being powerless to being the single most powerful individual in the whole of Chinpan.

Nothing and no one could stand against me.

When I had been peacelord, I had known invincibility. That might have been another reason why I was so utterly without hope. Having been able to accomplish everything, how dispiriting, how debilitating it was to go from that to being unable to accomplish anything.

That was no longer the case, though. I was unstoppable once more.

But I had learned. Ohhhh, how I had learned. I had succumbed as peacelord to the temptations of power and, as a result, had become a mere shadow of my former self. That was not going to happen this time. I was not about to embark on some broad-ranging campaign of destruction and conquest. Those ambitions had no attraction for me.

No. I simply wanted revenge.

Yes, I know. I had considered acts of vengeance to be a hollow pursuit. But that was before I actually had the means to *achieve* that vengeance. Now that I did, the entire concept suited me just fine, thank you very much.

Revenge. Revenge upon the Imperior for the way he had treated me. Revenge upon the Anaïs Ninjas for their slaughtering of my teacher. Revenge upon . . .

Veruh? Veruh Wang Ho?

My love.

My true love.

I had gotten to my feet, my imagination caught up in the giddy anticipation of piles of body parts everywhere. My unleashing of the demon to cause havoc amongst the ranks of those who had done me ill was joyously tempting.

But Veruh was allied with the Anaïs Ninjas. Veruh, who was the first woman I dared consider to be a true love. Veruh, for whom I felt an attraction that bordered on the mystical. My belief in the notion of fate was dodgy at best, yet I had come to embrace the notion that Veruh and I were truly fated to be together. If I unleashed the power of the demon sword upon the Anaïs Ninjas, would that cost me her love?

How could it not? I mean, really? How could she go on loving someone who destroyed her allies?

Except . . . well . . . I was going to destroy the Imperior as well. And she very much wanted him gone.

What it came down to, I reasoned, was which was more important to her: the death of the Imperior, or the lives of the Anaïs Ninjas.

It took me no more than an instant to answer that one for myself: the death of the Imperior, certainly. Veruh aspired to power. She wanted to take over Chinpan, to give it over to the Forked Tong. And she was evil. Evil alliances never hold. Ever. Sooner or later, the participants in such alliances turn upon one another, and the alliances are transformed into "last man standing" scenarios.

If I disposed of the Anaïs Ninjas through the power of the demon sword, that would only benefit Veruh. It meant fewer people with whom she would have to share power. And really, who had any desire to share power with a group of women who could sneak into and out of the shadows and probably kill you in your sleep whenever it suited their priorities? She'd be better off without them. Hell, she'd thank me for it.

I felt as if a great weight had been lifted off me.

I was not going to kill myself. I was going to accomplish exactly what I had set out to do. And the need and reason for vengeance had gone far beyond that of avenging the death of Chinpan Ali. Now there was the entire village of Hosbiyu to avenge. Every man, woman, and child had died in the name of the pointless quest involving the Imperior's honor. Well, that was going to be turned around against him.

In a way, it saddened me. As much contempt as I normally held for philosophies involving self-sacrifice and noble aspirations, I had an inkling that a well-placed sense of honor might not be such a bad thing. To try to live by an ethical code of personal conduct which demanded nobility and the preserving of a public persona that one could count on.

What was wrong with honor, really? Nothing. And perhaps somewhere there were countries where it was maintained in its good and pure form, and helped shape a society of decent and civilized behavior.

Not here, though. Here it was simply used as a weapon. As a means of abuse.

And it was going to stop.

I was going to stop it.

I crouched over the ashes that had been a small girl, and sifted them through my hand. Then I took them and smeared them upon either side of my face, leaving angry streaks upon it.

"This is for you," I whispered, and headed off for Taikyo while the crows descended and prepared for their feast.

BOOK THREE

Peons of Mass Destruction

Chapter 1

Playing the Palace

*A*s peacelord, when I had embarked upon conquests, I had often formulated complex and involved military plans in doing so. That had been necessary not for myself, but for my forces. I myself was invulnerable to harm, but my army was not. So I had to make accommodations in order to minimize losses. After all, what kind of commander would I have been to march troops mindlessly into battle, uncaring of what happened to them, while I went on my merry way impervious to all injury.

But this was a different situation. The only person I had to worry about was me. And with the demon sword in my hand, I wasn't all that worried. For that matter, even without the demon sword, I wasn't worried.

As peacelord, I'd considered myself above petty concerns such as morality. Because I could get away with anything, and not have to worry about punishment, I felt that good and evil didn't apply to me any more than they applied to hurricanes or floods or other forces of nature.

This was a very different circumstance. I knew there were risks. A long-distance archer who saw me coming could still put a brace of arrows in me before I uttered a word. I could still probably manage to say the magic words, but it wouldn't do me much good if goose-quill shafts had rearranged my innards in the meantime. For that matter, if the Slojinn of the demon sword was busy battling over-whelming odds, I might still be cut down while he was occupied elsewhere. The demon sword did not confer invin-cibility upon me. All it did was help assure that if I was to be destroyed, my opponent's destruction would be mutual.

In my state of mind, that was more than enough.

As much as I had taken pains to hide myself on the trip to the now defunct village of Hosbiyu, that was how little I worried about being spotted as I rode back to Taikyo.

And I was indeed spotted.

On two occasions, I found myself accosted by groups of Hamunri.

The first time, I was on horseback. I saw the riders approaching before they saw me, and I reined up my horse, angling it crosswise across the road to make it clear I was going to be squarely in their way. Not only did I make no effort at concealment, but I threw back my hood to reveal my features. Then I drew the demon sword and waited.

They came to a halt a short distance away and stared at me, apparently unable to believe their eyes. When one is hunting for someone, one usually assumes that the hunted will at least make some effort to stay out of the way. It is certainly not expected that the hunted will be waiting for you, staring you in the eye and almost daring you to make the first move.

"Po," said one of them, sounding a bit tentative.

"Yes."

This emboldened them. One would have thought that, considering they outnumbered me five to one, they would have been utterly confident from the beginning of the encounter. But the unusual nature of the way I was facing them down had been briefly disconcerting. Perhaps they'd simply decided I was insane, and were going to proceed from that assumption.

"You have dishonored the Imperior," said the same man, a bit more robustly this time.

"So he says." I paused.

"You will die for that action. You will be given one chance to do the honorable thing."

"Honorable thing," I echoed, shaking my head. "Back in that direction," and I pointed with the sword, "there was a village of farmers. I once resided there. The entire populace was murdered in the process of being questioned as to my whereabouts." I waited a moment, allowing that to sink in. I wanted to make sure we were all clear on the subject. "My question to you is: Do any of you have any problem with that?"

They exchanged looks. It could be they thought this was some sort of trick question. The spokesman said, "This has nothing to do with the dishonor that you—"

"Just answer the damned question. Or are you afraid to do so?"

Their scowls deepened. "No one questions our bravery."

"Then answer me."

"No. I have 'no problem' with that. Do any of you?" He looked to his associates. They all shook their heads.

"So you don't care," I asked.

Again shaking of the heads.

"Then I don't care," I said, and braced myself.

Then came the heat, and the pain that burned while not burning. My horse bucked in fear, and I nearly got myself tossed right off. Even as the demon ripped free of its imprisonment and tore into the Hamunri, I was busy making a mental note to myself that next time I unleashed the demon, I had to make certain not to be on horseback.

Within seconds, the small group of Hamunri had been torn to shreds. Apparently Aulhel had broken loose with an even greater vengeance this time. That didn't bother me in principle, although I was slightly concerned that the creature's ferocity could build to the point where I could no longer control it. But as long as I could maintain dominion over the Slojinn for the time that I required its services, that was all I needed. After that . . .

Well . . . after that, who knew? Once my immediate concerns had been attended to, why not continue to utilize the blade? What was wrong with having a weapon that could annihilate my enemies ten times over? Twenty times over?

It wasn't as if I would use it for evil, or for dominance. I had already been down that road, knew the mistakes that could be made and the pitfalls to be avoided.

The second time I employed the blade along my journey, however, a problem arose. One that I had not foreseen . . . and yet, strangely enough, had in fact predicted. Whether it was a lucky guess on my part, or some intuition I'd developed because I'd been carrying the sword for a time, I really couldn't say.

The incident occurred when I had decided to stop for a brief rest along the way. I was seated along the side of the road, leaning against a tree, devouring some simple breadstuffs I had in my pack. There was a peddler walking slowly down the road, pushing a small cart filled with knickknacks that swayed gently as he moved. He smiled toward me, tilting his head in greeting. I waved in acknowledgment.

Then the peddler stopped, and I could see him reacting to that which—at that moment—I only heard: The oncoming of horses. Four this time, by my estimate. Somehow I knew that it was going to be more Hamunri. I was right.

They rounded the corner of the road, started to move in

formation around the peddler, and then spotted me. They stopped, glanced at one another, silently concurred that I was who they were looking for. Then they started to move toward me.

I pulled the demon sword, and much of the conversation I'd had with the previous group of would-be attackers was repeated, almost word for word. It was nicely ironic—or perhaps pathetic. I couldn't quite make up my mind which.

It reached the exact same point as the other, with my uttering the magic words that unleashed the Slojinn. "Slo" he might have been in name, but certainly not in deed. He tore into them with the same ferocity and efficiency he'd displayed the previous day. I sat there and watched, and smiled, and enjoyed every moment of it.

If vengeance is a hollow pursuit, the joy of that is, since it *is* hollow, one can dine upon helping after helping and never fill up, so one is always ready for the next course. Sort of like an endless banquet.

Technically, I supposed, this had moved beyond vengeance. These soldiers, after all, had done nothing to me, any more than the set I'd encountered on the road the day before had. But my reasoning was simple: If they didn't consider the travesty visited upon the good people of Hosbiyu to be a crime of the first order, then that meant they endorsed it. If they endorsed it, then it was acceptable within their code of conduct. That being the case, there was a possibility that—sooner or later—they would do something similar.

Better then for all concerned to get rid of them before they had the opportunity to do so.

But when Aulhel was finished with the Hamunri, he turned his attention toward the peddler. The poor fellow let out an alarmed shriek, and immediately I shouted, "No! Leave him!"

The Slojinn stayed rooted to his spot for a moment, and looked at me with a combination of contempt and frustration, as if he hated having to explain something to me. "When I am summoned, all I see, die. That is my way."

"I don't care!" I shouted.

He staggered, twisted, as if bands of invisible force were trying to insinuate themselves around his body. He took several more steps toward the peddler, and then turned and faced me with obvious frustration.

"Beware of sending mixed messages from mixed emotions," he snarled. "Lack of focus may well be the death of you . . . and of others."

And then in a burst of blue flame and a wave of heat as he discharged energy, the Slojinn vanished back into the sword. The blade was intact once more, although I could have sworn—looking upon the blade—that I could see the snarling face of the demon reflected in its polished surface. Then it vanished.

The peddler was lying on the road, trembling. For a moment I thought he, too, had dropped dead from stress or something similar. But no; he was fine, albeit shaken. I went to him and extended a hand to help him up. Instead of taking it, he pulled away from the offer of help as if my hand held some great disease in it.

"You could thank me for saving your life, you know," I said, sounding a bit testy.

"Shall I . . . also thank you for endangering it?" he asked.

Well, it was a valid enough question, I suppose, but it still annoyed the hell out of me. I walked away without pressing the point.

I knew then that what I had told Veruh Wang Ho was correct. Once the demon was unleashed, bottling him up once more could present a problem. He would attack indiscriminately, killing everyone who was in his immediate field of vision, and he was not at his best when being made to obey orders that involved holding back.

This required a slight rethinking of my original plans regarding the Imperior. Demons are, by their nature, not to be trusted, and this Slojinn was no exception. It was clear that I could not simply ride up to the outside of the palace, unleash Aulhel, and tell him to fly straight as a crow to the Imperior and dispatch him for me. The odds were far more likely that Aulhel would annihilate not only the Imperior, but everyone else in the palace. Every servant, every woman and child. Yes, even Mitsu. And all of that mayhem, blood, and destruction would be on my head.

Well . . . fine. That was hardly an impossible problem to deal with. I would simply have to make certain that the Imperior and I were in the same room, and no one else who could remotely be considered an innocent was.

I was prepared for that. Really, I was prepared for anything. I was prepared for my mission to be a success. I was prepared for it to end in bloody failure. All of it was the same to me, for I had lost the capacity to care about anything . . .

. . . except . . .

. . . except . . . Veruh. Veruh Wang Ho, the mysterious woman who had so fascinated me, captivated me.

As I continued my ride toward Taikyo, I wondered whether what I felt was genuine. Was it all motivated by some desperate desire to experience that which Mitsu had made sound so tantalizing? The embracing of a soul mate, the dizzying rush of love at first sight?

No. No, I was convinced it was more than that. There in the darkness, we had come together, bonded in ways I had never thought possible. What we had done transcended mere sex. We had not simply been using each other for release, or benefit, or to try and maintain a particular rank. We were two souls uniting as one.

How pathetic that must seem to you, the reader. After all I had been through, to find me capable of the same giddy, pathetic failings as others who are far less cynical than I. How disappointed you must be in me. "Oh Apropos, what were you thinking?" you must be demanding. "Where is the unsociable, alienated fellow we've come to loathe and despise with the fiery passion of a thousand suns? You have succumbed to a pathetic, obsessive love that could befall any foolish, callow 'hero.' You disappoint us, Apropos! You have truly let us down!"

Have I? Have I let you down?

Ah well. Why should you be different from everyone else in my life?

I was expecting a welcoming committee when I entered Taikyo. Such was not to be the case. I moved through the streets on horseback, my back straight, my head held high. I saw that I was being recognized, pointed at, discussed as I rode past. It gave me a sense of smug superiority.

I also noticed something else rather interesting: All the wanted posters had been taken down. The only conclusion I could draw was that Veruh Wang Ho had instructed her Skang Kei friends to take them down because . . . why? They offended her sensibilities, perhaps. Or maybe they wanted to make it a bit easier for me to move about the town.

Well, I wasn't planning on a lengthy stay. I knew exactly where I was going and, although I was not one hundred percent certain of what I was going to do once I got there, I had enough confidence in my ability to think quickly that I felt I'd be able to figure it out.

I briefly considered heading toward the dark side of town to see if I could seek out Veruh. Ultimately I decided against it. Best not to prolong matters. I had business with the Imperior, and I could see no advantage to putting it off.

The palace loomed in front of me. I headed for the towering bridge that would carry me across the moat, bracing myself for possible difficulties in terms of getting in. I saw several Hamunri guards ahead of me, at the entrance to the bridge, about the same time they saw me. There was quick, excited talk between them that I didn't quite understand. As fluent as I had become in Chinpanese, I still had difficulty comprehending it if two or more natives were uttering it at full speed among themselves. Between the excitement in their voices and the distance I had yet to cover between us, this was one of those occasions.

I drew within range and stopped. As I looked down at them from atop my horse, my hand started to wander toward the hilt of the tachi sword. The magic summoning words were poised upon my lips.

And then the guards separated, the four of them stepping two to each side, allowing me full access to the bridge. To make matters even more curious . . . they bowed.

I didn't know what to make of that. A bow was a display of deepest respect. Why would they be displaying respect for me? What possible motivation could they have?

I had been expecting them to, at best, announce that I was their prisoner and they were to bring me before the Imperior at once. If they had done so, I would have willingly accompanied them, since to the Imperior was precisely where I wanted to go.

If they had attacked me, or tried to divest me of the demon sword, I would have been prepared for that as well. It was not my preferred course of action. I didn't desire to tip my hand too soon. Why alert them to my possession of a devastating and irresistible weapon before I'd even set foot within the palace proper?

But this response on their part was just . . . strange.

Nevertheless, I was hardly in a position to ignore it or dismiss it. So I bowed in reply, snapped the reins, and headed the horse over the bridge. Its hooves clip-clopped steadily on the wooden surface.

And now I could see others peering out the windows, or stepping out onto balconies and pointing. My return to the palace was definitely not going unobserved. I wasn't certain, but I thought I even saw the princess standing in one of the balconies and looking down upon me.

Did she know what was to come? Was she expecting the assault, the mayhem that I was preparing to inflict upon some of the palace denizens, including her own father? I had no way of knowing. I certainly hoped she did, because otherwise she was in for one hell of a shock.

Even as my horse strode across the bridge, I also kept careful watch for archers. Perhaps the plan was to try and pick me off from a distance. The thought made me squeeze tighter the hilt of the demon sword, so hard that the carvings of the bird's folded wings in the hilt itself were pressed into the flat of my hand. But I saw nothing. No threat was presenting itself from any direction.

We crossed the bridge and got to the main entrance. There were a number of Hamunri waiting for me, and the only way to distinguish them from the Hamunri who had been trying to kill me during my sojourn was that these were bowing. I dismounted and, slapping my hands against my thighs, bowed in reply. They seemed quite delighted by the quality and depth of my bow. So naturally they bowed again.

At which point I bowed again.

This went on for a couple of minutes, although it actually seemed more like forever. Apparently realizing that this could occupy the rest of the day, one of them indicated to the other two to cease what they were doing. "The Imperior is expecting you," he assured me.

"Is he now," I replied, sounding sarcastic. "Somehow I tend to doubt he is expecting what I am prepared to give him."

I allowed the Hamunri to serve as escorts into the palace, even though I certainly knew my way around well enough. My horse was taken away to be housed in the stables. If their intention was to isolate me, they were succeeding. But their success would be short-lived, as would indeed everyone who tried to get in my way.

It could not have been easier. It was so easy, in fact, that I was starting to feel guilty about it. I had some passing familiarity with quests or adventures, and this one involved such lack of risk that it was like insulting the memories of all those who had gone on, and died upon, quests. But then I thought, why not? After everything I've gone through, why shouldn't something be easy one time? I deserved a fragment of luck, did I not?

We went straight to the throne room, and there was the Imperior, much as he'd been when I first met him. He sat upon his dragon throne and was watching me with steady, warm eyes.

"Po," he said softly. He rose from his throne, came down off the small platform, and walked toward me. There were personal guards standing about, but no one seemed especially concerned. That was incredibly odd considering I had enough weapons upon me to cut down the Imperior where he stood. "Po," he said again, and to my shock, opened his arms and wrapped them around me. My hand was against the demon sword's hilt in readiness for an attack. This might have been many things—a trick, the act of a demented mind—but an attack it definitely was not.

"Po, my boy . . . it is good to see you." He stepped back and steadied himself. "Forgive a grateful old man's sentimentality. It was brilliant. Brilliant. But why did you not tell me?"

I had no idea whatsoever what to say in response to that. My hand slipped off the hilt of the demon sword. The Imperior didn't appear to notice or care. He was oblivious of any danger. His personal guards actually seemed pleased at the insane interaction that was occurring. I felt as if I were hallucinating. None of this made any damned bit of sense.

"Tell you?" I echoed.

"You do not have to respond. I know why . . . and I suppose in some ways, I had it coming."

He stepped back, shaking his head. "For so long," he said, "so long I have held myself up as the Divine One. The One who is told by the gods what is to be, what is to come, and all that is. Yet if that were really true, I would have known instantly the true nature of your plan. The brilliance of its execution. And you knew that. Because of that, you did not tell me. Perhaps you counted on me to know because you too thought me to be omniscient. Or perhaps you were testing me . . . and if that is the case then, dear boy, I have truly been found wanting." He stared at me, looking briefly puzzled. "You are pinching yourself very, very hard. Why are you doing that?"

Realizing that the gesture was not causing me to wake up, I muttered, "It . . . is a traditional gesture for self-congratulations in my country."

"Ah. Well . . . go question others' traditions. All they do is make our own look sane in comparison."

He was walking in a small circle around the room. "And to think: I believed it to be some sort of insane mistake. A miscommunication caused by ineptitude. Instead it was a dazzling, brilliant defense maneuver. The greatest in the history of Chinpan . . . and it is all thanks to you. Had I only been the truly omniscient individual you thought me to be, or that I wished me to be, I would have divined your intent and a great deal of aggravation could have been avoided."

"I . . . think you're being too hard on yourself, Divine One," I managed to say. I realized that I was actually following him. "There is, uhm . . . no way you could have known. And I . . . suppose I could have been more forthcoming. Really. I cannot dismiss my responsibility in this matter."

"Well, all I can say to you is that it worked to far greater a degree than I think anyone could possibly have expected it to."

"Certainly beyond mine," I said.

I heard a bustling at the doors at the far end, and for a moment I tensed, thinking that the true attack was now to be forthcoming. That they had endeavored to put me off guard. But no, it was merely the Imperior's councilors, with Itso Esi leading the way. They were all talking at once, rendering it impossible for me to understand exactly what any of them was saying. It was clear, though, that they were all echoing the Imperior's words of praise. Except I still had no clue what the hell I was being praised for.

Itso Esi's voice managed to carry above the others as he stopped and bowed to me, as did the others. They remained that way until I bowed in response, and then Itso Esi said, "I must say, honorable Po, on behalf of the council . . . we wish that you had taken us into your confidence when you conceived your brilliant plan. But since you chose not to, we respect your wisdom in this matter. We collectively wonder, though: How did you come up with the idea?"

There was expectant silence. "The idea?" I echoed.

"Yes, the idea. For the Great Wall."

"The Great Wall?"

"Of Chinpan, yes."

"Ohhhhh, the Great Wall!" I said, doing everything I could to act as if we'd simply had a mere communications error, rather than that I was just now learning about the brilliant strategy I had supposedly unilaterally developed. I spoke with grand, sweeping gestures, as if I were a grand orator speaking to a crowded amphitheater. "Yes, of course, the Great Wall, well . . . I, uhm . . . I studied the situation, and tried to discern just . . . what we needed. And I thought, 'Hunh. Well . . . obviously, only a Great Wall will do the trick.' "

There were nods and murmurs of "Of course. It's so simple the way he tells it." I smiled gamely, and then added in an almost offhand way, "Now . . . obviously I've been somewhat occupied in the past days, so I couldn't monitor the situation myself."

They gave one another grim, almost accusing looks, silently admitting that they themselves were the cause for my being "occupied."

"So I have to wonder," I continued, "how, exactly, did the Great Wall work out? In regards to the situation, I mean."

"Better than even *you* could have anticipated," said Itso Esi, as the others bobbed their heads. "I wish you could have seen the effectiveness with which it halted the Mingol hordes. How did you know they were coming?"

Oh my gods.

"Ahhhh," I said slowly. "Well, gentlemen . . . and Divine One . . . that is a most . . . most interesting tale. The Mingol hordes . . . they were, in fact, in league with the Forked Tong."

There were cries of "I knew it! Those bastards!"

"The Forked Tong sought an alliance with the Mingol hordes in the hopes of overthrowing the Divine One. They carefully analyzed where Chinpan was most vulnerable . . . provided aid, weapons, and staging areas for the hordes . . .

and then sat back and waited for them to do all the heavy-duty conquest."

"Little suspecting," intoned the Imperior, "that when they came charging up to our borders, they would discover a massive wall, miles long. They never stopped building, Kan Du and his men. They must have shared your vision."

"Of course," I said hollowly.

"And since the Hamunri and I were so intent on trying to find you, no one was paying attention to Kan Du. They kept building the wall, and building, and building. They're still working on it, you know. I've authorized continued work on it. All the materials, all the funding they need, to build a wall that will block Chinpan from all invaders all throughout our borders. Good walls make good neighbors, I say."

There were bobbing heads and "They do indeed, Divine One" coming from every quarter.

The Imperior was shaking his head in wonder. "Would that you could have been there to see the culmination of your vision, Po. The battle was spectacular. We suffered no casualties at all. There were the bewildered Mingols, slamming up against the impenetrable Great Wall. They tried to shatter it, to climb over it. None of it did any good. And there were our people, atop the wall, pouring down hot oil upon them, or loosing arrows. The Mingols' casualties were astronomical. The ground ran red with their blood. Their corpses were as numerous as grains of sand upon the beach. It was one of the most splendid sights these old eyes have ever seen, and we have none but you to thank for it. A man of true vision. A man of wisdom. Why, after such a shattering defeat when they doubtless thought we would be easily conquered, it is likely that the Mingols may never recover. We may well have heard the last of those harassing barbarians. What do you say to that, Po?"

"Huzzah?" I said weakly.

"Huzzah!" they repeated, stumbling over the unfamiliar word but managing it as best they could.

The Imperior rested a hand on my shoulder and said solemnly, "Young Po . . . you have earned more than a seat on my council. You have earned a place at my right hand. Go Nogo is gone. Until now, he had been my most trusted advisor. Yet he was so blinded by his hatred for you, that even he was unable to fully grasp the subtlety of your genius. You will take his place."

"Imperior . . ."

"What?"

I stepped away from him, trying to remain focused. They were all looking at me expectantly, as if I were the wisest individual in the history of the country, about to impart more morsels of my great wisdom upon them.

"Do you have . . . any idea . . . how many people have died because of this? Because of me?" I said.

"We're still endeavoring to get a count," said the Imperior. "Thus far the Mingol casualties stand at—"

"*No!* I'm speaking of innocent people! People who have done no harm to any!" I said. I strode toward him, my body shaking with passion. "Several days' ride from here, there is a village . . . or there was. Populated by innocent farmers. Your Hamunri came through there looking for me, and they slaughtered them. *All of them!* Men, women, and children!"

"Really?" He didn't seem upset so much as curious. "And why did they do that?"

"Because the Hamunri were looking for me, and didn't feel the people were cooperating."

"Ahhh." There were head nods and looks of understanding from them all. "Well, given the outcome and our subsequent realization of how you were, in fact, not dishonoring me at all," said the Imperior, "that is somewhat unfortunate."

"*Somewhat unfortunate?! They're dead! They're all dead!*"

"Po—"

I was ranting, stumbling around the room, gesturing so wildly that I almost knocked myself off my feet. "The men! Dead! The women! Dead! *The children!* Dead! A little girl who never harmed anyone in her life, Imperior! If you could have seen her, held her . . . you would have seen! Seen the depths of depravity, the perversion that concepts such as honor have been put to! The entire concept of loyalty to the ruler of the country, and the country he represents . . . that's fine as far as it goes! But it's being taken by those in power and used as a club to subjugate anyone and everyone who gets in their way! It's sick and twisted and how can you ask me to be a part of a ruling class that would condone and accept such horrors, and dismiss them as 'somewhat unfortunate'? It—"

"Enough."

He spoke sharply and with great strength, one hand upraised, and even though my chest was heaving with fury and emotion, I still halted my tirade. I leaned upon my walking staff, feeling drained and frustrated.

And I thought, *This is it. This is when the battle starts. He will order me dead for daring to speak so to him, and I will strike him down with my demon sword, and—*

"A child, you say?"

I was stunned by the softness of his voice. The change had been so abrupt that it was almost impossible to believe. "Yes," I said slowly. "A little girl. Four, maybe five years old."

The Imperior's mind seemed to wander away. Even his closest advisors were looking at him curiously. "Divine One," one of them said tentatively after a lengthy silence had passed. "Divine One, are . . . are you all ri—?"

"Mitsu was once four . . . maybe five years old," said the Imperior, sounding as if he were addressing us from another time, very long ago. The edges of his mouth twitched in an almost-smile. "I was still quite angry over the fact that she had dared to be a female. For the first four years of her life, I did not wish to know from her. I did not comprehend how her mother could do such a thing to me. My brother . . . he claimed that it was my seed that had determined the child would be female rather than male. I nearly had him executed on the spot. Perhaps I should have. It might have been preferable." There were knowing nods from the others. I did not nod knowingly, but mostly because I really had no desire to know.

"And then," continued the Imperior, "one day I saw this child dashing about the palace. I was thunderstruck. There are occasionally children seen in some parts of the palace . . . offspring of the staff. But they know their place. They conduct themselves quietly, with proper deportment. This child, though . . . she was running in circles, her arms out to either side, her head tilted back. And she was laughing. Laughing with the pure joy of life.

"I had never seen any such thing in the palace before. Possibly in my previous existence, for all those who are presented to me know to bow and scrape and act in a subservient manner.

"I should have been outraged. Instead, I found it charming.

"I walked over to the child. She saw me and immediately stopped right where she was. I waved to her, like this," and he gestured in a vague manner, "and said, 'Please. Continue if you wish.'

"I thought she would be too self-conscious. No. Not at all. She instantly resumed her running and careening about. I had never witnessed a human being so consumed with the sheer thrill of living. And I said to her, 'Where are your parents? Your mother? Your father? Did your father never teach you proper conduct in the palace of the Imperior?'

"And she said, 'No,' and then gave this . . . this odd, tittering chuckle. 'What do you find so funny?' I asked her." He looked at me. "You know, I assume, what she found so funny?"

"Because you were the father who had never taught her."

He nodded ruefully. "Four years old . . . is a very magical time. I realized that at that moment. Anything is possible in the world at the age of four."

"So you taught her? Became closer to her?"

"Of course not," said the Imperior. "That is a woman's work. I had more important things to do."

"Oh," I said, a bit disappointed in the way that anecdote had concluded.

"Still . . . it displeases me to consider another child that age, cut short in her life for no real reason. It . . . seems rather brutal, does it not. Brutal and unfair."

"That's what I was trying to say."

He took a deep breath and then let it out slowly. "It seems to me that perhaps we are reaching a point as a civilization . . . where we must reassess that which we consider important. We must reconsider what constitutes honor, and loyalty, and devotion."

"Imperior . . . where would we start?" asked Itso Esi. The others looked equally bewildered.

"You could begin with rethinking the entire concept that life is cheap," I said. "You could do away with ritualistic suicide in the name of honor."

The advisors gasped visibly, but the Imperior merely looked interested. "Why would we wish to do that?"

"Because it only allows for one sort of redemption," I said. "In the land where I come from, there are many, many ways that one can go about making restitution for poor or inappropriate behavior, or even criminal action. Someone who is . . ." The ironic self-reflection was not lost upon me. "Someone who is a great villain one day can do things to benefit the public good another day. But those opportunities will never arise if the only acceptable form of penance is death."

It looked like the advisors were about to respond, but then they immediately held their peace as they waited to see how the Imperior would react. He was simply nodding, apparently considering my words.

"Change," he said slowly, "does not occur overnight. Matters that go to the very core of who we are must be weighed, measured, and considered. Even I, divinely inspired by the gods, do not turn a society on its ear overnight. But you have given us much to consider, Po. Very much." He rested a hand on my shoulder, and he looked more tired than I'd ever seen him. "It is difficult to know the difference between those who are dedicated, and those who are friends . . . and those who are simply using you to achieve their own ends. Knowing whom to trust is never an easy business, Po."

"Yes. I know."

"Come."

Although it was one word, it was immediately understood that it was addressed only to me. I followed him, curious as to what was happening. The advisors stayed behind, looking at one another, but making no attempt to ask what was going on. Itso Esi must have been dying with fury. He knew, as did I, that I had engineered no brilliant defense. The Great Wall existed through his attempt to sabotage me. But he had to go along with the perception that I was responsible, lest he admit his sinister intentions.

We went through a door into a much smaller room. Then the Imperior turned to me. Although he still looked elderly, he also appeared regal and dignified and quite, quite sure of himself. If Veruh Wang Ho had been an old man, she'd probably have been a lot like him. Which could explain why I wanted to like the old bastard, despite everything that had happened.

"There are things we need to discuss," he told me.

And we discussed them.

Chapter 2

Crouching Tigress

*S*omething told me the Princess Mitsu was not happy to see me. Perhaps it was the way she hit me in the face that gave it away.

I had been given far more luxurious quarters than during my previous stay. Quarters that were commensurate with the status of someone who was the savior of all of Chinpan. I had unpacked the few belongings I had, but made sure to keep the demon sword with me, strapped securely to my belt. Granted, only I could unleash the demon within, for only I knew the words that released it. But I was certainly not going to let the best chance I had of getting out of this situation alive be stolen out from under me.

I was just getting settled in when Mitsu literally burst into the room. It was not that difficult; the door was made from paper. She simply smashed right through it. As entrances went, it was pretty impressive.

"Oh," I said. "Hello."

She was across the room in record time. She didn't bother to walk; she did several handsprings, propelling herself forward, and it was a miracle that I was able to get out of the way in time. I did so by throwing myself to the floor to avoid her as she sailed over me.

She landed gracefully, bounced an inch or two to absorb the impact, and then whirled to face me. *"How could you?"* she snarled, and came right at me.

I was still holding my walking staff. I angled it in her direction as she barreled toward me, and the four-inch blade snapped out of the mouth of the dragon. Mitsu realized her mistake too late, caught up as she was in the force of her rush at me, and she twisted her body to try and prevent the impact. She failed, and her chest slammed against the end of my staff.

She gasped, anticipating the metal jamming into her. Then she froze there a moment, not quite understanding what had happened.

"You're all right," I told her. "I retracted the blade an instant before you hit it."

Mitsu stepped back to see that I was telling the truth. The blade was gone, pulled back into its place of concealment. She rubbed her chest in irritation, scowling at me. "I should kill you for that," she said.

"I *could* have killed with *that*," I reminded Mitsu. "I don't desire you dead."

"I wish I could say the feeling was mutual." She was still angry, but she made no further attempt to attack. Instead she stalked the interior of the room, never taking her angry glare from me. "After everything we've discussed, all the time we spent together . . . I thought I knew you, Apropos."

"Nobody knows anybody," I said. "We only know those aspects of others that they let us see. The true individual remains hidden from the world. And that's as it should be. Otherwise we'd all probably want to kill each other."

"That's certainly true in this case." Her fists were clenched and shook with suppressed rage. "You swore loyalty to the Forked Tong, Apropos! And the next thing I know, you elect to serve my father? Why? Why are you doing that, when you carry the demon sword?"

"What does that have to do with anything?"

She dropped down onto a pillow on the floor. "Veruh Wang Ho told me there was a great likelihood that you would return to the village where you found the sword. That if you didn't know the magic words that released the demon, you'd learn them there so the sword can be used to end my father's reign and perhaps force him to . . ."

"To what?"

"To do as the Forked Tong demands. His oppressive rule . . ."

"Mitsu," I said in a very low voice lest someone overhear, "I'm still on the side of the Forked Tong."

That stopped her cold. "What? What are you—"

"Veruh's suspicion was correct: I didn't know the magic words. But I've learned how the sword works. I know what to do to unleash the power within."

Her eyes widened at that. "You . . . you know? You found out?" I nodded. "But . . . how did you . . . ?"

"By accident. The same way, I suspect, that Ali, my teacher, found out."

"What is it? What do you say to—?"

I raised a finger and simply shook my head. "No. No, for the time being, that remains my secret. However, you are here as a representative of the Forked Tong. So my question to you becomes: What do you wish to do now?"

"I . . ."

"Well? Come now." I sounded annoyed with her. "We have this weapon at our disposal. I have managed to put your father off his guard. He has no idea where my loyalties lie."

"Nor do I."

She sounded suspicious. I shrugged. "What would you have me do to prove my loyalty? Would you have me execute your father? I could have done so earlier, you know. It would have been no great difficulty. But you could have done that. You live here in the palace. Certainly the opportunity presented itself, as I've pointed out. Instead what I'm told is that you've no immediate desire to do so. Why is that?"

Mitsu looked a bit confused, a swell of emotions playing across her face. "Why . . . is what?"

"You call your father a tyrant. A brute. To you he is the most evil creature that ever walked the planet." I started to raise my voice. "And yet I sit here now, telling you that I possess a weapon that could easily put an end to him. Why are you not interested in that?"

"Shhh!" she said with some alarm. "Keep your voice down! You never know—"

"No, I never do," I said. "I never know what you want from me. I never know what's truly going through your head. I never know what you or any of your shadow associates want. But I'm going to damn well find out."

"Find out?" Her face was a question. "How?"

"Tonight I go to kill the Imperior. I've had it with the lot of you. No one seems to know what they want around here. There's all this talk of honor and sacrifice and changes in power, and manipulation and secrets, so many secrets. Well, I'm flushing it all out into the open. It ends tonight."

"It can't!"

"Why?" I reached over, grabbed her by the wrist. "Tell me why. Why can't it?"

"I can't!"

"Why not?"

"None can know!"

"Know what?"

And suddenly there was a flap of wings, and Mordant sailed into the room like a thrown javelin. He struck me in the chest with such force that he knocked me flat on my back. I looked up at him in surprise as he hovered over me and said, with more anger than I'd ever known him to display, *"Leave her alone."*

"This is none of your business, Mordant."

"Oddly, Apropos, I get to choose what is and isn't my business."

"Fine. You choose your business, then." I stood and straightened my clothes, endeavoring to recapture some degree of dignity. "Mine is with the Imperior. Tonight."

"You can't!" she said with great urgency.

"I can. Why? Do you plan to stop me?" I tapped the demon sword with one hand. "I would not advise it. Matters could prove ugly."

She stared at me for a long moment. It seemed as if she were trying to bore deep into the recesses of my mind with her dark eyes.

"You're bluffing," she said abruptly. She turned to Mordant. "He's bluffing."

"No," I assured her. "I am not."

"You will not go and utilize a weapon as devastating as the demon sword against my father."

"Mitsu," I said, and it took me a moment to muster the strength to say what I was about to say. "You have no idea of the horrors I saw when I was out on the road. The innocents who suffered. You have no idea what those sights . . . did to me. Whatever you think you know of Apropos . . . whatever you think motivates me . . . it's gone. What remains is a man who can only still the sobbing voices of your father's victims by putting an end to your father himself. I hear them, you know," and my voice cracked slightly.

"The voices. The dead villagers . . . all of them, gone, dying brutal, horrible deaths. And your father," and I pointed in the general direction of the palace where he resided, "your father has the nerve to tell me that he wants things to change. He wants them to be different. Then he takes me into another room, speaks to me privately. Tells me of his grand plans for Chinpan. And within minutes, he's already sounding like his old self. Talks about ritual suicide in a nostalgic way. Nostalgic!

"Do you comprehend the irony of that? The man hasn't even done away with the practice, and he's already dwelling in sentimental fashion upon the 'good old days' that haven't even left yet! He's insane, Mitsu," and I made small, circling motions at the side of my head. "You were right all along. You were always right. The man is too dangerous to live. You have my condolences that he is your father. Obviously, however, the fact that he is your father is proving too much of an obstacle to get past. That's fine. I can understand that. I spent much of my youth dwelling upon how I would love to kill my father, if I only knew who he was. When I did discover it, did I kill him? No. I didn't have the stomach for it. And if you don't have the stomach for this, I completely understand.

"But this is not the time for lack of fortitude, Mitsu. This is something that has to be done. And if you are not prepared to do it, then I most certainly am. The only question is do you desire to be there when I do it or not?"

She wavered, looking uncertain. Mordant looked from one of us to the other. "Mitsu," he said, "perhaps it's—"

"Yes," she said quickly, interrupting Mordant, who looked a bit surprised. "Yes . . . I will be there. If it is your desire to kill him on my behalf, then the least I can do is be there to watch. To bear witness to the end of the tyrant."

That was what she was saying. But I was positive there

was more going through her head than that. She was making some sort of alternate plans. I couldn't know what they were, although I had a guess or two. It was pure speculation, however. I wouldn't know for sure until the actual moment came.

"Very well," I said. "Tonight, then."

"How do you plan to sneak in?"

"Sneak in?" I laughed at that. "My dear princess . . . I am to be an invited guest."

"Oh!" Mitsu then joined in the laughter, her slim shoulders shaking with amusement. "How very clever. You needn't worry about gaining entrance, for you are already invited. But . . . what about his guards?"

"There will be none. He trusts me, you see."

"And the sword? In private conference, he will not permit any weapons to be brought into his presence."

"Oh, he will allow this one."

"Why?"

"Because," I smiled, "I said I would make a present of it to him. He has no idea of the sword's true nature. He simply admires the craftsmanship of the hilt. But he will find out. Yes, my dear Mitsu," and I smiled very unpleasantly, "he will most assuredly find out."

I was standing in a garden outside the palace, watching the setting sun. The stunning fragrance reminded me in so many ways of Veruh. I wondered what she was doing right about then. I thought of wandering through the garden with her, an arm draped about her shoulders, and making love to her under the scented trees that dotted the landscape.

The brief rustling of wings was more than enough to inform me that Mordant had perched somewhere nearby.

"Hello, Mordant."

There came no immediate answer. I turned in the direction I thought he was, and he wasn't there. I frowned, and then his voice came from a tree behind me.

"What are you up to, Apropos?"

I turned and saw him there, nestled in among the branches. "I'm not sure what you mean."

"Yes you are, and yes you do," he said. He shifted his position slightly to make himself more comfortable. "I know you too well, have known you for too long. You do nothing unless it's for yourself. So what is there to be gained for you by killing the Imperior? There's certainly much more to be gained if he lives."

"Peace of mind, to start," I said. "If he dies, no more innocents will perish—"

"Innocents perish all the time, Apropos. They perish, they suffer, they're treated in horribly unfair ways. The death of one man, no matter how powerful he may be in local circles, isn't going to change that. Except I shouldn't have to tell you that. You know it already. Which brings us right back to my wondering what it is you have up your sleeve."

"I'm tired, Mordant. That's all."

"Tired of what?"

I sighed heavily. "Of letting the bastards win. Of not doing anything about it because I think it threatens me. Of believing that, because I can't save the entirety of the world, I shouldn't bother to try and save any of it. You have no idea how exhausting it is, always seeing the worst in everything. I want to try and make a difference. I want to try and be something."

Mordant uttered a curt, disbelieving laugh. "Can I accept the evidence of my own ear holes? Are you actually aspiring to be . . . *a hero?*"

"I don't know," I said thoughtfully. "I don't think so. A

hero is filled with altruism, and lives on a high moral plane. I'm simply someone tired of not giving a damn, so I figure I may as well try and give a damn about something. Because not giving a damn about anything isn't making me happy."

"Well, I'm impressed. I am indeed impressed," said Mordant. "There is just one thing that the two of us have to completely understand."

"And what is that?"

"If you in any way try and hurt the princess, the last thing you will feel will be my teeth upon your throat."

"Mordant!" I said with feigned shock. "And here I thought you were my friend."

"I am. Were I not your friend, I would not have warned you. Now that you are warned, what you choose to do with the information is up to you."

"You are too kind to me, Mordant."

"Yes. I know. It's my single fault," said Mordant, and he launched himself away from the tree and angled away toward the palace.

Mitsu came to my room as I adjusted the sword upon my belt. My bastard sword was standing upright neatly in the corner, and the sai were crisscrossed on the floor in front of it. I would have no need for them that night.

She was dressed differently than I was used to seeing her, outfitted in a green silken kimono which did much to set off her eyes. She appeared apprehensive, as I had anticipated she might. "Are you quite all right, Princess?" I asked her.

"Yes. Quite all right," she echoed.

"Come," I said. "Your father is expecting me in his private quarters. We would not want to do something thoroughly impolite, such as be late."

"Waiting for you?" she said. "But not for me."

"I did not mention to him that you would be accompanying me. Why?" I asked. "Does that present a problem, do you think? He is your father, after all. Certainly he should be glad to see his only daughter, even if it is unexpected."

"Yes. Yes, of course he would," she said.

I nodded approvingly.

We passed through the vast hallways, strangely devoid of guards. I admired the statues, the tapestries depicting great moments in the history of Chinpan. Mitsu walked beside me, head held high. She didn't seem to walk so much as glide across the floor, as if she had runners strapped to her feet and was moving across ice.

We reached the doors of the Imperior's quarters, and it was nice to see they weren't made of paper. That would afford more privacy. The doors instead were large, lacquered wood with carvings of birds and snakes upon them. The snakes had their mouths open and were moving toward birds who were desperately trying to get out of their way . . . and did not seem, by the looks of things, to be destined to succeed. I found the imagery rather disturbing.

I knocked, and heard the Imperior's voice from within. "Enter," he said. I gestured in an "after you" manner and Mitsu, with a quick nod, entered the room.

Her father was seated on an elevated chair at the far end, his hands resting lightly on the carved armrest, which also had the heads of snakes on either one. He was smiling gently, one eyebrow cocked when he saw that Mitsu had come in with me. "This is unexpected. Greetings, my child."

"Hello, Father," said Mitsu neutrally. I eased the large doors shut behind me. "It has been a little while since we chatted."

"Much has happened," replied the Imperior. "Po here has said many interesting things. He—"

"We're here to kill you," I interrupted.

The Imperior did not appear surprised. "I see. With that?" He nodded toward the sword on my hip.

"Yes."

"You said you would make a gift of it."

"And so I shall. I'll deliver it point-first."

For someone who was about to die, the Imperior seemed quite calm. "Indeed. And may I ask why you are about to take this murderous action?"

I turned to Mitsu. "Tell him."

She looked from him to me and back again. Her face hardened. "Because of all you've done, Father. Because of what you did to the boy in the marketplace—"

"Oh, Mitsu, not that again," sighed the Imperior. "When will you grow up? When will—"

She strode toward him, her voice growing harsher, angrier. "I *have* grown up, Father. I've made powerful allies. Allies who are enemies of yours. It's about time you realized it. It's about time you came to understand what it is you've done, and what it is you've brought upon yourself."

"Allies? Enemies? What are you going on about . . . ?"

"The Anaïs Ninjas, Father. The Forked Tong. They are my family now," she said heatedly. "They support me. They love me in a way that you never did."

"I don't believe you," the Imperior replied, but there was clearly building anger in his face. "A princess would not associate with such as they. You could not be—"

Abruptly Mitsu reached up and ripped open the front of her kimono. Beneath it was the distinctive black outfit of the sisterhood of the Anaïs Ninjas. She tossed aside the kimono, lifted up the cowl, and tied it tightly across her face in one smooth move. She did not have a sword strapped across her back, but she did have a knife tucked in her belt.

"Return to your room and dispose of that costume at once," the Imperior ordered her. He was standing now, clearly irked. "This is intolerable behavior, and I—"

"I would not speak in such a condescending tone if I were you, Father," said Mitsu. "For at this moment, I am the only thing standing between you and certain death."

"Standing between?" I looked at her in puzzlement.

"Actually," replied the Imperior, "*I* am the only thing standing between *you* and certain death. And to be honest, my daughter, my stance is not especially firm."

With that, he clapped his hands briskly.

The Hamunri came in from everywhere. Hidden doors opened from everywhere. Even the chair slid aside with a rough, scratching noise to reveal a hole in the floor from which more of the Hamunri appeared. All of them had their swords out, and all of them were focused upon Mitsu.

She looked around desperately, and then shouted, "Apropos! Now!"

And she waited.

And nothing happened.

I simply stood there, looking at her sadly.

It took her about two seconds to figure it out.

"You lying bastard!" howled Mitsu, and she yanked the knife from her belt and came at me. I wasn't standing all that far away. Had we been alone in the room, there was every chance she would have been able to gut me before I could make a move.

But the Hamunri, the cream of the crop, were far faster and more fleet of foot than I. Barely had she taken three steps before five of the soldiers had piled upon her, bearing her to the ground. Two grabbed her arms, two her legs, and one threw himself directly across her torso. She struggled and howled and cursed my name, but it did her no good as the Hamunri tossed her knife aside and hauled her to her feet.

"I'll kill you, Apropos! I swear, I'll kill you myself, you betraying piece of slime!" Mitsu shrieked at me.

"Mitsu, he knew."

"You promised the Forked Tong! You—"

I was upon her then, grabbing her face with my hands so I could look straight in her eyes. "*Mitsu, he knew!* Listen to me! He knew what you were up to! He knew—or at least very much suspected—your alliance with the Anaïs Ninjas! He confronted me with his suspicions, as a concerned father! What was I supposed to do?"

She spit in my face. I stepped back, trying to wipe the liquid from my eyes.

"What were you supposed to do?" she demanded with venom. "*Lie!* It's what you do! It's what you're best at! It's what you did to me, and to Veruh Wang Ho! To all of us! You swore fealty—"

"To murderers, Mitsu!" I snapped back at her. "To murderers and thugs and criminals, who would eventually turn against one another. Believe me, I know. Such alliances never last. I had to get you out."

"Get me *out?* You mean get me *killed!*"

"No," and I shook my head fervently. "No, your father doesn't want that for you. And I don't . . ."

"You bastard!" she said again.

I rolled my eyes. "Considering I am a bastard, you might want to give up on the idea of trying to wound me with that 'insult.' Mitsu . . . it's a cult. These women . . . it's a cult movement that's dragged you in. And you'll come to a bad end because of it. I couldn't just stand by—"

"So you betrayed me!"

"I didn't betray you. I told you, he already knew. . . ."

"How? How could he?"

And a low voice said, "I told him."

It took a moment to register upon me who had spoken even as I turned and looked in disbelief.

Go Nogo, the deceased head of security, swaggered toward me. His face bore that same scowl as always, and he barely looked at me. Apparently he was reserving his contempt for the princess. "May the gods save us from pretty young women who are not remotely as clever as they think they are."

"You said he was dead," Mitsu snapped at me. "Another lie . . ."

I was shaking my head in disbelief. "No. No, I saw him die. I saw him . . ."

"A sword wielded by a woman, kill me?" Go Nogo's voice was filled with contempt. "Stun me. Send me into shock, so that I had to withdraw deep into myself, into meditation, to heal myself." He scratched at his chest. "It still itches, I'll give that to the black-clad bitch who did this. But kill me? No."

"You . . ." My lips were suddenly dry as I felt matters beginning to spiral out of control. "Imperior, you said nothing to me about his being alive . . ."

"You did not ask," the Imperior pointed out. Which, I had to admit, was true enough.

Mitsu struggled to break free once more, but their grip upon her was too strong. "So what did you think was going to happen here, Apropos?" she demanded. "My father was going to embrace me? Forgive me the error of my ways? Don't you understand? He's going to try and use me to destroy the Forked Tong. To bring down the alliance . . ."

"I already told you, Mitsu. An alliance of thieves and murderers . . ."

"And still better than he is! A tyrant! A dark sorcerer, enforcing his reign of terror . . ."

"That," said the Imperior with surprising softness, "is enough. Go Nogo," and he nodded.

Go Nogo immediately stepped behind her, pulling out a cloth sash and drawing it across her mouth. Her protests were reduced to muffled, unintelligible grunts.

"Imperior, is that really necessary?" I asked.

"Yes. Yes, I believe it is," he said after seeming to give the matter a moment's thought. "So . . . we apparently have in our hands a sister of the dreaded Anaïs Ninjas, and a close ally of the legendary Veruh Wang Ho as well. Go Nogo . . . what do you suggest we do with her? Bait, perhaps?"

"There is a slight possibility that would work . . . but only slight, and truly, not very likely," said Go Nogo. "Despite her importance to their cause in terms of her connections, I doubt they would risk themselves to save her."

"The alternative?"

Go Nogo shrugged. "Torture would seem to be the best way to proceed."

This time the Imperior did not hesitate at all. "Very well," he said.

I suddenly couldn't get enough breath into my lungs. "Imperior! That's . . ."

"Yes?" He stared at me with open curiosity, as if he couldn't imagine what I could possibly say or, even worse, what objection I could put forward.

"Torture? Your own daughter?"

"Why not? She would have killed me."

"No, I . . . I don't think so. Remember," I said, moving toward him pleadingly, "she said she was the only thing standing between you and death, back when she thought I meant to dispose of you myself. Didn't that prove her loyalty? Her determination to keep you alive?"

"No. It only proved her selfishness." He nodded once

more, obviously coming to a decision. "She will be tortured for information and, if she does not provide it, she will die. It is no more involved than that."

"It bloody well is!" I fairly exploded. "Imperior, we talked a long time! Spoke of many things! Of compassion, and changing the way things were done, and—"

"Honorable Po," said the Imperior, his voice dripping with sarcasm, "I would have said whatever was required to reveal my daughter's duplicity, and to encourage you to help us gain a wedge into the Forked Tong. Why else do you think you were welcomed so willingly?"

The chill settled into me then, and I slowly looked around the room, saw the smirks and smiles of the Hamunri as they readied their swords with great anticipation.

"A trick. It was all a trick," I said hollowly.

"We had about given up on finding you," Go Nogo informed me. "And then what should happen but that you walk right up to the palace, swaggering and big as life. We would have been fools not to exploit the opportunity. Rather than sending men out to attack you . . . why not welcome you? Praise you? Treat you as a long-lost man of greatness?"

"So . . . what you told me? About the Great Wall holding back the Mingol hordes . . ."

"Oh, no, no, that was quite true," the Imperior assured me. "We know, however, that you did not intend for that to happen. It was simply luck on your part. Still, we benefited from it, so I did wish you to know that I was most appreciative of it."

Go Nogo advanced on me then. His face could have been carved out of stone. "One thing you will tell me . . . and I suspect that torture will not be necessary, for it is my belief that merely the slightest hint of potential pain will be enough to get you to speak freely. A number of my men have not returned. Where are they? Did your Forked Tong allies dispose of them?"

My face was grim and determined as I looked around. "Do you want to know?"

"Yes."

"Do you *really* want to know?"

"This is not a joke, Po," Go Nogo informed me. "The amount of cooperation you provide me now will determine whether you die quickly and mercifully . . . or slowly and agonizingly."

"To die quickly or slowly. Hmmm," I murmured, and my hand went to my sword hilt. "Tough choice."

The other Hamunri automatically tensed, ready for a battle, but Go Nogo simply smiled. "Please, yes, by all means. Draw your weapon. I would welcome a fight with you."

Obediently I drew the bird's-head sword. The noiselessness of its departure from the scabbard clearly surprised Go Nogo ever so slightly, but he covered it deftly. "Now . . . you will tell me what I want to know. And for every minute that passes that you do not give me answers I like, I will sever a body part."

"Seems fair. Perhaps you might want to start with your balls. I'd love to see how you sound as a eunuch."

"Not *my* body parts!"

"Oh," I said, as if just comprehending it. "You mean *my* body parts."

"Yes," he said, obviously under the impression he was talking to an idiot. "Perhaps I will start with your tongue."

"If you insist. But you're the one who will have to deal with your wife's complaints when I can't give her oral pleasure anymore."

This actually drew a combination of raucous laughter and startled gasps from the assembled Hamunri.

The point of Go Nogo's sword trembled a foot away

from me. He was clearly doing everything he could to fight an impulse to behead me right then. "Do you not care," he demanded, "that I am about to kill you as slowly as humanly possible?"

"Funny you should ask," I said, and gripped the hilt as hard as I could. "No . . . I don't care."

He raised up his sword to have at me, and then the demon sword began to tremble. The Hamunri stepped back, bewildered, and suddenly the Imperior shouted, "*Kill him! Quickly!* That's no ordinary tachi blade! He's discovered Kumagatu, the demon sword! I should have recognized it immedi—!"

And that was all he had the time to say before the blade twisted and bent back upon itself and the demon Aulhel broke loose once more.

The others were astounded, shocked, brought their weapons up and tried to engage in combat without having a clear idea of what they were facing. I, however, knew, and was already one step ahead of them. I charged forward as they were distracted by the hissing, spitting demon, and I brought my walking staff up and around and slammed it into the nearest of the soldiers who were holding Mitsu. He staggered, and the moment his grip was less than firm upon her, Mitsu yanked her arm completely free and slammed an elbow into the face of the guard on the other side.

The right half of her body was free, and then the Hamunri who had been endeavoring to hold her captive released her as they grabbed for their swords. I didn't have to see why. I knew.

The demon unleashed a bellow of undiluted rage and then he was upon them. Even as he proceeded to shred them in his customary unstoppable manner, I was shoving Mitsu toward the door. It was imperative I get her out of the room before the demon spotted her, or I was going to have to do everything I could to haul him off her before he sliced her to ribbons. And I didn't want to bank on my being able to stop him.

Mitsu barely resisted. She was watching the berserk demon in shocked horror. My back was to him, but I could hear the rending and tearing and screams, and could imagine what she was witnessing. At the last moment, just when I had her to the door, she started to push back.

"You have to get out!" I shouted at her to make myself heard over the shrieks and howls and dying. "If he sees you in here, you're dead!"

"But—!"

"No buts!"

"My father! You have to save him! I need him!"

Mixed signals, thy name was Mitsu.

"No promises!" I told her, and slammed the door in her face. Then I turned to see what the damage was, just as Go Nogo's head rolled up to my feet. I didn't hesitate, taking the opportunity to swing my good left foot and kick the head halfway across the room.

Then I turned to see the demon's progress.

As always, the Slojinn had been thorough.

Pieces of the Hamunri were everywhere. The room was a literal bloodbath. At that moment, Aulhel was holding an unfortunate, screaming soldier over his head, gripping him by the right leg and the left arm. With one fierce pull, he ripped the soldier apart and then used the leg of the man he'd just dismembered to club another into submission.

Then he turned and faced the Imperior.

The Imperior had gone deathly pale, his back up against the chair, but his face was a mask of concentration. He had his hands in front of him, his fingertips facing one another, and he was speaking quickly in a tongue

I did not understand. Blue crackling energy was jumping from one hand to the other, and suddenly he flung open his hands and the energy leaped across the room and crashed into Aulhel.

For an instant a look of triumph appeared on the Imperior's face, but then the Slojinn was on his feet, and he growled, "Your shi is weak, sorcerer. Look at you. You can barely stand."

Aulhel was correct. And not only that, but the Imperior looked measurably older than he had moments ago. His face more wrinkled, his eyes more sunken. His hands trembling, he tried to mount a defense, but it clearly was going to do no good. Aulhel advanced on him, his long pointed talons clicking together in anticipation.

"Save me!" screamed the Imperior.

I considered it coolly and decided I was not so inclined.

Aulhel lashed out and the Imperior fell back, desperately trying to avoid the Slojinn's attack. He turned to run, and Aulhel's talons raked across his back, tearing through his elaborate robes and hitting flesh and bone beneath. The Imperior screamed and fell, hitting the floor hard, blood welling up upon his back, and Aulhel moved in for the kill.

Suddenly there was an earsplitting screech, and Mordant dove down from overhead. He whipped around, getting between the Slojinn and the Imperior, and darted at Aulhel's face. Aulhel let out a scream of rage and lashed out at Mordant, trying to catch him. The drabit was fast, however. He swept in, slicing fast with his claws fully extended. Aulhel swept an arm around, almost caught him, but missed.

"Mordant, get out of here!" I shouted.

"No!" Mordant cried. "We need the Imperior alive— unhhh!!!"

That last outcry was because, as fast as Mordant was,

Aulhel was faster. The demon had snagged Mordant, and it was only going to be a moment's work for him to rip the drabit's head free of his neck.

"Dammit!" I muttered even as I held the sword tightly and shouted, *"I don't care!"*

Aulhel let out a furious howl and staggered as magicks swept from the hilt, trying to re-form him into the sword. He released Mordant and turned to face me, and he snarled, "I warned you once, boy! You keep trying to use a few words to bottle up forces that you've unleashed! It doesn't work that way! The forces of nothingness are not yours to tamper with at your whim! I am ultimate destruction, boy! You cannot toy with nihilism, nor dabble with the abyss, for sooner or later, it will swallow all, whole! *Whole!*"

And then there was roaring and howling of wind that sent me crashing to the floor. My breath was heavy in my chest, and I wasn't sure, but I thought I'd gone slightly— although, ideally, only temporarily—deaf.

I lay there panting, trying to catch my breath, and looked across the room to see the Imperior lying there, not appearing in particularly good shape. I didn't think he was going to make it. At that moment, I didn't give a damn.

Mordant was lying on the ground near me. He looked a bit battered, but otherwise he was fine. His eyes glowed as he looked at me. "Thanks," he said.

" 'Twas no problem," I lied.

The door to the room was shoved open and Mitsu entered quickly. She ran toward Mordant, picked him up, and cradled the banged-up drabit in her arms. She looked at the Imperior, with the blood covering his back, and screamed, *"Father! Oh, no! No!"*

Then she looked down at me and kicked me in the small of the back.

"Ow!" I yelled in protest. "Was that really necessary?"

"I told you to protect my father!"

"Well," and I hauled myself to my feet, "I was unaware I took orders from Princess Spits-In-My-Face! The only reason your father is still drawing air into his lungs at all is because I sent the demon back so he wouldn't kill Mordant. My sympathies are not with dear old daddy at the moment."

"We don't need your sympathies," said Mordant. "We need your help."

"There's only one healer in all of Chinpan who can help him now," Mitsu said. "Veruh Wang Ho."

"You can't be serious," I said. "She'll never come here."

"We can bring him to the Noble Ho. There are ways out of here," she said, her voice growing increasingly desperate-sounding. "Secret ways that I've used to get in and out. The Noble Ho will be able to cure him. To—"

"Why?" I demanded. "Tell me why. I deserve to know. Why in the world should we be going out of our way to help this . . . this so-called ruler."

"For me," said Mordant. "I need you to help him for me."

"For you?" I was lost. "Why for you, Mordant? What interest does he have for—"

"He's my lover!" Mitsu cried out.

"Hush!" Mordant snapped at her. "You promised—!"

I was appalled. I looked at the fallen Imperior and then at Mitsu. "Your father is your lover? Gods, that . . . that is the most horrible, hideous—"

"Not my father, you idiot!" Mitsu shouted, and cuffed me in the side of the head. "Him!" And she pointed at Mordant.

I stared at her blankly, convinced she'd lost her mind.

And then I realized. It all snapped into place.

"Oh . . . my gods," I said. "Oh my dear gods. You," and I pointed with a trembling finger at Mordant. "You're . . .

you're the peasant boy. The boy from the marketplace. The one Mitsu said she fell in love with. You . . . you were human . . ."

"Of course I was human!" Mordant said, immensely irritated. "*I'm a talking dragon, for gods' sake!* Have you ever met any talking animal in your life?"

"Well . . . no . . ."

"And it never once occurred to you to ask me how I was able to converse with you? Not even once?"

"I just . . . I thought you were magic. Once I accepted the notion that you were magic, anything seemed possible. So I . . . I . . ."

"Apropos," sighed Mordant, "for someone who fancies himself to be exceptionally intelligent, you can be astoundingly stupid sometimes."

"I told you my father was a powerful wizard," Mitsu said. "When he discovered my true love, he called up a deep and powerful curse and placed it upon him." She walked quickly over to her father and knelt, examining his wounds. "He transformed my beloved into what you see here, and sent him away . . . far, far away. But he came back to me. . . ."

"Took a while. A couple of years," said Mordant.

"But why didn't you tell me?" I demanded.

"Because although my father unleashed the curse, he didn't know what sort of animal my love had been changed into," said Mitsu. "We didn't want to take any chance that he might find out. . . ." She shook her head as she looked up, her face getting pale. "We have to hurry. We have to bring him to Veruh Wang Ho. He is the only one who can remove the curse upon my beloved. If that doesn't happen . . ."

"You're a drabit forever," I guessed.

Mordant nodded dourly. "Not a bad fate if you're born this way. Somewhat unfortunate if you once possessed another form."

"All right, fine!" I growled. "Let's get out of here. But with something slightly less noticeable than the bloodied body of the ruler of all Chinpan."

It was but the work of a moment to tear down a tapestry and wind the Imperior up in it. He was in no shape to protest, his head lolling and looking deathly pale.

With the Imperior obscured from sight, I said, "All right, let's get out of here. Do you know where Veruh Wang Ho can be found?"

"The Noble Ho will meet us in Darktown," said Mitsu, and I immediately took that to mean the section of the city we'd been to before, with the overhanging roofs and the sense of perpetual blackness.

"How do you know she'll be there?"

"I'll make certain of it," said Mordant. "Although my guess is that Ho'll know before I even get there." And with that, he leaped skyward and flapped out of the room. I was sure it would take him no more than a minute to find a window and be on his way to wherever it was he was going to go.

"My love is right. The Noble Ho has eyes and ears everywhere," she assured me. "By the time we're approaching the dwelling of the Anaïs Ninjas, the Noble Ho will be prepared for us."

Which was fine, of course, for those whose loyalty to the Forked Tong and its associate members was unquestioned. For one such as me, however, I was concerned over the likelihood of my life being extended much beyond its current measure.

"Do not concern yourself," said Mitsu as we headed

down the hallway, with a bloodstained tapestry slung over my shoulder. "Nothing useful ever came out of worrying."

"Sudden death," I said.

Mitsu stared at me. "How is sudden death useful?"

"Better than a slow, lingering death."

I just hoped I'd never have the opportunity to compare methods.

Chapter 3

Hidden Draggin'

I never thought he would survive the trip.

I'm not sure how he managed it. We're talking about an elderly man, badly wounded by a demon creature, wrapped up inside a tapestry and hauled across the length of Taikyo. I kept waiting for him to wake up, to shout for help. But he didn't. Which then led me to start worrying that when we eventually unwrapped him, he would be a corpse tumbling out.

We went straight to my quarters where I packed my things within seconds. I'd gotten rather skilled at that. Someone like me had to be prepared to depart a place at a moment's notice, since I never knew when someone might be coming to kill me. I didn't know for sure if I was going to be returning to the palace or not, and better to play it safe. "All right," I said when I was ready. "Which way?"

"This way," she said, and headed over toward one of the panels of the wall.

Mitsu certainly knew what she was talking about when it came to hidden passages. Apparently they had been there long before her father became Imperior. They had been built by predecessors who were trying to anticipate a time when they might have to leave as quickly as possible, because of either invasion from without or uprising from their own people. I wasn't entirely surprised. The castle of King Runcible had had similar secret passages, constructed for much the same reasons. It was intriguing that those who were ostensibly the most powerful individuals in the land always seemed to fear for their lives and plan for escapes. Whereas the least powerful individuals in the land resided in single-room huts and were quite content to do so, going to sleep every night in relative peace. Not easy to determine, when considering that, who was truly in charge of their own destinies.

The princess had discovered a moving panel on the wall of her room when she was very young, and from that point on had used the secret passages to explore the palace and go wherever she wanted, whenever she wanted. It was one of the few things about her life that ever made her feel powerful. She would sit and watch her father's meetings from hiding and be smug over never being seen. And on several occasions, she witnessed dark rituals her father performed, and they chilled her and frightened her and made her realize just what it was she was dealing with.

"Even before I saw him performing the rituals, I would know after the fact he had done one," she told me as we moved like ghosts through the walls. "He would age."

"Age?"

She nodded. "The magicks he channeled were so powerful that they would drain life energy from his body. He would dispose of enemies, achieve alliances . . . transform people when he desired to make their lives a living hell," she added grimly. "But it would always take something out of him. That's why he did it less and less as time wore on. My father looks so old to your eyes, does he not.

Ancient, even. That's deceptive. In terms of how many years he's been in this world, he's not really all that old."

We descended a long, narrow stairway that was hewn directly into the rock. It led to a subterranean passage, with a trickling stream running through. We walked along the bank, and I shifted the Imperior-in-the-tapestry from one shoulder to the other. This was not the easiest endeavor I'd ever engaged in. My arms were strong, yes, but it was starting to cause serious wear and tear upon my lame leg.

I shook my head as I contemplated the follies some people would engage in for the purpose of obtaining and retaining power. And then I started to think about everything that Mitsu and Mordant had gone through . . . and I chuckled slightly.

"What's so funny?" she asked.

"I am. This situation is."

She shook her head, uncomprehending.

"I'm a side character. *Again*," I told her.

"A what?"

"An incidental individual. A throwaway cast member. A sidekick. One who thinks his own life really matters, and who is experiencing his own great adventure . . . and it turns out that I'm experiencing yours."

She stepped carefully over some slime that had gathered on the shore. Not too far ahead of us, I could see moonlight filtering through. We were drawing nearer to an exit. "I still cannot say I understand what you're talking about."

"You, and your heroic young man in the marketplace . . . or, as I call him, Mordant the snide and occasionally annoying drabit," I explained. "You and he have this grand and great tragic romance that I've been pulled into. Your story is the truly interesting one. I'm just . . . just this foolish individual who's been trying to change his life, find love, make something of himself . . . in short, operate in a manner contrary to his nature just to have—if nothing else—something different to think about and do and contemplate. And you . . ."

I sighed heavily, readjusted her father around my shoulders once again, and said, "I can see that what I'm saying remains impenetrable to you. Do not concern yourself with it."

"No, it's not impenetrable at all. I grasp what you're saying now. You liken your life, and the lives of those around you, to great literary adventures or tales of mythic accomplishments."

"Yes, exactly."

"And you consider yourself to be something other than the central figure. A subordinate 'character' who participates in the lives of others who are far more interesting and unique, while constantly being frustrated that he himself amounts to nothing."

"You *do* understand," I said with satisfaction.

The exit out was so narrow that we could only emerge one at a time. In fact, it was little more than a hole, so we had to crawl through it. Mitsu eased herself through first, and then I slid her the wrapped form of her father, which she pulled out from the other side. I took a deep breath and shoved my head in, twisting and insinuating my body through. When my head poked out the other side, I sucked in fresh air and then muttered, "So . . . this is what birth is like."

"Very funny," she said, and helped pull me out the rest of the way. We sat there for a moment, resting from the exertion. Actually, I was the one who had exerted himself. Mitsu wasn't even breathing hard.

"You're wrong, you know," she said.

"About what?"

"About what you're saying. About your point of view," said Mitsu. "Our story, the tale of my lover and I, has been seen and told and retold any number of times. Look at us: Star-crossed lovers. The hero transformed. The heroine in disguise. It's all been done before, by people far more intriguing and clever than we. But you, Apropos . . . you're unique. I've never heard of anyone like you. You're much more interesting than we are. Much too interesting, in fact, to be a 'supporting character.' "

"Do you truly think so?" I asked.

"Oh, unquestionably. You have a personality. Supporting, incidental characters have personality traits. But you are much more than you're crediting yourself."

"And yet . . ."

"And yet?" She looked at me expectantly.

"And yet . . . I still have nothing. In many ways, still am nothing."

She shook her head sadly. "Do not underestimate the joy of nothing. The problem with having something is that some-one else always wants to take it away from you. A man who has nothing has nothing to lose, and everything to gain . . . unless he's wise enough not to gain it." She got to her feet, her face suddenly serious. "Come. Time is running short."

No one gave us a second glance as we walked quickly through the darkened streets of Taikyo. There was every likelihood that by this point, the alarm had been sounded back at the palace. But many, if not all, of the formidable Hamunri had been disposed of by the Slojinn. Matters would be in disarray. They would likely be searching every corner, looking desperately for the Imperior, not realizing that he was gone. And with any luck, by the time the search spread into the city, matters would be resolved.

Then again, I thought grimly, when did "with any luck"

and "Apropos" ever live in comfortable harmony with one another?

We entered the shadow city. I had come to think of the darkened section of town as another place entirely, separate from Taikyo, with a life and energy—or lack of life and sucking of energy—all its own. I did not fear the shadows this time, however. I welcomed them.

And they welcomed us.

Literally.

We passed a shadow and from within came the word, "Welcome."

I almost jumped as I saw one of the Anaïs Ninjas emerge from hiding and fall into step behind us. And then from another shadow came a second, and then a third. The shadows in front of us, too, birthed more of the warrior sisters. They were giving us an escort of sorts. Or perhaps they just wanted to make sure there was no trickery on my part.

"Word really did get around," I said under my breath.

"As I said it would."

I saw their eyes glittering in the darkness. None of them were looking directly at me. Instead they were fascinated with the bundle I was carrying, obviously intrigued and delighted at the notion that the great, mighty, and divine Imperior was being treated with the dignity usually accorded to a load of laundry.

Suddenly they stopped, which naturally caused us to halt as well. "Here," said Mitsu, pointing, and I wouldn't have been able to tell you if it was the same place we'd gone before, or somewhere else entirely.

We entered and this time the illumination was a bit more festive. Paper lanterns hung around the room, and there was Veruh Wang Ho, seated on a thronelike chair that was in some ways similar to the dragon throne of the Imperior. Her eyes glittered coldly when she saw the tapestry I had slung over my shoulder. Mordant was perched on the back of her chair, watching impassively.

"Remove him immediately," she said. "This is not appropriate."

I was stung by the criticism. "Would you have preferred we walk through the streets of Taikyo with an unconscious ruler slung across—"

"Remove. Him." Each word was as ice.

I lay the tapestry down upon the floor. The Anaïs Ninjas moved in quickly, rolling him out as smoothly as they could. Unfortunately the blood upon his back had dried against the tapestry, making a sticky mess. His skin was terribly pale, and for a moment I thought we were too late. But then his chest rose and fell ever so slightly, and I heard an ugly rasping from within.

"Can you heal him, Noble Ho?" asked Mitsu.

"Do you think I should?"

"Yes."

"Because you hope that he will be willing to undo the spell he placed upon your lover."

"Yes," she said again.

"Is there any other reason?"

Mitsu looked down and said softly, "Because of who he is . . . to me . . ." and she looked up. "And to you."

To her, I wondered. *Who is the Imperior to this woman whom I love with all my—*

That was when it struck me with the force of a thunderbolt.

The bond that clearly existed between Veruh and Mitsu. The affection that I felt for Mitsu as compared to the far greater intensity of feeling I held for Veruh. And I realized at that point, even though it had not been as evident thanks to the white face makeup that Veruh wore, that there was a resemblance between the two.

Veruh Wang Ho was Mitsu's mother.

I was in love, not with the princess, but with the queen. A dethroned, displaced queen, but still a queen to be sure. Or perhaps an Imperiess. Whatever it was she was called in these parts.

And I thought, *Huh. Well done you. Moving up in the world, I daresay. No more falling in love with the daughters when you can be heels over head with the mothers.*

Even as I tried to deal with this revelation, Veruh was looking down at the Imperior, her face inscrutable. "He once had potential, you know," she said. She looked up at Mitsu. "If you," and then she glanced around the room at the assembled sisters, "if any of you had known him in his younger days, when I knew him. So much potential. But his urge to retain power became a sick need within him."

"Are you to eulogize him, my love, or help him?" I asked.

She turned her attention to me. "And you. I understand that you endeavored to betray Mitsu. To betray all of us. Is there any reason that I should not have the sisters kill you where you stand?"

I looked around as they glowered at me. Then I drew myself up, fixing a steady gaze upon her. "I did what I thought was best for her. I wanted better for Mitsu than this . . ." and I pointed around, "this shadow existence."

"And what would you know of it?"

"Because I've lived a shadow existence most of my life," I said. "I just carry mine within rather than without. And I wouldn't wish that upon anyone . . . much less Mitsu. You spoke of the potential the Imperior had. What of the potential of his daughter? Is this," and once more I pointed around the room, "is this a measure of her full potential?"

"Interesting," said Veruh Wang Ho. "I thought you would say that I should not kill you because you love me, and I love you, and our souls are intertwined—"

"Why would I waste your time with that which you

already know. I could not . . ." I paused, tried to find the best way to phrase it. "Veruh . . . I have utilized in my life every trick, every contrivance, every deception I know for the purpose of staying alive. I could not take what I feel for you . . . and what I hope you feel for me . . . and turn it into just another tool in my tool chest."

Her gaze held mine steady for an eternity, and then she smiled. "Well said." She nodded toward the Imperior. "Take him in the back," she said to the sisters. "I will attend to him. And then . . . we shall see what we shall see."

The Anaïs Ninjas did as they were instructed, although some of them still fired annoyed glances in my direction. But I didn't care. At that moment, my soul was singing within my breast.

She had accepted what I had done. She was not angry. If anything, my actions had brought me closer to her than ever before. The notion filled me with so much joy that I thought my heart would literally explode from my chest with joy. Then I got a mental image of just what exactly that would look like, and that dampened my enthusiasm. But even so, my passion for her was boundless, my certainty that we could be united forever growing with each passing moment.

Except it all hinged upon what she was going to do now with the Imperior. She needed to do more than just save his life. She had to mend the broken fences between them. She had to . . .

Shite.

She was going to have to get back together with him.

How could they mend fences, after all, if she was continuing to lead a crime family? How could they possibly be allies if they remained estranged as man and wife? For my true love to be able to do what had to be done, I would have to lose her to the man who had tried to have his soldiers kill me. Well, I supposed I didn't resent him all that much over the killing part. Too many people had tried to have me killed or tried to kill me themselves for me to single out one individual for the transgression.

But how could we have any sort of future together if she were to reunite with the Imperior?

So . . . what was I to do now? Hope the Imperior died? If he did, Mordant would forever stay a transformed dragon, and very likely Veruh would remain as head of the Skang Kei family. With the death of the Imperior and no one apparently in line to inherit the throne—since Mitsu, as a "mere woman," would not be allowed to rule—there would probably be a struggle for power that would leave many dead. Chaos would conceivably descend upon the whole of Chinpan.

But if the Imperior lived, and matters were sorted out between them, then I would lose my love.

It will all work out for the best. No matter what, it will all work out for the best, my inner voice assured me, even as frustration washed over me.

The next hours stretched on interminably. The silence did not help. All the Anaïs Ninjas simply stared at me, as if waiting to be told what to do. I thought I spotted the one I'd known earlier. She was looking me up and down, and I noticed that her hand seemed to be sliding into the top of her trousers, descending downward toward her privates.

I didn't need to see that. And I certainly didn't want to imagine what she was thinking about as she did it.

Even Mitsu said nothing. She simply sat there in what appeared to be a deeply meditative state. Mordant had curled up next to her, and she was idly running her fingers along his scales. He would look up at her every so often with a gaze of pure adoration. Here I had treated him like a pet, or a talking oddity, and he was a human trapped in this form. Unaccountably I felt guilty. It wasn't as if I could have known. Still . . . I felt as if I should have figured it out somehow, with the same type of intuition that had enabled me to divine Veruh Wang Ho's true identity.

Then others began to arrive.

Men, mostly. Men who seemed cut from rough cloth. Men who appeared to be, at the very least, criminal types. They arrived one by one until they numbered roughly a dozen.

Each of them, I saw, had a tattoo on the back of his hand: a snake, its tongue lashing out, curled around a pair of what appeared to be grasping scissors.

The Forked Tong. They had to be.

When they were assembled en masse, one of them stepped forward and said to Mitsu, "Where is he? Where is the Imperior? We know he is here."

"The Noble Ho is attending to him. Trying to save his life."

"The Noble Ho should let him die." There were nods of agreement from the men.

Slowly Mitsu rose to her feet. Mordant, perched upon her shoulder, flared out his wings and conveyed a threatening air.

"You see before you the assembled might of the Anaïs Ninjas," she said. "Furthermore, the might of the Skang Kei family is in the next building, being held in reserve lest you attempt any . . . ugliness."

"What are you saying?" demanded the spokesman.

"I am saying that if you desire to maintain our alliance, then you will do nothing until—"

At that moment, there came a noise from the doorway through which Veruh Wang Ho and the Imperior had passed. A scuffle, a soft footfall. The attention of everyone in the room was drawn to it.

Slowly the Imperior moved forward into the light of the lamps. He looked around the room, his face dark as a thundercloud, his gaze malevolent.

"So. The Noble Ho healed you."

"Yes, daughter. I did not ask it, nor did I desire it. But it was done." He appeared to be glaring at everyone all at once. His life had been saved, and it did not appear to have improved his disposition one bit. "I am going to depart now. Unless one of you desires to get in the way of the anointed of the gods."

"You," said the leader of the Forked Tong, and he started forward.

The Imperior looked up at him and there was something in his eyes that froze the man where he stood. Nothing happened for a moment, and then the criminal backed away.

"Father, wait!" Mitsu said urgently, desperately. It hurt me to hear her speak in that manner, but she had tossed aside considerations of personal dignity. "Wait . . . please. The Noble Ho cured you. Saved your life. I ask a boon, in the name of honor. Restore him," and she indicated Mordant, who was looking at the Imperior hopefully. "Only you can do it. Please. In honor's name, you owe us . . ."

"What do you know of honor?" the Imperior grunted. He looked around. "What do *any* of you know? Honor is all! Honor is above everything! It is even above petty considerations of personal gain!"

"And who determines all that?" I asked. "Who sets the standard for honor? How does anyone know . . . ?"

"It is determined here," said the Imperior, and he touched his chest. "That is all you need to know."

"But that's not all you need to know," I said, standing in his path. "Mitsu is right. You owe her—"

"I owe her nothing. If not for her, I would never have been in danger. And I certainly owe *that* nothing."

He pointed toward the doorway. Veruh Wang Ho was standing there, hands on either side, looking tired. Whatever she'd done to minister to his needs and cure him of his wounds, it had taken a good deal out of her. My feelings were so torn. Clearly she was not going to reunite with her husband, but still . . . the alternative was not going to be pleasant. But at least she would be mine, and we could be together.

"So after all this time," said Veruh Wang Ho, "I am simply to be referred to as 'that'?"

"It is all that you deserve and more," said the Imperior with greater force than ever. "You are a disgrace. A travesty, a—"

"Hey!" Fury was building in me. I was becoming so angry with the Imperior that I was starting to reach a point where I didn't trust myself. Where I might actually assault him for his abuse. "Hey, that's enough! How dare you? How *dare* you? Whatever it is you believe she did to you, or you to her, Veruh deserves better treatment at your hands than this. She saved your life, and gave you your daughter. You may not think much of Mitsu simply because of her gender, but still, this woman," and I pointed at Veruh, "is the mother of your child. A woman that I love with all my heart, and who loves me as well! At least I can appreciate her for the wondrous creature she is! How can you not also—"

There was a chuckle then, from one of the men of the Forked Tong. A guffaw from another. A snicker from several of the Anaïs Ninjas.

"What?" I demanded. "What's so funny?"

The laughter grew and grew. I looked at Mitsu in a quandary. "What are they laughing at?"

Mitsu appeared chagrined. "I . . . I thought you knew."

"Knew?"

"You . . ." She lowered her voice . . . why, I don't know,

since everyone could hear her anyway. "You said your time with the bathing maiden . . . it meant nothing to you. That you wanted something else. And all that time with me, you never . . . tried to touch me, or . . ."

"Because I thought of you as a friend! I didn't want to presume, to . . ."

And the laughter was getting louder still. Above it, I fairly shouted, "What does any of this have to do with your mother!" and I pointed at Veruh.

"You idiot," snapped the impatient Imperior. "That is not my daughter's mother. That is my daughter's uncle . . . my sick brother. Except I have no brother."

A faint buzzing started in my head, behind my eyes. Just as everyone else was laughing, so did I start to laugh, even as my mind began to shrink away in horror. Veruh was smiling at me sadly, shaking her head. Her head. Veruh's head her head she . . .

She . . .

She . . .

"Yes. No, I . . ." I laughed louder than any of them, for it was driven by mounting terror and nausea. "Yes, this is . . . this is a joke! An amazing joke! Some . . . sort of indoctrination, or ritual of acceptance, I understand that now. You . . . you wacky Chinpanese! I'd never have thought that you—"

"When you disappeared," said the Imperior to Veruh, "I thought you had the good grace to go somewhere private and kill yourself, and not even leave us a body to clean up. I never dreamt, when I heard of this 'Veruh Wang Ho,' that it was you. Would that I never had."

She . . .

She . . .

Veruh continued to shake her head and stepped back into the adjoining room, and she . . .

She. She was a woman. Of course she was a woman. She was my soul mate, the love of my life, the creature of my dreams, and besides, any number of times, Mitsu had referred to Veruh as "she" or "her," why, there was the time that . . .

. . . that . . .

And I ran our conversations through my head with the same type of copious memory that lets me write down my memoirs now, and desperately sought for Mitsu using the female pronoun in reference to Veruh Wang. There must have been one time . . . one . . .

"No," I said, and I wanted to vomit, I wanted to scream, and I charged after Veruh with the hysterical braying of the most villainous beings in all of Chinpan ringing in my ears.

I staggered into the next room, and Veruh turned to face me, and there was such sadness in her eyes. Me, I was still giggling, which was all I could do to force down my temptation to scream, because I was afraid that if I did, I would never stop.

"It's a mistake. Tell him it's a mistake," I said, sounding crazed.

"*We* were not a mistake, Apropos," Veruh said softly. "We are as one. We saw each other truly from the moment we set eyes upon each other. What do the details matter?"

"This is . . . this is taking a joke too far."

"He never understood, Apropos," she said, slowly coming toward me. "Never. But you . . . you understood me more in our short time together than all the time when the Imperior and I were brothers . . ."

"*We were lovers!*"

"Yes, we were. In new and exciting ways for you. Isn't that enough? Isn't that—"

"But . . ." I shook my head desperately. The laughter was still resounding from outside. Me, I had stopped. "But it simply can't be, because I would never fall in love with another man! It couldn't happen! That is the province of . . . of sick, demented men! Of perversion! Not of normal . . ."

"Has it never occurred to you, sweet Apropos, that 'normal' is not an absolute? That we are what we are? And we must accept ourselves for what we are? You accepted me. You accepted our bond."

"The . . . the only way a man could make me fall in love with him—and not that it's possible, you understand, but if it was—was to do something to sap my mind. Brainwarping perfumes, or trick lights or—"

"No," she said. "No, I did nothing like that. The fragrances you smelled, the dim lighting . . . simply atmosphere. I would never have done anything to impair your judgment, sweet Apropos. What we have is real. What we have transcends physical limitations. What we have—"

"You're not a man!" I shrieked. She reached toward me, and I stumbled backward and fell. *"You're not the Imperior's brother! You're Veruh—"*

She threw open her robe, revealing her nude body.

"—Wang Ho," I finished weakly.

She . . . he . . . it . . . looked at me with infinite sadness, allowing the robes to drop, covering the indisputably male body she . . . he . . . it . . . possessed. "Apropos . . . you love me. I know you do, for I love you." He reached toward me. I backed up, crab-walking across the ground, shaking my head furiously. "And what we had," he said, "we can still have, only greater than ever, for we know each other now fully. No more hiding. No more uncertainty."

I couldn't think. Couldn't feel. I wanted to rip my body away and leave it behind and run off into oblivion.

"Apropos . . . there is so much good that can be between us."

"I don't care," I whispered.

"But don't you see? It—"

"I don't care," I said again, this time a bit louder. There was a warning vibration at my hip. At that moment, I didn't notice. All I was trying to do was get myself as far away from him as possible.

"Apropos, I love you!" cried out Veruh Wang Ho, baring his soul to me since he had already bared his body.

It was the words no one had truly spoken to me and meant since the death of my mother. It was the words that could have filled my life with meaning.

And I looked at the face of the man who said them, and screamed, *"I don't care! I don't care! I DON'T CARE! I DON'T CARE I DON'T CARE I DON'T CARE! I DON'T CARE!* **I DON'T CARE! I DON'T CARE! I DON'T CARE! I DON'T C—"**

And then the blinding white light exploded.

The world crashed and smoked around me, and burned into my inner eye was the image of a cloud going up and up and up, spreading outward in all directions like a giant toadstool. Something burned at the side of my head, and then nothingness enveloped me.

I welcomed it.

Chapter 4

The Trinity Test

I floated peacefully, wondering if I was dead, hoping that I was, because if I was simply dreaming or sleeping, then inevitably I would have to awaken. And I had no desire to do so.

I saw an image floating toward me. It was my mother. She was shaking her head, and she looked disappointed in me, but also appeared to understand. "It's all right," she whispered to me. "Everything is all right."

"What happened? Am I . . ." I hesitated to ask. "Am I dead?"

"Oh, no, my love. No, you're not dead."

"Then . . . then what . . . ?"

"You were warned, my love. Warned about intensity of emotion. Warned about what it could do, especially when it came to unleashing of power."

"But . . . but I don't . . ." I was trying to understand. "The sword. I . . . didn't pull the sword. It shouldn't have . . ."

"Ah, that's the problem with destructive power," she assured me. "You think you control it. You think, 'As long as I don't intend to use it, it won't be used.' But it does get used. In this case, because of the intensity of your denial. You wanted Veruh gone."

"No."

"You wanted all of them gone. All of them. Their laughter, their pity, their knowledge of what a complete and utter fool you'd been. It ripped a hole in your heart greater than any that had ever come before. Your antipathy for their very existence, your revulsion for your own, was so overwhelming that it activated the demon sword even when you weren't planning to do so. But because it was still within the sheath, the energy built and built and then just . . . just released. And now they're gone. Just like that."

"No," I whispered. I wanted to push her away, but I felt as if I had no body with which to do so.

"It's all right. Don't be concerned. You were right. Eventually they would have just killed one another anyway. Gone to war in a long, protracted power struggle. By unleashing the power of the ultimate weapon, you avoided that war. You did them a favor."

"A favor?"

She smiled at me with all her mother love. "Yes, my dear. It was for the best. It truly was." She patted my face. Her hand felt cold. All around us was pure, stark, white nothingness. "There's only one problem."

"Just one?"

"The power is unleashed now. More power than the demon sword even knew it was capable of. It loves that power now. It wants to release it again. And again."

"I'll . . . I'll destroy it!"

"You can't."

"Throw it into the sea!"

"If you wish," she said. "But the seabeds shift, tides come in and out. Sooner or later, the weapon will surface. Who knows who will have it then? Anyone could acquire the power. Anyone at all."

"It could . . . it could obliterate the world . . ."

She considered that a moment. "Yes," she decided. "Yes. It could. That would be . . . interesting . . ."

"But . . . you said I'm not dead. It didn't destroy me?"

"No. You are its master. For the moment, in any event."

"So I'm . . . unscathed?"

"I didn't say that, my love," she said sadly. "Such power as you unleashed does not come without a price. A pound of flesh, as it were. The sword chose the price. And you will have to live with it."

I started to sob. I had never felt so miserable. She clucked disapprovingly. "Oh, now, Apropos . . ."

"I ruined it, didn't I, Mother," I said.

"Yes. But that's all right, my love. You ruin everything."

The last words had been said with a deep, fearsome growl, and it was no longer my mother standing there, but Aulhel, and he was laughing, loud and long, and others began to join in, also laughing at me, and my head was swimming in laughter and humiliation, and then I awoke.

I was lying right where I had been, except that sunlight was streaming down upon me. That should not have been possible. This was the shadow town, where the sun never shone.

The buildings were gone.

All gone.

There was a faint ringing in my ear. I reached up automatically to touch it, and came away with dried blood on my fingertips.

My right ear was gone.

Something sharp had violently cut it away.

The ringing . . . which nowadays is reduced to faint background noise, but I can still detect every now and then . . . continued.

Among my possessions was a small tapestry I had been given. It showed me as older, grim-faced . . . and missing an ear.

Was it all fate, then? Had all of this been completely out of my hands? Could it truly have been that, no matter what I had done, the same appalling fate awaited me and everyone who had been near me? Could the gods truly be that cruel?

Sadly, I knew the answer to the last question instantly. And that was enough to answer all the ones previous to it.

I had collapsed upon my walking staff. Under my "friendly" auspices, it too was spared. Slowly I hauled myself to my feet.

Veruh Wang Ho was dust at my feet. At least I was reasonably certain it was him . . . he . . . her . . .

Her.

I took in a deep breath and let it out slowly as I saw the anguish that had been reflected in her face, trying to defy that which the gods had given her in one of their typically cruel jokes. Yes. Her.

The ground was burned in all directions. I took a few steps and stopped once more. The faint wind was continuing to blow ashes all about, but I saw one thing upon the ground that seized my full attention.

Burned into the ground was a scorched silhouette. A young woman, it appeared to be, embracing what seemed to be the outline of a dragon.

Mitsu. And Mordant. All that was left of them, blasted into the ground by the force of the energies released. I didn't know why they had been singled out. Perhaps because Mordant had magic in him. Perhaps because of where they'd been standing, or who'd been standing in front of them.

Or perhaps the gods were even bigger bastards than I'd credited them.

I stood there for a long moment, waiting for the tears to start.

Waiting for something.

Nothing came.

Nothing.

And then I started to laugh.

I didn't know where it came from, or why, but I continued to laugh. I turned away from the scene of lethal devastation and started walking, and I kept on laughing until I finally figured out why.

Because I was nothing. Finally and completely, because I was nothing.

That used to upset me.

It didn't anymore.

I moved through the city then. The farther I got from the blast point, the more I began to see signs of life. It had been a devastating blast, but it had not torn apart the entire city. There were survivors, many survivors.

Except they didn't appear to be happy that they had survived.

Buildings had been knocked down, flattened. Entire blocks had been obliterated. And the people . . .

The innocent people . . .

They wandered about aimlessly, or simply sat in one place and stared off into space, wondering what they had done to deserve this. Many of them were horrifically burned.

I felt nothing.

I heard the sounds of children crying, of dogs barking. So much pain, so much pain.

And I felt nothing.

When I had been holding the dead Kit to my breast, I thought—in my cries that I did not care—that I had embraced the totality of nothingness. I had been wrong. I had barely scratched the surface, not even begun to realize the remarkable strength that came from utter nothingness.

I had hated the notion that I was known as Apropos of Nothing. I had wanted to have something, love something, stand for something. How typically Apropos, to want to rid myself of that which was, in fact, my greatest strength.

Something makes you weak. Something makes you second-guess. Something makes you doubt. Something makes you love, or hate, or fear, or make mistakes.

But nothingness . . . in nothing, there is no love or hate or fear. Nothing never makes mistakes.

"Nothing ventured, nothing gained." "Nothing for nothing." "Nothing to fear." "Nothing matters."

In the beginning, there is nothing. We come from nothing, we go to nothing.

The message was clear in day-to-day life, and I had been too blind to see it. Ali had tried to teach it to me, and I hadn't been fully ready to appreciate it or understand it. I had thought the strength I sought from Ali came from the sword.

It didn't. It came from nothing. The sword was simply a tool.

Nothing was impenetrable. Nothing was invincible. I had nothing to fear but something.

Darkness was nothing. One could hide in darkness, strike from darkness.

Something always bogged you down. Be it emotions or sentiment or inordinate possessions. But you were never slowed by nothing.

"What are you doing?" Nothing.

"What are you looking for?" Nothing.

"What are you thinking about?" Nothing.

"What's the matter?" Nothing.

"Ah, that damned son of mine! He's good for nothing!"

That's what I was going to be. Good for nothing.

Finally.

Here I'd been chagrined that I was known as Sir Apropos of Nothing, as if that made me less than others when, in fact, it made me so much more.

I had been walking slowly at first, but the more people I passed, the more I embraced nothing, the more confident I became. I didn't care about the blood on the side of my face. So I was missing an ear. So what? I had another. And besides, it wasn't as if a lot of people in the world were saying anything so damned interesting anyway.

Once I would have felt terrible for all these people, whose simple lives had suddenly been sent into disarray.

Now I didn't.

Once I might have tried to stop, to help them, all the time rationalizing that I was doing it for myself. Yet now I didn't have to engage in any such subterfuge for the simple reason that I wasn't remotely interested in trying to help them.

Why?

Nothing doing.

If I did nothing, the world could not hurt me. Never, ever again.

Finally . . . finally . . . I was at peace.

There was only one lingering problem, and that was the sword at my side.

It was something.

It was responsibility. It needed to be guarded against, maintained. The other weapons I carried, they were just for defense. To defend myself from what? From something. And from those who wanted to give something, namely death.

Death was something. Death was peace. Death was release.

Life . . . life was nothing. I had seen that all too clearly, knew that beyond any hope of denial. I knew that the moment I saw the dead Kit. Life was nothing. Arbitrarily assigned, not cherished by nearly enough, not comprehended by those in power who would take that which they had not been given in the first place. Oh, perhaps life wasn't actually nothing, but it was treated as nothing by enough people—kings, rulers, brigands, thieves, monsters—that it became nothing by default, because everything in the world is defined by humanity.

So my weapons would enable me to hold on to the nothing called life.

But I didn't want the demon sword because of all the somethings attached to it.

I didn't know what to do with it, however.

And then, as I made my way out of town, I came upon two people approaching.

One was an overweight warrior. He had stern, pitiless features, a sword tucked through his belt, and he looked at me with—well, with no curiosity at all, unlike everyone else I had encountered. This fat man did not seem to care about me. He seemed to have an appreciation for nothing.

Even more curious was his companion. It was a little boy, being pushed along in a sort of cart. The boy stared up at me, and he also was not curious. His dark eyes merely fixed upon me. Obviously the fat man was the boy's father.

We stopped and faced one another: the fat man, the little boy, and myself. The father, the son, and me . . . a mere ghost of what I had been when I first washed up upon the shores of Chinpan. And yet, I was not bothered by that.

Because nothing bothered me.

"Did you see what happened there?" I asked, nodding toward the devastated city behind me.

"I saw a cloud," rumbled the fat man. "It seemed like a giant toadstool."

"Yes. I saw it too."

"It's gone now."

"No," I said. "It's still there. It will always be there." I studied him a moment further. "Tell me," I asked. "Would you ever be in a situation where you would give up? Where you would not care about anything?"

"Never," said the fat man. "I have a son. Not caring is a luxury I do not have." He paused. "Do you have a son?"

"No," I said, not realizing I was mistaken. "Which is fortunate, because if I did, he would probably want to kill me," I added, not realizing I was right. "Here." I held up the tachi sword. "Take this."

He looked at me askance. "Why?"

"Because I am giving it to you," I said reasonably.

He took the sword from me, eyed it. He pulled it from the sheath, whipped it back and forth through the air. "It is a fine blade," he allowed and deftly slid it back into the scabbard. "What do you wish for it?"

"Nothing."

"Then I will give you nothing."

"Accepted."

And so we parted ways, we three. The fat man, who had something to live for, namely his little boy.

And I, Apropos, struck out for the north, knowing at long last that I truly had nothing to live for . . . and was finally looking forward to living it.